The Big Day

and other stories

A collection of short and
not-so-short fictional works

Dave Lauby

BookLocker
Trenton, Georgia

Copyright © 2023 Dave Lauby

Print ISBN: 978-1-958890-09-7
Ebook ISBN: 979-8-88531-525-8

All rights reserved. No part of this publication may be reproduced, stored in a retrieval system, or transmitted in any form or by any means, electronic, mechanical, recording or otherwise, without the prior written permission of the author.

Published by BookLocker.com, Inc., Trenton, Georgia, U.S.A.

The characters and events in this book are fictitious. Any similarity to real persons, living or dead, is coincidental and not intended by the author.

Library of Congress Cataloguing in Publication Data
Lauby, Dave
The Big Day and other stories by Dave Lauby
Library of Congress Control Number: 2023909890

Printed on acid-free paper.

BookLocker.com, Inc.
2023

for Danny, in lieu of a decent inheritance

CONTENTS

GERRY AND BIRDIE 1
ESCAPE PLAN 19
UNSTARTED STORY 63
TAKE IT 92
THE WOBBLY LEG 112
RATS IN HER HOUSE 150
THE HOME BOARD 200
TICKET TO HEAVEN 264
THE BIG DAY 301

GERRY AND BIRDIE

```
``````````````````````````````````````````````````````
```

The big sedan which was swerving and speeding like mad around the sharp bends of the narrow logging road was a brand-new four-door burgundy red 1982 Buick LeSabre, Limited Edition. A luxury automobile. Definitely a city car, which was why it looked so out-of-place way up in the back country, kicking out twigs and gravel as it careened wildly on its reckless descent down the heavily-wooded mountain. Another thing that looked out-of-place was the driver, because it was a fourteen year-old boy. And the little fucking maniac was driving like he wasn't afraid to die.

"Slow down Birdie, please!" The driver's accomplice, Gerry, also fourteen but so small that he looked more like eleven, was afraid enough for the both of them; he sat in a scrunched-up ball in the front passenger seat, both hands gripping the overtightened seat belt which was doing nothing whatsoever to keep him from being thrown about like a crash test dummy by every pothole and ravine. "If somebody comes up the other way we'll crash 'em head on!"

"Then we need to go even faster and get to the bottom before somebody comes up!" A short straightaway lay just ahead, so Birdie gunned the big V-8 like he'd done it a million times before, which he hadn't. He had never driven a car before, ever, not even once. Birdie was always doing things he'd never done like he had done it a million times. So this new thing was no different.
```

Birdie glanced into his rear view mirror. "Think he's dead?" Gerry turned his head to look behind him, but a sudden switchback at the end of the straightaway flung him over to one side before he could catch a glimpse of the body of the man who was lying on the back seat. "*Pleeeease* Birdie slow down!"

Despite the violent jarring of the ride the cigarette in the corner of Birdie's mouth held its place. Birdie had been smoking like a pro for over a year, while Gerry was still too afraid to light a match. "Quit cryin' Gerry. You *want* me to slow down? He's your dad not mine!"

Gerry turned his head once more toward the back seat but could not bring himself to look, whimpering "He's dead, I know he's dead." Now the road was skirting along the edge of a deep ravine which fell below the driver's side, the sheer precipice dropping off just a few feet away from the gravel-spraying tires. Gerry peeked out over the drop-off and instantly felt sick. "How much farther is it?"

"How should I know… oh shit hang on!" With a jerk of the steering wheel, Birdie fishtailed the big car's rear end just inches from sliding off the edge of the ravine, then left their near-death experience behind them in a cloud of gray dust. Birdie's steady cigarette glowed like a headlight. "Look back there and see if he's breathing."

Forcing himself to face the worst, Gerry twisted himself around once again, and his sick feeling returned, this time from seeing the blood which was oozing from the back of the man's head, blood which was creating a two-tone red effect as it smeared against the glossy burgundy leather. The body was doing a lot of moving around back there but only because of the bouncing ride, not on its own. It bothered Gerry to see the fishing poles slapping against his dad's face but there was nothing he could do to stop it. "I can't tell. I can't tell if he's breathing."

"Well he was breathing when we put him back there so he still might be." Gerry remembered how hard it had been, dragging his dad up out of the trout stream and up to the car, amazed at how heavy a knocked-out grown man was (now he knew what they meant by "dead weight"), and how they couldn't help but keep bumping his head again and again against the ground as they dragged him, the same head that was already bashed in from hitting the boulder when he had slipped in the water and fallen. Just before he fell his dad had told them how awesome the fishing was going to be since it was a weekday so there'd be nobody up there to bother them for miles around; a few minutes later, with his dad lying maybe dead in the stream, it wasn't so awesome that there was nobody up there for miles around because it meant it was up to them and them alone to get him help. And while Gerry was screaming into the trees as loud as he could hoping somebody who knew how to drive would hear him, Birdie was already behind the wheel starting the car and yelling for Gerry to get in or get left behind.

"We're almost to the bottom. I can see the main road down there between the trees." Risking more sickness by taking another look out over the ravine, Gerry peered out his window, but all he was able to pick out was the passing rush of bouncing forest which seemed to be growing sideways thanks to Birdie's roller-coaster assault of the gravel road. That was always the way it was with him and Birdie, Gerry thought to himself. Gerry was never able to see past the trees, while Birdie always saw things all the way through to the other side. Birdie was always plunging into that forest, hacking away, not afraid of thorns or spiders or of getting lost, with Gerry following, well, dragged against his will usually, kicking and crying the whole time. And one way or another, Birdie always made it through the trees, afterwards laughing at Gerry's crying and laughing because it was fun and laughing because they almost died but didn't. Birdie was Gerry's biggest hero, bigger even than Johnny Bench or Davey Concepcion. Those guys were just baseball players after all. Birdie was a god.

"Okay, we're at the highway. Is your dad dead yet?" But before Gerry had a chance to check the back seat for an update, Birdie was veering them onto the two-lane highway, not checking for oncoming cross traffic or slowing down in the slightest, a maneuver which sent the tires to screeching and whose centrifugal force body-slammed Gerry against the passenger door. It was open road now, and Birdie had the pedal to the floor and the Le Sabre flying like a rocket down the wrong side of the two-lane road. "Gotta head back toward Beckley. There's a hospital there." After rubbing out his cigarette in the ashtray, Birdie lit up another with the car cigarette lighter as if he'd done it a million times before, which he hadn't, and then leaned back comfortably, his head against the headrest, enjoying what for him was just another pleasant and relaxing drive in the country at 104 mph. "Hell, driving is easy. Gerry, find something on the radio."

"Wh- what?"

"The radio. Find us some music."

"Music?" Gerry stared up in amazement at Birdie, who was staring right back at him, already such a veteran of driving that he didn't need to watch the road. "Music Birdie? Now?"

"Yeah. And no country shit."

Gerry stared dumbly at the car radio like it was the control panel of an alien spaceship. Outside the hurtling craft, trees and telephone poles flew past at the speed of light. "Maybe first we should just get my dad to- "

"Goddamn, never mind, I'll do it!" After first returning his cigarette to its designated mouth corner, Birdie pushed one button, and the warm drawl of Merle Haggard came crooning across the airwaves. Gerry knew the song; his dad played it on the stereo at home. The title was *I'm Always on a Mountain When I Fall*. It pissed Birdie off. "No dammitt, *no country shit!*" He punched another button, and a song which was definitely not a country song came out, another which Gerry knew because his older brother played it on the stereo when his dad wasn't around. It was from this new Irish group called U2, from an album called *Boy*. The song was *I Will Follow*. "That's better." Birdie glanced into the rear-view mirror and whistled. "Goddamn! That's a lotta blood." The reminder of the blood made Gerry feel sick again, and Birdie noticed the smaller boy's discomfiture with amusement. He looked down at Gerry and grinned. "So whaddya say? Feel like doin' some driving?"

All Gerry could do was roll himself back into a ball and close his eyes. "Just let me know when we get there."

Raleigh General Hospital was the biggest hospital in Raleigh County, right on Highway 3; it was definitely big and obvious enough that if you drove by it you'd know right away that you were at a hospital. But no matter how hospital-looking it was Gerry had no idea how Bertie got them there, but somehow he did, hurtling the big Le Sabre into the entrance marked Emergency Room and lurching it to a screeching stop across two parking spaces. Gerry had quit keeping track of the traffic violations after the third blown stop sign, and despite his constant praying that the police would pull them over and take his dad the rest of the way to the hospital, Birdie got away with the drive the whole way, just like he always got away with everything. With the car no longer tossing its human cargo up and down and all about, Gerry, could finally check if his dad was making any movement of his own effort. He was not. Birdie put the car in "park" and flicked his cigarette butt out the window.

"Well alright! You grab him by one shoulder I'll grab the other."

"Wait!" Birdie was already standing outside the car and opening the back door. "Let me do the talking in there Birdie."

Birdie was the picture of innocence. "What? Don't I always?"

Gerry was out of the car now too, at the opposite back car door. "Well, yeah, but you always, kindof… take over."

"And why is that Gerry?"

"Because…" Gerry stared down at the pavement. "Because I always mess it up."

"Because you always FUCK it up Gerry! And then I have to step in and talk our way out of your fuck-up!" Gerry was still staring at the pavement, nodding his head in agreement. "Meanwhile, your dad is bleedin' all over the back seat. Now come on!"

After running around to Birdie's side of the car, the two boys grabbed Gerry's dad under his armpits and began to pull him across the seat. Behind them, a nurse who was coming into work passed behind the big Le Sabre.

"What happened here?"

Birdie zipped his lip and let Gerry take the lead. "It's my dad. He fell on the rocks when we were fishing."

The nurse hurried over and looked at Gerry's dad's head. "And you were just gonna drag your dad across the parking lot without a gurney or any help?"

Gerry stared back at the nurse dumbly, his tongue stuck between gears. Birdie swooped in like a falcon. "Ma'am, you're right, it was really dumb. Could you find someone inside to help? Thanks!" In a moment the nurse had jogged up to the hospital and gone in; a minute later, two orderlies were lifting Gerry's dad out of the car and onto a wheeled stretcher. Gerry couldn't help but notice how strange it looked, seeing other people carrying his dad without his dad carrying himself. Gerry had never seen his dad helpless like that, needing someone else to do something for him. It seemed to Gerry that if anyone should get carried in it should be himself, because as long as he could remember, his dad had always yelled at him for needing other people to carry him. Like in any sport he'd play for instance. In basketball, the opposing player who Gerry was assigned to guard would dribble toward the basket; Gerry's dad (he was the coach for, like, every team Gerry played on) would yell "Pick him up Gerry, pick him up!" and Gerry would spread his arms and feet like his dad taught him and cut off the lane to the basket like his dad taught him, but no matter what he did the player always found a way around Gerry, which left it up to his teammates to stop the opposing player, to stop the man Gerry was supposed to have stopped. And on his way back to the other end of the court Gerry would hear his dad hollering at him, "Gotta pull your own weight out there Number Fourteen, don't make your teammates carry you!" And it was the same thing in baseball and football- some teammate would have to chase after the ground ball that went under Gerry's glove or recover the football that Gerry had just fumbled. But it wasn't just in sports that Gerry needed carrying. Bigger things, like doing chores around the house or helping on his grampa's farm or earning all the badges it required to someday make Eagle in Boy Scouts, it seemed like Gerry always needed bailing out, needed somebody else to carry him. But nobody carried him more than Birdie of course, Birdie doing all the flying with Gerry on his back. At the same time, nobody got him into trouble more than Birdie. It was always Birdie that got Gerry grounded or punished in any way. And his dad never blamed anybody but Gerry. When this mess at the hospital was over with, Gerry had already decided he would lie to his dad and tell him that it was he and not Birdie who had been the hero and drove the car to the hospital. If his dad lived that is.

As soon as Gerry's dad had been taken into the examination room, a nurse told Gerry and Birdie to go sit in a little room off to the side, where another nurse who wasn't dressed like a nurse sat behind a desk and pecked away at her electric typewriter. "Randall Tabor. Two L's in Randall?"

"Yes ma'am."

The woman looked down at Gerry. "And he's your dad?"

"Yes ma'am." He could feel Birdie's eyes on him, just waiting for him to fuck up.

The woman went back to typing, but then abruptly looked up from her keyboard with a puzzled look, darting her eyes all about the waiting area. "Wait now. How old are you?"

"Fourteen ma'am."

The woman cocked her head. "Well then where's the adult who drove you here?"

The first nurse who had met them in the parking lot poked her head into the office. "No adult. This boy did the driving. How 'bout that?" Birdie grinned up at the nurse, his face beaming with pride.

The woman behind the desk crossed her arms and stared sternly through her horn rims. "Well first things first then. We need to call your mother. What's your phone number?"

"Three oh four, eight one six, five- " As he reeled off his home phone number, Gerry imagined his mother sitting at home, doing her house work, and then getting the phone call from the hospital telling him that his dad was hurt bad and it not looking too good. It wouldn't be a nice phone call of course, but Gerry wasn't really worried about it. His mom wasn't all that bad about hearing bad news, even bad news that had to do with him. It was like his mom was always sortof expecting to hear bad news about Gerry; she would just listen and nod while the assistant principal told her about Gerry's latest fight in the cafeteria which had made a huge mess and gave one kid a nosebleed which Gerry swore up and down he didn't start because it was Birdie who started it but of course he couldn't tell her or the teachers that because Birdie would get him for it. After the phone call his mom wouldn't go flying off the handle or smack him in the head or anything like that; she'd sigh and in her quiet mom voice remind him what the counsellors had said about him needing to straighten up and fly right because this was high school now, then she'd give him his two-weeks grounding punishment or some extra chores and that would be it (most times when she gave him her talking-to Gerry would walk past the kitchen a few minutes afterward and hear a sniffle or two from his mom which always made him feel like crap for making her cry yet again). But his dad, holy shit, when the phone rang and it was his dad who went to answer it Gerry would run outside and hide behind the shed and wait for the bomb to drop, which would only be a few minutes later when he'd hear *"Gerry, goddammitt, get your punk ass in here!"* And when Gerry went crawling in there'd be no chance to explain because right away he'd get thrown against the wall like a bean bag and wouldn't even need to get grounded because he wouldn't want to leave the house for two weeks anyway until the bruises had healed and gone away. And Birdie? Oh, well, Birdie was never to be found when Gerry's dad was in ass-beating mode, even though it was always because of Birdie that his dad got those phone calls which turned into ass beatings. But there was no way of course that this hospital phone call would turn into an ass beating, because this time the ass-beater himself was laying on a gurney almost dead in a hospital room. And his mom probably wouldn't be all that upset about the news anyway because she didn't like Gerry's dad much more than Gerry did.

"I bet I can get away with smoking in here."

They were sitting in the waiting room with a handful of other people who were also waiting for someone to get fixed up. About a half hour had passed and Birdie was sneaking out a cigarette and digging in his pocket for matches while Gerry was freaking out in general.

"He's gonna die Birdie I know he's gonna die."

"Prob'ly." He had found the matches, and was now darting his eyes about to check if anybody was watching him. "Hit his head pretty damn hard you know."

"Yes I do know! I was there too! And *please* don't smoke Birdie you'll get us kicked out!" Feeling himself getting more fidgety by the second, Gerry wished the emergency room had magazines to look at like at his dentist's office, just something, anything to distract his brain. So when he saw the office nurse waving toward him to come see her he was more than happy to hurry up to her desk and find out what she wanted. And since Birdie didn't trust Gerry to handle things by himself, he came up to her desk along with him.

"Okay Gerry. We've talked to your mom and she's on her way to the hospital."

"How? Our family only has the one car."

"Your neighbor's bringing her." The desk nurse looked down at her papers. "A Mrs. Martindale?"

Gerry rolled his eyes in anguish. "Mrs. Martindale!" As the boys made their way back to the waiting room, Gerry felt his stomach getting queasy as he thought of the neighbor lady who would soon be bringing his mom to the hospital. The Martindale's lived right next door to his house, and their oldest daughter Rickey had been Gerry's first and only big crush all through middle school and had been for most all of the other 8th grade boys as well. Birdie was too cool to let himself get actual crushes on girls; he just said that this one had a good ass or this one had some really nice high school-sized tits on her, dirty stuff like that, but even Birdie agreed that Rickey was the best looking girl at Stratton Junior High without a doubt. At the end of the school year was the 8th grade prom, and all that night Gerry couldn't take his eyes off Rickey Martindale in her shiny lavender-colored dress which fit her like mermaid skin and how the mirror-balled lights sparkled like fish scales and showed off all her better-than-8th-grade curves and cleavages. Birdie meanwhile couldn't stop looking at Rickey either, or at every other girl at the prom for that matter, and if Gerry hadn't stopped him time and time again Birdie would have felt all of them up like melons at the grocery store, trying to grope half the cheerleading squad and even one time rubbing up "accidentally" against Miss Larson the Home Economics teacher. It was just as they were leaving the dance that Birdie told Gerry his big idea: as soon as Rickey gets home she's gonna want to get out of that tight dress, so what if we were there to see that happen? And before Gerry could get out one word of argument there they were, outside her house in the dark of night along with the crickets, hunkered down in the wet dewy grass right underneath Rickey's bedroom window, waiting for the light to be turned on in her room and for the show to begin. Gerry said he was getting cold feet, actual cold feet from the dew, and that it was a dumb idea and so he started to go home, but Birdie said Come on, I'll even let you have the first look. So when Rickey's bedroom light came on there was Gerry, up on Birdie's back so that he could see in, just like he was always riding on Birdie's back in everything he ever dared to do. And Rickey started peeling off one thing after another, and she was almost all the way down to nothing when Gerry bumped his stupid head against the glass and Rickey heard it; she looked and saw Gerry's mooncalf face in the window and screamed like hell which brought her mom running in and sent Gerry and Birdie scampering away. Of course Rickey's parents were at Gerry's house a few minutes later, and from under his bed where he was hiding (while Birdie sat on top of the bed calmly flipping through a titty magazine) Gerry could hear his parents out in the front room apologizing over and over and telling the Martindales that Gerry would be dealt with severely don't you worry about that. But what his punishment was that night was different than other times; Gerry wished right away that he'd been tossed like a bean bag into walls instead of what his dad did to him that time because it was sick, the way his dad made Gerry strip completely naked to "see how you like it you little shit," and where his dad made Gerry stand while he was naked and for how long and who all saw him and how he was shivering in the dew, with Birdie doing nothing except laughing at how tiny Gerry's wiener looked dangling out in the shriveling cold air. And now it was the same Mrs. Martindale who was bringing his mom to the hospital, who he and Birdie would have to sit with in the car on the long ride home, her angry scary eyes in the rear view mirror keeping an eye on him in the back seat. Gerry knew that it was just him who Mrs. Martindale would be watching in the mirror, not Birdie, even though the whole Rickey thing had been Birdie's fault. Nobody cared that Gerry could never have been able to see into Rickey's window if he hadn't been on Birdie's back. His mom and dad didn't care what Birdie did because Birdie wasn't their kid after all. That was maybe the coolest thing about Birdie, the fact that he wasn't anybody's kid, didn't have to answer to any parents whatsoever. Birdie didn't need any parents because he could do whatever it took to get through life all by himself. Birdie was Just Birdie, nobody to answer to; no teammates who ever had to carry him, no mom who he was always disappointing and making her cry herself to sleep at night, no dad to smack him around and make him stand naked in the cold night air. And since Birdie was Just Birdie, Gerry was super grateful that a somebody like Birdie would let a nobody like himself hang out with him. So if getting in trouble because of Birdie was the price Gerry had to pay to be able to hang out with him, well then, it was worth it. Being in trouble with Birdie was way better than being nothing at all.

About fifteen minutes later the door of the examining room where they had taken Gerry's dad finally opened, and out stepped a young doctor who had apparently been working on Gerry's dad the whole hour or so since coming to the hospital. Gerry and Birdie watched the doctor closely, to see if they could get a clue from his face as to whether Gerry's dad was dead, but the doctor had that no-expression blank doctor face which told them nothing. A nurse came over and whispered something to the doctor; then they both looked over at Gerry and Birdie which made Gerry feel really nervous for no exact reason he could think of. The doctor whispered something else to the nurse, who then left the doctor and walked over to the desk nurse where more whispering happened, with the desk nurse finally picking up the telephone and making a call. The other nurse walked back to the doctor, and after one more whisper they both made their way to where the boys were sitting.

"Gerry?"

Gerry nodded his head.

"Hi Gerry. Nurse Harris here told me that your mom is on the way. I'm Doctor Kalber. I've been taking care of your dad."

Birdie was the one who blurted it out. "Is he dead?"

Doctor Kalber took a chair and placed it so that he could face them both, then sat down. "No. Your dad's not dead. He has some really serious injuries though. Do you know what a skull fracture is?"

Gerry remembered all the blood that was probably still wet on the back seat of the car. "Yes."

A second doctor had come to the emergency room now, and quickly stepped into the examining room where Gerry's dad was. "Well that's what we're dealing with. He's lost a lot of blood. It's too soon to know if there's brain damage of course, what we're most concerned with right now is making sure there's no fluid leakage, preventing infection, that sort of thing. Pretty soon he'll be going into surgery." Dr. Kalber glanced out at the parking lot, then back to the boys. "They also told me about how you drove the car."

Birdie's voice was too loud, as always. "So I'm in trouble for that now I suppose?"

Doctor Kalber regarded Birdie with a quiet curiosity. "No, you're not in trouble for that. So tell me, what happened today? You were fishing, and he fell?"

"That's right." In a quieter voice than Birdie's, Gerry told the doctor the story of what had happened, how they were fishing at the mountain stream, and how Gerry's dad had slipped on the rocks and hit his head, how they dragged his dad to the car and then drove to the hospital. Doctor Kalber listened very carefully throughout, and when Gerry was finished the doctor looked up at Nurse Harris, and then pulled his chair just a little closer to where the boys sat.

"So Gerry..." Doctor Kalber was leaning in now, his voice low and even. "Was there any part of the story that you... left out?"

"Um, why?"

"Well because..." Across the waiting room, two police officers had just come in from the parking lot and were walking toward the desk nurse's office. "I mentioned the skull fracture Gerry. At the back of your dad's head, when he fell and hit the rocks. But there's a second skull fracture Gerry. On the front of your dad's head. *Two* skull fractures, one back, one front. How is that possible?"

"Uh..."

"Because he couldn't fall twice Gerry. Only once. Right?"

Gerry was speechless. Worse than speechless; his mouth was unable to move at all, let alone make a sound. But weirdly, Gerry wasn't that worried about that, because he knew that this was when Birdie always saw that Gerry was fucking it up and would take over, would carry him the way he always carried him. So while Doctor Kalber and Nurse Harris waited for Gerry to explain two skull fractures, Gerry waited too, for Birdie to step up and tell them the whole story: about how they were fishing, and how Gerry had asked if he could carry the tackle box and his dad had said Okay but just don't drop it, and how Gerry had thought he'd seen a snake which made him totally drop the tackle box even though he promised he wouldn't, dumping all the lures and hooks and what-not down in between the rocks; how his dad then lost his shit and whacked Gerry upside his head with his coffee thermos, and when Birdie saw the drop of blood in Gerry's ear, Birdie suddenly got red-hot angry, and pushed Gerry's dad as hard as he could which made him fall and crack open the back of his head. And while his dad was lying there on his back Birdie had stood over him, and had said to him, "That one was for Gerry." And then Birdie had picked up a big rock and held it up high, and looking down at Gerry's glassy-eyed dad, had said "And this one is for me," then smashing the front of his dad's head with the huge rock. This was the part of the story that Gerry was waiting for Birdie to tell the doctor and the nurse. But Birdie wasn't saying a word. Because there was no Birdie anymore.

"Who are you looking for Gerry?"

The police officers had been whispering with the desk nurse the whole time, and now one of them went into the room where Gerry's dad was while the other walked up to where Gerry was sitting and stood over him.

"I'm Officer Harmon. Your name's Gerry?"

"Yes."

"My partner and I need to talk to you about what happened with you and your dad today."

"Okay."

"Let's go sit in the back of my car until your mom gets here."

"Okay."

Getting up from his chair, Gerry began the walk across the waiting room with the two police officers on either side of him. He could feel the eyes of everyone in the emergency room watching him, all of them surely wondering what he could have done, not understanding that Gerry hadn't done anything at all, ever. At the front door Gerry saw the police car which was waiting for him; and as they walked across the parking lot, Gerry and the cops passed by the big Le Sabre, where through the window Gerry could see his dad's blood, dark and thick, covering the back seat like a swirled sheet. Little sparklers began to flash behind his eyes, and he could feel a warm rush tingling across his face and into his knees.

"Whooah! He's goin' down, catch him!"

When Gerry woke up he was still in the parking lot, but he wasn't standing, was floating through the air somehow; then he noticed the two orderlies who were on either side of him, who were carrying him to the police car.

Gerry began to squirm in mid-air. "No! Don't carry me!"

"You fainted is all, we gotchoo, relax-"

"No! I don't need anybody to carry me! Don't carry me! I don't need to be carried!"

Sitting in the back seat of the police car, Gerry finally began to calm down somewhat. He had never been in a police car before, and it felt really big and empty in the back seat, bigger probably because he was so alone in it. But for Gerry it wasn't really that bad, being alone as he was. His mom hadn't showed up yet, so at least she wasn't there in the back seat with her sniffling and sobbing and making him feel guilty. At least there was no Mrs. Martindale, with her eyes watching him in the rearview mirror. At least there was no pissed-off dad sitting next to him to always be afraid of. And since Birdie had evaporated and left him to deal with all this shit alone, Gerry figured he might as well just be alone altogether, except of course for these cops. He would have to talk to these cops alone now, without Birdie. But Gerry knew he couldn't tell the cops about how Birdie was the one who did it. No way. Birdie would find out if Gerry told on him. Because Birdie would be back. Birdie had never really left. Birdie would always be there in the Birdie side of his brain, one way or another. No matter where this police car might carry him.

ESCAPE PLAN

From the one and only window of his third-story apartment Jason stared out upon what had to be the ugliest, busiest, noisiest and shit-stinkiest street in the entire north side of Chicago, and despite the fact that it had always looked and sounded and smelt like shit from the first day he'd ever heard and smelled and seen it, Jason had chosen it above all those other streets as the one where he would live. If "live" was the correct word. Which it wasn't. But Jason wasn't surprised in the least that he had ended up on Shit Street. What in his life had not gone to shit? Settling for a shithole like the one he presently stared out of therefore was almost a foregone conclusion. It was Saturday, the day when most people are happy to be home away from their jobs, and as much as Jason hated his own shit job he knew he should be happy to be home as well. But when he was at his shit job he at least had something to occupy his brain for eight-ish hours, while at home he had nothing more going on than looking at his phone or down at the street below and wishing he was at work where at least he was too busy to dwell upon his deep despair. But what did he wish for when he was at work? That he was at home instead. And so turned his shitty world.

He could see them all from his window down there on Shit Street, all the people walking into this store and coming out of that one, going about their business, living their lives. That was what Jason hated the most about them, that they had lives to live, and dared to live them. He had been down among them just an hour before, puttering through his meaningless little errands in and out of those same stores and shops. He tried to imagine himself down there now as he'd been then, moving among his species-mates, mingling his antennae with those of the other ants, but try as he might his mind couldn't picture himself there, could not see himself as one of them. This made complete sense, he decided, for he knew that he was not the kind of person who ever left much trace of himself having been anywhere, not the sort to make his mark, let alone leave his mark, as evidence of his existence. At least ants left pheromones. What was his existential residue? Yes, his errands had no doubt been very similar to all of theirs, and yet he knew that those people were so much more than just their errands; he knew that other people had goals and the initiative to pursue them, had families and the intestinal fortitude to provide for them, had futures and the courage to sail into them. Courage. That was what they fucking had. Courage and the pheromones they left. What Jason left was shit.

Scanning up and down the sidewalks for anyone or anything worth looking at *searching for Her should be rounding the corner into view any minute now*, Jason thought it ironic that he should have ended up spending so much time staring out at a street which offered so little to see; ironic that as a man whose sole activity was watching others doing things he should then be so bored with watching the things they did. But doing things himself was not an option. It came back to that word again, courage, that missing piece he'd never possessed, like the baker who had all the ingredients except the yeast and so his bread could never rise. Jason knew he understood courage in a way other people didn't, for the very reason that they possessed it without even knowing it. Other people took their day-to-day ability to function for granted; other people, when they thought of courage, assumed it to mean something dramatic, like diving into burning houses to save children or leading your outnumbered platoon into a firefight. Jason scoffed at such fairy-tale notions of courage. Courage, as he understood it, meant opening your bills when they arrive in the mail and daring to read them. Courage meant walking into a room full of people and remaining there, knowing they will all look at you, and keep on looking. Courage meant coming right out and talking directly to a girl *where was She anyway did She run an extra mile this morning?,* a real girl, not the nameless nametag girl who takes your croissonwich order every morning but a true specimen of a girl as they appear naturally in the wild, like that frightened doe who was sitting next to you in the dermatologist's office waiting room who you were trying not to look at and who was trying not to look at you but you just knew she was begging to be preyed upon but of course you didn't. Courage meant finally taking your driving test or trying a frightening new food or wearing the bright yellow shirt which you're afraid to take out of the dresser but which you can feel is down there in the bottom drawer, throbbing and glowing and waiting for you; courage is all those enormously small giant little things which by doing them announces to the world that you're the captain of your ship and you are sailing it bravely into the terrifying headwind of bill reading and shirt wearing and social interaction and risk taking instead of sinking like a lump into the drowning depths of your pathetic inability to act.

Courage meant pulling the trigger when you point the gun at your head.

Such were Jason's thoughts on this Saturday morning, staring down on his Shit Street vista of nothingness from his vantage point of nowhere. But those thoughts included more than just the generalized brooding over his sorry state of affairs which had preoccupied his mind his entire adult life. Today, and for some time now, his mind had been occupied by a far more specific and unwavering thought, an action-based, unshakable resolve: that enough had finally become enough, and enough was too much. No single, definitive final-straw event had occurred which brought him to his determination to end it all, but rather the cumulative weight of waiting, hoping against hope, for some semblance of a life to appear, then the eventual understanding that nothing at all would appear, nothing would ever change- because Jason himself would never change. Despite his youth he was experienced enough to have grasped the nature of existence and its blunt realities, i.e., that all systems trend toward decay and disintegration, and human animals, like all other animals, do not gain in life force with age but lose their strength and energy, succumbing more and more to the creeping onset of unavoidable fatigue *is it raining it is that means it's raining on Her now i'll see what She looks like wet.* Jason knew that despite his overwhelming feelings of powerlessness he was at the height of his powers, such as they were, and was therefore enjoying the comparative resilience of youthful vitality. A better stronger healthier version of Jason therefore was not waiting to be born. No magic potion existed which he could drink that would reverse his miserable trajectory. The mirrors in his life were only going to get harder to look at with time, not easier, and at the tender age of twenty-eight it had already come to the point that those mirrors were reflecting an image so distorted and twisted by anxiety and pain that he found it difficult to believe it was really himself he was looking at in the glass. What's more, the comprehensive emptiness of his life provided him no good reason not to relinquish it- unencumbered by friends or family, there was no one who would feel the pain of his removal from their lives (except his parents of course, but after years of Jason's clinging dependency on them to constantly bail him out of one financial or emotional strait after another, surely they'd rather be rid of their Jason problem than hold onto their Jason son. After all, if *he* was this tired of putting up with himself, how tired must *they* be?) No, there was nothing about his life which offered a good argument against ending it, no hopes on the horizon, no prospects for improvement, no regret of leaving, no purpose for staying. There was only one obstacle which had prevented him from carrying out his plans for self-destruction, the same obstacle which had prevented him from doing anything remotely impactful during his entire time on earth. For if he lacked the courage to live his life, how could he expect to find the courage to end it?

From the moment Jason had begun to consider suicide as his only option he'd been fascinated and frustrated by those who found the wherewithal to actually carry it out. Was it just that they were appreciably more unhappy than he and were therefore more motivated? No. Jason was certain that he was just as fucking miserable as the next guy. After all, what seems to be said more often than not after a suicide are things like "but he had so much going for him, his life seemed so great!" Well, there was nothing "going for him" in his life, so a lack of motivation wasn't the problem. It was lack of courage and nothing else keeping Jason undead, pure and simple. What a misconception it was that people considered suicide to be the "coward's way out." Suicide, cowardly? Anything but! If it were really the coward's way out then how could he, the ultimate coward, not have leapt before now at the chance to take it?

What could be braver and bolder than the ultimate act of making the final determination over one's own mortality? So much chatter about all the "courage" it takes to stay alive and "face one's problems head-on," but isn't the survival instinct the strongest instinct we possess? If so, then how could it take "courage" to merely submit to it, to put down your gun and surrender to it? How much more courage it takes to stare the survival instinct in its relentless eye and say "No, Survival Instinct, I dare to resist you! I stand up to you and reject you, I fight you, and I defeat you!" How on earth, he wondered, could the single most irreversible act one could take, the one road where truly there was no turning back once it's taken, be walked down without a massive dose of courage fueling each fateful step? *finally here She is coming around the corner puddlerunning splashingrunning soaking wet little water nymph* He was fascinated therefore anytime he heard or read about a suicide taking place. What circumstances led up to it? Where did they *get the courage* to do it? What had they found- or what had they lost- to get them to the point of taking the action he himself was unable to take? How frustrating it was to learn about the many suicides for which no backstory was given, where no clue was provided as to what the ultimate motivator had been. Some were easy cases to understand, like the terminally ill who lived in round-the-clock, bone-crushing pain, the Wall Street gamblers who lost it all in a crash, the paranoid schizophrenics, the acid-tripping window leapers, etcetera etcetera. But the overwhelming majority of suicides, it seemed to Jason, were not so easy to figure. They were people not unlike himself, living unremarkable lives in unremarkable circumstances. How then had they accomplished (yes, it was an *accomplishment*) such a remarkable thing? Surely they had been afraid, just like he was, to pull that trigger, to swallow those pills, to dive from that balcony, yet some triggering thing had switched their petrified muscles into the "on" position *Her muscles were not switched on now Her muscles were resting stretching on the sidewalk rain sprinkling Her back rain running fingers down Her legs.* Whatever catalytic agent had made the difference for them had gone with them to the grave, never to be known, leaving Jason paralyzed by his lack of courage, too miserable to live but too frightened to die, suspended in a limbo state of unfulfilled death wish. His life, though unbearable, was still just bearable enough to leave him mired in it, cementing him in a monotony of quicksand, so that the .38 revolver he'd purchased several months earlier always remained just out of reach, even when he held it in his hand; even when he rested his finger on the trigger it was beyond his grasp, for the pulling of that trigger was a step toward his escape which the bog of quicksand cowardice just wouldn't allow. And thus did Jason's existential incarceration drag on, a sentence of life without parole and without reprieve, himself an unwilling participant of one day followed by another in a studio apartment jail cell, staring out upon Shit Street where courageous people seize the day *and sees Her now She's on her feet She's at the door She's in the building on the stairs just underneath me right below me underneath me.*

    The long-awaited solution to his deathless dilemma had come to him as a revelation of sorts, the unexpected by-product of his frequent internet searches for anything and everything pertaining to suicide and its commission. He'd come upon the sordid tale of one Howard Elkins, part owner in the 1960's of a New York plastics factory, who had carried on an affair with a young El Salvadoran immigrant employee, gotten her pregnant, and then murdered her to prevent her from having the baby. After stuffing the girl's body into a 50-gallon drum and adding extra weight (so that it would sink to the bottom of the East River, it was later theorized), Elkins found that it was too heavy for him to remove from the crawl space, and so he simply left it down there, pushed into an out-of-the-way corner. The house was eventually sold and Elkins and his family relocated to Boca Raton. Decades later, the then-owner of the house who had always wondered about the mysterious barrel in his crawlspace which he'd never opened *but wouldn't I like to open it not too heavy coming up the stairs floating up the stairs* finally decided to get rid of it, but when the trash collector refused to take it due to its 350-pound heft, the homeowner angrily popped the lid and found the drum's decomposed occupants with whom he'd been unknowingly cohabitating. When the authorities investigated the gruesome contents of the barrel, forensic evidence provided sufficient clues for them to connect the history of both the barrel and its contents to the missing El Salvadoran girl and her employer/lover/father of her unborn child. When the police came to his home in Boca to interview the now 70-year-old Elkins, he of course denied everything, as well as refusing to provide the cops a swab of his DNA. The police said they would leave for the time being, but not before informing Elkins that they would obtain a court order to have his DNA forcibly taken, and when his DNA proved that he was the father of the unborn baby in the barrel they would come back to collect him and send him to jail for the rest of his life. The police left, and that very evening Elkins drove to his local Wal-Mart, purchased a shot gun, then returned with it to a neighbor's garage, where he positioned the weapon between his knees and blew his head clean off. Jason was much impressed by the solution-oriented abruptness of Elkins' self-disposal; it was such a clean and decisive step, one over which Elkins obviously hadn't waffled back-and-forth; he had experienced none of the cold feet temerity which always bound Jason with uselessness. In one moment, Elkins was living a quiet life in retirement, having put the sordid ordeal from thirty years before well behind him, and in the next moment he was loading shells into his exit strategy and positioning his big toe against its trigger. Quite obviously, the police visit was what it took for Elkins to push the ejection seat button and jettison him into that great dark night. The fact that Jason had been searching high and low to find such a mechanism while Elkins wished it had never found him was immaterial- the Harold Elkins story gave Jason irrefutable proof that such buttons existed, sought after or not. He tried to picture this unassuming old man standing there in his kitchen when the cops had told him he would soon be taken away from that kitchen forever. What a tsunami of panic must have washed through his dry old veins, a wave sufficient in strength to carry him *to the door I crouch behind it listen to her in the hall her feet so small her gentle footfall in the hall* all the way to a superstore's sporting goods department; clearly, prison had been for him The Great Unbearable Thing which trumped all other considerations, even survival. And when Jason, simply in an effort to better understand the mind of Elkins, imagined what it would feel like if he were told he would soon be locked away, a surprising reaction occurred within: that tsunami of panic which he imagined had washed through Elkins washed through himself as well, shocking him with its intensity and power. What was this feeling, this sensation of ultimate terror? Prison as a change of residence was nothing he had ever imagined, if for no other reason than that he'd never committed any crimes which would make imprisonment a possibility. But now, having assumed the mindset of the found-out murderer, Jason felt himself repulsed to the point of nausea, just as Elkins must have felt at the prospect of such a fate. Might this be it then? Could it be that the promise of a prison cell was the sought-after fate worse than death he'd been seeking, the threat which might finally make his trigger finger strong enough to do what Elkins' finger did? This unexpected moment of self-discovery told him that of all the scary things which Jason the coward could never face, hearing the cell door slam behind him was the scariest. But no sooner had he come to the realization that the prospect of prison was the plot development needed to close the curtain on his lifelong tragedy did he dismiss it with despair- what the hell would he ever be going to prison for? Nothing of course. He could imagine the overwhelming dread of prison all he wanted, but it was only that, his imagination. Jason wasn't going to prison. Which meant in prison he would have to remain.

That's when he decided he had to commit a crime. A really really bad one.

It was the first day since the long-dead days of his boyhood that he had felt real excitement about something to look forward to, that day several weeks ago when it occurred to him he must commit a big-boy crime in order to effect his escape plan from life. It was thrilling for him to think about his new scheme; picturing himself sitting in his chair, gun hidden down in the cushions, himself having just performed some dastardly criminal deed (and what a verrry dastardly deed he'd decided upon!), knowing the police would be coming, just waiting for them in his loaded chair, then the knock on the door, with Jason calling out "Who is it?" but of course already knowing, and the knockers answering "Chicago PD," Jason then replying "Come on in," and in through the door they would walk, maybe even with guns drawn (the crime he'd chosen was considered a violent one after all)- and before they could finish with "Jason Withrow, you're under ar- " his gun would fly up to his temple and the "Pow!" would punctuate the cop's unfinished sentence (he had briefly considered the option of pointing his gun at the cops and letting them perform his "suicide," but what if they weren't good shots and left him merely wounded and not dead?) Over and over Jason replayed that movie in his mind, himself its tragic hero, the snuff film which through fear of imprisonment would free him with a liberating death. There were certain obstacles to overcome of course in order to get to that ultimate goal; the first obstacle being that he wasn't a criminal and had never harbored any desire to become one (oh, there was the occasional wistful fantasy of keying the cars of his coworkers or burglarizing his parents' home to steal his mom's prescription pain meds, but after keying their cars they would still *have* cars, unlike Jason, and allowing his mom's pain to go untreated wouldn't make his own pain go away, so, nah...) Other obstacles existed with the crimes themselves; each of the "big crimes" which were sufficient to ensure long prison sentences were problematic in some way. Murder, in its many forms, was out altogether, for although he understood that while earning a prison sentence might mean having to make someone else enjoy a very bad day, well, so be it, but he wasn't ready nor able to make it someone else's very *last* day. Only his. Armed robberies, including the bank variety, were too fraught with complications for him to be sure he could pull it off and get away; for getting away, escaping from the scene, was an absolutely essential requirement, in order to park himself in his death chair and await arrest per the screen directions of his snuff film. Robbing stores or banks or even individual people meant the very real possibility of being overpowered and/or arrested on the scene, thereby landing him not in his death chair but in the very jail his suicide was designed to avoid. Arson, grand theft auto, acts of terror, child pornography- one after another Jason considered all the major crimes and dismissed them as either too repulsive or too unworkable to achieve his purpose. Only one crime- the crime of rape- seemed a viable possibility, the one crime which met his strategic requirements and which, after coming up with certain rationalizations and self-deceptions, he could justify to himself as an acceptable crime to commit. Rape, though he knew it to be loathsome, was not life-ending for the victim. In the end she would walk away from it, albeit a little gingerly. Rape, while it did take something from the victim, took only that which was emotional, psychological, and therefore intangible; after being raped, the woman was not deprived of her wealth or property. Rape also was a crime that, if the rapist planned it properly, afforded a high probability of a clean getaway. Well, a getaway at least. Only one consideration had presented a stumbling block which for a time had threatened to disqualify rape as the crime of choice: what woman deserved to be raped? Well of course, no woman really deserved to be put through the ignominy of such treatment. But as he listened now through the wall to the voice of the girl next door *is chatting on her phone I hear the chatty little water nymph is laughing speaking tiny twittering phone girl running through the puddles through his mind the girl who splashes in the rain and swims up the stairs and past his door the nextdoor nereid is running and she's laughing and she's swimming and she's drowning* he was reminded of how his mind had been changed in that regard, and how, on so many occasions, she'd proven herself deserving, proven herself well worthy to be cast as the leading lady in his snuff film, she the protagonist and antagonist and tragic heroine all rolled into one, so tiny to play such a big role in his startling denouement. And all because the little bitch wouldn't talk to him.

A grumbling of thunder now accompanied the rain as Jason's thoughts turned the way they always turned eventually, to the many chances he'd given her to prove herself to be a nice person. By now he had moved to his usual sitting spot on the floor, his head strategically *pressed against her wall*, where the vibration he felt buzzing through his ear seemed to be caused not by the rumble of the passing L train but by the warbling of the tiny titmouse chatting away on the other side. It had taken so much for him to overcome his fears and attempt to speak to her, three frightening attempts no less, only for her to confirm each time just how justified his fears had been. It had played out the same humiliating way on all three occasions- watching patiently from his window for her to return from her run, then positioning himself behind his door as she entered the building where he lay in wait behind it, listening for her to make it into the hallway, then the sound of her footsteps getting nearer, followed by his perfectly timed "coincidental" stepping out of his apartment just as she was putting her key into the door lock, counting on her key activity to delay her there just long enough for him to deliver his pre-rehearsed ice breaking sentence, an inane remark about the weather on attempt #1, a lame joke about the neon brightness of her running shoes on #2, then back to the stupid weather for #3. And each time- each fucking time- Jason would make it no further than his first three words when her phone would ring and she would raise her hand apologetically with a sheepish look on her face which said "Sorry I've got to take this," leaving him hanging in mid-sentence like a dangling participle, disconnected from the noun, giving him no recourse but to mumble and fumble his way back into his apartment as she blithely disappeared into hers, unaware of the leveling devastation she had caused. He was grateful, truth be told, for the multiple snubbings, for they provided him just enough grist to turn his mill of resentment, offenses which he convinced himself deserved a measure of retribution; and while he was aware that raping the little wench just for not speaking to him was a punishment not fitting the crime, he also knew his crime would ultimately fit her punishment. For though she would in fact be raped, he would then be shot dead for having raped her. And thus the last word of retribution would be hers.

And so had Jason decided he would rape his neighbor. Purely from a strategic vantage point his plan boasted many selling points. The proximity, of course, couldn't be better, either for the facilitation of the attack or his unproblematic getaway following it. He would have his own building to maneuver in, not some remote location where he didn't belong (it would be difficult enough maneuvering between two legs where he didn't belong); his plan was to stage yet another "coincidental" meeting as she was unlocking her door, only this time he would escort her into her apartment with a bum's rush, then rush her bum, then simply walk next door and await the arresting officers (he had first contemplated dragging her into his own apartment for the deed, but decided that raping her in the familiarity of her own home rather than a stranger's was a more considerate gesture). As for a victim, his little lovebird was a sitting duck, so conveniently placed that if Amazon had delivered her to his door she couldn't have been more readily available. He would of course not disguise himself in any way, for the whole point was for her to know exactly who her attacker was and thus easily identify him to the police to ensure that they'd promptly pay him a visit. Even her tiny size fit his purpose- Jason's hulking mass would easily overwhelm her, despite the squishiness of his physique. A bigger girl would fight back hard, and while he would probably still win, he would very likely have to hurt her in the process, and above all Jason didn't want to hurt anyone. The rape itself would be unpleasant enough- why add injury to insult? But aside from the purely practical aspects of his escape plan, there was a more personal angle not to be ignored, a psycho/sexual/emotional one, which both troubled and pleased him in equal measures. The strategy of his suicide plan thrust him into the mindset of a rapist, and as a result, a forbidden room of his thought life had for the first time been cracked open, allowing its contents to be aired out; now that his desperate circumstance had cast him in the role of a rapist, he was allowed, required even, to think the thoughts of a rapist, and he could not help but admit to himself that, to his surprise, he was liking those thoughts just fine thank you. It now seemed to him that he'd always wanted to rape her, had harbored that desire all along, but the straitjacket of his cowardice had prevented such thoughts from wriggling out of his mind. It was his impending suicide, his escape plan from life, which had smashed the lock and liberated him from cowardice. Here he was, brave enough finally to dream his darkest dreams, and to make those dreams come true. He would finally attain to his apotheosis. He would be the Martyr Rapist.

    The apartment next door had gone quiet by now, but Jason's ear remained pressed up against the wall, listening to the soundlessness, imagining all the silent private things his hummingbird might be about. How surely she must believe her private life belonged to herself alone- how could she know that soon she would meet the Martyr Rapist, who would insinuate himself into her privacy and claim its highest hill? He marveled at how dramatically his escape plan had changed him, to be transformed from an ineffectual nobody into a force-of-nature somebody, indeed, a somebody who would actually force himself *on* somebody. And here Jason was posed with a philosophical question: if special circumstances, in this case his escape plan, had provided him the courage to discover his inner rapist, then how might other special circumstances, had they been thrust upon him, have given him the courage to discover yet more hidden Jasons, and thereby set them free to pursue a whole panoply of bad behaviors? Had he thought about it before, he'd have assumed that his good (non-criminal) behavior was attributable to his morality, his personal code of honor and virtue, a conscious choice of right over wrong. But now, here he was a rapist- yes, he already was one, for he'd rehearsed the act with her so many times and had so enjoyed the rehearsing that his status as an accomplished rapist was now a foregone conclusion- and by acknowledging himself an accomplished rapist he understood that he'd been a rapist all along, merely a dormant one, and that his "moral opposition" to the crime had been nothing more than self-deceit, or at best, self-ignorance. What other crimes and atrocities, then, were his other dormant Jasons willing, perhaps even eager, to commit, if only the conscious Jason would provoke them? And he expanded his question to a broader context: how much of what the world calls law and order, how much human behavior which we deem civilized and peaceable and considerate and law-abiding and all that shit, is not the result of innate goodness or virtue in the animal, but rather of a species-wide lack of courage to follow through on the darkest and most selfish of its desires- in short, the fear of getting caught? For those who believe in an afterlife, the fear is twofold: the fear not only of consequences in this life for being caught but also consequences in the next even if they get away with it on earth. Should human animals therefore congratulate themselves on getting along as well as they do when so much of that "getting along" is just a product of their timidity? Shouldn't they instead be ashamed at what cowards they are by not taking what they really want from life? Hadn't all expeditions, forgings of nations, conquests and colonizations- the great "advancements" of civilization- necessarily depended upon forcible invasion and subjugation, non-negotiable appropriation and occupation in order to succeed? Taking what one wanted- rape, if you will- was the way of the world, the real essence of its core, despite the world's polite veneer of playing nicely with others. So who was Jason then but one of those brave ones daring to acknowledge humankind's true nature, to bravely take what he wanted, just as Alexander and Pizarro and Genghis Khan had? A lifetime spent throttled by the stranglehold of cowardice had given him an appreciation for courage as few others could ever understand. But while he had indeed found, finally, the courage to snatch up and grab a prize during his otherwise prize-deprived life, Jason did not forget that the ultimate prize would still remain, that being the end of same. For though he'd found inner strength to do his courageous crime, he was not brave enough by half to do the time. At least his death would be on his own terms.

    The ear which Jason was not pressing against the wall could no longer hear the rain falling outside; the departing of the storm was now permitting an emergence of sunlight into his apartment, sunlight which he resented, and he squinted shut his eyes. Then his wall-pressing ear picked up a new sound, another rain shower; not really a rain shower, but his water nymph's shower, where he pictured her standing behind steamy glass, Aphrodite-like in dripping marble nakedness. The shower was steady and gentle, and it sounded very distant to him, yet he knew just how close to the rain he really was. She was so near, his water nymph, standing in the rain now as she had been standing in the rain just before on the street below, but here the rain was just a few feet away and *just a few days away, the rain was getting nearer, and he would bring the rain and the storm, she was so clean now but that would all change for he would invade and subjugate and appropriate and occupy and he would sow the wind, but he would reap the whirlwind sure enough; he will be dead and gone but he will have left something behind a residue of his existence even though he would disappear down the drain where his water and hers would mingle forever.*

The Saturday morning next was the day of the crime, the day he had chosen when he would attain to his ultimacy as Martyr Rapist, and it found Jason sitting earlier than usual at his window, staring down on Shit Street; and as he regarded the ants going about their shop-to-shop business, he noticed that he was smiling as he watched, not feeling his usual resentment toward the ants, for he was one of them today, a worker ant who, like they, had a meaningful task to perform and would be leaving some pheromones of his own very soon. That he was excited was a simplification of course; it was a stirring of emotions, of thoughts, expectations, fears (yes, the fear was there, but it was manageable and he was sure he could work through it), all blended into something which he imagined must be what happiness felt like for non-raping people. Indeed, he considered ironically, if every day of his life could only feel like this then there would be no reason to be escaping it, but of course this morning's giddiness only bubbled up within him because he was. It was not so much ironic but pathetic to him that this happiest day of all days would occur as a result of tearing a girl's clothes off, but even the self-loathing this generated was advantageous, since self-loathing was essential to getting that trigger pulled. But it was the giddy excitement, not the self-loathing, which had brought him to his window an hour earlier than usual, excitement and vigilance, to make sure he didn't miss her when she left for her run, and so to be on point for action when she returned from it. He had watched her and waited for her and listened to her and was even convinced he had smelled her every morning of the preceding week in fact, not so much out of necessity to document her comings and goings but to immerse himself in the anticipation of the event, to get into the zone as it were, and to make himself available to this increased level of surveillance it had meant skipping work the entire week previous. To miss a week of work without calling in meant certain termination, which was exactly what Jason was after; he had decided that such a burning of his bridges made retreat from his resolve that much less an option. It was just another bullet-point on his final "all in" checklist- the planning was made, the mind was focused, the job was quit, and both his guns were loaded. He had rehearsed every step, imagined every angle, and explained away every misgiving. But now it was time to stop explaining and imagining, because here she was, coming around the corner, breathing nearly as hard as he was, glistening and slippery, not with rain this time but with sweat. The rehearsing was over. It was time to start the show.

Having confirmed that his water nymph had begun her cooldown and stretching routine on the sidewalk below, Jason made a quick self-inventory for the umpteenth time to make sure all was in order. His flip-flops had been kicked off in deference to barefoot's added agility (no socks, for what if she had slippery tile on her floor?); he was wearing his fastest "pull off/pull back on" shorts, but then again, would he even bother with putting them back on after?; a final sniff-check, catching a whiff of his earlier splash of cologne (an old birthday present from his mom, the first time he'd ever worn it, today was his first date with a girl after all); one last rub of his newly-bald head (his shoulder-length hair, he reasoned, was just something for her to pull on, so in a "night before battle" ritual he had shaved his scalp clean); then a final few hops up and down as a warm-up, knowing that the next however-many minutes would be the most exercise he'd done since wrestling in high school gym class (when he lost every match *no don't think about that*). She was finished with stretching and with drinking her water; she was up off the sidewalk and standing again, which meant she'd be coming back into the building at any moment. A rush of adrenaline surged out from his chest, then trickled down into his gut, reaching finally to the tips of his lower regions, as though the regimental bugler had sent out the assembly call to all the glandular and muscular and tubular troops who were about to be marched headlong and head first into the most mortal of combats. Finally she walked up to his building's door, and when she disappeared inside Jason's adrenalin chilled in a single moment to ice water. A thousand terrors swarmed over him in a whispering cloud, all telling him in no uncertain terms to retreat. But there could be no retreat now- he had quit his job and shaved his head, had shaved his balls for god's sake, had swallowed the Viagra he'd burglarized from his father's medicine chest (and swallowed his mom's tramadol too after all), and he had loaded his Glock .38 with the one and only bullet he would need and wedged it between his seat cushions. Jason had tied all that he was and all that he wanted to be to his ankle and thrown it off the cliff of this rape, but more than that, he had in the days before this day found the courage to dream of this day, to believe in himself as the rapist, to become the rapist, whether he went ahead with the rape or not; and if he didn't do the rape he would still *be* the rapist but could not be the *Martyr* Rapist for no police would come which meant having to go on living as a rapist in waiting rather than dying the Martyr Rapist's death he so desired. For the Martyr Rapist's death must be earned, this he knew. And so the newly-brave Jason shooed away the cloud of fearful whisperings, and in the silence of his resolve he was able to hear the footsteps, squeaking down the hallway, creaking and creeping nearer and nearer.

With his ear against his door and a hand on each of his respective doorknobs Jason listened as the footsteps passed by his apartment, then came to a stop. She was at her door now, and all that remained was to listen for her keys coming into contact with her door lock. There it was, the tinkling click! It was time. Opening his door, he was shocked at seeing her so very close-up, shocked by the presence of her physical body, still wet with sweat, as if her flesh had only been a dream up till now, and she appeared much bigger than she had all those times down on the sidewalk, bigger even than the other times at the door when she had made him feel so small. This time he felt smaller still- well, not smaller everywhere- and she looked at him and smiled as her key went in and turned in the lock. The big moment was at hand, for her door was opening now; once it was open wide enough and she turned to go in, that was when he would have to make his move. He was ready. But before the door had fully opened the girl looked back up to him, still smiling, as if waiting, expecting him to say something, just as he had tried the three times before. But Jason wasn't here to speak to her this time. She had wasted all her speaking chances. Now he was here to act. Now the door was open. Now he would step right through-

"Hi. We haven't really met. I'm Tina."

Jason's dick retreated to its cave.

"It's Jason right? I saw some of your mail, your name was on it." Her smile revealed a trace of embarrassment; she seemed a little nervous, but still smiling.

"So... it's Jason?"

All he could do was nod. It was his turn to sweat.

Tina smiled again *fuck her name is Tina I didn't want her to have a name!* and when she threw her hair back off her face some of it remained stuck to her still-wet forehead. She really was a water nymph. "God, I must look terrible, just went running, sorry." She was beautiful, so suddenly beautiful, wet and shiny and arisen from the sea, eyes fluttering and open mouth smiling from the deep and staring now at his stupid bald head. "You got a haircut?"

Again, a nod was all he could manage. Rubbing the stubble of his scalp self-consciously, Jason fought to remember why he was out in the hall in his bare feet. She was speaking to him. He had to *say something*. But his mouth was having none of it.

Still Tina persisted. "When I was on the swim team in college I thought about shaving my head. You know, to cut through the water. And it's so bad-ass besides." She was already bad-ass.

Bad-ass and beautiful. "But I guess I just wasn't brave enough to go through with it."

His head was an empty attic; his tongue tasted dust instead of words. *Why can't I say anything???* Those previous three times he'd been so prepared, so ready, pumped and prime for those conversations which never happened. Now it was happening! And still Tina was smiling at him. How many hours did it feel like they'd been standing here and here she still stood, not having given up on him yet! But then something suddenly dropped into the empty attic. A tasty line to say! *I'll tell her, "You wouldn't be brave to shave off hair that beautiful, you'd be crazy!" Yeah! Here I go...*

"You wouldn't be brave to- "

A twittering chirp cut him off in mid-line. It was her phone, her fucking phone, showing up right on time, heckling him from her fanny pack, gagging him and stumbling him up. It was happening again. It was all playing out as before. The encounter, the nerves, the line to deliver, then his delivery ruined by the chirping. He stood there impotently, waiting for the inevitable next thing, for the apologetic eyes to tell him "Sorry, I gotta take this." But her eyes merely flickered toward the phone with annoyance for a moment, then came back to meet his. The phone kept chirping. Tina was ignoring it. She was waiting for *him*! She was choosing him over the chirping. Now she was speaking to him over the chirping.

"I wouldn't be what?"

But all Jason could do was stare at the fanny-pack. His tasty line had dried up in his mouth. The attic was dust again. The phone had brought him back to himself. Back to where there was nothing.

The phone kept chirping. And now appeared those apologetic eyes, just like the times before, but this time they were not so much apologetic as exasperated. With him.

"Sorry, I gotta take this." As Tina began to fumble into her fanny pack, a fissure of emotion ripped open somewhere in Jason's chest. Tina and her phone had torn off a scab inside, which allowed the rage to begin bleeding, flowing, gushing through all those places where thrilling adrenalin had coursed only moments before. The phone was in Tina's hand now, still chirping away, a mocking magpie who had stolen his chance. The rage was everywhere, in his legs and arms and especially in his trembling hands. Just before she could answer the phone one of his trembling hands made the decision all on its own to swat it out of her grip, the phone landing on the carpet inside her apartment. He was nearly as startled by it as the girl, who screamed out in shock.

"Ahgh! What the fuck asshole???"

Jason stared at the still-chirping phone on her living room floor. Out of nowhere he had up and slapped the thing right out of her hand, an action which had slapped him back to his senses. Suddenly he remembered why he was in the hallway. He had crossed the line by striking out in violence. Swatting the phone had pushed him off the cliff. There was no climbing back onto it at this point. It was on.

Grabbing the ugly little fish by the fin he threw her into her apartment, slamming the door behind him. His hand was wrapped around her mouth before she could scream; she screamed anyway, but a sound too muffled to be heard. She was flopping on the floor and he was flopping right on top of her. She was slippery and strong. But he was winning.

"Shut up! Just shut up!"

"Mmrrmrrmmghrm!" She was still trying to scream, but Jason only pressed his hand harder against her mouth. She was writhing and grinding to escape from under his weight; she kept grinding, and she could not know that the grinding was strategically placed, right where Jason's dormant accomplice was waiting to be awakened and re-activated for assignment, which now it was. An actual girl was grinding against him! This was nothing like gym class wrestling, those bodies were just obstacles, immovable objects. This was a girl, the first girl he'd ever touched, and now his hand was under all the clothes and finding wet nipples and softness. He was in awe and in terror, so enjoying it and not able to enjoy it. He was pulling at tank tops and running tights and fanny packs and sports bras and himself while feeling hard rubber running shoes kicking his shins and he was making progress against it all, even with only one busy hand, the other hand muffling her biting mouth, the same mouth which had made the mistake of telling him "sorry, gotta take this," somehow even getting his own shorts pulled down, then kicked off, which she noticed, which he was glad she noticed. Despite the sticky resistance of her sweatiness she was mostly naked now *jesuschrist look at slippery white glistening everywhere* only the panties remaining, which he would chew off if need be. He was going to rape her by god! And he would die for it too! But he wasn't thinking about the dying part at the moment because she was pulling hard at the hand which covered her mouth and moving it just enough so she could

Ahghghghghhrrrrrhhghg!

"Shut up!" Covering her mouth again and pressing it harder to send a message Jason slid the other hand down her stomach *ohmygod that's a girl's belly button leave a finger there for a second* where he found the panties and was in and under just like that, maneuvering through the jungle just like someone who had been in jungles before and wasn't afraid of what he would find. Everything the internet had told him would be there was there but it felt nothing like his keyboard and now those panties had to go, the last remnant of her defenses, and they were down her smooth legs and *the stupid fucking shoes are still on* and now she was all his, all meat and magic and flesh-hairy namelessness, her name torn off and thrown aside like her clothes, and he was ready, she would try to wrench and twist away like any captured nymph but he was the mythological one now the rutting faun the Martyr Rapist... the martyr! All of this would be pointless if it did not result in his destruction. He had to be sure of her therefore, to make sure she would tell them afterward.

"You know my name don't you? I'm Jason Withrow!" A pair of wide-open eyes nodded "yes."

"You're gonna tell them I live right next door aren't you?" The eyes grew even wider. He could feel that every muscle in her soon-to-be-penetrated body had suddenly gone tight with tension.

"You're gonna tell them it was Jason Withrow aren't you?"

She was not wriggling about anymore, but had gone frozen and stiff, lying very still but remaining fully flexed. He had yelled really loudly at her, which must have frightened her, he realized, judging by her sudden stillness, and he instantly regretted that he'd used such a harsh tone. But he couldn't apologize to her at the moment because it was time to force his dick into her. Her rigid tenseness wouldn't be a problem as long as he was able to pry open her legs. He would need both hands though, which risked a scream; but when he tentatively removed his hand he was relieved to see a mouth which was frozen in suspended animation. His hands were in place, on the insides of each thigh. But as he was about to force the stiff legs open, he was surprised to feel the tension suddenly drop entirely, and then the soft legs opened for him all by themselves, spreading wide, and then wider still, her muscles no longer pinched but pliable, her door unlocked and inviting, her privacy no longer protected.

"Well? Go on!"

Something which Jason knew could not possibly be a smile had found its way onto her face.

"Go on?"

"Yes, go on!" Tina's hands began to run up and down his arms affectionately.

"Let's do this Jason." She reached up to his shoulders and gently pulled him toward her.

"Now that my phone isn't interrupting us, right?"

He hovered in place, landing gear retracted. "Your phone…"

She laughed. "Oh don't apologize! You just surprised me is all when you slapped it. I'm glad you surprised me! I'm glad you threw the phone down." She began stroking his arms once again. "I'm glad you threw *me* down."

He was sure he was dreaming, but the new place she was now stroking him was way beyond his ability to be dreamt. "I-ooo, ohhh- I didn't hurt you did I?"

She nodded. "Oh yeah. It hurt. It hurt sooooo good." By now her other hand had joined the first in the stroking operation. His eyes rolled to the back of his head. "And all the kicking and fighting back I was doing- did I hurt *you*? Was it too much?"

"Me? No, I- "

"Because I wanted to make it believable, you know? Like I was really resisting." As one hand continued to choke his chicken, the other took his hand and placed it on her breast meat. "Because if there's no resisting then it's not much of a rape is it?"

It was too much stimuli for either of his heads to handle. "So you- you don't mind that I'm raping you?"

"*Mind?*" It's a fantasy come true!" Now wrapping her hands around his back, Tina pulled his torso down with a quick jerk so that the full weight of his upper body landed heavily atop hers. "Ughgh! Oh yeah! That almost knocked the breath out of me!" In an instant she was kissing him, swallowing his tongue, her lower half grinding against his in a manner which was not only deliberate but delicious. As Jason felt himself increasingly entangled by the tentacles of his suddenly-eager octopus, the truth of the situation, impossible to believe though it was, could no longer be doubted: she wanted him to rape her! Whether she had wanted it from the moment he slapped her phone or from the moment he spoke to her or from the moment he had first become her neighbor he could not know, but she most certainly wanted it now- and he was more than willing to give it to her. With redoubled dedication to the demands of his role Jason shook off his stage fright and forged ahead with his performance.

"You like me on top of you don't you?" *that was a good line but where's the hole?*

"Yes I like you all over me." *maybe she'll help me and put it where it needs to go.*

"You've always wanted me to fuck you didn't you?" She wheezed instead of responding, and Jason realized that his clumsy body was squeezing the breath out of her. But she probably got off on not being able to breathe so he laid even more heavily against her lungs.

"Yes" she finally gasped. "Ever since I saw you. It was my little secret." *aren't there supposed to be lips in all this damn... wait, there it is! Shouldn't it be wet though! Fuck it, who cares, it's goin' in-*

"- and it'll stay our little secret. Only you and me will know."

The locomotive stalled at the tunnel. "Nobody?"

"Nobody." She wheezed again through a mischievous smile. "My lips are sealed. Well, sort of!"

A feeling of foreboding began to seep in through the cracks. "You... you're not going to tell anybody about this?"

"Nobody. Like I said, our little secret." A playful hand rubbed across the stubble of his shaved head. "We'll pretend like it never even happened. Which will make it better for the next time we play rape, right?"

"The next time?"

"Well, yeah! I was hoping tomorrow maybe."

"Uh, yeah. Tomorrow maybe." As Tina repositioned herself to better facilitate his anticipated entry, a rush of realizations flooded his thoughts. This would be their little secret! She had just made it clear that despite his bad intentions his attempt at doing crime was not a crime to her at all, but rather, a pleasant way to spend a Saturday morning. What then was the point? All his miserable life he'd never been able to do a single good thing, and now, he couldn't even successfully do a bad thing! With Tina not considering herself the victim of a crime there would be no crime for her to report, and Jason would be no closer to his ultimate goal whatsoever; he would not be a rapist after all and, as a result, would not be a martyr either. He was nothing but a bald-headed beached whale prostrated atop a wheezing mermaid.

He could feel Tina groping about as his now-blubbery business end. "Hey! What happened?"

"Sorry, I'm... I gotta... gotta go." With a clumsy lurch he brought himself up onto his knees.

"Go? Whaddayou mean?"

An acrid updraft of his stale cologne sickened him. "I'm- I can't. I'm sorry." He was standing now, swaying above her precariously, causing him to become suddenly aware of his nakedness; and his overrushed attempt at pulling on his shorts resulted in both legs being pushed into the same pant hole which sent him crashing back onto the floor, narrowly missing her.

"Be careful! Are you okay?" By now he was already headed for the door on his hands and knees, his shorts dangling from one leg like a baby whose diaper had come undone. "Can we still try again tomorrow maybe?" But Jason had already crawled butt-naked down the hallway and into his own apartment, the door shutting behind him and his pheromone-less trail, but not closing before he heard once again the bright chirping of her cellphone which was wishing him a merry Saturday afternoon and an even merrier rest of his life.

\\

The afternoon sunlight which filtered in through the window overlooking Shit Street revealed nothing but emptiness as it passed unimpeded through the dismal space, its brightness offering no remedy for the heavy darkness which defied any and all attempts to be lifted by illumination. As for the occupant of the sad apartment, the light could find no trace of him either; indeed, had a cave become available after the sordid events in his neighbor's flat some hours earlier, Jason would have shrouded himself in the darkest depths of it, such was his determination to shun the light. But with the north side of Chicago boasting no abandoned mine shafts, he had opted instead to sit on the floor of his tomb-like apartment, far from the window, his back against the door, and had remained there unmoved the entire time since his ignominious retreat from what he had so hoped would be the scene of his big crime. Crimes aplenty had taken place of course, felony crimes, of this he was not in denial, and over the hours following his failed mission he'd replayed in his mind all the criminal activity which had occurred. It was criminal of Tina, first of all, to have behaved so badly as a victim, deceiving him and turning the tables in such an unfair way. He had come to her sincerely and honestly as a rapist, with no hidden agendas, and for his good sportsmanship she had paid him back by cruelly welcoming him into her home once it had been invaded. It was then criminally feeble of him, in the moment of being faced by her double-dealings, to have succumbed to panic and shock and fled the scene with his flaccid tail between his legs instead of standing his ground and doing *whatever it took* to make her not enjoy her raping. Had he only found the courage to rough her up a little he was sure he could have served her in ways which weren't in keeping with her fantasies; he should have slapped that smile off her slutty little face and really given her something to call the police about. But the greatest crime of all was to not only fail in the execution of his escape plan from life but to guarantee himself an even more unendurable rest-of-his-life than the life he'd led up to that point. Before today he at least had a miserable job and a full head of hair. Now he was unemployed and bald. Before today he had a neighbor girl to secretly fantasize about; not only was that fantasy shattered, but he found himself living next door to a crazy woman who he must always avoid due to his pathetic failure between her welcoming legs. But the most unendurable aspect of the life which lay ahead for him was that he would have to continue living it after having come so close to finally ending it. It had been in his grasp, near enough to taste it, and now, having tasted the nearness of his demise, he knew that nothing could ever remove his missed opportunity's bitterness from his mouth. If only he hadn't tried, then he would never have known the shame of failure! Yet for all these downgrades to the quality of his remaining life (downgrades which afforded him more motivation now than ever to end it) Jason knew he was no closer than before to making his death happen. Without the flipping of the switch mechanism- his morbid fear of prison- no deterioration of his circumstances, however dismal, could move him to fatal action. The absurdity of their escapade would remain "our little secret," and so he would remain slumped behind his door, eternally immovable. No amount of afternoon sunlight would brighten his cave. The window of his escape plan had shut forever.

"'Our little secret.' That's what you told him?"

"That's what I told him." Tina drank from her water bottle and wished the lights in the windowless room weren't so bright. "Hey it worked, didn't it?"

"Looks like it. I mean, here you are." The detective powered on his iPad while his partner, a woman not much older than Tina, took a seat beside him. "Did he leave any marks on you, any visible injuries?"

"Oh yeah." Standing up from the table, she showed the detectives the rug burns on the backs of her shoulders and on her elbows, even baring a butt cheek to show an abrasion there.

"That's all from when he threw me on the floor. And I know you probably think it's nothing but believe me it fucking hurt!"

Detective Niddrie typed on his device. "No no, it is something. If he did that then he injured you."

"Oh. Well okay then." Tina sat back down. "Also broke my table when he almost fell on me. The pieces of it are at my apartment. If you don't believe me just go there and see for yourself!"

"Of course we'll be going over there." The female detective leaned in closer. "Now when he started to attack you, you said you knew he was going to kill you. What made you think that?"

"Oh I don't know, maybe because he was *fucking attacking me!*"

Niddrie's voice was dad-like. "Tina, we know our questions are a pain but we gotta ask 'em. What Lieutenant Montrose meant was, did he say or do anything *specifically* that told you he was there for more than... than just attacking you."

She closed her eyes, exhaled deeply, then began. "Sorry. Okay. So like I said, he smacks the phone out of my hand, throws me on the floor, flops down on top of me like a big-ass walrus and starts tearing off my clothes. And I'm fighting like hell because I wasn't going down like that, I just wasn't gonna lay there and take it."

"Risky choice" said Montrose.

"Didn't care. Motherfucker pissed me off."

"Were you screaming?"

"I was trying. But he had one of his walrus flippers over my mouth so I couldn't." Tina took another hit from her water bottle, then continued. "So I'm fighting, and he's pulling off clothes, and then he's naked, and of course I can see that the only part of the fucking walrus which wasn't soft was his big red dick coming straight at me." She paused and looked up at the detectives. "Too much detail?"

Niddrie fought back a smile as he typed. "Big red dick. Noted."

"Okay. So anyway, he's getting ready to go to town on me, and I'm kickin' at 'im with my running shoes 'cause that's all I was still wearing by that point, when all of a sudden he starts yellin' shit to me like 'You know my name don'tchoo?' and 'You're gonna tell 'em where I live aren'tchoo?' Like that. And then it hit me- who rapes somebody when the woman knows exactly who he is and where he lives and doesn't wear a mask and even says his name to her unless he's gonna kill her when he's done, right? I mean, who rapes his next-door neighbor and lets her live unless he *wants* the fucking police sorry the police to come and get him?"

Montrose glanced over to Niddrie, then back to Tina. "So that's when you told him it would be the two of you's little secret?"

"Ha! I wish it would have been that simple." She leaned forward, elbows on the table, her face in her hands. "No, when I realized he was gonna kill me after fucking me I just stop fighting and sortof gave up, you know, like, damn, I'm a dead girl, no way out. And right then it all of a sudden didn't matter anymore if I was gonna get raped because what was that compared to getting killed, right? So like in a split second I thought, well, anybody this fucking bold has done this shit before of course, so maybe if I give him like the best motherfucking rape he ever had, maybe if I pretend to really *get into it* as if all I ever wanted in life was to someday get throwed down like a sack of shit and walrus-fucked on the living room floor, then I might have a chance to not die afterwards. And so… I got into it."

"You went along with the rape then?"

"Went along? Hell, I started raping *him!*" Tina leaned in toward the detectives, her eyes wide and her palms on the table. "I start kissin' him and grindin' him and jerkin' his dick and rubbin' his head and tellin' him 'Yeah baby make it hurt throw me down squish the breath out of me' just to make him *think* I was enjoying myself."

Niddrie chose his words. "And was he… convinced… that you were into it?"

Tina tilted her head to the side in thought. "Well you know, that part was weird, because the more I pretended to get into it, the more he seemed, I don't know, not into it. And then when I played my big escape plan card, when I said it would be our little secret and I wouldn't tell anybody, he just quit altogether. Done."

Niddrie typed as Montrose spoke. "And then he stopped trying to rape you?"

Tina sat back triumphantly. "Yep. Checked out. Fumbled around for his fucking drawers and crawled, no shit, crawled out the door. And I even yelled after him, 'So do we have another date for tomorrow?' just as a final little fuck you."

Niddrie had stopped typing and was nodding with what could only be described as fatherly pride. "And that's how you stayed alive?"

"Stayed alive *and* un-fucked!" She took a victory swig from her water bottle.

Montrose sat back and regarded the girl across the table from her. "Well I gotta say, it's not something we'd recommend any other woman do in that situation, but you're clearly not just any other woman."

"I'm not?" Tina's mouth betrayed just the slightest tremor as her eyes began to blink. "Then how come I feel just like any other woman?" Suddenly her face was in her hands again, elbows on the table, her shoulders shaking as the sobs came tumbling out one upon the other. For perhaps a minute she allowed herself to cry freely in this way, oblivious to the detectives and her surroundings, but then just as abruptly she pushed her chair away from the table and exhaled loudly as if shouting away the emotion, her head and hands twitching rapidly to shake off the tears. "Arghghg! No!! Fuck that sonofabitch!" After throwing back an emptying swig from the water bottle she regained her composure with one long breath. Her voice was calm now but her tone was grim, cold-blooded. "He's gonna do major time for this won't he?"

Montrose squirmed as Niddrie sighed audibly. "Well Tina, all we do is catch these guys and charge 'em. We aren't involved in convicting and sentencing them."

She looked rapidly from one face to the other. "So what are you saying?"

"What he did to you today was a major felony" Montrose said. "You don't have to convince us of that. The problem is..." She looked to her partner for assistance, and finding none, she went on. "... the problem is that crimes like this- sexual assaults- are like the hardest ones to... to get good outcomes in the courts."

"But this motherfucker- "

"There were no witnesses" interjected Niddrie gently. "That's the first thing. There was also no forced entry- your door was already open, right?"

"Well, yeah, and he flung me airborne *through* that open door!"

"- which is your side of the story" continued Montrose. "His defense would be that you invited him in- "

"- and that you initiated the rough sex- "

"- which he then became uncomfortable with- "

"- without even raping you."

"Yes" concluded Niddrie. "Without even raping you. Which is why… he might not get any jail time at all." The two detectives gazed sympathetically upon the shell-shocked girl who stared back at them in wide-eyed disbelief.

Tina spluttered to find the words, running her fingers through her hair in exasperation. "Yeah well it wasn't for his lack of trying! His big red battering ram just couldn't find the hole fast enough is all!"

"Let's be thankful for that. More water?" Montrose handed her another bottle, which Tina nearly tore open, throwing the cap clear across the room. "But let's deal with one thing at a time. We'll do all we can to build the case. We promise."

"Thanks I guess." Tina drank from the water bottle, then shook her head with a bitter laugh. "Wow. Tries to walrus fuck me and won't even go to jail. His lucky day."

By early evening the darkness Jason so longed for had finally established itself across the moribund confines of his silent flat, while the newly-lit streetlights out on Shit Street announced another Saturday night in the big city. But for him, nothing about the hours to come would resemble a Saturday night or a Tuesday night or any other night with a name for that matter; all his days and nights would go on being just as nameless and indistinguishable as they had always been, and would proceed even more interminably. He had gotten up once or twice from his seat on the floor against his front door to shuffle to the bathroom and drain his failure of a dick, and had returned each time to his spot of shame like some misbehaving boy who had imposed upon himself an indefinite punishment of time-out. At some point the phone had trembled, probably his mother calling, no doubt to accuse him of stealing her pain meds. She could have them back as far as he was concerned; the four hours of tepid euphoria they afforded him earlier that afternoon had only served to mock him with its artificial pleasure, in that the drug took him to heights of blissful painlessness which, at its peak, merely reminded him just how inaccessible such altitudes of contentment really were for the likes of him without the help of chemicals, then dropping him crashed and abandoned at the foot of its mountain after the effects of the opiate had worn off. Jason had no need for redundancy when it came to falling to the depths. He had proven himself quite capable of crashing and burning all by himself without a drug come-down adding more steepness to the fall. His miserable ass was already planted on the floor. It was clear he could fall no further.

A soft pink and blue neon was blinking vaguely into and throughout the apartment, the light coming from the marquee of a movie theatre just across the street from Jason's building. He had never cared to see any of the films there, but the lights were blinking now with an irony, in that the film of his recent misadventure which had begun playing in his mind when he first closed the door on his retreat had not ceased to repeat all these hours, and showed no signs of scrolling to a merciful end any time soon. But would his mind find any relief if it were no longer forced to revisit over and over again the scenes of his pseudocomical tragifarce? For what better thoughts would replace that film once the screen went dark? Some happier film waiting to be loaded onto the projector? Not possibly. But it was not lost on him how other people, normal and happy other people, might watch the scenes of his Saturday matinee and see a somewhat different film, certainly no less obscene and poorly acted than the one he saw but a film which, with a little squinting, might almost be construed as having a happy ending. Because a normal and happy person, having behaved as despicably as he had but knowing he'd totally gotten away with it and would suffer no consequences, would be relieved and thrilled by such an outcome rather than thrown into despair. A normal and happy person, rather than sit for hours on the floor in a puddle of his own humiliation, would celebrate and party after having dodged such a portentous bullet. Indeed, he had dodged not just the figurative bullet but the actual one; for while the normal and happy person would never have included suicide as the terminal destination of his itinerary, Jason had, and but for the mathematically impossible luck/misfortune of choosing as his victim the only person in the 60640 zip code crazier than himself, he would right now be sitting in his chair, gun in hand, waiting for sweet release. It was nothing short of miraculous really, his dodging of that bullet; and as he thought more about the unlikely chain of events which had occurred, or rather, the non-events which had not, a slowly-stirring realization began to peek through the clouds and cast light upon the landscape of his mind where no light had shined before. It *was* a miracle, an actual miracle, that the bullet which had been all but guaranteed to find him was no longer to leave his weapon but would remain there, allowing him to remain as well. It was a miracle, nothing short of a divine intervention, an eleventh-hour stay of execution when no reprieve had been in sight. He had been the classic Isaac of old, neck pinned to the slab, awaiting sacrifice beneath the knife of Abraham, and Yahweh incarnated as Crazy Bitch had reached down from the heavens and held the knife at bay. Yes, a miracle had saved his life today, Jason understood this much at last; and as the growing light of his epiphany brightened his comprehension with greater and greater clarity, he also came to see that no miracle of such magnitude was granted to any man merely for that man's life to be spared, but for that life to be lived- and lived as it had never been lived before. The scales of his obtuse blindness now fell from his eyes. How could any man be granted a second chance at life and not seize it by the short hairs? An entirely new perspective, a positive and hopeful one, was presenting itself to him like a welcome stranger. So what if he was unemployed and bald? Jobs as shitty as his were a dime a dozen, and hair grew back. Yes, he was still a virgin, but having found the courage to attempt what he had attempted (and having learned just how badly girls wanted the attempt to be made) he knew that his next try would be more successful and that his virginity would soon be a thing of the past. As for that failed attempt, he had not raped Tina, nor had she expressed anything but eager gratitude for the attack- and so his criminal record remained clean! As far as the law and Tina and the god who spared him were concerned he'd done nothing wrong (except for breaking the little table, he'd pay her whatever it was worth of course). *He was a good guy after all!* He was on his feet now, pacing back and forth in the neon dark, his optimistic energy bouncing him about like a pinball. He was Ebenezer Scrooge on Christmas morning, a new man reconfigured and redeemed by lessons learned from a nightmare. *He had dodged the bullet!* His life lay before him to be lived!He ran to his window and gazed out over the streetlit activity of Shit Street and suddenly wished himself to be among it, to be down there celebrating the first Saturday night in his memory that finally felt like one. Until this moment his profound feelings of alienation had left him with no desire to share his existence with any part of the human race, but now, having emerged as a butterfly from the cocoon which had held him, Jason longed to open the window and test his untried wings, to flutter down to the sidewalk and participate in the game of pollination. There they were, he thought to himself, all of them having their Saturday night date nights, with him actually feeling just a little bit datable for the first time in his life but stuck in a room which was suddenly too small to contain him. Long ago he'd given up on the notion of anything so normal and healthy as a real relationship with a something called a girlfriend, but now, as the beneficiary of a life-changing miracle, his thoughts dared to swerve into that lane for the first time in the longest. Why shouldn't a relationship be a possibility? The miracle of his salvation had given him ample reason for all kinds of hope. So why not hope to find a girlfriend?

That's when Jason realized he already had one.

Tina! Wasn't Tina his girlfriend? What was it she said to him while making his hasty retreat? "Can we try again tomorrow?" *Try again!* She wanted him to try again! He had buried the memory of the words she'd said in those moments when she turned the tables and he fled in panic, but now he dug them all up and let them sound aloud. *Try again tomorrow!* He had thought at the time it was finished and done, but for her it was, well, just the beginning. And wait- she had also spoken of "the next time we play rape." *The next time!* Once again he was pacing his flat, his heart pumping like a jungle drum, now and then even laughing out loud as he giddily entertained the exciting possibilities. She was his, his to have, his to return to, she'd said so herself. She had seen him at his rubbery worst, yet she spoke of tomorrow night. *Tomorrow night!* As Jason's pacing took him back to his window overlook on Shit Street, the spark of an idea began to glow in his brain, an inspiration of the moment, the kind of idea that, once it whispers itself into existence, only grows in volume, until the insistence of its purpose cannot be shouted down. Tina had wanted their date to be tomorrow night- but hadn't she also said she was glad he surprised her? If so, then why not surprise her again? What if- he was giggling aloud again- what if he and Tina were to have Saturday night date night just like everyone else? Yes! The people on Shit Street had conventional relationships, wrapped in the drabness of planned events and predictable behaviors. But what he and his Tina had was something unpredictable and surprising, even dangerous. So tonight, not tomorrow night, he would wait for her return, just as he had earlier that morning, and would surprise her at the door once again. He would attack her again, this time not as the Martyr Rapist, but as Boyfriend Rapist, the Man Of Her Fantasies Come True *she had said those very words herself* Rapist, and this time, without the burdening pressure of a criminal agenda, he would succeed like the man she believed him to be. He would succeed like the man *he* now believed himself to be.

    It was nearly nine pm when Jason assumed his lookout position at the window and awaited his second date with his new girlfriend. He was worked up with excitement the first time of course, but that emotion had been muddied by dreadful purpose and fear of the unknown. His anticipation this time was purely-distilled enthusiasm, a 100-proof liquor of single-malt exhilaration, an intoxicating eagerness further fortified by the self-congratulating certainty that his second plan was so very obviously superior to his first. It turned out that Jason had not begun his vigil too soon, for at the corner of the block a figure turned the corner and came walking toward his building, and sure enough, the streetlights confirmed that it was His Tina, striding up the sidewalk. Merely her presence served as confirmation for him as to the correctness of his assessment of things, for what girl who considered herself attacked by a real rapist would even think of returning that same night to her apartment right next door to her assailant? His eyes were locked on his beloved target, she a victim of his love just as he was of hers; and when he watched her disappear into the entryway into the building he rushed into position, hunkering down behind his door just as he had earlier that morning, leaving little left for him to do but wait for the sound of her step in the hallway, hoping he would be able to hear it over the drum which was pounding in his chest.

Seconds which seemed like hours refused to pass; finally he heard the familiar creak of the door at the end of the hallway. She was here! He realized that in his haste he'd forgotten to swallow the last of his dad's Viagra, but from what he could feel down below it was not needed. He also found it unnecessary to wear his raping shorts or any other clothing for that matter, having decided in a moment of naughty inspiration that he would rush her this time just as naked as Adam. The sound of her steps grew louder as she neared her apartment door; he was standing now, one hand on the doorknob, the other holding his best idea of all- a sex toy of sorts he'd chosen for the occasion, a little something he grabbed at the last minute to heighten the drama and thus add some extra spice to their lovemaking. The key clicked against her lock; after one last eager giggle, Jason threw open the door. There in the hallway stood Detectives Niddrie and Montrose; Jason had not seen that the detectives were behind Tina on the sidewalk and had followed her into the building, for he had rushed to hide behind his door before they had appeared in view behind her, and Tina had only come back to the building to check her mail downstairs and then, after handing her apartment key to the detectives to do their investigation, left again to stay the night with friends. At the bursting open of Jason's door, the detectives were suddenly confronted with a wild-eyed naked man with a raging red erection aimed directly at them. Also aimed directly at them was the aforementioned sex toy the man had brought out merely as a prop, his .38 Glock revolver, hoping that it would bring an added element of delicious danger to their date night, which it definitely did. With not one but two loaded guns pointed at her face Detective Montrose had no choice but to shoot the naked man straight through his heart, a heart which only hours before had found the courage to begin beating for the first time ever, and which now spilled itself out across the thresholds of both his door and the door of his one true love. And as the naked man lay dying at the feet of the detectives who had come to arrest him but had instead set him free, it was not his freedom, his long-desired and finally achieved escape, which was on the naked man's mind and which moved him to utter his final words as the date night lights on Shit Street grew dim and finally went dark. On his mind was a question whose answer was obvious, and a self-realization whose truth was not. "Why did you have to shoot me?" Jason gasped. "I had so much to live for!"

UNSTARTED STORY

One of the kitchen girls who worked the breakfast said he lived west of town, out Ballincollig way, for she swore up and down she'd seen him in greatcoat and high boots walking a Newfoundland as tall as a pony down Spur Hill Road where all those big fancy estates built during the Celtic Tiger lay peppered about in Doughcloyne, one of several Cork City suburbs where the kitchen girls hoped to live one day. But then Casey the desk clerk told her no, it was east of town, in Blackrock where he lived, next door to the castle on Lough Mahon no less, because he was sure he'd seen his vintage BMW pulling through the iron gates of a humongous plantation right there on Millionaires Row and disappear down the treelined drive. To Roisin it was all one; be it Doughcloyne or Blackrock or Ballincolig or Bishopstown, the fact of the matter was that with her meager waitress job at the Imperial Hotel, in Lafayette's Brasserie Café, those iron gates would stay just as locked shut against her as they were shut to her kitchen girl colleagues. As for him, well, Roisin was full ready to believe that he called one of those high-brow places home; wasn't everything about him high-brow and toney after all? But Mister Stuart wasn't an arrogant man like so many rich could be, not in her dealings with him to be sure. Mister Stuart (was it Mister or Mr. no one was sure, or perhaps it was Stewart, for when he'd first introduced himself it was unclear whether or not it was his first or last name) was there every weekday morning, impeccably attired and tastefully appointed, arriving right on the button of ten am, the time of day when only the lucky folks who no longer have to go to a slaving job are able to sit about in cafes and sip cappuccinos and tap away on laptops for several leisurely hours, which is what Mister Stuart always did. He had one particular table which he clearly fancied (she suspected that it put him in the best position at the big window next to South Mall Street to watch the foot traffic coming in and out of the hotel, for he gazed out that window at least as much as he typed on his keyboard), but if he found that table already taken he was far too lovely a gentleman to grouse about it of course. Still, Roisin tried to avoid seating others at his favorite spot, because she always wished him to have the most agreeable morning possible. Because he was without doubt her best customer, by that meaning, her favorite customer; the one whose "good morning" always sounded sincerest in her ear, the one who was always understanding and never grumpy if his cup came out late, the one who could compliment her hairstyle without sounding the least bit creepy, the one who tipped her generously but not so much as to make her blush, the one whose table was just as spotless when he left it as when he sat down and the one who never left the shop without saying his polite goodbyes. Any day at work was a better one of course when it didn't rain on her walk home or if she hadn't dropped a plate of food or if the time went by quickly and she'd been rewarded with good tips- but the one and only aspect of her working day at Lafayette's which Roisin could say she truly looked forward to was the sight of elegant but not-quite elderly Mister Stuart sweeping in from the street and tipping his flat cap to her in his dignified, old-fashioned way. As for Roisin, to think about Lafayette's without thinking of Mister Stuart sitting at his window table was a thing she couldn't do. And those rare mornings when Mister Stuart was not present were days Roisin could do without.

Where he lived in Cork was but one question which everyone at the Imperial debated; where he'd lived before he came to Cork stirred up more disagreement still (what they all *could* agree on was that he certainly was not Irish). Some clearly heard London in the neatly-clipped precision of his speech, while others were sure they caught just a whiff of a French accent around the edges. Martin the doorman had noticed a New York Times tucked under his arm one day and immediately declared him American, while Shauna detected a subtle trill to his "r"s which to her could only be German. Mister Stuart himself seemed intent on complicating matters, for it was his mischievous habit of mixing up his way of saying "good morning" in a never-ending exchange of differing languages- on Monday he might ring out with a *buon giorno*, on Tuesday you could hear *buenos dias*, on Wednesday perhaps a *goedemorgen* and on one Thursday he surprised everyone with a *dzien dobry*, which nobody understood until Andrzej the Polish day porter expanded everyone's knowledge. Roisin was just as intrigued as the others by the enigma, but preferred to leave it unsolved; she was happier to think of Mister Stuart as not hailing from any one place but from all places somehow, the ultimate citizen of the world, embodying all the qualities (all good qualities to be sure) of the many far-flung lands Roisin had never seen and, as she told herself sometimes when her mood was at her lowest, would probably never see. But her mood was never low when she waited on Mister Stuart, and her fondness for the older man had struck her as a curious thing, as much a mystery to her as his uber-worldly provenance. There was nothing romantic in her feelings for him, yet there was a romance about him; none of her beaus or crushes had ever held her interest in such a way. And it was more than just his pleasant nature which had won her platonic affections- there were plenty of perfectly nice male patrons who cleaned off their tables and left ample tips for whom she'd never given a second moment's thought. What her fondness for him came down to, she had finally concluded, was more than who he was and how he behaved, but what he represented: Mister Stuart was to her a finished product, a completed thing, an ideal fully realized, a man who time and careful effort had brought to perfected completion, like a bottle of 30 year-old single-cask Middleton whisky which, according to her father who could never afford to buy it, stood well above the Seven Wonders of the Ancient World as the highest achievement of the human race. That she herself was so much Mister Stuart's opposite, just an insignificant little nobody living in a council flat up the hill in Knocknaheeny, was reminded to her whenever she was in her favorite customer's presence, her life so pitiably unstarted and unbegun by comparison. Thanks to a family of perpetually underemployed ne'er-do-wells which depended on her financial contributions to keep a roof over their heads (which included her petty-thieving brothers who needed bailing out of jail from time to time) Roisin found herself stuck in the grind of full-time work, affording her no time for college or any other training program which might launch her on her life's trajectory. But even if college were an option she wondered what she would do when she got there, for academics had never held her interest much; and as for something like technical school, she felt even less inclined, seeing the career options they offered as tickets to a lifetime of dreariness- a better paying dreariness than her present one, yes- but dreariness all the same. And so Roisin found herself unstarted in life in two ways- not only had the train which might carry her future prospects not yet left the station, but which track that train should take remained undetermined. What Orient Expresses, what 20th Century Limiteds, what Trans Siberians and Bullet Trains and Flying Scotsmans and Golden Arrows must have carried Mister Stuart in his well-travelled life? The only train Roisin had ever taken was the train to Limerick to visit her bad-tempered grandmother twice a year. And all that train ever did for Roisin was to bring her straight back to Cork City.

But while her perfected ideal of Mister Stuart served to cast his fully-flowered existence in stark opposition to the unsown barrenness of her own, Roisin was not shamed or troubled by his proximity, for the sweetness of his nature prevented one from feeling anything in the way of condescension or patronization when in his presence. She found it an irony, each time she handed him his croissant, that the likes of her, a girl with so little to offer, could deliver something which a man such as him might value, and that it was *he* who thanked *her* for delivering it. It was her pleasure, her privilege, to carefully set the saucer before him or to take it away after, for it was the nearest Roisin came to touching what she believed to be greatness (there was of course the time when Shirley Manson the lead singer of Garbage had stayed at the hotel and Roisin had served her a pear salad, but how could any singer whose band had a name like Garbage be considered "great?") And it was those near-brushes with Mister Stuart's greatness, the times when she'd come to his table for whatever reason, which piqued her sharpest curiosities about the man, for there was yet another mystery about him which, for her, was far more interesting than wondering where he lived now or in the past.

For those trips to the table brought her near his laptop, the thing which provided Mister Stuart his one and only occupation when sitting in Lafayette's. He was a writer of some sort, that much she'd determined, for her surreptitious glimpses at his screen had never observed a spreadsheet or an article from the internet or anything other than his own unbroken, uninterrupted word processing. Yes, Mister Stuart was writing something, and it was clearly creative and original in nature, for he worked from no books or reference materials of any kind. From the occasional smiling and self-satisfied nodding of his head as he typed, now and then exhaling into a wistful sigh, even chuckling to himself from time to time, Roisin knew that whatever he was composing gave him fine pleasure, and its content clearly mattered greatly to him in some private way- and anything which mattered greatly to one such as Mister Stuart, she surmised, should matter greatly to herself as well. Could it be possible that what he was writing might be as well put-together, as nuanced in its detail, as curated in its style, and as lovely in its temperament as its author? Then again, how could it not be? Watching him work from her observation post behind the glass pie case, Roisin found herself looking upon a man who had obviously found, who was actively finding right before her eyes, *something*, while she to this point in life hadn't found anything at all. Whatever it was he was typing into his device was coming from him and him alone, from a private place in his well-appointed mind, and knowing that his rarified essence was being pipelined directly into the laptop rather than being shared with her made Roisin more jealous of that lucky machine than she'd ever been of any romantic rival, for those bitches had battled her for the attentions of mere schoolboys who wanted only to reach up her dress, while this laptop enjoyed exclusively the intimate familiarities of an avatar. It was Roisin's nature, being an Irish girl, to come right out and ask him just what his fingers were typing about, but for all she knew he frequented Lafayette's because no one there ever bothered him about his business, and so the fear of running him off and never seeing him again kept all her questions unasked. She was left then with little to do but wonder, to imagine the confidential details of his relationship with her electronic rival. But it was also in her nature to not mope about with frustration at being barred entrance into his holy-of-holies- it was instead her nature to find a workaround, a back-door plan to get behind the curtain if you like- and having devised just such a plan, she had merely to await her chance for carrying it out. So the back-door plan which she'd come up with became her little secret, just as the wonders of Mister Stuart's mind remained the laptop's secret. And at one o'clock each weekday afternoon Mister Stuart zipped his digital confidante into its shoulder bag and carried it home to his secret palace, while Roisin trudged her way across the River Lee and up St. Patrick's Hill to her family's flat in Knocknaheeny.

It was pouring rain the next morning when, at 10:01, Mister Stuart breezed into the café without a wet spot to be seen on him.

"Ohayō!" After standing his brocaded umbrella in the corner, Mister Stuart found his place at his favorite table. Roisin waited patiently for him to unpack his laptop and power up before approaching, never wishing to rush the gentleman until he had a chance to settle in.

"Good morning Mister Stuart" she said, handing the menu which he had memorized long ago. "And what was that one you dropped on us today?"

He cocked his head with a grin as he removed his cap. "Oh yes. That was Japanese Roisin. Incredible city, Tokyo. Finest subway system in the world. Bailed me out of more than one sticky jam, I can assure you!"

Like everything else he said it begged her to ask him more about his sticky jams. But she remembered who she was. "Cappuccino?"

"You know me so well!" As she returned to the counter to make his coffee, Roisin watched Mister Stuart go through his well-rehearsed ritual: first a preparatory sigh as he glanced out onto the street, then on with his bifocals, then opening up the document he was working on, followed by looking out the top half of the glasses for another sighing glance onto South Mall, then through the lower half to begin work. It was a matter of professional pride to her that she always perfectly timed the delivery of his cup at the punctuation point of his routine. "Thank you dear."

A low rumble could be heard as passing headlights on South Mall flashed across Mister Stuart's laptop screen. "Woo! Thunder, in October yet. You drove through quite the rain Mister Stuart."

Now it was the eyes of the older gentleman which flashed teasingly. "Oh Roisin, that's not the only rain that's been pouring!" He made a roguish gesture toward his computer. "I'm in the middle of my own steady shower. It started this weekend and it's been raining ever since."

"What you're writing you mean?"

"Oh that's exactly what I mean!" There was a twitch now in one of those flashing eyes, but then she realized it wasn't a twitch at all- it was intentionally and unmistakably a wink. A wink! Was he actually inviting her to ask him about his work?

But it was as if he read her mind for he quickly added "But it's not something I can really talk about."

"No no, sorry, I wasn't- " The polite man smiled back warmly as the headlights from the street exposed her. "I'll let you get to it then Mister Stuart."

"Thank you Roisin." As Mister Stuart repositioned his glasses for work, Roisin retreated back to the safety of the pie case to ponder the meaning of their curious engagement. So his work was something he couldn't talk about, that was what he'd said. But why not? Everything else from the man had betrayed his eager desire to tell her all about it. With any other person she'd have been quick to call him out on his mixed message- "No no mister, you don't go hintin' about and winkin' and smilin' and pointin' to your screen with eye-rich glances and then say you can't tell me what the screen is sayin'. Out with it now!" Yet she had simply whimpered her apologies and scampered off. It was obvious that asking him point-blank would not have run him off from the café as she had feared in the least. He *wanted* to be asked! Yet he couldn't speak about it. Why? He was staring at his screen now, smiling, nodding, occasionally typing a word or two which moved him to still more nodding and smiling. As Roisin spied on her strange customer and wondered about the private world of creative pleasures which he was clearly inhabiting, an explanation for his contradictory behavior began to form in her mind, one which only served to deepen both the richness of his enigma and her fascination with it and him. Had Mister Stuart told her that he would not talk about his work? Not at all. What he had said was that he *could* not talk about it. Simply could not. So inexpressible then must be the wonders of his work that any attempt on his part to discuss or describe it would fail even a man of his multi-lingual word power; what's more, speaking of his work was not only impossible for him but would only serve to diminish its lofty essence and break the charm of its magic, reducing it from an artistic statement to a common topic of conversation. She looked at him again, and his eyes were closed now, lost in some virtual reality, more likely something much better than reality, fingers rested on the keyboard as if that physical touch provided him the connection to the inner source of his outward tranquility. Clearly he was transported, carried off to a distant somewhere which was so unlike the nowheres of Roisin's stuck-in-neutral existence. No, Mister Stuart's work was not a thing to talk about for talking could not begin to touch it; and with him telling her about it so very much not an option, Roisin appreciated that much more the value of the workaround she'd come up with which lay in reserve, awaiting its opportunity should it arise. And if the chance of being transported to a Stuart-esque somewhere meant the risk of getting fired from her nowhere job as a result of employing that risky workaround, she was prepared to accept the very worst.

By the time the lunch hour arrived it was still raining steadily; and after taking Mister Stuart's order for seafood chowder and heading back to the counter, Roisin heard a scraping thud somewhere out on South Mall. The eyes of Lafayette's handful of customers looked out the window, including those of Mister Stuart.

"What's this now?" He was up and standing at the glass for a better look.

"What happened Mister Stuart?" Roisin was beside him at the window as well.

"Looks like our rain has taken a casualty. See that?" Where Mister Stuart pointed Roisin saw that a car had apparently slid out of its lane and struck a car which was parked just across the street. The driver of the car which slid was stepping out of his vehicle, opening an umbrella and looking things over.

Roisin started. "Oh wow. Smacked its rear pretty good. Doesn't look very serious though. Still, whoever owns the parked car is not going to be too happy."

Meanwhile, Mister Stuart was grabbing his umbrella from its stand. "Oh I don't see that a little fender-bender should alter my happiness in the least."

"*Your* happiness?" She looked out again and then gasped. "Oh! Shite! That's your car got hit Mister Stuart!"

He was smiling from ear to ear. "None other!" The driver was on his phone now, standing in the rain and looking about, as Mister Stuart put on his cap. "Actually Roisin, it's that gentleman who's not too happy I'm afraid. Back in a few." He unsnapped his umbrella and started for the door. "Watch my things will you?"

"Sure, no worries." As the driver finished his phone call, Mister Stuart crossed South Mall and upon reaching the cars immediately shook the driver's hand; the two then went round to the back of Mister Stuart's BMW and inspected the minor damage. Roisin watched them for a moment, smiling to herself at how lucky the driver was to have crunched the bumper of the most agreeable person in the world, then turned back to the window to check her tables. At once a surge of electricity buzzed through her- there, unattended on Mister Stuart's table, sat his open laptop, his work-in- progress still up on its screen. Her opportunity! It had arrived! Dashing a glance first at the street to confirm Mister Stuart was well occupied with the accident, Roisin scanned the café and saw that the lunch crowd had paid and left, all but one table with two old ladies seated at the far opposite end of the room. Feeling the thump of her accelerated heart rate she checked the pocket of her apron- there it was, her workaround, the external zip drive she had begun to carry the past few days in the event that a chance like this might drop into her lap. Checking that no one else of the staff was nearby, Roisin nonchalantly sidled up to Mister Stuart's chair and, after another look about, quickly plopped down in the chair with the zip drive in her hand. Fumbling to find the USB port and then finally getting it plugged in she quickly reminded herself of the sequence she'd planned out: first determine the document's file location, then save it, close it, open File Explorer, find the file, drag it into her zip, then reopen the file on his desktop as though she'd never been there. While performing these steps she took great pains to fight the temptation of reading or even looking at the document's contents, not only because there was no time to waste on enjoying a preview but also from a desire to not spoil the thrill of discovery until she could be alone with the work in the privacy of her room. Closing and saving the document revealed the file's name, which was but one word, simple yet forbidding- *MINE*- but the twinge of guilt it triggered was only momentary. She was surprised at how quick and efficient her fingers were at performing the crime (and couldn't help but think of how she really was her thieving brothers' sister after all); after a quick glance at the old ladies and toward the kitchen, Roisin was just about to drag the file into her fob when red and blue lights popped up on the street and flashed across the laptop screen with an accusing glare. The Garda! For just an instant she felt the panic of her imminent arrest, then realized stupidly that they hadn't come for her but to work Mister Stuart's accident of course. Refocusing on her task, Roisin captured the file to the zip and, after removing the drive from the laptop and dropping it back into her pocket, reopened the file so that his desktop appeared just the way Mister Stuart had left it. Out on the street the police were talking with the driver of the car, but Mister Stuart had left them and, to Roisin's horror, had already made it back to the door of the hotel. With a scurry and a hop she was on her feet and safely away from his table just as he re-entered the café.

"Well, what a way to spend a lunch hour!" As he returned his umbrella to the stand Roisin touched her apron pocket- yes, it was there. "Perfectly nice fellow. Too bad he's getting a ticket."

"How's your car?"

"Just a crumply bumper and a tail light." As Mister Stuart sat down at his computer Roisin watched him carefully, praying that he found nothing amiss. With a bemused sigh, Mister Stuart raised his cup. "The only real casualty of the affair was that my coffee went cold!"

Roisin was quick to take up his cup. "Here, let's get you a new one, and your chowder too, no charge."

"No no, that's very kind of you Roisin, but I think I'll call it an afternoon. I'm a little- " he gestured toward his keyboard "- out of the zone now. I think instead my crumply car and I shall repair to the repair shop."

She watched him nervously as he closed down his document on his laptop. All was well. Her crime had gone undetected. "Well I can't say that I blame you. Hate it that you have to quit early though."

His eyes twinkled. "Oh, it's quite alright, believe me." Raising a brow, he tapped his fingers on the folded laptop. "Plenty of good progress made here today. Plenty!"

"That's right!" Mister Stuart gazed back at her with a tilt of his head. "I mean, if you say so then it's so, yes?"

He laughed as he shouldered his computer bag. "Ah Roisin, Roisin. You're a good soul through and through."

One of her hands held his cup; the other was in her apron pocket. "As far as you know at least."

"Ha! Yes dear. As far as I know." Now his cap was back on his head, his umbrella poised to open. "And what do we really know about anyone, right? All we really know is what's ours." He pointed first to his own breast, then to hers. "What's ours and ours alone. Until next time Roisin." With a tip of his cap, Mister Stuart was out the door, walking briskly across South Mall with a lightness of step which defied the gloom of the rainy day and the damage to his BMW. And for the rest of her shift and over her long walk home through that same rain Roisin's step was brisk as well, lifted and lightened by the untold wealth of a pirate's treasure which she carried in her pocket.

The narrow streets and lanes of Knocknaheeny were quiet that evening, the lingering rain providing the perfect underscoring to the silent film of an uneventful Tuesday night on St. Patrick Hill. By contrast it had been nothing short of a madhouse in the little flat of Roisin's family on Hollyville Road; from the moment she'd come through the door in the afternoon to nearly 10 o'clock that night it had been an uninterrupted goat rodeo of barking dogs and howling brothers and grousing mothers and drinking fathers, all pinballing about the too-small rooms which provided Roisin no escape from the racket and no way to read the words of her own thoughts, let alone the digitized words which awaited her on the zip drive. But as the revelers eventually wore themselves out into inert and inebriated layabouts lumped together before the television,

Roisin finally found her calm after the storm, and behind the closed door of her room she eagerly powered up her laptop and loaded the zip into its data port. After finding the drive in the quick access toolbar and opening it, she was startled somewhat by the sparseness of its contents- just one file, the one named *MINE*, and nothing else. But of course it could contain nothing else, since she'd only just bought the zip and had never used it; still, to have it shown to her so starkly that the one and only thing she possessed was something which didn't even belong to her was somewhat disconcerting, causing her to consider renaming the file to something less incriminating. But then it struck her another way: yes, when she had opened the file on Mister Stuart's computer, *MINE* had obviously meant *HIS*, but now, opening the file on her computer, the naming of *MINE* was changed to mean *HERS*, and so the file's name, she reasoned, was perfect just as it was. After taking a deep breath to ease her nerves she clicked on the file, and there it was, Mister Stuart's work-in-progress, laid out before her like a stolen diary.

As soon as her eyes scanned the document's content Roisin was shocked by its overall appearance. Unlike previous times at the café when stolen glimpses at his laptop had revealed long passages of unbroken prose, this new piece was in a threadbare state, consisting of seemingly random words and phrases loosely assembled in the form of notes rather than fully realized paragraphs or even sentences. To call it a work-in-progress was clearly an understatement; it seemed to her that Mister Stuart's progress with the piece had gone no further than a beginning, and not much of one at that. There was little more to read than geographical place names, names of cities and countries, names of regions and territories and landmarks, with no syntactical connective tissue provided to link them into any meaningful context. At once Roisin's heart sank with disappointment. She had waited all afternoon, well, much longer than that of course, to dive head-first into the deep end of Mister Stuart's word pool and snorkel about in his thoughts; instead she found herself merely ankle-deep in the shallows. For this she'd risked the embarrassment of getting caught stealing and losing her job? Yet earlier in the day, oh, how he'd winked and smiled and told her he had made "plenty of progress." *This* was his idea of progress? A stream-of-consciousness smattering of sightseeing spots and a paltry scattering of city names? How he'd looked all morning while he was at work, so happily immersed, so carried along by the current of creativity. And this was the boat he'd been floating in? From where she sat on her unmade bed Roisin looked up from her laptop screen and stared about sadly at the dimly lit walls surrounding her. The room looked small to her, smaller than usual, for they seemed to hold her prisoner more tightly now than ever. She had hoped for herself to be transported by his writing, just as Mister Stuart had been transported by it; she had so envied the finished completeness of the man yet what she'd stolen from him was no less unstarted than herself. Perhaps the question could be asked: how finished and complete was he then after all? Where, if anywhere, had his heart and soul been transported? What a fool she had been, she told herself bitterly, what a naïve little girl she was, to allow herself to be so taken in by his two-tone waistcoat with the scrimshaw pocket watch and his noble posture and his cultivated ways, all just an outward dog-and-pony show which girls even dumber than she would have seen through in a moment. His *MINE* file was all bits and pieces and chicken scratchings, nothing more! Roisin had been so self-impressed by her daring criminality at stealing a pearl of such great price, but she had only collected a few shells from the seashore. She laughed out loud at herself, remembering the way she'd checked her pocket every few minutes all afternoon and evening to make sure she hadn't lost the zip, only now to learn just how very little value the plastic device really held. There was a life lesson or two to learn from this shameful experience, of this she was sure, perhaps nothing more profound than the old adage "crime does not pay;" and having quickly made the decision to just write off the day's events as a daydreamer's folly borne of youthful silliness, Roisin closed the document and powered off the laptop. But as she was sliding her computer underneath her bed a word from the closed document refused to power down in her mind, lingering still on the screen of her thoughts. Even as she made for the door to rejoin her family the word refused to let her depart in peace; and so, a moment later she had dragged the laptop back out from under her bed and was rebooting it so that she might give the annoying word the attention it demanded.

MINE. The name of the stupid file, this was the word which was locking up the operating system of her full attention and insisted to be dealt with. *MINE.* That the word no longer meant *HERS* was a fact she'd already resigned herself to; she was more than happy to let the contents- or lack of same- of the file to go back to belonging to poor deluded Mister Stuart. But as she reopened the file and stared at the troublesome word, it looked different to her now, as if its spelling had changed or was taking on a different meaning right before her eyes. But what? There was nothing in the document which meant anything to her at all, let alone its name, so devoid of value was it, like some forlorn and empty landscape strewn about with non-descript boulders and the occasional tree. Landscapes like those at least held the potential of wealth beneath them, for though such wastelands lacked surface appeal they often sat upon vast deposits of precious ore which only awaited the work of the miner to bring it out. At this she started with a gasp. The miner! That was it! In this way the word *MINE* was redefining itself for her: the mine, the substratum reserves of untapped wealth which lay hidden below an otherwise unremarkable surface. Roisin now regarded the *MINE* document from a new vantage. Could there be more to these names and places than what their one-dimensional surfaces suggested? The cities which Mister Stuart included in these notes, Paris, Los Angeles, Rome, Berlin, Melbourne and others, all of them he had no doubt visited or even lived in at some point in his life, and as a result of his experiences he had, in his way, mined them of their value. But what of Roisin? She had neither seen nor taken anything from them, and so they lay before her as unmined potential. But the potential for what? It was all swirling in her head now, these spinning thoughts of faraway cities and subterranean digging, as she struggled to focus her mind upon some idea which made sense. She'd been so let down to learn that Mister Stuart's document held nothing but a beginning, but wasn't a beginning just what she needed? What if she were to... but she stopped herself short of allowing the crazy thought to develop into a plan of action, since she'd never in her life written anything more than a grocery list or a break-up email to a bad boyfriend. Still, the plan insisted itself despite herself. What if... what if she were to find her own shovel and dig out her own story, mining the claim she had stolen from Mister Stuart? It would be a flight of fantasy of course, utter fiction, but if perhaps those far-flung locales of his served as a framework upon which she could hang her first attempt at a narrative, she might just be able to pull it off. With his notes at her disposal, now viewed by her not as strewn boulders but as so many wrapped gifts which had been dropped into her laptop for her to open, those places might carry her to a place all her own, an invented, imaginary place, yes, but one for her to inhabit nonetheless. In this way *MINE* could really and truly mean *HERS*, for she and only she would be christening its bow for its maiden voyage, not Mister Stuart. And so, feeling both the excitement and the trepidation of an explorer who sets sail with neither compass nor map, Roisin bravely climbed back up onto the wheelhouse of her unmade bed and, with only the stars and a stolen file to guide her, set her typing fingers forth upon the unfamiliar task of banging out a finished something from the formlessness of her mentor's unstarted nothing.

As could be predicted, Roisin's project was launched with its beginner's share of fits and starts, but her process rounded itself into form more and more each day. She learned right off that she couldn't work the way Mister Stuart did, sitting in public view for others to gawk at her (she tried it, spending her first official afternoon as a writer at a table in Alchemy Coffee on Barrack Street surrounded by Cork College students, only to fold up her laptop and flee after an uneasy hour of self-consciousness). It was one thing to be lost and struggling, but to feel as though others were watching you struggle was not pleasant, and so she opted for the privacy of her room. With regular discipline she labored over her story every evening (once the decibel level of the frantic house lowered enough to allow her), working sometimes past midnight if either the words were flowing too freely to stop or if she was stuck in the mire and didn't want to quit until she'd worked herself free. Each workday morning she'd go in for her shift at Lafayette's, brimming with the accomplishments of the evening before, then hurry home in the afternoon in anticipation of that evening's work to come. Coincidentally, Mister Stuart's smiling face had been absent from the café ever since the day of Roisin's crime; each morning she'd look forward as always to his arrival, only for 10:00 o'clock to come and go without him. But this was by no means a concern for her; every few months his habit was to disappear for a fortnight or so, only to return bright and cheerful, reporting happily that he'd been travelling here there and elsewhere but offering no other details, leaving her imagination hanging. He was certainly on one such adventure; for her part, she was always disappointed at not seeing him of course, but the timing of his current travels was particularly inopportune, for she longed to be watching him write his *MINE* story at the café during the day while she, unbeknownst to him, was writing her *MINE* story at night. At the same time however it struck her as apt, symbolically, that her always-considerate benefactor had graciously taken himself out of the picture for a time to allow his newly-feathered fledgling the liberty of making her first flight from the nest unsupervised. And so in this way did Roisin stay at it, freely and faithfully, half a page one night, perhaps two or even three pages the next, until finally, one quick month after that initial evening when the idea to write first struck her, Roisin felt her eyes fill with emotion as she watched her fingers type the words "The End." Her story was completed. But what manner of thing had she written?

    The initial spark from Mister Stuart's notes which had started the fire in her soul to write had been the almost mystical resonance she found in the names of all those cities, laid out before her in a way which seemed to beg some unspoken itinerary, one which Mister Stuart had no doubt experienced for real but was as foreign to Roisin as the cities themselves.

Thinking once again of how her own travels had been limited to that dreary train to Limerick, a "what if" had presented itself to her: what if, in some magical and wholly impossible way, the heroine of her story (who could only be herself of course) took that train to Limerick and, after an uneventful ride across North Cork which she passed entirely in a daydream of distant longing, stepped off the train when it arrived, but instead of Limerick's Colbert Station found herself standing in the middle of the Gare Montparnasse in Paris, with the Eiffel Tower on one horizon and Notre Dame on the other. While in Paris she is embroiled in a series of incredibly whacky events, putting her very life deliciously in danger, and after diving back onto the train to escape her fantastical predicaments, takes the train back home for Ireland, only to leave the car and step smack into the middle of New York's Grand Central, where still more perilous hijinks ensue. And so the story proceeds, one calamitous encounter after another across a laundry list of international cities, until our heroine, physically exhausted but emotionally satisfied, decides it's finally time to go home; and after launching herself into one final daydream of walking along her well-worn route of St. Patrick's Quay across the River Lee, steps off the train and finds herself back in old familiar Cork City, which for the first time in her life she sees in a richer aspect with the newly-acquired eyes of deeper wisdom. As short stories go, it wasn't one; almost from the beginning it had redefined itself as a novella, for her little idea rejected limitation, expanding and spreading its reach in keeping with the unlimited expanse of its heroine's adventure. As a personal accomplishment she was quite simply amazed at it and with herself; how recently it had been that she'd never dreamt of attempting such a thing, and now, here was her finished creation, conceived and birthed and raised by her, a child of her imagination who belonged to her alone. That it was no longer Mister Stuart's in any way was patently obvious; comparing her finished story to the scattered bits of his original confirmed just how little the one had to do with the other. By the time Roisin had finished her story she had deleted all of his original notes and renamed the file to *Changing Stations,* the title of her story, which held for her the double reference to both the many train stations encountered by her heroine and to the way she'd "changed the station" of her inner radio to her own wavelength in order to receive the signal of personal inspiration which Mister Stuart's disconnected wires were unable to send. Indeed, were he to read her story he would make no connection between it and his original file either; and reading her story was precisely what Roisin was so very eager for him to do upon his return to Lafayette's. She knew she'd no longer be just his waitress after he read it- Roisin would be his comrade, his kindred spirit, a girl who Mister Stuart would see with new eyes, just as her heroine came to see her old familiar Cork with new eyes. Roisin would appear to him now in fuller, added dimension, a young woman he couldn't help but see as so much more alive both through her story and because of her story. For the writing of it had raised her from the dead; and so, after taking up the same zip drive which she'd first employed to steal a forbidden glimpse into Mister Stuart's soul and downloading into it the story of her new heroine, Roisin returned the zip to her apron pocket, and eagerly awaited her chance to offer a glimpse of the newly-born Roisin to her hero.

At 10:30 the next Friday morning Roisin cleared the saucers and cups from a table and, before returning the dishes to the kitchen, glanced for the tenth time that day toward the parking spaces which lined South Mall, and for the tenth time saw nothing but empty spaces. A week had passed since she'd finished *Changing Stations*, and every workday that week she had carried the zip drive in her apron pocket and kept one eye on the window, hoping and waiting for Mister Stuart's overdue return. Five weeks had elapsed since his last visit on that rainy morning; and though it was a longer stretch than he'd ever been away before, Roisin had stubbornly refused to entertain the possibility that he might not return at all. Such a deflating outcome was simply too sad to consider; she had so much to share with him now, so much more of herself for the sharing, and the little zip in her apron pocket seemed fat and heavy, pregnant as it was with the unborn Roisin in its electronic womb. The glow she'd first felt upon completing the story had not diminished during the ensuing week, but had intensified rather and deepened, filling her with a self-confidence and sense of well-being which she found to be nothing short of transformative. Her smile felt several inches wider and made more frequent appearances; her posture was straighter, her stride was surer, and the little flat in Knocknaheeny no longer seemed a prison to her but a launching pad, for she was certain that the fantastic voyage of her fictional self was but a shadow of the actual adventures in her real life soon to come. After leaving the cleared dishes in the plastic bin behind the counter, Roisin walked over to the café's entrance where an older couple waited to be seated. As she greeted them, her peripheral vision detected activity outside the window on South Mall. Turning for a better look, she watched the unrepaired bumper of Mister Stuart's BMW pulling into an empty parking space. The unthinkable was a thought no longer. Her hero had returned!

Fighting the temptation to run straight out the front door of the hotel and bear- hug him in the street, Roisin took her place at an appropriate distance from his favorite table (thank god it was unoccupied!) and stood by impatiently, waiting for him to enter. It was always Mister Stuart's habit, once he'd parked his car, to instantly pop out of it with great energy and come bounding across South Mall as if in a race to get to his work. But today, Roisin stood in place for several uncomfortable minutes, until finally, there he was, making his way from the hotel lobby through the Lafayette's entrance. At once her mouth fell open in shock. Yes, it was her Mister Stuart who stood in the entranceway, of this there could be no debate. But this version of him which now hesitated uncertainly before coming fully into the café appeared different to her in so many ways that she found herself wondering if he could really have changed so or if his long absence had simply caused her to remember him incorrectly. Gone was the crisp and curated fastidiousness of his clothing and accoutrements; he looked slapped together, slovenly even, as if he'd been digging in his garden and hadn't bothered to change out of work clothes before coming into town. His hair seemed whiter than before, and she was certain there was less of it; conspicuously absent from the balding head was his customary flat cap, and the incompleteness which this brought to his newly-disheveled look revealed him with a naked vulnerability Roisin had never seen in him before. His face looked drawn, creased and hollow, and wherein his eyes had always sparkled with humor and intelligence, they now blinked and squinted with a nervous timidity, as if unsure of what they were seeing and afraid of what they might see. He even looked shorter by some inches, which she knew to be an impossibility; and yet, as he began the transcontinental trek across the floor to find his seat, Roisin noticed that a crooked bend had replaced his familiar upright posture, and he shuffled now with the tentative step of an old man who no longer trusts his feet. Mister Stuart made his way to his favorite table, but then ambled right on past it, continuing across the room and away from the window; and when he did finally sit, clearly exhausted from his perambulation, it was at an isolated table along the far wall with a view of nothing in particular, which, after catching his breath, he commenced to staring at with blank eyes, his back to South Mall. For several awkward moments Roisin could do nothing but stand in her spot, so deeply affected was she by this picture of Dorian Gray who had just come in off the street. But she'd waited five long weeks for this moment, a reacquaintance which meant far too much to allow a few outward changes in her hero to keep her from it or him. Fearing that her zip drive might jump completely out of her apron pocket all by itself, Roisin held it down, and after steeling her resolve and reconstructing her smile, strode happily and confidently across the room to Mister

Stuart's table and greeted him broadly.

"Dobroye utra!"

"Ex-excuse me?" His voice, always so clear and sonorous, was thin and small. The portrait of his general diminishment was thus complete.

"That was good morning. In Russian!" His sad eyes drifted up to meet hers without comprehension. "I looked it up and I practiced it. For when you, you know..." But his gaze had moved away from her already, staring off into some other nowhere.

"Cappuccino as usual?"

For several seconds Mister Stuart stared about at the surface of his table, as if the answer to her question could be found there. Finally he looked up. "No. Tea. Just tea."

"Tea. On its way!" Grateful for the chance to escape, Roisin returned to the counter, and in between troubled glances toward his table prepared her old friend's never-before-ordered tea. What had happened to him? There he sat, a spent cartridge of a man, as if these five weeks had been five years in the gulag. She had so many questions for him, but the fragility of his condition was an off-putting factor to say the least. Had he been ill? Was he still? Regardless what had happened, it was abundantly clear to Roisin that her zip drive would have to wait until she'd gotten to the bottom of things with him. Which she would. But she would need to tread carefully.

As she approached his table with her tray she noticed that his laptop was not with him. "Here's your tea. A croissant or something?"

"Roisin." It came out strangely, the utterance of a wistful memory, as if he'd been trying to remember her name all these minutes and finally succeeded. "No. Just tea. Thank you."

As he turned his face to the wall it was obvious to her that no further engagement would be offered. But she was not ready to leave it at that. "So Mister Stuart. Have you been… travelling to more exotic places?"

"Travelling? Ha!" He shook his head sardonically, his eyes registering the first flashes of fire since his entrance. "No. I haven't been travelling. I didn't go anywhere." Now he began looking about the café with some agitation, his eyes seeming to search it out. "I wasn't the one who left."

The one who left? The mystery was deepening. She poured his cup for him as his eyes continued to float about from here and there. "So, I notice Mister Stuart, you've no laptop with you today."

"Left it at home."

"Ah." He lifted the cup but it never made it to his lips, falling back to the saucer with a clatter. "This is a first then. I could always count on you working on your computer every day, without fail."

Again he shook his head bitterly as he pushed the saucer away. "Yes. I used to work. Every day, without fail." There was desperation in his voice as he stared at her directly, emphasizing his point. "Without fail, Roisin!"

Though his words clearly held some sort of pain which went unspoken, Roisin was sure she could hear through them his badly-veiled desire to speak of it. So she pressed further. "I remember, your last day you were here, when... that day, you were working on something. You said you'd made great progress."

"I did say that. Yes."

"Yes. His eyes resumed their unfocused searchings. With the thumb of her pocket hand she rubbed the hidden zip drive like a talisman. "So... how's that coming?"

"It's not."

"It's not... not what?"

He stared up at her with exasperation. "It's not coming Roisin. It's going."

"I'm sorry, I don't- "

"Coming and going. Coming, and going... and finally, gone." His exasperation was now replaced by sadness and resignation. "It's gone Roisin. Gone."

She felt an ominous twinge in the pit of her stomach. "What's gone?"

His hands were on the table, spread apart laptop-width, and he stared at the conspicuously empty space between them.

"What I had. What I was working on. My idea. It was there, and when I went back to work on it… it was gone."

"You mean… from your laptop?"

Looking up to her, Mister Stuart touched his hand to his head. "From here. It's gone. I just lost it somehow."

She could feel the hollow spot in her stomach beginning to spread. "That's… that doesn't seem- "

"How is it possible Roisin? Where did it go?" He was shaking his head with perplexity, running his fingers through his thinning hair. "This idea, it had come to me, come *from* me, the beginning of a… of a something… but then, when I looked again at my notes, they were reduced to just words, nothing but words. That something wasn't in them anymore. It was as if *I* wasn't in them anymore." He laughed bitterly, staring at the empty space on the tabletop where his laptop should have been. "And to think- I had even given it a name. Do you know what its name was? MINE. I had named it MINE." His hands cradled the teacup without lifting it, his eyes once again moving in all directions about the café. "I thought perhaps I could find it again if I came back. If I came here. But…" Outside, a wintry rain had begun to fall on South Mall, and Mister Stuart's wandering eyes now noticed the wet sidewalks. "It's raining. It was raining that morning, do you remember Roisin? And my car…" With a wavering effort he was on his feet once again, a forlorn and lonely island, gazing out Lafayette's front window as Roisin stood helplessly by. "My bumper. Need to get it repaired. Need to get fixed. Shouldn't be driving." As a murmuring of thunder rolled its disconsolate accompaniment, Mister Stuart began to make his unsteady way across the café, an unanchored shard of driftwood floating aimlessly toward the door.

"Mister Stuart!" But the tide continued to take him, farther out to sea, carrying him all the way through the entranceway without any word of goodbye, until he was across South Mall and standing next to his little car; as the hunched and unfortunate man stood hatless in the rain and stared in silence at his crumpled bumper, Roisin watched it all from inside the café, watched as he gradually dissolved before her eyes, her face pressed against the window whose cold glass offered stinging contrast against her warm, wet face. And later that afternoon, as the rain continued to flow in tiny rivulets down gutters along the streets of Cork, a tragic heroine of a stolen drama trudged home along St. Patrick's Quay, a penitent thief of original thoughts and of mysteries unwritten whose heart now felt as void of content as the pocket of her apron. For what she'd carried in that apron pocket had grown too heavy to hold, so she had tossed it from the bridge into the River Lee, where it floated downstream, farther and farther away, past Cork Harbor and in the Celtic Sea, its adventure into the wide world bravely launched, but whose fate it was to merely sink to the bottom of the cold Atlantic from the weight of its own plundered cargo.

TAKE IT

I was sixteen years old at the end of my sophomore year in 1979 when I went down south where my dad lived to work with him that summer and make the kind of money a kid my age could never hope to make up in my small town in Illinois. It wasn't going to be any fun and I knew it. My dad had basically run out on my mom and me the year before, just up and left, and now, after being as good as dead to us for all that time, I was the first member of the family who would be laying eyes on him in the place where he had run away to hide. There was no other way to say it: run away was what he did, when his drinking and his hell-raising got so out of hand that my mom said that she'd had enough. For some people, maybe most people, that would mean that maybe you should clean up your act just a little bit to keep house and home together, but for my dad, it only meant one thing: get the hell away from that "damn nagging cow" as I heard him call her more than once and be free, whatever "free" means. When I had answered the phone and it was him I was shocked; I was double-shocked when he said it was me and not my mom he wanted to talk to, and then topping-it-off shocked when he said he could get me a job as a mason-tender laborer (my dad was a bricklayer) at the new hospital his company was building down in Mayfield Kentucky. It would be $400 per week, cash money, with an extra time-and-a-half for overtime, which my dad told me was union-scale but without having to be in any union which meant no union dues deducted from my check. When I told my mom she was, to my big surprise, all for it; I had assumed she'd say something like "How can you go work for that son-of-a-bitch after he abandoned us and left us next to nothing?" But when instead she said it was a great idea I figured it was because of two reasons: one, that she hoped I would bring back to the family some of what I earned, which was exactly my plan, and two, that some contact with my dad, any contact, would give her some reason to hope that things weren't really over and done between them. Why she even wanted things to not be over with the sorry bastard was a mystery to me, but I didn't ask her to explain. There are some things you don't ask your mother to explain when you're only sixteen.

I took the Greyhound down to Mayfield, over 400 pain-in-the-ass miles, where at the bus station my dad would be picking me up. During the ride I thought about why he was doing all this, going out of his way to land me a good job and help me out when he hadn't sent a single penny up to us for almost a year. Mom was forced to work two jobs now (she wouldn't let me work during the school year because I was an A student and, as she put it, I was going to stay an A student), driving a school bus during the day and working in a department store in nearby Rockford as many hours as she could get on nights and weekends. Luckily I was not a child anymore, which meant she didn't have to worry about finding time to "parent" me. But I could tell it was kicking her ass something frightful, so that when my dad had called with the job offer, I came very close to just saying Forget about a job for me, how about supporting Mom like you know you should? It made me mad as hell that she wouldn't divorce him and legally require him to help, and even madder to know that he knew full well that she wouldn't and that he could get away with being a deadbeat. But whatever his reasons, he was offering now, and I knew that mad as hell or not it was for me to accept. It would be ball-busting labor to be sure, working as a mason tender, with constant heavy lifting in the summer heat, shoveling cement and setting up/tearing down scaffolding, but I knew that if it didn't kill me it would probably put some muscle on me. But the toughest conditions wouldn't be at the job site- it would be sharing a single-wide with my hard-drinking old man who had probably only become an even worse drunk from living alone (I could tell he was pretty lit up when he had called on the phone). Still, for only three months I figured I could live with a grizzly bear if I had to if it meant being able to buy a car and pay a few months of my mom's rent.

When the bus crossed the Ohio River into Paducah I pulled my backpack up from under my seat and got ready for the big happy family reunion, because I knew Mayfield wasn't very much farther south. When we pulled into the town it was just what I expected, straight out of *To Kill A Mockingbird*, and on the west side was the Greyhound station. I got off the bus, and after the driver tossed me my duffel from storage I went into the terminal where my dad said he would be. He wasn't there yet, and so I sat down to wait. Then a clerk wearing a Greyhound blazer walked up to me.

"Are yew-" now he read from a card "- Gordie Drennan?"

"Yes sir."

"Here. Yer dad told me ta give yew this." The hillbilly clerk handed me the card, and I could see it was my dad's handwriting. It said:

WELCOME TO MAYFIELD 418 PASCHALL ROAD #17
HAVE FUN GETTING HERE

I was so mad I could shit. I walked up to the counter. "Excuse me, how do I get to Paschall Road?"

The clerk looked me up and down. "Yew got a corr?"

"No."

"Ya mean yer *walkin'*?" Instead of giving him the smart-ass response he deserved I just nodded. The clerk grinned. "Dang boy, wud you dew ta git yer dad so mad at'cha?" Then he wrote out the directions, chuckling like it was the biggest joke ever the entire time, and off I went with a backpack and a duffle bag in the 90 degree heat of five in the afternoon, walking five miles like a damn hobo until I came to the Whispering Creek Mobile Home Park. At lot #17 I knew I was at the right single-wide, because there was my dad's mostly-rusted Chevy van parked next to it. I remembered how, just before he ran out on us, he had promised it would be mine on my sixteenth birthday, but like everything else that he promised my sixteenth came and went and he still drove it. Setting all that aside, I walked up to what would be our happy home for the next three months, provided no murders were committed.

He had just gotten home from doing his daily best to help build American healthcare and was still in his work clothes but already pie-eyed. Not seeing him for a year had made me forget how big he was; he completely filled the door. "Holy shit, look at this sad-sack draggin' up to my house!"

"Yeah. Thanks for picking me up."

All he did was grin and nod. "Startin' tomorrow you'll wish all ya had ta do was walk five miles. You'll be doin' that walk but with a load of bricks on your back and a bucket of mud in each hand." Mud of course was cement, which is where I wished his head was at the moment. He got a beer (he knew full well that I had already had many such beverages by my age and would not mind having one now) and dropped into the mobile home-quality easy chair that was caked with cement dust. "I'd give you a beer but beer's for workin' men."

"Right. So where are my slave quarters?"

"First door on the right." I took a step or two down the hall, and then I heard behind me, "How's your mom?" I turned back. He was still just staring straight ahead at the TV as if he hadn't said a thing, as if the voice had come from the sitcom he was watching.

"She's good."

"Good." And that was it. For him, that was enough for him to think he'd bridged the entire space of a missing year; by those four words, he had performed his due-diligence. I turned away and went looking for my room. Expecting that when I opened the door a bucket of water would be rigged up above to dump on my head, I went in and found that, for once, the thing he said he had for me actually existed. It was a normal room with an adequate single bed and a chest of drawers. This would work. At least I would have a place to shut the door and get away from him every night for these next three months. It was a thought which struck me as funny in a pathetic way, that after not seeing my dad for a whole year I was already looking for ways to hide from him. Well, it wasn't time to hide quite yet, because I was starving and I could smell something edible in the kitchen. I came back down the hall.

"So what's for dinner?"

All I could see was the back of his chair and the TV screen which he refused to turn away from. "Dinner? Dinner's for workin' men."

The next morning we were at the job at first light, and it was quite an operation, with big cranes and cement trucks and the whole shittery (it always made me mad that I picked up so much of my dad's upper Midwest slang but some of it was just too good not to incorporate into my otherwise standard American English). There was a foreman named Johnnie who was technically my boss, and he was snarly and short with me from the beginning, treating me like I shouldn't be there, which made me suspect that my dad had pulled some behind-the-scene strings to get me the job and that the foreman had been forced to take me on. But Johnnie gave me my gloves and some clunky kneepads and took me over to the bricklayers I'd be laboring for. There was one weird thing I found out even before I shoveled my first pan of mud, which was that my dad was The Shit around here. I had always known he was a good bricklayer, a stone mason really, but I had never been on a job with him and just assumed he was the same ridiculous prick at work that he was at home. But no. Here, he knew everything; here, if there was any question, they asked Ernie (I just realized that this whole time in this story I haven't even mentioned his name. Wow. A psychiatrist would have a fucking field day with me.) Even though there was a foreman in charge it was my dad who really ran the job, from the brick saw which he operated so well it was more like sculpting than sawing; when the other bricklayers needed a brick cut they would mark it and send it with a laborer to my dad, at which point my dad would ask the laborer how far that bricklayer had gotten on the wall and then send a message back to the bricklayer as to what to do next, who should go help who, etc. And from all parts of the job these cut requests would come to him, and in that way he would be on top of the entire operation from his central location. It was somewhat brilliant. It was insane, the Jekyll/Hyde switch with him that I saw on the job site. He was respected, even admired, and I wanted to go up to all these dopes who were kissing his ass and tell them "Yeah, well, at home he gets so drunk his face drops into his mashed potatoes." But for all I knew this was really "at home" for him, so I just shook my head at the marvel of it and got on with keeping my own head out of the mashed potatoes.

There were no formalities of introduction to say the least; it was "Everybody, this is Gordie, alright Gordie, help them with those scaffold frames." As I was working and trying to copy what they were doing I was meeting everybody one by one, and nearly everybody would say "So, you're Ernie's kid?" and then smile funny like they knew something I didn't. The truth was they knew everything that I didn't because I was green as grass, and I learned just how much of a weakling I was when I saw how much they could lift and throw compared to me. But I was hanging in alright when foreman Johnnie walked up all pissed off as usual.

"Why is this man working without a hardhat?"

Some guy with a hardhat came up as if he had been waiting for his cue. "Sorry, here it is." I put on the hardhat, and when I did, I immediately felt something thick and wet oozing down my head, then glops of red hitting my boots and my arms. Was it blood? I freaked and hollered like a bitch, throwing the hardhat off my head, which was when everybody around me started cracking up. I looked at it closer, and what someone had done was to empty a bottle of ketchup into the hardhat but hid it underneath the liner, so that I wouldn't see it when I put the hardhat on but would come squishing out the sides and running down my head once I wore it. Now I was pretty much a tomato-bloody mess from the shoulders up, and when I turned, there was my dad laughing more than all of them and getting high-fives; he had obviously been the engineer behind it.

Then he pretended to get very serious and yelled at me. "Hey, that's your hardhat boy! Don't throw it on the ground. It's yours dammit, put it on!" I realized in an instant that this was the kind of rookie hazing that's better to go along with so that you fit in instead of fight against and only cause more problems for yourself, so I put the disgusting mess back on my head and went back to work as if nothing had happened, if for no other reason to not give my dad the satisfaction for having stuck it to me. But he had won, and out of the corner of my eye I saw him strut like a hero back toward his saw, still getting high-fives and pats on the back for a job well done.

And that was only Day One. Little did I realize just how much more of the same was in store for me. Later that week was the dead mouse in my lunchbox. Then came being locked inside the Port-O-Pottie the entire afternoon break period. Next was my dad jumping into the van and speeding off at the end of the day before I could get in and making me walk home (making me walk was a real favorite with him, he never seemed to get enough of it). Cardboard in sandwiches, my coffee thermos glued shut, the axle unscrewed on my wheelbarrow so that it collapsed and dumped as soon as I pushed it- everything was designed and executed by my dad who made sure that none of it happened without a big audience around to witness my humiliations. Not that he didn't also play similar reindeer games back at the trailer for his enjoyment only mind you. He would offer me a bottle of beer which he'd already emptied and tapped the cap back on to make it look full. He would know when I'd be taking a shower and make sure the hot water to the trailer was cut off. Assorted refrigerator sabotages, Vaseline in boots, pillowcases full of rocks; there was no daily activity that did not come with the risk of blundering into an ambush, and I blundered into a shitload. But the cash was rolling in, and I had already Western Unioned $800 to my mom back in Illinois. As long as I was able to do that I could put up with both my bedroom door and my old man being unhinged.

About halfway through the summer we had one day which was trying its best to be a record-setter for heat. It had to be a hundred out, humid as hell and not even a tickle of a breeze. Guys were taking salt tablets (which I learned years later was just about the worst thing you could do under those conditions) and stuffing wet rags under their hardhats, and there wasn't a face that didn't look like it wasn't in pain even though everyone was too much of a manly-man to admit it. Even though I was a lightweight compared to the older laborers I was holding my own, and I had even perfected the art of being able to carry not just one hod of bricks on my back but a double-hod, one slung over each shoulder, which required perfect balance and just the right angle of lift from the legs. Even grumpy Johnnie told me it was impressive, and when the more experienced mason tenders tried it and they were too clumsy to pull it off they opted for the sour grapes reaction, saying it was a stupid kid's stunt and I'd probably end up busting my ass. Nevertheless, having my own special ability helped make me feel like I belonged finally. Anyway, my bricklayer's supply was getting low and so I went back to the brick pile to get him a new set-up, and after I loaded my two hods I positioned them for the lift and, with one smooth move, got them on my back and headed off. Between the brick pile and where my bricklayer was working was a long plank bridge that you had to cross over a muddy puddle area; the plank was maybe only a foot above the puddle but narrow and wobbly. I came up to the plank and made sure I was steady, then started over it with my two hods. It was then that good ol' Ernie stepped up with the water hose.

"Need some coolin' off?"

Before I could say or do anything he turned that blaster on and hit me straight-on in the chest with the water. A little breeze would have been enough to knock me over, so I had absolutely no chance of staying up, especially with the spray instantly making the plank as slippery as grease. I was falling before I even had a chance to pick a landing spot, and just like that I had wiped out ass-over-appetite (*fuck my dad's slang!*) flat in the mud with a double-load of bricks on top of me. I was up on my knees and screaming before I even checked to see if I was dead or not.

"You fucking asshole! Asshole!"

Now the rest of them were laughing, but I had noticed that everyone had waited to laugh until they knew if I had any broken bones. I was too mad to know if I did or not. Then foreman Johnnie walked up.

"What the hell is this?"

My dad turned all business. "Damn kid of mine, doing that double-hod stunt, we told him he'd fall on his ass one day and he did."

"Goddamn it I- "

Johnnie wasn't hearing a thing I had to say. "I should've shut it down first time you tried it. OSHA would fine us a thousand bucks if they saw you. No more. Carry bricks the right way from now on." When he was gone I laid into the imbecile again.

"You coulda got me killed! How was that funny?"

But my dad was already walking away. "Ah, the only way you might could get killed is if you don't get that load a bricks over t' Jerry before he runs out." Then everybody just went back to work, leaving me there to flail myself up out of the mud and get the load of bricks over to bricklayer Jerry. But in two trips now instead of one.

It was a few days later at morning break time, and after inspecting my lunchbox for tripwires I was eating my crackers and coffee with another laborer named Devonne, the only black guy on the crew. He had been a laborer for more than twenty years and he didn't even have to stretch his fingers to easily hold four bricks in one hand. He was laughing about all the shit my dad had been giving me on the job, but not in a cruel way, almost sympathetically. "Man, that ol' man of yours wearin' you out!"

"And he's been wearin' me out like that all sixteen years."

Devonne stopped chewing. "Sixteen years? You sixteen?"

I didn't like advertising that I was a kid compared to all the others, but now that I had slipped I had to 'fess up. "Yeah. Sixteen."

Devonne started looking around as if making sure no one was listening in. "Dude, how you get this job at sixteen?"

"Whaddya mean?"

"You can't work a mason-tender job if you under eighteen. You know that right?"

Immediately I was afraid Devonne would bust me and I'd be out of a job. "You gonna tell?"

Devonne laughed out loud. "Man, I ain't no snitch! Hell, more power to you, to pull it off!" Devonne went back to his chewing. "Shit, if I coulda got me a job at sixteen that paid me five-hunderd take-home I'd a tol' any ol' lie."

Now I stopped chewing. "Five hundred?"

"Yeah. After taxes. Ain'tchoo?"

Somehow I was quick enough to lie. "Yeah, just wondered if you were getting as much as me."

Devonne shook his head. "Trust me kid, if it was up to these white boys here in Mayfield they wouldn't pay a nigger a single dime."

We both went back to chewing as I started to put some things together. *Five* hundred? I was taking home four hundred. And his was "after taxes," which meant he was being paid like in a normal job, with a pay stub and deductions and all that. My dad had worked it out for me to be paid straight cash, and it wasn't until that talk with Devonne that it struck me as weird. How did my dad work it for me to be hired under the table? And why was I getting a hundred less? At afternoon breaktime I held my nose and approached foreman Johnnie to interrogate him a little.

"What?" That was Johnnie's way of saying hello.

"Johnnie, um, I wanted to ask you about my pay- "

He was boiling over before the fire was even lit. "Look, you're lucky to have a job at all, don't be complainin' it ain't enough!"

I ignored the bit of bologna sandwich he had spit on my chin. "No no, not that. I was, just, wonderin', why I don't get an actual paycheck with deductions and what-not."

Apparently everyone on this job stopped chewing when they were caught off guard. "That's between me and your dad. And you. Nobody else. You got it?"

It was only getting weirder and weirder. "Yeah, sure, but when I talked with Devonne- "

The bologna bits started to hit me like birdshot. "You don't need to be talkin' to that nigger about the arrangement! Now I went an done what your dad told me to do and that's that. I done my part! Just be happy with your five hundred and shut the fuck up about it!"

When I went back to tearing down the scaffolding I kept thinking about all the bits of info mixed with bologna which I had collected during break. It was pretty obvious that I was correct from the start, that my dad had some heavy-duty blackmail shit on Johnnie which was why he was forced to go along with my dad's arrangement (and why my dad was able to get away with all the wild-ass pranks he was playing on me on the jobsite). But why did I get a hundred less than the other guys? And why had Johnnie said "be happy with your *five* hundred?" Well, today was payday, and with a bad explanation for what was going on beginning to cook up in my mind, I decided that once we were back at our happy home my dad would be the next star witness I would call to the stand.

We got out of the van and started toward the door. "Hey," he said, "get my lunchbox for me." I went back to get it, and when I did, I heard the screen slam shut and when I made it to the door my dad was already inside grinning, and the screen door- which only locked from the inside and had no key- was locked.

"You lookin' for this?" Now the dick was holding up four hundred-dollar bills and taunting me with them. "I can't pay you if you don't come on in!" And with that he went off into the house, leaving me to sit on the step until he decided the joke was over, which was about an hour. After he finally let me in and I ate something and took a shower, I decided it was time to confront him before he got too liquored up. As I walked past the kitchen I checked the counter where he always left me my pay, but it wasn't there.

"Is it okay if I get a beer?"

He was docked as usual in the cement-dust chair in front of the TV. "Beer is for workin' men."

"Uh, yeah, my point exactly."

"Workin *men*."

I didn't want to push it so I left the refrigerator and came into the living room. "You got a minute?"

He started singing. "If you got the time, we got the beer, Miller Beeeer..." Well, so much for confronting him before he got liquored up. I went to the other chair and checked the seat for thumbtacks before I sat in it. He laughed like a giant weasel. "Damn, boy, whatchoo afraid of?"

Having a conversation with you, actually. "Never know around here. You keep me on my toes."

He belched with approval. "Good. I'm tryin' to toughen you up some. Can't be a mama's boy all your life."

His "mama's boy" mantra was something he had started back when I was thirteen. I hadn't heard it in over a year. It was so great that he was picking right up with it after all that time. "So that's behind all the fucking up of my lunchbox and spraying me while I'm carrying bricks, so I won't be a mama's boy?"

"Damn right." By now we had already reached the point of our longest conversation I could ever remember. "Hell, it's why I broughtcha down here. T' make a man outta ya."

I could feel some boiling going on which I tried to ignore. "How does taking the blades out of my razors make me a man?"

His eyes started to wander off a little from the TV screen. "Shit, my old man did way worse to me growin' up and it didn't kill me."

Things were straying off point and my patience was running low. "I noticed that my pay wasn't on the counter."

"Ya noticed that huh?" He was back to grinning again. "You like it when it's all easy like that dontcha? Just layin' there for you t' pick up."

"Is there another option?"

It was precisely the question he hoped I would ask and I got precisely the answer I didn't want to hear. "Sure. You could come over 'ere and take it."

I recalled a story he had told about a year before he skipped out on us, a story prompted by alcohol and not from any desire on my part to hear it, about how at my age he and his dad (my legendary grandfather who I never met) used to come to serious blows out on the front yard, a story which he did not tell with any apparent anger or bitterness but out of sentimental pride, that he had survived some necessary rite of passage. I was by nature a bookish quiet kid who avoided confrontation at all costs and so I always knew I'd be able to avoid that kind of stone age crap, but now, with this drunk volcano making noises like it might erupt, I was thinking that my luck might be running out. "I'm not about to 'come over there and take it.'"

He kept pretending he was watching TV. "Well, okay then. Damn shame to work all week and not get paid."

"Is this more of the 'to make a man out of me' nonsense?"

Now he semi-focused his eyes straight at me. "Nonsense? You think it's funny?"

"Could you just pay me?"

"You think I'm funny, for tryin' to make a man out of you?"

It was obvious at that point that anything I might say would only shake the can of soda more, so instead of making it burst I decided to drop it, let him sleep it off and try again in the morning, which might not be necessary because the pay would probably be on the counter by then anyway. The question of the discrepancy in the amount would have to wait. I stood up and headed back toward my room.

"Yep. Run off. Just like your mama taught you."

Now it wasn't clear to me if The King Of Running Off only thought that would be a good last line to zing me with or if he hoped it would be what it took to turn me back around. But it was definitely the latter which he got. I sat back down in the chair.

"How come I only get four hundred bucks?"

"Huh?" He kept looking at the TV but I could tell I had just landed a good one.

"Four hundred bucks. The other laborers take home five."

This brought him to something close to sitting up straight. "Wud that sonofabitch Johnnie tell you?"

"Why, did you get him to swear to secrecy about something?"

It was the first time I had ever seen my dad look like he was nervous and flustered. He threw his hands up in surrender. "Alright alright, fine! Go on, you can drink a beer!"

For a second I had to process what the hell it was he just said, because it was a little hard to believe. But it was true. He had just let me know that he thought me so shallow that letting me drink a beer like a big boy was all it would take to shut me up and stop asking questions. Up to that point I had always known he was a shit father. Now I knew he was a stupid one.

"Johnnie said he pays me five hundred a week. Why do you give me four?" He took a drink from his beer and just stared straight ahead at the TV which only made me more direct. "Johnnie gives you my five hundred, and you keep a hundred, don't you?"

I had just accused my dad to his face of scamming me out of a hundred bucks every week. I had never called him on any of the shit things he had done to us ever in my life, avoiding confrontation. So now I expected the eruption, and I had my fists clenched just waiting. But that wasn't it at all. He just smiled a queer way like he thought himself the cleverest motherfucker of all time.

"So? You still get four hundred."

I didn't expect it to glance off him that easily and it made me mad as hell. "I earn five hundred. That hundred you steal is mine."

"Really? You ain't been man enough to take your *four* yet."

I felt a flinch, just a flinch mind you, directed toward him, some long-suppressed impulse that wanted to lunge at his neck. But I had practiced my suppressing skills long enough to hold it back. But he saw that flinch. He was a better animal than me. I had read Oscar Wilde and even Plato by this time so I was working on living like a human being. But he still lived and always lived like an animal. So he saw that flinch in me before I saw it in myself, and he went in for the kill.

"Oh, gettin' a little worked up are ya'? Well come on Mister Where'sMyMoney! Come take it!"

"Goddammit..."

Now he stood up. "Goddammit huh? Ooo, gettin' all mad. Yeah! So, come and take it! Take what's yours!"

He was hovering all around behind me as I just sat in the chair. I was feeling buzzy and hot all over. "Just stop alright?"

He whined my words back at me. "Just stooop, alright? Waaaa! Mama's boy! Come take what's yours!"

Somehow I was standing now and facing him. "You didn't bring me down here to make a man out of me or to help me. You saw a chance to make a hundred bucks a week off me. That was your plan!"

It was like I had recharged his battery. "Woo! Yeah! Be a man! Come take what's yours!"

Things were breaking up like melting glaciers and falling over the cliffs. "I wonder what mom would say is "being a man"- taking what's yours or giving her what's hers!"

A new surge of rage mixed in with his mania. "She's too afraid to take what's hers either, afraid like you. She's too scared a me to divorce me! Come on mama's boy, take what's yours!"

He was poking me in the chest by this point but I stayed with it. "Yeah, big man, steals from his own son and his own wife!"

"Gettin' mad aren'tcha? Come on, take what's yours!" The pokes were harder now.

"Stop it!"

"Take it!"

"Stop it!!!"

By this point the poking and screaming in my face had become too much, and my suppressing skills were finally overwhelmed by the need to punch. But still I wouldn't, or I couldn't, punch my dad- and so I screamed in frustration and punched the closet door instead, which of course was mobile-home quality, and so my fist went all the way through. The surprise of it stopped him, and everything got quiet for a few seconds. But only a few seconds. Like a silverback gorilla he started hopping up and down. "Oh you can punch holes in my house can ya? Huh? Well little mama's boy, this is my house, and I'm the one gets to punch holes in it!" With that he lumbered over to his tool bag, grabbed a brick hammer, and rushed up to me. So this was it. Death by brick hammer. "Here, this is how I put holes in my own goddamn house!" Without another moment's thought (obviously) he took an epic chop and bashed all the way through the wall. "Like that!" For a split second I figured well, that was it, he got it out of him. But no. He started down the hall, bashing through the wall with the hammer every two or three feet, all the time hollering "My house! I make the holes!"

The violent absurdity of it made me have stupid thoughts. I yelled ridiculous shit at him like "Stop, it's a rental!", but he just kept chopping and hollering. Finally it was too much; I grabbed his arm just to stop the chopping, but of course he took that as the starting bell for the fight. With a big sweeping flail he chopped at me with the point of the brick hammer, but it turned in his hand just enough so that what glanced off me- on the side of my neck, a shot meant for my head- was the blunt end and not the sharp end of the hammer. At that point I had the single fastest and clearest thought of my life ever: there are times when you can no longer take it, and then, you have to Take It. With one clean right hand I slammed him in the mouth; the hammer dropped one way and he dropped the other.

"Whu- whu di yuh duh..." His mouth was barely opening at a warped angle. His jaw was broken.

I had taken the punch and so I kept on taking. As he laid there moaning I pulled his wallet out of his pocket. "I'm doing what you said! I'm taking what's mine!" I found the four hundred, then I pulled out a few hundred more. "My pay. But all of it this time! I'm taking everything that's mine!"

"Yu boke ma juh."

Sixteen years of being mocked and abused was blowing out like an oil well. I did my best Ernie impression right in his bloated face. "Dontchoo know why I come down here to Kentucky, boy? T' make a man outta ya!" I went to his wallet one last time and took out all the cash that remained and waved it in front of his bloody mouth. I could see that tears were mixing with it. "That's for your wife! Don't it feel good t' be doin' the right thing? Don't it feel good t' finally be a man?"

"Why dih oo bake muh juh?"

He was flat on his back and sobbing like a child. I was hoping the slam of the door was loud enough so that he wouldn't hear that I was too.

On the ride back home to Illinois there was this thought that wouldn't leave me alone, that even though I had taken what was mine it felt like I had still left something of mine with him. Then I knew what it was. He had taken my self-control, and I couldn't ever get it back. It was like he held it in his hand and was waving it in my face from behind the screen door. He had won somehow, or to be accurate, I had lost. It wasn't a good thought, but it was a good night at least for driving on the open road and thinking, way better than riding the bus. I thought about what my dad would do when he saw I had also taken my van. I wondered, as I made the merge from I24 onto the Dixie Highway north, if he would be man enough to let me keep it like he promised. Or maybe he would be man enough to come try to take it.

THE WOBBLY LEG

vvvvvvvvvvvvvvvvvvvvvvvvvvvvvvvvvvvvvvvvvvvvvvvvvvvvv

Sitting in the coffee shop, as Gary would tell you if he would risk speaking to you, isn't as easy as you might think. The sitting part isn't so difficult- even a coffee shop novice can sit well enough- but where to sit, well, that's the critical decision which distinguishes the casual visitor from the every day regular. Because, as Gary would explain to you as he had to imaginary table mates at The Daily Grind many times, the table you choose, and the chair at that table, becomes your home. Not just your home away from home, because that would suggest you had some other home, which of course you don't. No, for the true coffee shop regular, That Chair at That Table represents your place in the world, your base of operations, your crow's nest perched high above yet safely amidst a hostile sea. And so, by choosing That Chair at That Table, the coffee shop regular enters into the most committed of relationships. By choosing, he becomes "the guy who always sits at that table every morning," and thus earns an identity all his own (and as he would point out, if an identity isn't all your own then it isn't an identity). That table, your table, becomes Who You Are. And so taking one's seat must not be taken lightly.

Gary hadn't taken his seat at The Daily Grind lightly, nor had he taken it easily. He had in fact taken many seats before he settled, literally, upon his seat. There had been problems with all the others, irreconcilable differences resulting in quick divorces. His first chair was certainly the prettiest, with an edenic clump of Ficus trees to its left and a bookshelf nook just behind, so falling recklessly into it was an honest, youthful sort of mistake born of animal impulse. Gary had bumbled bee-like into its bouquet, and for a short time had buzzed happily. But soon, it troubled him that he couldn't see the door; it was at his back, preventing him from monitoring the in-and-out traffic, and this would never do. They, that traffic, those people to whom he would never speak, were the reason he was here after all. So he left that table, as youthful lovers often do, without so much as a goodbye. His second table, though not providing the romantic thrill of his first, was solid and sensible, strategically placed triangularly between door and counter. But there, the window overlooking the street was obscured, and without that window he felt as cut off from the outside world as he did sitting in the unemployment office each month (one may in fact be cut off, but who wants to *feel* like it?) Realizing after all that this second table was really nothing more than a rebound relationship, he left it as well. Now cynical and experienced, Gary moved through the remaining tables with a devouring detachment, and the furniture which succumbed to his advances amounted to little more than notches on his laptop bag. There were deal-breaking problems with them all: this table, too close to the ever-screaming "Kidz Zone," that table, downwind of the restroom; another table was the long variety which must be share *with others*, and still another was too far from the wall to reach the power outlet. Ceiling fans, drafty doors, crowded corners, swallowing armchairs- Gary began to think he might possibly be too choosy, too neurotic and sensitive, to ever find a table which could be his and his alone, and so he... okay no. He didn't begin to think that at all. He knew the problem wasn't him. The problem was with The Daily Grind. Yes. It wasn't him.

It's often said that there's someone for everyone. This isn't true of course. But Gary was one of the lucky ones; at the end of his dreary run of unfulfilling one-cup stands one table proved a keeper, surviving his withering vetting process and measuring up to his exacting standards. Through sheer persistence he had finally found his table. It gave him everything- a lovely setting, protection from draughts, adequate workspace for the work he pretended to do, even a tiltable chair (a bad habit of his, tilting back in his chair, but he found it exhilarating to lean back onto just the rear legs and raise the front legs skyward, imagining his jet lifting off the tarmac, and best of all he could fly above the earthbound seated around him without them being any the wiser). But most importantly, his table was strategically situated where he was the audience of two simultaneous shows: the one on the street which he observed through the window and the one in the shop, each acted out between the proscenium arches of his peripheral vision. His table provided him separation without banishment, immersion without involvement, privacy without exclusion. It was his dream home, and Gary made sure to leave that other place where he kept his things early enough every morning to be at The Grind when its doors opened, ensuring that he and no one else would sit at the table which he had rightfully won as his own, the table whose real value only he could truly understand and appreciate.

But his table had a problem. His table had a wobbly leg.

And this was a problem which, under any other circumstance, would have led to yet another messy breakup. But such was the rare combination of charms possessed by his otherwise perfect table that Gary knew he could never find one better, and so he endured and accepted the wobbly leg. And soon he came to regard the wobbly leg in a philosophical light;

remembering Shakespeare's admonition that "the course of true love never did run smooth," he concluded that it probably didn't run level either, and so he welcomed the wobbly leg as his cross to bear, the test of his devotion. At first, he allowed his table to wobble at will, celebrating his beloved's irregularity as a mark of distinction. But after the third spilt coffee ($3.58 each!) he gave in to necessity, and was forced to level out the leg, telling himself he wasn't correcting it so much as caring for it. Clearly, this table was placed in his life that he might be the one to steady it. He'd often seen others sitting at wobbly tables, and it made him anxious to watch them wobble, the water glasses sloshing about so close spilling and the sitters at those tables doing nothing about it, unconcerned or unaware of impending disaster. Well, Gary resolved, he would not be numbered among the unconcerned and unaware. And so, armed with plastic furniture wedges stolen from the hardware store, he began each morning at The Grind by wedging up the short leg, viewing the act as more than mere maintenance but his way of telling his table Hello my love, Good Morning, the push of the wedge nothing less than a kiss on its cheek. This ritual performed, Gary would arrange his tabletop and assume the pretense of working which concealed his people-watching which was, of course, the true reason for his being there, settling in for the surrounding show, proud to be known as "the guy who always sits at that table" and content with his level of participation in an activity which was by its very nature non-participatory.

So the weeks went by, with Gary and table installed as fixtures of The Daily Grind's décor, each helping the other stay level in an uneven world. There were bad mornings of course, wrenches thrown into the gears of his routine; for example, there was one morning each month when he could not be at The Grind at opening time, required instead to report to the unemployment office. After telling the woman at the desk what she needed to hear he would hurry to the shop and enter with the dread expectation of seeing some interloping squatter seated at his table. Invariably, the squatter's chair (*Gary's* chair!) would be turned stupidly away from both counter and window, betraying the oaf's disregard for his table's strategic placement. The noble qualities of his table meant nothing to these squatters, interested only in their electronic devices, mindlessly spilling bran muffin crumbs on his violated tabletop and, most horribly, insensate to the wobbling of his table's unwedged leg. Gary, forced to park himself across the room at an inferior alternative, could only watch in pain as his table wobbled cruelly, the swaying so pronounced beneath the squatter's dead-weight arm that the table seemed to cry out, "Gary, look what he's doing to me, please come wedge me!" Eventually the squatter would shamble to his feet with a violence that delivered one final shuddering blow, sometimes with force enough to screech the table several inches from the spot Gary had so carefully placed it. The clumsy beast finally gone, Gary would rush to his table, restore its positioning, wipe away the crumbs and set the wedge, saying nearly aloud "It's okay. I'm here now." With that the wobbling would cease, and man and table were restored to stability.

    The day when everything changed for Gary and his table had been a wobbler from the start. It began with getting out of bed an hour late, thanks to an overnight power outage which reset the clock to a blinking 12:00, throwing off the alarm; while rushing frantically to make up the time he had grabbed his laptop bag and, not realizing it was unzipped, dumped all the contents onto the floor. Having recovered from his disaster but still doing too many things at once he had knocked over the orange juice, creating a HASMAT situation on the floor all around the refrigerator. When he was finally ready to run out the door he'd made up much of the time but was still eighteen minutes behind schedule, and for a brief moment he considered driving his car to The Grind rather than take the slower bus (his car was reserved for emergency use only due to its precarious mechanical condition and his precarious ability to pay for gas). But in the end he rolled the dice with the bus, and despite the morning's best efforts to thwart him he arrived at the front door just as the owner (after two full years they did not know each other's names) was opening up. Once inside he saw his table, and in that moment the dead alarm clocks and dumped bags and spilled juice were forgotten, and his mood improved instantly.

Gary sat his laptop bag in the chair (never on the tabletop, for to place a top-heavy load on the unwedged surface would be as insensitive to the table's feelings as it would be physically precarious) and then opened the bag to find a leg wedge. As always, the wedges were buried beneath cords and pens and eyeglass cloths and nail clippers, and as he dug about, he told himself for the ninety-seventh day in a row that he needed to designate one compartment in the bag just for wedges where he could find them every morning. On the previous ninety-six mornings he had never gotten fully through that thought without finding a wedge; today, he'd finished the thought and was still digging. Where are they? He removed everything from the laptop bag, item by item- still no wedges. He knew this was impossible. Just this Sunday he'd shoplifted a whole new jar and put them in the bag that same evening. They had to be here.

And then he remembered: this morning's string of disasters, and among them, the dumped laptop bag! In his haste to gather up everything that dumped the wedges must have disappeared under a bed or a chair and he'd missed it. A wave of panic washed through him, and as he returned everything to the laptop bag he could feel his table tremoring, not only in reaction to the activity but expectantly, silently looking up to him, asking for its morning wedge. He sat and began to talk himself out of his state of agitation. "This is not an emergency Gary. It's a wedge. That's all. Breathe. Just find something else to use this morning. Find a wedge." Digging about in his laptop bag once again he found several envelopes, any of which would work perfectly. But those were unopened bills, stashed away out of sight because he was afraid to look at them- and even more afraid of them looking at him- so he could never bring them out into the light and have their guilt-generating eyes staring up at him from the floor the entire morning. A credit card? No. He'd cut them all up and thrown them out months ago. Folded napkins? As unseemly and image-damaging as toilet paper trailing from a pantleg. There was surely something behind the counter he could use, but that would require asking someone for it. Ugh. Ideas followed ideas, and one after another he eliminated them. Meanwhile, his table wobbled. A crisis was at hand.

    Now certain he was being stared at (and would soon be kicked out for not purchasing anything) Gary considered leaving, just taking a mulligan on today's misadventure and starting over properly tomorrow. Instead he could spend the rest of the morning... spend it how? Nothing came to mind. His inability to answer terrified him, and his desperate search for a wedge continued. Surely there was something in his bag. An index card or a matchbook, a business card, a dime or a quarter, a- that's it! A business card! He spun his head to the far wall, remembering the cork board above the cream and sugar which was used as a public posting board for events and lost dogs and found cats and... lots of business cards, any of which could wedge his table leg perfectly. Gary leapt to his feet and nearly ran across the room. But midway enroute he skidded to a stop. "What are you about to do Gary? Take someone's business card? Really? A card which someone stuck on the board to attract customers to the business they've taken the initiative to start up and are now hoping against hope that this card on this cork board in this coffee shop will bring in the revenue to help them stay afloat? Who are you to steal their card, you who never had the initiative to start anything? You're about to sabotage their business, and why? Because you were too stupid to bring a wedge this morning. Nice Gary. Very nice." Held in place by these guilty thoughts he found himself standing in the middle of the coffee shop only halfway to the cork board, conspicuously stranded in a no man's land of indecision and failed purpose. Now fully exposed and vulnerable to the sniper fire of surrounding gazes he scurried back to his foxhole and fell into the safety of his chair, his table wobbling expectantly as he sat.

    Acutely aware of the situation's urgency, Gary regrouped. "Alright. Let's consider this. Your table is wobbling. Your table needs you. The solution is right over there on that cork board. After all, those cards are there *for the taking*. Who cares why you take them? This is no time to be squeamish. Think of your table." He stood, and with dark determination headed once again toward the cards. And as he neared- as the moment of being able to read the cards grew nearer- Gary squinted his eyes so that, upon reaching the board, he wouldn't be able to read the cards he was about to assault and would thereby spare himself the horror of looking into the eyes of his victims. Now he was there, standing before the wall of push-pinned cards. Knowing that someone would be coming for cream and sugar any moment, he made his move and grabbed at the fuzzy outline of a card. But his squinting distorted not only the printed words but his depth perception, so instead of just one card he ham-handedly brought down more than a dozen, which fell all over the counter with a cardboard clatter. Panicking, he fumbled about to repair the damage, but made no progress due to his unwavering commitment to the squinting. Finally, certain that the suspicious owner would be at the counter any second, Gary scraped up a random card and, abandoning the wreckage, fled the scene of his crime and made a clumsy getaway back to his table.

Not daring to move until his breathing returned to near-normal, Gary warily lifted his head and looked around- everything was fuzzy. So he stopped squinting and looked again- all was quiet on the western front. As casually as he could manage he risked a glance toward the cork board and saw no activity at the sugar counter. It seemed he had gotten away with it. Breathing a sigh of relief he leaned against his table, and it wobbled severely; remembering the purpose for his pillaging raid, Gary felt the pirated card in his hand for the first time since grabbing it. Making sure to not read it, he folded the card in half and wedged the leg. It was perfect. His beloved table was restored to health, as was Gary, who could now finally go buy his coffee and resume, or rather begin, his normal morning. As he walked up to the counter he replayed in his mind the film of his adventure, how he'd faced calamity and prevailed. Indeed, he had grown from merely "the guy who always sits at that table" to "the guy who fought for his table and prevailed." Standing in line, he smiled as he glanced back at the wedged table leg. There was the card, or rather, the barely visible edges of it, now out of circulation, no longer serving its intended purpose, folded and mutilated, never to be read again. A wave of admiration and respect for the fallen soldier stirred in the pit of Gary's stomach; it seemed a shame this card's sacrifice had been so anonymous, without recognition or acknowledgement. And despite his determination to know nothing of the identity of the card's business, he was now involuntarily possessed by a desire to learn just that. Who, what had just given its life for him? To whom did he owe his gratitude? He was next in line for coffee but it would need to be forestalled once again. Before he could set a cup of coffee on his table, he needed to know who was holding it up.

Leaving the line and sitting again, Gary first checked that no one was watching, then furtively reached down and pulled out the folded card. Laying it open he noticed the background, depicting a man standing solidly on a round earth, feet spread wide, hands raised skyward and face turned to the heavens, and across the image the name of the business- "Firmer Foundation Counselling Group." Flipping the card he read the following: "Firmer Foundation, empowering you to balance your life, strengthen your relationships and achieve your long-term goals." He dropped the card as if it were electrified. This was the card he picked at random? A counselling center? Gary was horrified. "Great job. You took the card of a business that exists to help people. People *in need* of help. Now some person who needs to 'balance his life, strengthen his relationships and achieve his long-term goals' will be at that board tomorrow, maybe today, and that card won't be there for him. Why? Because *you* have it now instead of that person who needs it. Nice." He looked back at the cork board, then felt a flutter of adrenalin across the tops of his hands. His trip to the board had nearly killed him, but he knew what he had to do. Standing abruptly, Gary marched with dread resolve toward the board, but this time, as the cards came into view, he did not distort his vision. With unflinching will, he first surveyed the damage he'd done on his initial trip, and realized that the dozen cards he imagined knocking down were actually only three. He re-pinned those, then re-pinned Firmer Foundation in the most prominent empty spot on the cork. Finally, after a deep steadying breath, he read across the other cards for a better one to use. A daycare- no, good daycare is hard to find, besides, its kids... yoga- somebody once told him that he should do yoga, it would help him chill the fuck out, probably true... dog sitting- a moving service- home catering- nothing jumping out, come on dumbass someone will be here any moment- real estate- home security- wait, real estate. Why not? Gary grabbed the card and hurried back to his chair. Once again he folded the card and wedged his table leg; again his problem was solved. Standing in line for his coffee he thought about the card and its business; it was a large real estate company with plenty of agents and offices. Surely their business comes from word of mouth, internet searches, For Sale signs in yards. How much business could they get from stupid cards? His guilt sufficiently defused, Gary returned to his table with his coffee, and as he set up for pretend-work he thought more about real estate in general, reminding himself of his life-long distaste for real estate agents, what with their smarmy spiels and forced smiles and annoying perkiness. The longer he thought about real estate the better he felt about using the card, so that, by the time he opened his fake Excel spreadsheet and set out for public display the books he wasn't really reading, he felt not only free from guilt but a sense of accomplishment and satisfaction at having given the real estate industry just the subtlest of middle fingers. Having begun the day as "the guy who always sits at that table" and then promoted to "the guy who fought for his table and prevailed," Gary had ultimately attained to "the guy who gave real estate the finger." Here he was, seated triumphantly, and here was the vanquished realtor's card at his feet, crushed beneath his table's leg like The Witch of the East under Dorothy's house. He smiled and sipped his coffee. The day's rocky start had smoothed considerably; having flown into the patch of early turbulence he had ridden it out, gliding across the remainder of the day atop the upstream of his improvised success.

The next morning Gary returned to The Grind re-equipped with proper wedges, relieved that his table wouldn't once again be put through the drama of the previous day. Their wedging/greeting ritual completed, he patted his tabletop reassuringly, purchased his coffee, and then settled into his non-activity. But despite having checked off every detail of his routine he couldn't shake the sensation that something was missing. But what? All was in order; he'd even gotten the coffee/cream/sugar ratio correct for the first time in weeks. Cream and sugar... glancing in that direction he noticed the cork board, then realized what was off. Yesterday had been the near-disaster of the lost wedges, and with that experience, the unfamiliar empowerment he'd felt from the sabotage of the realtor. Today by comparison was too easy; there'd been no risk, no adventure, and certainly no sense of making an impact like the one he'd made the morning before. He dismissed his feelings as ridiculous. "All you did was stick a business card under a table leg dude. That's not 'making an impact.' You didn't *do* anything." His focus on work restored, Gary redirected his attention to the female scenery on the sidewalk. But his thought life blocked his view of them. "No, you did do something Gary. In your own private way you made a difference. Completely on your own, from no one else's prompting, you went rogue and foiled one realtor's attempt to place her card where it might attract business. A house *may not be sold now* because of you. Because of what *you* did. On your own. And it felt good. Don't deny it." Still staring at the street but seeing nothing, Gary realized it was true. Try as he might he could not dismiss the significance of yesterday's feat. He had tasted power, and he could not for the life of him un-taste it. It had been a petty and covert act, but it was all his. He looked down at the wedge, and with heightened introspection considered the piece of plastic as he'd never done before; its design, he realized, was to look like nothing, to blend with the floor and serve its purpose with no one aware of its existence. Suddenly he was repulsed by the wedge's simple functionality, its lack of character. For these many months he'd been satisfied to level his table and leave it at that. But yesterday he had combined that purpose with a bolder one, and now, it was all to obvious that mere functionality would no longer suffice. Again the adrenalin bubbled across his hands; once again, he looked toward the cork board. Before he knew it he was there, scanning the cards, and when his eye settled on a buffed-out body-builder with a smile as broad as his shoulders, curling a dumbbell on a card which advertised personal training, Gary didn't hesitate snatching it away and returning the captured card to his table. "I hate those fucking guys, with their sickening rah-rah 'come on gimme one more you can do it!' bullshit." He jammed the folded card under the table leg. "There, let's see you lift that!" With the euphoric drug from the day before once again streaming through his veins, Gary returned the plastic wedge to his bag, knowing he would never use it again. Looking back at the board he could see the empty space where the personal trainer's card had been, and the rush of accomplishment he felt at seeing that empty space vibrated straight through the seat of his chair. "That empty space- I did that!" he thought to himself. "That's me. That empty space is *me*!"

And so began his thrilling secret identity as "the guy who thinned out the business cards." Each morning presented an opportunity for new adventure. *Who will be crushed beneath my table today?* Appreciating the weight of responsibility his choices carried he approached the board each day with the sobriety of a hanging judge. Despite the hit-and-run nature of his guerrilla raids, Gary didn't grab cards at random but, using a split-second vetting process based on his gut instincts, chose those cards which seemed most deserving to be purged. Some were easy kills; his first victim, the real estate industry, remained a favorite target (he never realized just how many people had, like him, missed their dreams and had, unlike him, fallen back on real estate). Insurance salesmen and financial planners were also granted no mercy, for as a man who boasted neither insurable possessions nor finances these industries were useless to him; indeed, they mocked his condition. A special vial of vitriol was reserved for temp agencies, since his long litany of temp job miseries were among the most recurring of his nightmares. Photographers, hair stylists, and the comic irony of business card services were summarily whacked as well. Like any addict, he sought ways to intensify his high- sometimes he would take one card, say for an ice cream shop, and instead of folding it he would pair it with another card especially chosen for its ironic effect, such as a weight loss counselor. He'd giggle to himself as he laid them face-to-face before wedging them, taking pleasure in imagining the poor miserable fuck whose life was wedged between the cruel sandwich of an insatiable sweet tooth and a spreading ass.

Then there were those businesses which at the very least gave him pause, and at the worst were strictly off-limits. Gary's conscience prevented him from sabotaging the special souls who did those jobs which were not glamorous but necessary, such as the mortician trade, senior care (although his mother had changed his diapers he couldn't imagine returning the favor), pest control, plumbing, junk removal, etc. The world was rotten enough without making it worse by leaving these thankless jobs undone, so their cards were left alone. Math tutors were also spared ("What, I want to make some kid do bad in school?"), as were community outreach programs (he had no idea what community outreach was but to mess with it seemed bad karma). That he was prudent and discerning in the death sentences he meted out was crucial toward assuaging the guilt he initially felt for committing what others might call (but he would never call) vandalism. But in no time the most obvious villains were thinned off the board, and with his addiction to card-killing not waning in the least Gary's noble standards of selection deteriorated, and he soon found himself plucking down the cards of home care providers, dog walkers, flood and fire cleanup services and physical therapists, ashamed as all addicts are of his wretched behavior yet fed by the power rush it provided. On some mornings his card from the day before would still be wedged where he left it, but as his mission at The

Grind was no longer limited to merely levelling his table he would remove the previous day's card and restore his table's wobble, thus renewing his opportunity to fulfill his greater purpose. On one particular morning he returned from the board with a card which had put up little resistance, a card which hadn't made even the faintest appeal to his integrity to be spared; it was a business which he was convinced only catered to crybabies who needed to get a grip on their lives and not waste their money paying others to hold their hands. After wedging it under the table he sat and, as always, gazed with pride at the new empty space on the board. This card which had now become easy to kill was for the Firmer Foundation Counselling Group. Corrupting power had corrupted him absolutely.

Through it all, Gary's new identity was acted out in complete secrecy; to be sure, the undercover nature of his mission was essential to the thrill he derived. That his actions went unobserved in plain sight excited him, like those summer nights when he was fourteen, cool dewy nights when he would sneak out of his parents' house at midnight, creep barefoot to the backyard, and with no light other than the moon would take off all his clothes and walk across the cold wet grass, naked as Adam but, unlike Adam, aware that he was, feeling himself swelling down below with the danger of knowing that neighbors' porchlights might snap on at any moment, revealing him in every sense of the word. But his secrecy involved far more than the mere physical act of taking the cards. Every aspect of the crime, every associated private thought, was a turn-on. "None of these people know why I'm walking up to the board," then "If these people only knew what I'm about to do to this immigration firm," followed by "These people think I'm just wedging a wobbly table, they don't realize I'm preventing Antonini & Cohen from defending job-stealing immigrants," and ultimately, "These people think I'm just staring blankly, they don't realize I'm looking a my beautiful empty space on the board," and so it went. And while his initial tactic was to only go for his card when no one was at the cream and sugar counter, Gary eventually flipped it, delaying his approach *until* someone was at the counter, thus intensifying the rush by going about his secret business elbow-to-elbow with his clueless coffee mates. Most titillating were those rare occasions when someone would post their card while he watched from his chair, or as he stood beside them at the board shopping for his next victim; his heart would leap into his throat as the unsuspecting wedding planner would pushpin her card, smile innocently at him, and then walk off. His eyes would watch her to the door, and once it closed behind her, he'd snatch away her newly-pinned card with a barely-containable sense of triumph. But soon, even this level of danger became passe- the ultimate bare-wire buzz occurred when he was able to remove the new card before the person who pinned it had even left the shop. One time he'd waited until the small Mexican woman who had posted the card for her husband's landscaping business had glanced back at the board before taking it down; holding it aloft he waved it at her as if to say "Thanks, just what I was looking for!" The woman smiled in return and nodded eagerly, pleased that its placement had not been in vain. *And when you need an immigration attorney* he said to her silently as she happily left the shop, *Antonini & Cohen won't be on the board for you!* He was making a difference, one business card at a time. Knowing he was changing the world made his coffee taste better.

This, then, was Gary's daily experience at The Daily Grind, and it was with zealous diligence that he carried out the duties of his various identities: "The guy who always sits at that table"- "The guy who had fought for his table and prevailed"- "The guy who thinned out the business cards." He wore his identities like medals earned in battle, and each empty space he created on the board was pinned to his breast like citations for bravery. His conduct in battle was exemplary and honorable; if he came to the counter and found cards fallen from the board he'd restore them to the ranks by pinning them back up rather than exploit their misfortune with wholesale capture (he refused to consider the most obvious thing, to walk up to the board one morning and simply take cards for the sake of taking them- the Geneva Convention of his mind stipulated that cards were to be harvested only as needed for the steadying of his table, and poaching above and beyond this end would amount to nothing more than a contemptible and dishonorable war crime). But of all Gary's achievements, none meant more to him than the knowledge that the card idea was his and his alone- no one else had suggested it, he had not waited for anyone's permission to begin it, and it wasn't just one more job he could be fired from. He was the initiator and the inventor; he was the creator of the business and its only employee. No longer was he a pawn, a piece to be moved about by higher Others. Not here. Never had the hours of his day been spent more profitably. Never had he been paid so well.

And then the inevitable happened. Gary saw it coming of course because, as he would tell you if he were the telling type, he wasn't delusional or a denier of the facts. His cork board, to his creeping horror, was running out of cards, and its empty places, those cherished voids which depicted the pock-marked history of his pillage, were connecting now, blending together, to the point that the open area of the board was now the general background while the remaining cards had been reduced to occasional islands separated by seas of unoccupied cork. Soon, there would be no cards left. What would he do then? Each day the surviving card total shrank, and in direct proportion to this shrinkage his panic grew. The absurd irony was not lost on him- because of his unwavering commitment to his calling he was incapable of staying his hand from slaughtering the cards, yet his very existence depended on saving them from extinction. Day and night he struggled to find an answer to his dilemma. He simply could not go back to his previous uselessness; he'd created purpose in his life, and to lose it now would amount to nothing less than the loss of life itself. Each morning he'd painfully remove one of the dwindling cards, wedge the leg, then brainstorm for a way out. If he could be absent from The Grind for an extended period of time then new cards would post and thus repopulate the board- but he just wasn't strong enough to resist his table's magnetism, not even for a day... well then, he could make himself ill, so ill to be physically unable to leave his apartment for several weeks, and during his recuperation period the cards would regenerate. But he recalled his many suicide attempts, how every time he tried to make himself sick enough to die he'd accidentally survived, which probably meant that if he tried to make himself sick but survive he'd accidentally die, so he gave up on that otherwise sound idea. What about recycling, re-pinning the cards he'd already used... oh sure Gary. What's next, bathing in last night's bath water? Then came a novel notion: get a job, become datable, find a girl and eliminate the need for the coffee shop altoge- he shuddered, amazed at being able to even conceive such madness. He forced his eyes to look at the board. By his estimation, perhaps a week's worth of cards, maybe fewer, remained. The situation was critical. If only the business owners could repeat their rounds after posting their cards in the other shops and come back here to pin more cards, then the problem would...

Gary's mind froze. *What did I just say? Other coffee shops. Yes!* In other coffee shops- in the surrounding blocks, all over town- were cork boards full of business cards. Boards crammed to overflowing with cards pinned on top of other cards which were pinned on top of other cards. He thought of these teeming swarms of business cards in dire need of herd management and realized instantly what lay ahead for him. His mission- his destiny, the ultimate apotheosis in his quest for identity- was to bring his winnowing fan of card thinning to the boards of the surrounding coffee shops. It was beyond obvious. That his work might be shut down at the very peak of his fever was unthinkable; here was the tailor-made plan for perpetuating his purpose. Besides, it offered him an adventure of the highest darkest order, to roam the streets as an angel of death, a secret ninja, specialist of the surgical strike, an assassin on assignment in unassuming disguise. As he waited for his coffee, Gary considered the logistical demands of his expanded mission, and understood that some shops would not be well served by mass transit, creating a difficulty. But wait- he owned a car. Of course! That familiar flood of adrenalin washed through his hands as he realized that this was the reason he'd held back his car all these many months, to be able to drive it to all the coffee shops! He had reserved the use of his car for emergencies- well, what emergency was more pressing than this? *It's as if a higher power has know all along the eventual purpose for my life,* he amazed, *and led me to save my car for that future need without my understanding why I was saving it!* That he could have been so in-tune with the universe to have yielded his subconscious will to its cosmic leadings filled him with a sense of affirmation he'd never felt before, and as Gary and coffee walked back to his chair to plan his strategy he felt, for the first time in his life, that he'd found that elusive ladder of self-actualization, there to be climbed rung-by-rung, and that an invisible Power awaited him on the first step with hand outstretched, ready to pull him upward.

There was no time to waste. His first step was to determine which coffee shops were where and then plot out his circuit in the most logical sequence. He dropped eagerly into his chair and began his internet search. "It would be helpful to make an Excel spreadsheet for them" he surmised, at once recalling the purely decorative spreadsheet filled with fake data he opened on his desktop every morning to give others the impression he was working "on business." He smiled. "How many weeks and months have I sat at this table pretending I was working, and now, finally, I have real work!" As he powered up Excel, Gary couldn't help but see it as yet more proof that he was in the perfect will of the cosmos, that by stumbling onto his destiny he was actually working for the first time since… well, since ever. He fantasized sitting at the desk of the terrible unemployment woman and telling her "Thanks anyway, but I won't be wasting my time shuffling in here hat-in-hand and staring at your face ever again- I don't need to find a job now. I'm self employed. Kiss my ass!" Leaning onto the back legs of his chair he could feel his life climbing with an upward trajectory, and imagined himself lifting off the tarmac of The Daily Grind and flying off into intrepid skies, leaving The Grind and the empty board and his wobbly table far behind.

Leaving his wobbly table behind.

His chair crash-landed back to earth. "Oh my god. Leaving my table! What am I doing?" As if awaking from a trance, Gary saw himself all too clearly. Like all addicts whose obsession with their drug causes them to forget and ignore those they love, he had forgotten his table. Overwhelmed by sudden panic he clutched onto his tabletop like a drowning man to a buoy. He thought of all his table had meant to him, how right it had felt the first time he sat in this chair after so many other chairs had felt so wrong. *And if it hadn't been for my table's wobbly leg I never would have discovered the business cards in the first place, never would have found my calling.* As his panic ebbed, guilt and shame took its place. *I owe everything to this table, and now I'm leaving it behind?* What would his table do without him? Could he really leave it to the squatters, who would treat his table like a piece of cheap furniture and then leave it wobbling once they had their way with it? Gary knew he was facing the crisis of his life. He was at a crossroads, and the direction he would take would define him forever. Who did he want to be? His table meant home, comfort, security, acceptance, unconditional love. But his business cards... the thinning of the cards was his and his alone, suggested by no one else, the truest, nay, the only, expression of himself he'd ever known. The great men of history, he reflected, had all left home and comfort and security behind in the pursuit of Destiny. "Why, now I see it" he suddenly realized. "My table isn't the landing point for my life. My table... is the launching pad!" He moved his hands affectionately and gratefully over his table top one last time and then returned to his coffee shop spreadsheet, now firmly confident in the correctness of his plan. And yet, as he sat typing at his table, he couldn't help but feel a little like the man sitting with his wife on a romantic date, clinking the champagne and kissing her across the table, even as he's planning to leave her in the morning.

To say that Gary found fulfillment in the carrying out of his mission to the coffee shops was an understatement. All the heights he'd imagined his adventure taking him were topped by the actual experience. His first stop had been the Corner Croissant, where upon entering his gaze had fallen upon a gloriously overflowing cork board twice the size of The Grind's. But at that moment he ran aground on a major stumbling block which, despite all his route-planning and preparations, he'd failed to anticipate. His Geneva Convention of procedure stipulated that cards were to be taken only for the purpose of levelling a wobbly leg- what if there was no wobbly table? He looked about; there was only one table available. Swallowing back despair, Gary grimly approached, aware that the fate of his mission, and his destiny, was on the line. He set his laptop bag on the table... and it wobbled! The table was badly out of balance, worse than (wincing nostalgically) his old table at The Grind; he knew it would need at least a double-card. *What more cosmic confirmation do I need* he mused, as he advanced upon the pregnant board, *that I'm smack in the middle of the will of the universe than to walk up to the only available table and have it wobble for me?* His month-long assignment at Corner felt more like a victory lap, and as it drew to a close he allowed the board's cards to dwindle to the very last one, no longer afraid of emptying a board but rather excited to do so, since today's empty board meant a new beginning with a full one tomorrow.

Next came the huge oval stickpin board of CaffeiNation, and once again, the kismet of a wobbly table conveniently greeted

Gary's arrival. In fact, there was never a shop along his circuit which didn't have a wobbly table in need of his assistance, so that in time he ceased worrying about the prospect that eventually one of his shops wouldn't provide him the necessary justification for his "clutter management." One worry which didn't disappear however concerned his finances; soon his unemployment checks would dry up and the gas for his car would be impossible to pay, let alone the $3.50 each morning for the coffee (some shops were as high as $3.90!) But Gary accepted, even welcomed, this looming threat as a test of his faith, just the sort of obstacle one must expect when undertaking a quest such as his (that the thrill he got from walking naked in all these new back yards made him forget such mundane concerns as income must also be noted). Now and then while wedging up yet another inevitably short leg, Gary would recall how hesitant he'd been to venture out, how he was so sure his identity was wrapped inextricably with The Grind and his first beloved table. But by so venturing he'd come to realize that his identity wasn't tied to any one thing or location; his identity was his to take anywhere, he'd created it himself out of nothing after all and could therefore do with it what he wanted. He depended on no one, needed no one's permission to thin out the cards and needed nothing from anyone except one thing- the cards themselves, and even that resource he had located by himself and was mining per a private claim. And as for that ladder of self-actualization he'd envisioned, he knew that each vanquished board was proof he was well on his upward-climbing way (the emptier the board, the fuller he felt) and that each new coffee shop represented the next rung toward reaching the very top. Whatever that was.

So the contented months rolled by, with Gary working each board down to a single card and then moving on. He was especially buoyed by the realization that he would never run out of boards to clear, for the simple fact that by finishing the last shop on his spreadsheet he would simply go back to the first and start over, since by that time it would have become covered once again with new cards (the spreadsheet now included an exhaustive list of all the businesses whose cards were removed in each coffee shop, serving no practical purpose but allowing him to glance at the list with the satisfaction of a grim reaper gazing across a growing cemetery). What's more, the universe had actually rewarded Gary financially for his leap of faith- the prospect of running out of money and not being able to continue his work so terrified him that he was motivated to find a job with a determination he'd never before possessed, landing a barista position in one of the coffee shops on his circuit (which he then removed from his list, since he considered the taking of cards from a board where he was employed to be unethical). Being employed by no means reduced his time at his target coffee shops however; on the contrary, Gary now made his visits twice a day, one shop before his shift and another shop after (only one shop per day was too easy for him by this point, preferring now the balancing act of hitting several different shops in a week and timing it so that, on what he called a "payoff day," two or even three shops would be down to their last cards and Gary, in one triumphant morning, could finish them all off before lunch). Before the start of his mission he had slept ten fitful hours each night and then dragged about like a sloth for the rest; now he slept six restful hours and awoke energized and focused, ready to balance work and spreadsheet and card thinning and even performing some do-it-yourself repair work on his car. Yes, thinning out business cards had given his entire life nothing less than a makeover. Now, as he sat people-watching at the unwobbled tables of his conquered coffee shops, he viewed those he watched quite differently, no longer a superior race who he, as an untouchable, was forbidden to approach, but as members of his same species, maybe a rung or two lower on the evolutionary ladder even. "After all, I know that I'm *doing* something- but what have they ever done?" For all he knew, these people were all business owners with their own business cards, but so what? Gary, in his secret way, owned them all.

One particular morning (a day off from work, three shops were targeted) Gary was at The Café Americano, where destiny had once again provided him with a very wobbly table which he'd just wedged with two cards folded over; he had chosen them with a perverse glee, pairing the accounting firm of Schwartzman, Grobstein and Green with a Palestinian bakery. Having picked up his coffee and, since he was gainfully employed now, a bagel, he returned to the board where the cream and sugar also lived. As he stirred his sugar he gazed as always with satisfaction at the two empty spaces he'd created, and then noticed on the board a plain white card, blank except for one sentence printed in a sold black font: **We Know What You're Doing**. He unpinned the card and turned it over- there was no business name or info of any kind, just a local phone number in the same black font. Adrenalin washed through the tops of his hands. Gary quickly re-pinned the card and returned to his table, then puzzled over the possible meaning of the card. "We Know What You're Doing." The slogan for a security service?

But then why no company name or information? And is that the marketing gimmick? No, it's too creepy. "We Know What You're Doing." A promotional teaser for a new film or web series maybe? Nah, there'd be a scan code or an Instagram page, not a phone number. He surreptitiously glanced at the faces of the surrounding patrons. "We Know What You're Doing." For all of an hour Gary thought and thought, but no explanation made any sense. He walked back to the board- yes, that's all it is, just that simple sentence on a plain card with a phone number. As he re-pinned it once again a bad thought, its own bold font enlarging in his mind, came into clear, irreducible focus. The card was not representing any business, This card, he was certain, was meant only for him. He looked around the room again. Surely he was being watched, but no face was turned his way. Then, in an impulse which violated all of his strictly observed rules of procedure, he snatched the card off the board and carried it back, then jammed it into his laptop bag. It was the first time he'd ever pinched a card without intending to wedge a table, and he was ashamed of his descent into common vandalism. But now the game had changed. Now, someone was watching him. Being seen, well, that was a necessary component of the thrill- but being *watched* was a whole 'nother matter. Being watched meant that the lights had come on in the yard and his wee-wee was exposed. But as he sat for a while his heart slowed its racing, and he gradually crawled back in off the ledge as he realized how ridiculous his conclusions were. "Come on man. No one's 'watching you.' And my god, even if they were they wouldn't print business cards to say it!" Laughing at himself, Gary booted up his spreadsheet and began planning the next stops on his circuit, now only vaguely curious about the cryptic card. *I should probably pin it back up.* But after another furtive glance about the shop he left the card in the bag and continued working.

Having sat for his allotted time slot at The Americano (during which he'd enjoyed ogling an impressive number of attractive women, any of whom would've surely talked to him if only they'd known he was a secret assassin with a job and car), Gary moved on to The Upper Crust, where of course the next wobbly table Destiny had unsteadied just for him awaited. "Probably needs a single fold-over" he assessed, and noticed the small but well-littered cork board across the room.. At the moment no one was standing at it and so he waited, preferring an unsuspecting bystander beside him when he took his card. Finally, a woman went up for sugar; Gary walked to the board, smiled at her, then scanned the cards. There, in the center of the board, was another one: **We Know What You're Doing.** He gasped. The woman looked at him askance; he spluttered something about having forgotten his coffee, then retreated to his chair where he sat heavily, his breath shallow, his wobbly table listing unsteadily. *What the fuck? Here too???* He looked around the room. There were a half-dozen other customers, none of whom seemed aware of his presence, nor were they remarkable in any way: a girl with earbuds studying a textbook, an older couple looking at magazines, two business-type guys looking at their phones, a college guy watching a video. Once again he could think of no other explanation for the card other than it being meant for him. And once again he talked himself down. "It's a business card Gary. Of course it will be in more than one coffee shop. They put them in many places. Totally normal." He relaxed a little, and felt the table wobble under his arm. "Come on. Let's get to work." Returning to the board (but this time waiting until no one was there to watch him) Gary attempted to scan all the cards but could only stare at the plain white one. Finally, inevitably, he plucked it away and scuttled back to his chair. Removing from his bag the similar card from the day before he compared the phone numbers on the backs of each- they were the same local number. Squirreling both cards away in his bag he determined to resume business as normal yet again, but by now, a queasy nausea had crept its way into his stomach and soured his resolve. He shook his head and gathered his things. *Take a mulligan son. Do-over tomorrow. You'll feel better.* As he left the shop he felt many eyes watching him depart. He did not look back for confirmation.

The next morning, Gary did feel better; his plan was to return to The Upper Crust since, after all, he hadn't really performed his duties due to the interruption of the plain white card. But halfway there came a sudden impulse to conduct a little experiment; remembering that The Java Joint was next on his list he redirected his route and arrived there instead. A wobbly table, of course, was available, and he located straight away the card-cluttered board. "Alright" he said to himself. "Let's see." Striding up to the board, Gary bravely looked it in the eye- and there in the center was **We Know What You're Doing** staring back at him. But this time he was prepared for it, expecting it even.

Okay. So it's here too. Fine. His experiment had confirmed the two suppositions he'd sought to prove: one, that the cryptic card was in fact everywhere he was, and two, that he could live with that and not suffer a meltdown. Feeling his strength fully returned, Gary blithely chose another card for his table and returned to wedge it. But as he bent down to the floor he was arrested by something he'd seen enroute at one of the tables, something his eyes had recorded but which his consciousness hadn't fully noted until now. Peering over his tabletop he looked back to the table in question, and sure enough, sitting there were the same two business-type men he'd seen at The Upper Crust the day before. They weren't looking at him now, but he was sure they had been when he passed them. Once again, Gary felt adrenalin wash through his hands, and without looking at the men, looked at them. Yes. They were the same two. The Java Joint was more than a mile away from The Upper Crust- why would these guys just happen to be there one morning but here the next? Were they wondering the same about him? Standing in line for his coffee (no bagel this time, the queasiness had returned) he felt the men staring at him, but when his eyes turned their direction, their eyes averted. Back at table with his coffee, Gary mechanically booted up his laptop and opened his spreadsheet. Pretending to gaze at something on the street he cheated another glance at the men. But this time they were staring back at him, concealing nothing. Pretending not to care he noodled meaninglessly over his keyboard, unable to focus on it or his people-watching due to being watched himself. After three or four interminably long minutes in the fishbowl he could take no more. Abruptly checking his phone as if something had just popped up and then rapidly typing to give the men the impression he'd received an urgent text, Gary powered down and stuffed his laptop into his bag, then jumped up to leave. And before he could think to tell himself not to he bent down to remove the folded card he'd just wedged as was his habit upon leaving every shop. "Idiot!" he said to himself, his face flushing with self-consciousness. "While they were watching you?" *You fucking idiot!!!"* Shambling out the door he hurried to his car, finally hazarding a terrified glance over his shoulder upon turning the corner. No one there; at least he hadn't been followed. Taking several deep breaths to calm himself he turned the key and started the engine- at which point the two men walked right past his car and, not seeing him somehow, crossed the street out of sight.

Gary and his car idled in park, unable to move. The men were gone, but surely they had just tried to follow him. *What the hell is going on?* Continuing on to the next coffee shop was out of the question; his fragile nerves at this point weren't ready for what he might find. But to neither dispel nor confirm his fears was unendurable as well. He removed one of the cards from his bag and rubbed it like a worry stone. As was always the case whenever he faced a stressful situation the tinnitus of his emotions was drowning out the sound of the logical thing to do, but finally, above the noise of his panic (and while staring at the back of the card) he heard it: *call the phone number.* Of course! With frantic clumsiness he dialed the numbers but then ended the call before it rang. "Hold on boy. Are you ready for this?" After shaking the bubbling adrenalin out of his hands he redialed. This time it rang; then, a bored woman's voice. *Chicago Police.* Something dropped into the basement of his stomach. *Chicago Police. Hello?*" He ended the call. So that was it. Although he'd fought hard from the start to suppress his consideration of this possibility, he had known all along somehow that the police were behind the cards. "We Know What You're Doing." Well that's it. They know what I'm doing. Or rather, they know what somebody is doing, and that card is the cops' message to whoever is clearing the boards that it's only a matter of time before we catch you. Before they catch *me.* He turned off the car. Flooding thought poured from his mind like bats from a cave at sunset. *They know what's going on in all the shops. They've tracked your movements. The saw you wedge that table today and they saw you take away the card. Busted. Now you'll be arrested. You'll lose your barista job because your crime is coffee shop-related. You'll have a record. You'll be even more unemployable than before. You'll be banned-* his hands flew up to cover his mouth to prevent the most terrible realization from escaping the cave- *you'll be banned from every coffee shop forever and you will lose your life's work and your newly-found purpose.* He was numb. Everything he had achieved, all the growth he'd experienced, was about to be lost. The fruits of his labor were about to wither on the vine. As he sat in his car, Gary understood that he alone had brought about his demise. Addiction had impelled him to take it one step too far and robbed him of his sense, had emboldened him and made him reckless; addiction's hunger for danger's thrill had pushed him to take the cards in full view, always with witnesses, and hadn't been satisfied until he'd stripped each cork board conspicuously (and thus suspiciously) clean. Now it was over; his drug would be cut off and he would have to kick, and he knew withdrawal's pain would be worse than death. He wanted to drive away, just drive, but did not trust what he might do behind the wheel. "So much for the ladder of self-actualization" he thought with finality. "Now I'm dead. Just one rung from the top, and I'm dead before I reach it. I'm a dead man." Over and over he repeated it to himself, and the thing which had dropped inside him turned to lead. "How could the universe play such a joke on me? To discover my unique purpose within the great cosmic will, to follow it passionately and wholly with confirmations and affirmations along the way, only for my purpose to die before reaching the end!" He slumped over the steering wheel, his pain exacerbated by the knowledge that his proven incompetency with suicide would rob him of even that relief. "I can't die, but I'm dead nevertheless."

There was no avoiding his impending doom, Gary realized, and no relieving the pain. All that remained was to give the pain its victory, to feel the full range of its power. "Just imagine, asshole" he lamented, "if you hadn't fucked this up and could have kept on, you might have… but he stopped. Although he knew that he'd come up short, he couldn't put his finger on just what it was he hadn't yet reached. He had sought identity and found it. He had tuned into the universe's wavelength for guidance on how to live it. He'd dedicated his life to his work and applied himself fully. He had fought the good fight. What remained but the end? His head slowly lifted up from the steering wheel as an idea began to form. "But I haven't reached just any end. Not just the end which follows that good fight, but the end… which is *caused* by that good fight." He stared at himself in his rear-view mirror. "All that remains is martyrdom! Of course!" In a rush he thought again about the great men from history whose achievements had been the loftiest and whose impact had been most profound, and to a man they had surrendered everything in the name of their causes, even died for them. From Christ to Lincoln, from Joan to Gandhi, martyrdom had been the great transcending event which had propelled their legacies from the merely momentous to the incorruptibly timeless. For him to lose everything now because of his great work would not signify yet another failure in his disappointing life but would stand as its crowning achievement. To be arrested, to lose his job and to be banned from the coffee shops would amount to a death of sorts, one which would represent the ultimate sacrifice made by the ultimate crusader. His martyrdom would mean reaching the unreachable star by crashing into it. He laughed out loud. Fear and gloom left him completely; he was filled instead with a joy unlike any he'd ever known. "I'm not coming up one rung short from the top of my ladder" he realized. "I'm already standing on it. All that's left for me is to jump!" As he joyfully imagined hurling himself triumphantly into the void, Gary recognized yet another accomplishment his martyrdom would represent, indeed his ultimate one: as a man who'd never been able to successfully kill himself physically, he had finally found the one form of death which even a failure like him could attain. His martyrdom, like his identity, would be his and his alone. And he would make it happen. He jumped out of his car and ran down the sidewalk. "Hey cops! Where are you? Here I am! Arrest me!" But no sooner had he exposed himself he reconsidered whether this was how it should go down. Ducking back into his car and out of sight, Gary realized that merely getting arrested wasn't enough; for his martyrdom to carry its full weight and achieve its ultimate legendary impact, his downfall must occur at the coffee shop, during the real-time commission of his crime. He would wait until tomorrow, when the two cops would surely be waiting for him, and give them what they wanted.

    Giddy with resolve, Gary drove back home and waited out the endlessly long day and sleepless night, and when the morning finally arrived, he was waiting at the door of The Java Joint ten minutes before opening. He'd chosen carefully what clothes to wear for his big day, opting for solid black and white (to show there was no gray area clouding his purpose). He had left his laptop bag at home, not wishing to clutter with superfluous props the stark image of a man sitting at his table awaiting his doom. So prepared, Gary took his place at the unwedged wobbly table and watched the door. Sure enough, an hour later the two men appeared; after buying their coffee, one sat at their table while the other walked up to the cork board where, just as Gary hoped, he pinned up a new **We Know What You're Doing** card. Now there was no doubt whatsoever that these two were cops, and the adrenalin electrifying his hands bristled up and down his arms. Both were seated now, and Gary stared at them, fearing and hoping they'd return his challenge. They did. After several stare down seconds, one of the cops nodded politely, and Gary returned his nod. *It's time son.* Rising onto numb feet he felt himself walk to the board, then remain standing before it at attention. Making sure the cops were watching he slowly and deliberately reached for the card the cop had just pinned, and while keeping his eyes fixed on the officers, plucked it neatly off the board. Like Cellini's Perseus holding the severed head of Medusa, Gary proudly held out the card, then walked it back to his table with an ease of bearing which belied the trembling in his knees. With the officers watching, their view illuminated by the floodlights of all the backyards burning hot, he methodically folded the card in half, bent down, and wedged it under the short leg. Then he sat, his hands lain comfortably on his cross, awaiting the nails. The cops looked at one another, then stood and approached Gary's table. Maintaining a stoic exterior he pinched back a surge of pee and smiled up to them benignly. One of the cops spoke.

"Hey."

"Hey."

"What's your name?"

"Who's asking?" He was so proud of his remark he almost asked the cops if they liked it too. The shorter cop showed his badge.

"Chicago Police." Gary felt the urge to run but held it back. His piss demonstrated no such restraint.

"Okay."

"Weren't you at the Café Americano a coupla days ago?"

He considered snapping back with "Weren't you too?" but decided one smart-ass crack was enough. "I was there, yeah."

"Then at The Upper Crust?"

"The Upper Crust, hmm..." Gary stroked his chin like a bad actor. "Isn't that the coffee shop on Webster?"

"Yeah, that's it."

"Guilty." The shorter cop actually smiled.

"We noticed you takin' the cards off the board."

They're coming straight at it Gary said to himself. He knew it was no time to defend himself or equivocate. This was martyrdom after all.

"Yes. I've been taking the cards."

The shorter cop glanced down at the folded card Gary had just wedged, then smiled back at him sheepishly. "It's kinda gotten out of hand, hasn't it? Gary decided the shorter cop was the nice one.

"I guess you could say that."

"I mean, normally we wouldn't even be involved in a petty matter like this" the tall cop added. "But when you get vandalism this widespread-"

Vandalism! They're calling my work vandalism? He wanted to jump up and get in their faces but feared revealing the wet spot. The tall cop looked down at the card, then back at Gary with weary eyes. "Kinda sick if you ask me."

"Well I don't know if I'd call it sick." *I DON't call it sick you dumbass cop. I call it dedicated. I call it focused. I call it inspired. I call it empowering. I call it-*

Now the short cop came on just as mean. "Where does a fucked-up idea like this even come from?"

Where does an idea like this come from? From a voice you've never heard sir. From a voice which whispers from high atop the ladder, heard only by those who dare to climb! He saw himself once again at the top rung, and vaguely knew that he was no longer sitting in his chair but had brought himself to standing.

"Anyway, enough's enough, It's gotta stop. Pretty sure you agree, right?"

Yes officer. I agree. The cold air of the ceiling fan hit the wet spot. All the floodlights had found him.

"So with you taking all these cards- "

"- in all these different coffee shops- "

"- and wedging up all these tables…" The cops were building up to it nicely, Gary thought. Even these dullards must somehow sense the import.

"… we figured that you might be the one- " This was it then. His moment of transcendence. He was ready to jump.

"- to help us catch him."

He held onto the ladder a moment longer. "Catch *him?*"

"The guy who's been going around making all the tables wobbly."

A chair scraped across the floor somewhere. The ceiling fan blew a card off the cork board.

"Yeah. We thought maybe you might have seen him."

"Since you've been wedging up all his wobbly tables."

"You must be getting' pretty sick of it, right?"

Gary's mouth turned to cotton. His wet spot was dry now.

"The guy's amazing. Going from shop to shop, making one leg on all the tables just a little shorter."

"Don't know how he's doing it. Does he have a rasp, or a file, or some tiny saw?"

"Doin' it right in broad daylight. Hiding in plain sight."

"Prob'ly gets off doin' his thing with people all around him."

"Like some kinda secret ninja, doing surgical strikes."

"I mean, look at this- " The short cop tipped the table as Gary felt his knees jellify. "Check it out. And they're all like this. But then you already know that of course."

"Yeah. You can't even find a level table now if you tried."

"And he's organized. Methodical. Doesn't miss a shop."

"Hey Steve, maybe the sick bastard's got a spreadsheet he's workin' off." The cops laughed. Gary felt the ladder begin to wobble.

"It's gonna kinda suck to shut him down though. He's a real artist."

"A genius."

"He got our attention, that's for sure."

Somewhere in the same room, Gary's hands slipped from the ladder, but instead of soaring into space he fell into nothing, making impact with nothing whatsoever, his body suspended as if dangled on strings, feeling only a vague sensation of strangers' hands reaching down but unable to lift him from the place where he had not landed.

RATS IN HER HOUSE

Maydelis Bethke loved animals. All animals. There was no reason for her to not love all animals, because she knew that there was no such thing as a bad animal. Or a good one. Animals were just what they were by no fault of their own, nor could they take any of the credit for their good qualities (unlike people, who are blessed with the above-animal ability to choose what they'll become in life and to behave either like angels or assholes as their variable moods move them). And since Maydelis possessed the exclusively-human power to choose her own behavior, she chose to love all animals. Whether it flew or galloped or wriggled or swam, every creature which lived, even a Chavista, was a creature which merited her appreciation. Even insects and arachnids were not beneath her favor; the sight of a garden spider's intricate web or the leafy-green twigginess of the praying mantis moved her to paroxysms of emotion no less than did the breaching of a whale or the scream of an eagle. If there had existed some universal language that all the critters could read and understand, Maydelis would have written "Welcome" on a sign and posted it in the front yard of the Bethke's three-bedroom suburban Atlanta bungalow years ago. In lieu of any such language she could only write out her invitation to the animal kingdom on her heart and in her thoughts, and hope somehow the animals could read the "Welcome" she extended to them there.

But in truth, Maydelis had found a way to give her "come hither" to the creatures of the earth a more tangible form than merely thinking and feeling it. It was not really a conscious effort to attract the animals so much as it was her desire to recreate the tropical paradise of her native Venezuela, where the separation between man and nature was not so well-defined. For upon the modest quarter-acre of the Bethke's residential plot, May had created a natural heaven, or as natural as she dared push (*ie* violate) the local compliance laws; over the years, she'd planted a truly breathtaking variety of fauna-attracting flora, apple trees and plum trees and peach trees and pear trees, flowering shrubs and feathering palms and clumps of ferns and grasses, fruit-bearing bushes and carpeting vines and even a thicket of black bamboo, a densely packed and multi-arrayed arboretum which spilled across the ground and filled the canopy above in an impenetrable display of botanical madness. Added then to her verdant oasis were the feeders of so many different varieties, an all-you-can-eat buffet line of sunflower seeds and mealworm treats and salt licks for the deer (yes, even deer, which lived in the wooded in-betweens of the neighborhoods, would slip into the yard in the gloaming hours through a door in the back fence installed specifically for their visits, and having found themselves surrounded by a garden of earthly delights were never in a hurry to leave it), nectar feeders for the hummies and peanuts and corn scattered here and there for the squirrels and chipmunks. The several birdbaths, by no means ornamental in their purpose, were splashed in and drank from year-round (in the hot months she went so far as to drop blocks of ice into the water in the mid afternoon to keep the temperature "swimmable.") This then, the exquisitely appointed garden and its all-you-can-eat salad bar, was how Maydelis beckoned to her non-human neighbors to stop in and stay awhile. But while May served as the mad genius who guided all the experiments in the outdoor laboratory, it was husband Brad, the dutiful Igor at her bidding, who performed the bulk of the heavy lifting; Brad, who also loved the critters but who loved them, shall we say, not quite so unconditionally as his more generous *esposa*, was the planter of the trees and the installer of the deer doors and the shoveler of compost and mulch. When Maydelis announced it was time for action in the fight to save the noble honey bee, that action was taken by Brad, who brought in for her the Langstroth hives and stacked them on the wooden platform he had built per her specifications; and when May observed two bluebirds on their mailbox and was concerned about the newlyweds' prospects for finding nesting opportunities, Brad was on his ladder a few days later, nailing up cedar bluebird boxes onto trees and fenceposts all around the yard. A bat house was his next project- or rather, May's next project, via Brad- and while Brad stood atop an even taller ladder screwing the cedar bat house into a tall tree, Maydelis reminded him of how many mosquitoes the hoped-for bat colony would eat. But by no means did Brad resent his role in the operation- on the contrary, he was genuinely thrilled to be able to construct an environment where not only the animals could be happy but even more so his wife, knowing that the degree to which his wife was made happy determined how much happiness he himself was to enjoy. And as a result of this joint effort by the Bethke's, May's beloved beasts RSVP'd her invitation with resounding enthusiasm; rabbits and birds and bees and butterflies and deer and squirrels and chipmunks and more all wedged in elbow-to-antler for a place at the table, with a delighted Maydelis welcoming them at the door. Word of beak had spread the news that a land of plenty awaited them on Glendale Drive, and the animals came to check it out by the flock and by the swarm. The Bethke's had all the critters they'd ever wanted. As well as some they didn't.

Yes, Brad and Maydelis had a small problem on their hands, one which was wholly predictable really. The success of their efforts had been indisputable but totally indiscriminate, like the hot new nightclub whose popularity soon fills it to overspilling capacity, necessitating the hiring of bouncers to turn away the common hoi-polloi and allow access to only the beautiful people. May's animal magnetism had been responsible for attracting the invading hordes, and it was Brad's shoulders where the chore of controlling them fell. And while Maydelis remained unwavering in her belief that no animal was bad, she was in grudging agreement with her husband that too much good was not always so great. First to be dealt with were the rabbits, whose appetite for anything and everything was nearly as impressive as their talent for multiplication. Natural repellents turned out to be the answer, in the form of garlic and vinegar and other spicy things the furry little locusts hated to smell, and per May's direction, Brad distributed his stink bombs, but only sparingly, so that her adorable little bunnies would not be entirely repelled but only somewhat discouraged. As a result the rabbits were put off a bit but not fully prohibited, a *detente* which struck a sort of "stay away/come hither" balance which Maydelis found acceptable. Next to be dealt with was Bambi and co., who posed a similar problem as the rabbits but a nocturnal one. May had decreed that the deer opening in the fence which Brad created should be left open day and night so that "they could feel at home anytime;" as a result, the time the deer chose to feel at home was while the Bethke's slept, so that come morning, everything too high for the rabbits' teeth to reach had been nibbled away by the whitetails. A compromise clearly was needed; and so, May agreed to trim back her open-door policy, which meant Brad would remove the fence section only on those early evenings when the Bethke's were awake to receive visitors (and then replaced again pre-nightfall before their visitors could defoliate the geraniums). Encapsulating the crawlspace led to their next crisis; when the workers crawled their way to the farthest reaches beneath the house they immediately reversed their crawling posthaste, and told Brad that no work could be done until the large and plentiful snakes their flashlights had discovered were removed. An exterminator was summoned, and after assuring Maydelis that the snakes would not in fact be exterminated but relocated to some happier habitat ("But they're happy *here*!" she had protested), she gave her reluctant blessing, and watched as no fewer than a half dozen seven-foot serpents were pulled out and carried off to reptilian exile. It also came as no surprise that the most densely populated quarter-acre in Cobb County for birds, squirrels and chipmunks was soon discovered by the apex predators, namely, feral cats; and when Maydelis the life-long cat lover looked out her kitchen window to see one such tigress belly-crawling her way toward an unsuspecting brown thrasher, she screamed and ran to the back yard with a broom to scare the cat away. It returned of course, as did others, but when they did, a large wire live trap which Brad had strategically placed and baited with a can of tuna awaited them. Three wildcats were trapped unharmed, which Brad relocated just as the snakes had been. But the moles were a different matter. The moles, attracted by the soft loamy soil which Brad diligently composted and fertilized to make it so, were themselves never actually seen, but their damage to the flowerbeds and shrub roots was all too evident. How they were a different matter lay in how they were dealt with, how dealt with, *bien sur,* by Brad; one day some weeks into the infestation he announced that said infestation had ended, and a delighted Maydelis asked how it had been accomplished. He said nothing, which told her the gruesome everything. How he had killed them was something she did not ask and certainly had no desire to know, and for a moment she couldn't help but think of those small and furry balls of sightless innocence, huddled together beneath the ground, trembling with fear beneath the feet of the cruel humans above, families of them, with babies, all painfully losing their lives for the sake of a few stupid roots and a hydrangea bush. But she quickly shook it off, literally shook her head to clear it, and was able to rid herself of the unpleasant image easily enough since after all she had never actually *seen* the creatures let alone witness the moments of their demise, and so she could tell the denying side of her mind that neither the moles nor their demise was a tangible reality. Perhaps they'd experienced no pain at all, she reasoned; perhaps their manner of death had been nothing more than a light switch simply turned off, just a click and then no more. This comforted her, to imagine the quick and painless efficiency of the light switch, and so Maydelis was able to switch it off from her thoughts with a similar efficiency. Existing, living, dead or dying, the moles would remain out of sight and out of mind beneath the ground. And it was Brad not her whose job it was to dig in it.

In this way then did the back-and-forth between the beasts and the Bethke's proceed in their popular if not overpopulated back yard, with the humans enforcing certain limitations and the animals obeying their instinctive drives to disregard them. It was both a difficult and contradictory operation for May and Brad to prosecute, to with one hand keep giving and giving and with the other take back again. But in time the creators of the verdant little world regained the upper hand over their creation, a one-sided negotiation establishing a coexistence which permitted the animals to eat at their house and home without eating them completely out of it. Peace had been brokered, the sort of peace which depends not on a mutual respect for boundaries but on the disrespected's ability to defend its boundaries against the disrespectful. Most importantly, Maydelis was happy, happy with the adjustments, happy with the still plentiful but more manageable numbers, and more than happy to have a husband who was so eager and able to maintain her level of happiness. It was during this newly-begun period of ecological harmony, one evening in late summer, that she and Brad sat on their living room sofa watching *Dateline: Secrets Uncovered*, when Keith Morrison's warm baritone narration began to sound uncharacteristically scratchy.

"Brad! What's wrong with Keith's voice?"

Brad took a sip from his bourbon and coke. "He's like 107 dear. The pipes had to go eventually."

"Don't talk shit about my Keith." Maydelis leaned closer to the screen. "You hear it too right?"

"Not even a little."

"Lean closer!"

Obediently, he leaned in. "Oh. Oh yeah. Can't believe they didn't edit that raspy sound out." As they both listened to Keith's smooth but scratchy summing-up of the segment, the show broke for commercial, but during the silent seconds between the show and the ads the scratching sound continued. Husband and wife regarded each other with matching furrowed brows. "What the hell is that?" Muting the TV, Brad stood and tip-toed closer to the screen. It was there, or behind the TV it seemed, an insistent *scratch scratch scratch* coming from some unseen place lower than the TV perhaps, down at floor level. "It's coming from back here somewhere" he whispered.

May shifted nervously on the sofa. "I'm turning on the light."

"No no, don't!" Creeping up stealthily to the wall behind the television, Brad got down on his hands and knees and put his ear to the wall. "Fuck."

"Fuck what?"

He was nodding his head as he listened to the *scratch scratch scratch*. "Yeah. In here. Behind the wall. Inside the fucking wall. Come hear it."

"Oh hell no!" She pulled her blanket up to her chin. "What's inside the wall?"

He was no longer nodding his head but shaking it, slowly. "Rats."

Maydelis quickly retracted her feet up off the floor onto the sofa and scooted to the far end. "Shut up!"

"Gotta be. If it was daytime then squirrels maybe, but not at night." He was back on his hands and knees now, crawling along the baseboard. "It's rats alright. Wonder where they're getting in at?"

The frightened blanket wrapped itself more tightly around her. "*They???*"

"They." Brad was back on his feet now, and sat next to Maydelis again on the sofa. "Probably many 'theys'."

She pulled his shoulder back to force him to look her in the eye. "Don't joke around with me right now. Do we really have rats in the house?"

His face was stone serious, but she detected a glint in his eye which betrayed his amusement at her discomfort. "No my dear. We do not have rats in the house. We have rats in the walls of the house."

"*That's in the house!!!*" She twisted herself away from him anxiously. "How? How did we get rats?"

It was more than Brad could do to not laugh. "How did we get 'em? How did we not get 'em sooner?!" He reached for his drink as the *scratch scratch scratch* continued. "Our whole yard is a nature preserve. It's animal paradise out there."

"Well if it's such a paradise out there why do they want to come in *here?!*"

"Your birdseed isn't enough for them." He brought his face in close to hers and brought forth with his most ominous Keith Morrison rumble. "They want your soooul."

"Stop it!" May glanced about the living room from wall to wall as if expecting the sheet rock to burst open at any moment. "So what are we going to do about it?"

Brad was matter-of-fact. "I'll set traps."

"Where?"

"In the basement."

"So the rats are in the basement?"

"We'll find out with the traps."

She wrinkled her nose. "Are they live traps?" His response was only a dark look, the same look as when she had asked about the moles. "How does it kill them?"

"I got snap traps."

"You *got?* You mean you already have traps?"

Brad drank from his beverage again, then nodded with grim sobriety. "Yep. I've been expecting them."

Maydelis shifted uneasily. "Will- will I be able to hear them snapping?"

Now it was Brad making sure that she looked him eye-to-eye. "May, would you rather hear the traps snapping, or... " Brad pointed toward the wall, and the *scratch scratch stratch* came right on cue.

"Fuck." For a moment Maydelis sat very still, just listening, imagining the tiny claws behind the sound, the sharp little teeth behind the gnawing. They were coming alright, not satisfied with birdseed but set upon invasion, on plundering the storehouse, her house, her home, where filthy rats were not allowed. But it was not their fault she reminded herself, they did not mean to upset her; the rats were only doing the thing they were created to do. There were no bad animals after all. Rats were not bad animals. The TV was unmuted, and Keith's sonorous voice was scratchier than ever.

"Brad."

"Yes?"

"Set the traps now."

And thus began the Year of the Rat, or rather, what the Bethke's hoped would turn out to be nothing more than The Few Days of the Rat. It had already lasted too long as far as May was concerned, right from that first moment when Brad identified the scratching. He hadn't set the traps that night when she had asked him to however ("Not tonight dear. I'm sober enough to drive but not to set a rat trap") but had waited until the next day to set them, two traps in the basement; as she watched Brad bait them with the peanut butter, the cruelty of the enterprise struck her, not only the obvious cruelty of a bar of metal snapping some poor animal's neck but the more insidious cruelty of the deception, the luring of the unknowing animal with something too yummy for it to resist and then, having drawn it in with the promise of yumminess, to take vicious advantage of the creature's vulnerability to the irresistible temptation by slaughtering it at the very moment the poor thing was thinking to itself "wow, peanut butter, my lucky day!" But the rats could not stay, that was beyond debate; and if they were to leave, then their departure could only be effected by their deaths. What, was Brad to play the flute and lead them Pied Piper-like out of the walls and off their island? No, she wanted them gone- they both wanted them gone- and to be gone they had to be goners. And so, after adding peanut butter to her shopping list (she could never again eat out of the jar they already had, for thanks to Brad, it was now rat food), Maydelis watched as Brad carried the traps down to the basement where he would load them however they needed to be loaded she did not want to know how and place them in suitable places she did not want to see where, and when he came back up, she made sure the basement door was good and shut behind him. Then she prayed the traps would work. And that they wouldn't.

The next morning, Saturday morning, found the Bethke's going about their every Saturday morning routine of making brunch, a somewhat elaborate affair involving lots of preparation, which for them was a big part of the fun; another part of the fun was the kitchen window, where between the onion chopping and the sausage frying one Bethke or the other or both would now and then stop to look out upon the scene of abounding bird and squirrel and chipmunk life cavorting about the many feeders which Maydelis (Brad) had mounted in the back yard with the view from that kitchen window specifically in mind (due to May's height limitations a step stool was placed on the floor near the sink to facilitate her seeing the entire show). It was a busy and entertaining sight to be sure, and a happy one;

no mention had been made yet by either of them about the subterranean traps, and Maydelis was happy to keep it that way, hoping that Brad had made the courteous and wife-considerate decision that he wouldn't go downstairs and check on the filthy situation until their brunch had ended. The sausage and toast and hash browns were cooked and ready, but before starting the omelets, May stopped at the window and climbed her stool once again.

"Brad! On the fence! Peregrine!"

Brad rushed to the window just in time to see the small falcon hop off the top rail of the fence and fly right past their faces and off into the woods. "Wow! And look, the yard is empty, as soon as she showed up everybody scattered off."

"Yeah. Nobody wanted to hang around and become peregrine breakfast."

With the threat having flown, the critters began to return to the feeders one by one as Brad resumed stirring the eggs. "One of these days you know, we're gonna be watching out here and wham, some fat unsuspecting dove is gonna get talons in its back right before our eyes."

She winced. "Nooo!" But before Brad had a chance to chide her she continued. "I mean, yes I get it, the doves come to the feeder for the seeds and the peregrine falcon comes to the feeder for the doves. It's just- "

"- you just don't want to see it, I know." He glanced toward the stove, then looked back at her and smiled. "May I remind you that you're eating chicken sausage this morning?"

"Yes. I am eating chicken sausage this morning." She was at the table now, pouring Brad's orange juice. "I know full well how double-minded I am about all this. But knowing it doesn't make seeing a pile of bloody dove feathers sound any better."

SNAP

Maydelis nearly dropped the juice bottle. "What was that?"

A crooked grin slowly grew across her husband's face.

"Oh god…"

"I'll be right back!"

"Brad!" But he was already at the basement door and scampering down the stairs. "Not during brunch!" Having been left holding the spatula, May stood anxiously in the kitchen, unwilling to participate in what was occurring but unable to escape it. Silent seconds passed. Then came the sound of feet clomping back up the wooden steps, along with her horrifying realization that he might not be coming up those steps alone. Running down the hall, Maydelis shut herself into the bathroom and hid.

"We got one!" He was right outside the door. No, *they* were. "It's a nice 'un too. Should I just take it outside or do you wa- "

"Just take it outside!" May did her best to not picture her husband on the other side holding a dead rat. She began to feel faint.

"I thought you might want to see it in case you didn't believe we really got one."

She was sitting on the bathroom floor now, unaware of how she got there. "I believe you, get rid of it!" After some amount of time spent on one side or the other of consciousness, May dreamt she was hearing Brad's voice once again. "Okay. All gone. You can come out."

She knew she needed to stand up but didn't quite know how. "Bring me a glass of water." Soon the door opened, and Brad was there with it. "Yes, I'm sitting on the floor. Don't ask why."

He handed her the water. "I wasn't going to. I'm just wondering why you brought the spatula."

After finally making it to her feet (and watching to make sure Brad had washed his hands, twice), Maydelis and her rat killer spouse went on with the rest of their Saturday. Some hours later a second snap was heard; after repairing once again to the bathroom floor, May quietly hyperventilated as Brad carried out a second rat, and after rebaiting both traps, the Bethke's hoped their brief domestic nightmare had come to its end. An extra glass of celebratory wine was enjoyed that evening on their date night, but later on, as they sat once again to watch SNL, it was Colin Jost's voice which this time was uncharacteristically scratchy.

Brad shook his head. "Aw, rats!" He elbowed his once again disquieted wife. *Aw, rats!* Brad elbowed her. "Get it dear?"

She was not laughing. "Fuck! There are more in there?"

"Yep." Brad's ear was down at the baseboard once again. "The word must have gotten out that we have peanut butter."

May's landing gear was retracted under the blanket. "You reset the traps, right?"

"Yes. You saw me do it." He sat back on the sofa as Jost delivered The Weekend Scratchy Update. "Don't stress dear, you saw that the traps work. I'll get 'em."

A new frightening thought now insinuated its way into his wife's already frightened mind. "So we caught two in the basement. And the basement is technically a room in the house." Her troubled eyes stared up at her husband. "That means the rats are in the house. They're already *in the house* Brad."

"The traps will get 'em May. Trust me."

But Maydelis did not trust him, not even a little bit. And her distrust proved prophetic; over the next three days Brad's traps which had proven so effective at the beginning now went undisturbed, while the scratching in the wall continued, got louder even, May was convinced of it. The services of an exterminator therefore were secured; his traps which were the same kind as Brad's and placed in the same spots where Brad had placed his were not ignored by the rats like Brad's had been but rather scored three more kills, much to Brad's irritation (*you prob'ly got your human scent on your traps, that's why they stopped workin' for ya* was how the exterminator had tried to console him). Beyond just killing the varmints, the exterminator performed what he called an exterior exclusion on the entire house, going from the foundation to the rooftop and sealing every possible crack and crevice and opening of any kind where the unwanteds were wont to enter. But when the exterminator recommended setting rat poison bait boxes around the perimeter of the house May put her foot down, not willing to risk the collateral damage of innocent chipmunks also being poisoned (that the rats were just as innocent for being rats as the chipmunks were innocent for being chipmunks remained a thorn in her philosophical side). At all events, the exterminator's triple execution and the exclusion seemed to do the trick, for after the service, three full weeks went by with no more scratching being heard during the evening TV hours, and the traps which the exterminator left baited in the basement lay unvisited and unsnapped. The Bethke's home was, via the exclusion, exclusively theirs once again, hermetically sealed and secured from any further incursions. Once again, Brad and Maydelis had defended their boundaries and restored order to their peaceable kingdom, an order purchased by considerably more violence this time than in their tug-of-wars with the other animals, yes, but an end which even the non-violent May believed justified the means. The five rats had needed killing, simply put. Rats were destructive and spread germs. Rat-borne disease had once killed half the world's human population. Rats reproduce early and often, and an unchecked and never-killed rat population could not be tolerated in a hygienic society. All these things she was fully convinced of and had no misgivings about. As for the things she did have misgivings about, they would no longer trouble her, for she wouldn't have to think about them anymore. The rats were gone and her problem was solved, and so her mind was free to forget the unpleasant experience altogether and focus again upon the happiness of her situation and the beauty of her surroundings. It was on such things which one's mind should dwell after all, she reasoned, and to allow unpleasant thoughts to enter one's mind was a very unhealthy thing. Nearly as unhealthy as rats in the house.

It was another Saturday brunch morning, nearly a month after the elimination of the unmentionables, when Maydelis stood on her foot stool and opened the kitchen window to invite in the fresh air of early autumn and noticed a problem.

"How good is my husband at repairing screens?"

Brad cracked another egg. "No good at all. By that I mean I don't want to, it's a pain in the ass. I'd just replace it instead. Why?"

May poked a pinky finger into the tiny hole she had discovered. "We've got one that needs replacing then." With the pointy end of a steak knife May began picking at the few broken ends of screen wire in a pathetic attempt to close the hole somewhat. "Well, crap. I wanted to let in the nice air but not the bugs too."

"So put a piece of tape on it until I get the new screen."

She made a face. "Bleh! Too ugly."

"What about clear tape?"

"Yes!" After skipping off to the utility room she returned with a roll of clear packing tape, then cut off a small square of it and stuck it across the offending opening in the screen. "Good, we can keep the window open now." Looking out toward the sunflower seed feeders, Maydelis watched the flurry-scurry taking place on the ground and grass where the not-quite empty seed shells were falling. "The chipmunks are tearing it up around the birdbath this morning. Hopping over the squirrels and each other and everything else."

Brad came up to the window to watch with her. "Somebody posted last week on Nextdoor asking if anyone knew a way to get rid of the chipmunks in their yard."

"Get *rid* of the chipmunks? Who would want to get rid of the chipmunks?" May drank some coffee and shook her head. "What's wrong with people?" As Brad returned to his breakfast duties, Maydelis kept her eyes on the life-and-death struggle for seed bits playing out before her. The thrashers and towhees were in the middle of it too, scratching and pecking and throwing elbows for *primo* position, and at a safer distance, the unwieldy doves bobbed and shuffled over the trashscape of cracked and empty shells, content with finding less to eat for the sake of not getting squirrel-tailed in the beak. Amidst the flipping flapping and hopping, May saw a very plump chipmunk sliding along through the grass as if hoping to go unnoticed. She leaned across the kitchen sink to improve her view.

"Brad! Check out this chubby little *cerdito* of a chipmunk! He's too fat to hop!"

"Where?" Brad leaned forward too, surveying the shell-littered grass.

"There, right next to the ground feeder. See him sliding up real cool and quiet like he's getting away with something?" Brad looked in that direction, then slowly stood up straight and with the droll beginnings of a grin looked down to his wife.

"Yeah May. That's one hell of a chipmunk alright."

The wry edge in his voice made her look up to him. "What?"

"Your chipmunk. Look again." May looked back toward the ground and watched the dark little hairball foraging about. "See anything wrong yet?"

She craned her neck. "Wrong? What's wrong, it's just-" Suddenly May's eyes became aware that the fat little chipmunk lacked the chestnut color, the white stripe, the bushy tail or any other damn thing which might have made her think it was a chipmunk. "Oh my god Brad, what is that?"

"I think its Latin name is *Rattus norvegicus*. A real cerdito of one all right."

She shrunk back away from the glass. "Nooo!" Looking once again at the chubby rat, she now clearly saw the long pointy tail. "But I thought we got rid of the rats!"

"We did. In the house." Again he brought out the droll grin. "There are other rats you know." He gazed out the window with a look which, to May's horror, resembled approval. "How diverse our little game preserve is becoming!"

"It's not diverse Brad it's infested!" Even more birds, squirrels and chipmunks had by now joined the scramble, but all May could see was the long pointy tail. "What are we going to do about it?"

"Well, nothing dear. I mean, what needs doing?" She was still shaking her head, even mumbling to herself under her breath, praying or cursing or both Brad couldn't tell. "May, you won! The rats are out of the house. And they can't get back in." He pointed out the window toward the ground. "That fat little fucker is kicked to the curb now. So why aren't we celebrating? I'm making mimosas." As he went to the fridge for champagne and orange juice, May's eyes remained fixed on the scavenging rodent who had crashed her backyard party and was now intermingling among the invited furred and feathered guests. Another rat! It was true of course what Brad said, that this rat was not in the house and would not be coming in. And she wasn't stupid, she knew there existed other rats besides the five they'd killed, and that a wildlife haven such as theirs might reasonably expect the rogue visitor now and then, attracted by the victuals. But one aspect of this visit was different than the inner-wall ones, an aspect which mimosas could not celebrate away from her thoughts: this rat she had actually seen, was seeing with her very own eyes right this moment, and as a seen rat was realer than any vermin she'd imagined while sitting on the bathroom floor. For all she knew it was looking at her now, staring her down with its black beady eyes, leering up at the window and into the house where the coveted seeds and mealworms and peanut butter were all stored. Did it know the big prize was inside her home? Was the exterminator's exclusion really and truly all-excluding? Were rats perhaps like prison inmates, who have nothing to do all day but think of ways to escape, but in the rat's case, the reverse, to look for ways of entry, always sniffing, always chewing, always gnawing and scraping and scratching with a hunger-driven insistence that sooner or later gets them inside? She and Brad were safe for now, fine, but there *it* was, on Bethke soil, separated from May's personal space by- well, by nothing thicker than a window screen really, and a compromised one at that. And no sooner had she considered this did the little piece of tape fall off the screen, fluttering down to the window sill and exposing the tiny tear.

"Here you go dear, have a mimo- "

She slammed the window shut, her recoil bumping into her startled husband and nearly dumping the drinks from his hand.

Later that morning following the Bethke's uncharacteristically alcoholic brunch, Brad's honey-do list underwent an urgent reshuffling, with the emergency repair of the window screen being moved up not only to Job One but Job Only, pain in Brad's ass that it was notwithstanding. But after the tiny tear in the screen was repaired, May's view through it still wasn't; gazing out onto her Eden had suddenly become problematic for her, due to the fear she now felt as to what her eyes might find. And this was a first for her, to say the least; the panorama presented by her kitchen window had always been a wholly idyllic one, a source of serenity and comfort, representing the best realization of her goal of creating the backyard zoo of her dreams, but now that dream had been *cauchemar*red. Her beatific biosphere was tainted, and she deeply resented the filthy rat who'd done nothing anymore harmful than to merely appear in it, to simply exist within her view. Why couldn't the thing have just kept itself in whatever unseen place it had been before she'd seen it? Had it stayed out of sight it would have remained out of mind; but her mind was full of rats now, teeming with them, the one portal which the exterminator's exclusion had not closed, and in the rats had rushed and were having themselves a shitfest. The dysphoria of her thought life was ridiculous, an overreaction, and she knew it. But these same thoughts also made her realize that what she'd previously considered to be "her house" was clearly not limited to that which was contained within its exterior walls; it included the exterior as well, the surrounding kingdom which she (Brad) had built, causing her to feel that this "excluded" rodent had made it inside her home all the same, and she chided herself for entertaining such a foolish attitude. But the following several days helped pull her back off the ledge; as the week progressed, each trepidatious climb onto the stool to peek out the window revealed no return of ol' Pointy Tail, and by Friday, Maydelis was once again happily observing her menagerie without any cautious wincing whatsoever, increasingly assured that the previous Saturday's sighting had been a one-off, more or less a random stopover. It was a Saturbrunchday once again, exactly one week following the sighting, which found May peering out her bucolic portal upon the battle royale being fought beneath the feeders as Brad wielded his knife against the broccoli.

"Did you want onion too May?"

"Yes. And tomato." A bright flash of yellow burst out from the cover of the rough leaf dogwood and perched upon a feeder. "Ah! There's our goldfinch, he's back."

Brad paused his assault upon the vegetables and joined May at the window. "Just 'he?' No 'she?'"

"Not yet. But just wait." As if it had only been waiting for May's introduction, the female goldfinch popped out from the dogwood as well and landed on the feeder, opposite her mate. "And there you go!"

Brad watched the two finches for a moment and then returned to the chopping block. "You called it. He never seems to go anywhere without her following his every move." He took up his knife and pointed it toward May. "Don't get any ideas."

"Just keep chopping." She watched as the goldfinches bobbed and pecked at the sunflower seeds, hopping about until they'd traded places on the platform. "It's true though with goldfinches. They always seem to be in multiple numbers. You never see one goldfinch without also seeing FUCK FUCK FUCK!!!

Brad was at his wife's side in a second. "Fuck fuck what?"

"Look!" Following the pointed direction of May's trembling finger, Brad stared at the grass beneath the feeders and saw not one but two fat gray rats, foraging for the leftovers amidst the other busy animals. "Two now! There's *two!*"

Brad was irritatingly undismayed. "Oh. Yes. You haven't seen 'em 'til now?"

Her eyes were wide with pain. "You mean you have?"

"Yes dear. Every day this week." Leaving his dumbfounded wife rooted in place, Brad strolled back to the block and resumed his chopping. "They're like goldfinches in that way. Hardly ever see one without seeing another. And then another another."

May spun around on her stool to face him. "Stop it Brad, it's not a comedy!"

He looked up from the broccoli and smiled at her serenely. "But it's not a tragedy either." He put down the knife to give the crisis his full attention. "Here's the thing May. The rats haven't just recently shown up. They've been there all along."

"What does 'all along' mean?"

"The whole time we've lived in this house. All along."

She could feel the beginnings of a headache. "How do you know they've been here?"

"Because I've always seen them."

"So why haven't I?"

Brad sat on a stool with a calmness which made her insane. "Because I'm outside doing the work dear. I'm in all the weedy places, the grungy under-the-deck places. They've been my buddies for six years now."

May's hands were pressed against her now-pounding forehead. "So why didn't you take care of the problem then?"

"What problem?"

"What problem?!!" Her hands were gripping the edge of the kitchen island to keep herself from sliding into the sea. "The yard is crawling with rats! Isn't that a problem?"

He remained unflappable. "It's also crawling with giant cockroaches and black widow spiders and field mice and mosquitoes and deer ticks and snakes and- "

"Rats are different!" She shook her head with exasperation. "I know, I know, they're not different. They're just animals doing animal things like all the other animals. I'm not going to try to justify it and you can laugh at me all you want but I can't live with them Brad! I just can't!"

"But you've *been* living with them!" He was on his feet now at the window, and he gestured expansively toward the backyard beyond it as he spoke. "There's a whole lot goin' on out there May, and you can only do so much to control it. By that I mean there's only so much I can do to control it." Only the slightest suggestion of frustration had found its way into Brad's voice, but now his tone returned to fully soothing as he sat on the stool beside her. "I can set some snap traps out there."

"But won't those traps also kill the chipmunks and the- "

"I'll only set them at night when all the nice animals are sleeping. Don't worry." After kissing her on the forehead, Brad returned to the chopping board and once again took up his knife. "It will be a surgical strike my dear. Not a random slaughter."

Maydelis finally allowed herself to exhale. "Thanks for taking care of everything."

"Well, I do my best."

She lifted her coffee cup with both hands, then shifted nervously on her stool. "So… are there really black widow spiders out there?"

"Yes. Also brown widow spiders. And brown recluses. And scorpions. And biting midges. And- "

"Just dice the tomatoes!"

That evening right after dark the snap traps promised by Brad were loaded and set in the general area of the ground beneath the seed feeders, and at the break of dawn Sunday morning he went out to check them before the "nice animals" were up and about. But his bad luck with the basement traps seemed to have followed him up the stairs and into the back yard, for the traps hadn't been visited; that night the traps were set again, in slightly different locations and with a variety of baits, but come Monday morning there was still no success. And so the week continued, with Brad religiously setting his traps at late dusk and finding them unsnapped the next early morning. Maydelis, meanwhile, was unsnapping a little bit more by the minute; each day of unsuccessful exterminating left her fragile nerves just that much more eroded, for she was aware enough to realize that the two fat rats she saw almost certainly meant they were a breeding pair. If there were more than just the two at the feeders she could not and would not know, for the unsettling sight from the previous Saturday had been enough to keep her from looking out the kitchen window even once since then; twice during the week Brad had seen the return of the peregrine falcon and called her to hurry come look, but her impulse to rush to the window was instantly squashed by the greater impulse to not see the remake of *Willard* taking place among the seed husks. Brad of course was well aware of the change in May, and knowing what a critical role the window had always played in his wife's domestic happiness- and that both the window and that happiness were now shuttered- it bothered him to no end. With the traps not working and the untrapped rats surely fucking themselves silly and popping out beady-eyed babies one after the other, May's feelings of helpless vulnerability were palpable, which in turn made Brad feel helpless as well, helpless and uncharacteristically useless. Keeping their cheerful little world turning contentedly on its axis was the job which had always rested on his Atlas shoulders, and to let her down for the first time ever by not being able to repel the rat invasion and reopen her window of happiness piqued him sorely. Moreover, while Maydelis had turned away from looking out the kitchen window, Brad had not; one early evening a week or so after the Saturday when the two rats were sighted he glanced out at the feeders and counted no fewer than five pointy tails, an increase which even he found startling and could by no means be reported to his already creeped-out spouse. The crisis, in short, was escalating, just as were the tensions in the Bethke home, and Brad was growing desperate to find some remedy for the problem no matter how drastic the measure. For although the first signs of autumn had not yet shown themselves in their vermin-infested back yard, the winter of his sad wife's discontent was clearly upon them.

    On a Sunday in late September May's car was turning up the Bethke driveway, returning home from visiting her elderly mother. May stopped in at her mom's house every Sunday for a few hours, but on this particular Sunday, Mom was feeling less visitatious than usual, so May had left Mom asleep in her napping chair and came home early. Opening the front door she walked into the house, and there was Brad, greeting her with a large black pistol in his hand.

"Hi dear. You're home early."

"Um... Brad?"

"Yes dear?"

"What the fuck?"

He pretended to not understand the question, then got around to looking at the weapon in his hand. "Oh. This? Yeah." He rolled his wrist back and forth admiringly to show off both sides of the gun, then dared to smile just a little. "You're home early."

"You already said that." As May stared at the handgun's barrel and guessed it to be at least a foot long, a gentle breeze blew across her face. Behind her pistol-wielding husband she noticed that the kitchen window was wide open, with the screen removed.

"So I have several questions. Let's start with the window."

"Oh, crap!" Hurrying over to the kitchen window, Brad closed it, then turned back to face his wife's apprehensive stare. "I was just doing some work in the yard."

"Before you explain what 'yard work' has to do with the window being open, could you put down the gun please?" After a compliant Brad laid the pistol on the countertop, May pulled out a stool and sat. "Okay. Explain."

"Right." Pulling out a stool of his own he began to sit as well, but then pushed the stool back and remained standing. "The window was open becau- "

"Actually I changed my mind. Explain the gun first."

Brad nodded and sighed. "I really was doing yard work May. Through the window." He picked up the gun once again. "With this."

She did her best to not look at his hands. "That's not explaining. What 'yard work'?'"

"The rats." The puzzlement on her face made him roll his eyes and then point toward the window. "The rats, May. I'm shooting at the rats."

She let the words sink in for a moment or two before responding. "Shooting at the rats... through the window?"

He nodded. "Yep. Through the window."

"But that's... that's not even *legal,* is it?"

He laughed. "Yes, it's legal. Because it's just an air pistol. See?" He reached into his pocket and pulled out a handful of tiny lead balls. "Pellets. That's what it shoots."

"A pellet gun."

"Yep." Brad returned the handful of pellets to his pocket, and came out still holding one pellet between his fingers. "See? They're like bb's. Only... deadlier."

Maydelis stared at him in disbelief. "I cannot believe my husband is trying to shoot rats out my kitchen window."

"Oh, not merely trying my dear."

She recoiled on her stool. "You've shot some?"

He beamed back proudly. "Three so far." He looked over his weapon with a furrowed brow. "I wonder how gunslingers carve notches into their guns..."

Maydelis could only stare at him. "So it's turned into the killing fields underneath the feeders now, that's what you're saying?"

The gun was at his side, pointed safely toward the ground. "May, don't start. You were happy with the traps when they - "

"I wouldn't say I was 'happy' exactly-"

"*- you did not object* when the traps were catching them and getting rid of your problem. So what's the difference? The snap trap kills the bloody fuck out of them, the pellet kills the fuck out of them too. The traps stopped working, so, here we are. I'm a solutions-oriented man May, you sortof like that about me right?"

She was leaning forward with her elbows on the island, her head in her hands as she shook it slowly. "But a gun Brad… it's more- it's more hands-on, it's more personal than just leaving some trap and going to bed and forgetting about it and checking it in the morning." She looked up at him. "It's you, looking right at the poor thing, and then pulling the trigger, then watching it as- " But she stopped herself, unwilling to watch in her own mind the outcome of the imagined shot pellet.

Brad sat on the stool opposite her. "I appreciate your compassion for the unfortunate little fuckers. I really do. It's a credit to you that you're humane and troubled by what I'm doing to them. But you said it yourself- you can't live with the rats, indoors or out. And since you can't live with them, then they can't live. What, do I instead go get a flute like the pied piper and just-

"I know about the stupid pied piper!" May stood and walked toward the kitchen window, preventing herself at the last moment from looking out it. She closed her eyes and sighed with resignation, then turned to face him. "I know. I get it. The only way to get rid of the rats is to kill them. Three already you said, right?" He smiled like a schoolboy. "All I ask is… just don't shoot them when I'm here. I don't want to see the gun or the open window or the bloody bodies or anything that goes along with it."

"You'll still have to see the guy who's doing the shooting."

"Don't tease me Brad."

"No no, I won't tease you." Picking up a small metal cannister from the counter which May hadn't noticed before, Brad removed the pellets from his pocket and poured them into the container. "Now, if I *was* gonna tease you, I might mention that someone who wants to enjoy the rewards of comfort and beauty and happiness but insists that her delicate eyes be spared from seeing all the unpleasant ugliness performed by others which is necessary to purchase for her that comfort and happiness is a very first-world elitist attitude for one to take and not at all what one would expect from a third-world egalitarian Venezuelan country girl like you. Is how I might tease you." With that, Brad took up his pellet gun and was gone, leaving May in his wake to process the non-teasing which he'd just dumptrucked into her lap. An elitist attitude? Well that was unfair of him of course. She knew perfectly well how the world turned, that there were those who made the world a more livable place by performing the thankless jobs, underpaid and underappreciated, and she'd made a point all her life to not take them for granted, understanding the debt she owed to the ones who labored "behind the scenes" as it were. After all, wasn't it she who always waved "hello" to the trash collectors when they came to her street every Monday rather than get exasperated with how their trucks congested the traffic or, worse, ignoring the guys altogether? Even so, she saw no need to deepen her acknowledgement of their service by going up and smelling their trucks nor had she any interest in visiting their colleagues out at the landfill to familiarize herself with the total trash experience. Who would? May was grateful for the trash collectors, saw them as heroes really, and as awful a thing as shooting rats was she was grateful for her hero Brad to be doing it- but did that mean she should stand at the window and watch him fill them with lead any more than she should drive to the dump and walk about through the refuse? No, she was not some entitled and insulated *gringo* elitist just because she didn't want to watch the shooting, Brad's implication was way out of line. And yet there was some unresolved issue in her mind concerning her attitude about it which nagged at her, some aspect peculiar to the rat situation which for some reason made the comparison between not visiting the landfill and not witnessing the backyard bloodletting a faulty one. Sitting on her stool in the kitchen, alone with her thoughts, that difference-making aspect revealed itself to her soon enough, in the form of a single word - guilt - and once that word appeared in her mind it refused to give way. Guilt, she understood now, was the difference; as for the trash, it was dead, inanimate and unfeeling, and so to have it removed to the landfill caused it no pain and required it to make no sacrifice. But the rats were living things, had life, in their simple rat way *had lives*, which meant that the removal of the rats required them to sacrifice those lives of theirs and thus pay the ultimate price, for no other reason but that May's view through the kitchen window might include only the "beautiful people" of the animal world. Yet this level of guilt was but the obvious one, the guilt she felt for requiring the rats to die so as to improve her quality of life. Her deeper level of guilt lay in her aloof unwillingness to do even so little as *pay witness* to those executions which her selfish cruelty demanded! Did not these innocent creatures deserve the honor of her presence at least for their final sendoff, to pay them the personal acknowledgement of a farewell salute? But no, here she was, the epitome of *can't even,* unable to lay her delicate eyes on such indelicacies. To think of herself as so pathetic nauseated her nearly as much as imagining the rats in her house. And at length May asked herself: if she couldn't bring herself to face these animals in their final moment, how could she face herself in the mirror?

Brad was out on the front porch loading a new spool in his weed eater when Maydelis came out and sat beside him on the loveseat.

"Okay."

He continued to fuss with the weed eater without looking up. "Okay what?"

"I'm ready to watch you shoot the rats."

"Really?" The weed eater was set aside. "That's fantastic!" He then regarded her carefully. "Um… what happened?"

Maydelis stared straight ahead. "I need to look in the mirror."

Brad knew better than to ask. "Good enough." He clapped his hands and stood up. "Okay! Let's load up." May followed him into the house and down the hall to the spare bedroom. "I'm glad you came around, especially today. Cool and cloudy, which brings them out and about during daylight hours." After lifting up a corner of the box spring of the guest bed he pulled out the enormous pellet gun.

"So that's where you've been hiding it." He then pulled out from under the mattress the box of pellets. "What else do have hidden around the house?"

"One skeleton in the family closet at a time dear." Leading his wife back down the hall and into the kitchen, Brad set his weaponry down and opened the window. "It's good you want to see how it goes with the pellet gun May. You'll see how quick and efficient it is." He removed the screen. "Way more humane than those poison bait traps, they take forever to die when they eat that shit." Holding the gun in his right hand he checked that the safety was engaged, then unlatched the pump bar mechanism with his left and began pumping up the air pressure. "Crossman P1377 Pneumatic. Bolt action, single shot. Up to four hundred sixty feet per second with ten pumps."

She shook her head. "Boy talk."

He squeezed the pump bar back into the gun with a snap. "But all we need are five pumps for what we're doing." Taking up a pellet from the cannister, Brad pulled back the bolt of the small loading chamber, and after setting the pellet in place closed it back up. "Alright. Time to assume the position. Uh, you'll probably need your step stool to be able to see. I mean, if you... really want to... to see them actually getting- "

"Gimme the stool." He quickly pulled her foot stool out from under the sink and popped it open. May got up onto it, bringing her to nearly his height.

Brad stood next to her and fixed his gaze toward the shell-covered ground beneath the seed feeders. "And now we wait." It was the first time in nearly three weeks since she'd last dared look out her window, and it was only after swallowing back a sizable lump of apprehension that she was able to do it now. There it was, her beautiful green world that she had missed so much all these many days, and behold!- to her pleasant surprise, there was no pointy-tailed lump of gray anywhere in the grass to spoil the view. Her beloved finches and towhees and cardinals, the rowdy gang of chipmunks and squirrels, all were present as if purposely assembled to welcome her home. And it did feel like she was home again, truly *in* her home for the first time in all those three weeks. As she watched her creatures romping and roughhousing around and about, she chided herself for having stayed away so long, and for so silly a reason. Several minutes later there were still no rats, and she began to wonder hopefully if perhaps they wouldn't come out again today at all, and that her dreaded dose of reality might be pushed back to some other day in the unspecified future. Besides, hadn't Brad said that he'd already killed three? Maybe that was enough. Maybe there were no more. Maydelis leaned forward now, her arms on the window sill, all her fearful restraint having vanished and desiring to be as close to her babies as possible, even wishing to be sitting out there among them. Two thrashers had joined the party now, and a wren, then a brown creeper, and then a long pointy tail connected to a lumpy gray body*AAAGHGHG!*

She stood up from the sill with a violent start, enough to have toppled off the stool had not Brad grabbed her by the elbow. "Be careful!" he whispered, shushing her with a finger. May's outburst had scattered all the critters, but within seconds the foragers were all scurrying back into place. Sure enough, the rat was back as well, oblivious to being the sole object of human interest in the nearby open window.

"He's a chubster" Brad whispered as he slowly lifted the loaded pistol. "Eeeasy target." Without making a sound he slowly raised the gun up to the window, then gently set its barrel down on the sill. He continued in whisper mode. "The sill gives me a steady aiming platform. If he sits still for even a second I won't miss." With the unsuspecting rat still sniffing for seeds out in the open, Brad used his free left hand to push the safety button to "off," then put his eye behind the sight. "Now you'll see" he whispered "what a quick and simple business this is my dear." As Maydelis held her breath and reminded herself of the guilt which had made standing on the stool at this moment seem like a good idea, Brad aimed, and then with a pull of the trigger the air pistol made a popping *pfff* sound.

"Oh no no no no no!"

A piteous scene of prolonged and miserable torture now unfolded before May's horrified eyes. Brad's pellet had found its mark- or rather, had somewhat found its mark- for the unkilled rat had only been wounded, struck at a spot just below its spine which caused the poor creature's legs to furiously twitch and jerk, flopping its injured body about in the dirt as if electrocuted while screaming with pain in a high-pitched yelp. As the little rat's spasming torment in the bloody dirt continued, May could only stare helplessly, petrified with shock and covering her ears to block out the wounded creature's screams

"Brad! Something, do something!" But he was already headed for the front door, pistol in hand, and for what seemed like hours Maydelis stood paralyzed on her stool, watching the screaming rat shiver and shake. Then Brad finally appeared in the window, coming into the back yard from around the corner of the house; and as he neared the flopping rat the other animals scattered, wanting no part whatsoever of the grim proceedings which were imminent. No film had ever unreeled in such excruciating slow motion, May was sure of it, as she watched him pump up the air and release the safety, then lower the barrel of the pistol toward the seizing animal. Then came another *pfff*, and in an instant, the kicking legs went stiff and all was still; the red-stained rat lay dead at last, a little deflated balloon asleep across its bed of scattered shells. Using the nearby shovel he'd employed three times before, Brad scooped up the limp furball from its bier and trudged off with the carcass down the garden trail, disappearing through the backyard trees toward a final destination which a teary-eyed Maydelis was glad lay beyond her window's view.

Some minutes later Brad was back in the kitchen, washing up in the sink. Maydelis had collapsed back onto her stool, her head drooping against her chest. It was Brad who finally broke the silence as he dried his hands.

"I swear that didn't happen with the other three."

Her head was not lifted. "Did you get all the blood off your hands?"

He sat on the stool opposite and attempted damage control. "It was really only a couple of minutes. It just seemed longer."

"I'm sure it seemed longer to the rat."

"*Are* you sure?"

Maydelis finally looked up. "What's that supposed to mean?"

He proceeded despite the thinness of the ice. "Well, just that... does anything really 'seem' like anything to a rat? I mean, you must admit that the level of their thought and emotion and understanding and what-not is way lower than ours, right? So then doesn't it stand to reason its pain and suffering is lower too?"

May sat up straight and pointed at the window. "I saw what that rat went through Brad! I watched it, I heard it, I still hear it! Don't try to minimize it!"

His voice was as mouse-like as he could make it. "May. It was just a rat."

"Says the big human with the *biiiig* gun- "

"Alright stop!" He was on his feet in a burst, and the equal-size burst in his voice startled her where she sat. His frustrated energy carried him across the kitchen in three loping strides, where he stopped with his face in the corner, hands on his hips, as if he'd put himself in time-out until he simmered down a bit. There was one audible exhale, a composure-gathering breath, and then he turned, clearly making an effort to measure his words. "By 'stop,' I mean you need to stop pretending that you don't know everything which you know very well that you know." After another collecting breath he continued. "You know full damn well that every day, all over the world, millions and millions of sweet innocent animals are having their heads cut off and their feathers pulled out and their skin ripped off and their scales scraped away just to make animal-lovers like you have pretty purses and yummy meals. Slaughterhouses are shooting cows with stun guns and hoisting them upside-down in the air to slice open their veins, little piggies are getting their throats cut, chickens are getting their necks snapped and lambs are being electrocuted, and every one of those murdered animals *you eat*. Test animals are being tortured with chemicals so that the makeup *you* wear doesn't make your skin itch, other animals are injected with diseases that break out their skins with oozing sores so that *you* can be cured of those diseases if you ever catch them- hell, ducks are gettin' their necks throttled just to harvest their damn livers for the foie gras *you* just can't live without when you go to Paris. Animals are screaming in pain for you everyday Maydelis Bethke, moaning and howling and bleating and bleeding just to put a smile on your face. So don't, please don't, act like that little rat with a pellet in its ass is really all that big a deal to you May. 'Cause there's a whole hell of a lot more pain and suffering going on out there on your behalf than that little rat. That little rat don't even rate." After a punctuating nod of his head which clearly said "so there," Brad took up his coffee cup from the counter, and before leaving the room put a hand on May's shoulder and leaned down just behind her ear. "I was really hoping I wouldn't have had to say all that. But I had it prepared just in case."

An hour or so later out on the front porch, Maydelis sat by herself amidst the falling leaves and considered one by one the many ways she was mad at her husband. She was mad at him for his rat shooting, not only the barbaric violence of it but that the execution of the brutality came to him so easily. She was mad at him for letting her see the rat get shot, especially since it was Brad who had shame-forced her into seeing it. She was mad at him for lecturing her after the shooting, mad too that it was clearly rehearsed. But the main reason she was mad at him was that everything he said was true. May was convicted by every word he said, the whole unsettling account he had presented of the relentless violence inflicted upon the animal kingdom in the name of her pursuit of happiness. How conveniently she had shielded her self-absorbed mind from thinking about the truth, the truth which Brad correctly pointed out that she knew but pretended not to know so that every bite of steak and every shoe she wore would not sicken her stomach and pinch her feet with guilt. And as she sat on the porch and stared dead-on upon those thoughts she had up 'til now kept her eyes averted from, she saw herself as well, with those thoughts casting her in a new and glaringly revealing light. For the first time, May understood that while Brad may have been the one who pulled the fatal trigger, it was she who had drawn the rats into the range of his sights by providing them such an irresistible oasis so near the pistoleer's window. She had maintained for them a never-ending supply of sunflower seeds spread across the ground- well, how had that been any less a baited trap than the ones Brad spread with peanut butter?

Would any rats ever have been seen out her window if not for Maydelis having drawn them out from hiding? What a cruel little brat she'd been, to have lured the rats to the house and then demand they be killed! And she had in fact demanded it, though she had been far too disingenuous to have come right out and said it. *I can't live with them Brad!* is what she'd petulantly cried out to her husband- well, what else did that mean to her "solutions-oriented man" than that the rats had to die? That so *many* had to die! Yes, there were many of them out there, and why was that? Because May had fed them so very well, thereby ensuring that the species would flourish and breed. Were the rats to blame for being so good at breeding? Job One for any animal, above all else, is to reproduce itself. What the rats were doing therefore was succeeding as a species. What then did that say about May? For she had never birthed even a single baby. So in the eyes of the rats and every other creature on the planet Maydelis was the ultimate failure of an animal. Yet here she was, insisting upon the extermination of the rats simply because they were successful at doing what they were put on earth to do! She was on her feet now, her thoughts agitating her off the porch and into her front yard; an English garden more or less, so much more trimmed and controlled than the jungle-like wildness of the Bethke's backyard arboretum. Here, walking down the flagstone pathway between the neatly sculpted shrubs and hedges, there was no fear of any rat underfoot, no beady-eyed lump which might dart across her path. And May wondered why it was, as she looked at the walkway before her, that if a chipmunk or a squirrel would at that moment rush from under the anise bush and scurry over her shoe she would be startled, yes, but then laugh, perhaps even wish for another to do the same, but if a rat were to brush her foot she'd soil her

Spanx. Yes, if such an encounter occurred she might very well lose control of herself; and at that word, control, Maydelis understood the reason why the rat and the chipmunk occupied such very different spots in her affections. The chipmunk was merely just another wild animal, an innocuous and neutral member of the living scenery, and as such was a pleasant feature of the décor; but the sight of a rat triggered within her what rat sightings have always triggered in humans from ancient times, that being, the uneasy feeling that our defenses have been breached and our control over the kingdom has been compromised. May recounted the book of Genesis, the Hebrew god's commission to the first man to subdue every creeping thing on the earth, and how enthusiastically the subsequent generations of mankind had carried out that task whether they'd believed in or even heard of that old Hebrew god; for thousands of years the overlord humans had subdued the animal kingdom with overkill, quite literally, and so the cheeky appearance of a rat inside the fortress walls represented a threat to human superiority, a challenge to the throne, taunting the ruling class by crashing their members-only party. Growing up in Venezuela, Maydelis had known the separate realms of the human world and the natural world as not so very separated, a land where man and animal encroached one another's personal spaces with matching relentlessness, resulting in a stand-off of mutual if not grudging toleration. But despite her South American upbringing, May had come to adopt a very North American attitude, clinging to the naïve belief that she could maintain control over her environment and exist in a safely sealed bubble of suburban impregnability, unthreatened by the random vagaries of an untamable natural world. And now these hideously innocent non-chipmunks had scratched through that bubble, squeezing their beastly and blameless bodies into the dark crevices of her mind if not into her actual home. She had always considered herself an animal lover, first and foremost; didn't her contributions to the Audubon Society and World Wildlife Fund prove it? But now, as she sat on the little wooden bench Brad had built just for her in the shade of the Japanese maple, May set in balance the two opposing forces which vied for position in her mind, her need to control her world and her empathy for the animals in it, and was shocked and saddened by which force carried the most weight. Humanity had proven conclusively over the millennia that its desire to control the environment was far stronger than its compassion for it, and May was forced to admit she was no better. Brad had accused her of hypocrisy, and he was right. She knew, knew with growing shame, that she'd go right along mourning the rats' demise while allowing the demising to continue. And her shame spread in expanding circles. She would continue to eat her veal scallopini despite knowing that young calves would be slaughtered to facilitate it. She'd go on eating all the innocent animals and wearing the makeup and carrying the handbags and wearing the shoes those animals had been murdered for, and would go on satisfying her unquenchable lust for more shoes and bags in the future. No amount of animal torture would dissuade her from her appetites. It was one thing that she had all these years prevented her mind from thinking of all the blood spilt on her behalf, but with Brad having jolted her brain into fuller awareness, it was a far worse thing that she would now commit the greater sin of *continuing* to do wrong when she knew full well how wrong it was. May sat frozen in place on the little bench, feeling no inclination to stand, as immobile sitting there on her selfish human ass as she was unwilling to move it in a better direction. As she remained rooted beneath the shade of the maple a mosquito landed on her arm; in a reflex the other arm raised to swat it. But she stopped her hand in mid-swing. *No,* she told herself, as she felt the bite of the mosquito and watched the tiny speck of red appear. *You deserve it.*

The lengthening shadows and chilly breezes of the North Georgia late fall brought changes aplenty to the Bethke back yard; not unwelcome changes mind you, for each season introduced its own unique charm to their quarter-acre slice of horticultural heaven. Along with the seasonal changes in the foliage came new visitors of the migrating variety; the summer's eastern peewees and great crested flycatchers made their exits south, replaced by twittering gangs of yellow-rumped warblers and pine siskins. Not that Maydelis was seeing any of it mind you; she had eschewed the kitchen window entirely the weeks following the botched execution, and it had become tacitly understood between her and Brad that neither that day nor the rats in general were to be mentioned whatsoever. Meanwhile, Brad had continued to... well, May could not rightly say what Brad continued to do or not do, for to call up on old Bowie lyric, he *kept his gun in quiet seclusion* whenever May was present. But her suspicions were strong that, when she was not at home, the window was once again opened and the pellet gun repositioned to resume its deadly purpose. Some weeks had passed since the day of his reproaching lecture, and as May reclined on the sofa while shopping for shoes on her cell phone, Brad came in from the kitchen and took a curiously upstanding position in the center of the living room. After several weirdly silent seconds, May looked up from her phone and regarded her conspicuously-placed husband.

"Um... yes?"

He cleared his throat. "Okay. So, it's been a few weeks, and I don't know if you... if you want to know, or not, or... Anyway, I just wanted to report that I have not seen a rat in the yard for two and a half weeks. Not one." Brad sat on the chair next to the sofa and leaned in toward his wife. "I think I've finally- I think the rats are all gone May. They're gone." He continued leaning in, awaiting her reaction.

"Thank you Brad." It was simple and sincere, and weighted with defeat.

"You're welcome." Leaning back in his chair, he nodded, his only effort toward filling the awkward space. May stared down at the carpet, having no better idea what to do with the clumsy moment than Brad. But then he proceeded. "Yeah. So, like I said, looking out the kitchen window, haven't been seeing any bad guys whatsoever. But, what I have been seeing lately, since, you know, since it's migrating season now... is a little flock of cedar waxwings." Her sinking head resurfaced, of which Brad took note. "Yep. Chowing down on the red cedar berries."

Her eyes widened. "On the cedars I had you plant specifically in hopes waxwings might find the berries some winter?"

The sign of life in her made him smile. "I think I counted half a dozen of 'em."

She risked a quick glance toward the kitchen. "When did you see them last?"

"Oh... about three seconds before I walked in here." With a little wink, Brad rose and walked into the kitchen, and just as he hoped, May followed, not running to the window but approaching it timidly, as if calling upon an old friend with whom one has suffered a falling out and now returns tentatively to seek a reconciliation. On the floor before the window her step stool was already in place. He shrugged his shoulders. "I kinda guessed you wouldn't resist cedar waxwings." It provoked her first smile of the day; stepping up onto her old familiar spot, Maydelis peered through the glass, and was struck by the foliage changes since the last time she'd taken it all in. At the feeders, all the usual subjects fought for seeds and mealworms, oblivious to the window return of their old benefactor and friend. Being careful to prevent her glance from dropping groundward toward *that place*, her eyes moved instead to the nearby clump of small red cedars, and there, popping in and out of the branches with flashes of brown gray and yellow were the waxwings, clearly enjoying the hell out of their North Georgia stopover en route to Mexico.

    Brad was by her side. "You called it May. You said if we planted the cedars the waxwings would find 'em." His hand was on her shoulder. "You got just what you asked for out there."

    She turned abruptly to face him, her shoulder pulling out from under his hand. "What?"

    His face was a clueless blank. "What?"

    "Nothing." Looking back out across the yard, May watched the happy waxwings picking away at the cedar berries; then a burst of black and red shot across her gaze, a redheaded woodpecker, which landed on the mealworm feeder where it angled and tilted its bulky body into pecking position. As the woodpecker tore into the treat with a machine gun burst of stabs, little bits of seed and mealworm dropped to the ground below, providing highly prized perks to the squirrels and chipmunks who waited there in hopes of such manna falling from the heavens. May's attention was irresistibly drawn to the activity, and as she watched one chipmunk stuffing her cheeks into an overinflated ball with the mealworms, it dawned on her that it was all taking place on the very patch of ground where her autumn and her moral equilibrium had been ruined, that distressing spot she had resolved to visually avoid.

Brad looked over at May as she stared out the window, and beamed with self-congratulatory pride at having restored his queen to her rightful stool throne. "See my dear? Nobody there. The rats are *gone*."

Maydelis continued to stare at the shell-covered ground without saying a word. She was unable to say anything really, at least not to Brad, unwilling as she was to ruin his happy mood with news he would not want to hear. For there among the seed husks, unnoticed by the other animals who were focused on nothing but their own greedy appetites, was a wounded rat, shot just below the spine, flopping and twitching upon the red-stained dirt in a painful unending torment which only May could see.

As the fall plodded along on its steady decline toward winter, life for Maydelis and Brad moved along in a similarly unhurried and unremarkable manner, a business-as-usual unfolding of things with nary a pothole nor bump in the road. It was a time which could almost be described as a wakeful hibernation of sorts for them, for with the growing season having come to an end and the plant life of the garden and arboretum asleep in their dormancy the Bethke's daily labors (Brad's daily labors) in the out-of-doors were reduced to a trickle, allowing time for the indoor hobbies of Mays' jewelry making and Brad's jigsaw puzzles. The animals had by no means taken a break from the feeders of course, as May could well attest; yes, she'd returned to her foot stool on her former regular basis again, not because she had forgotten her reasons for avoiding it but because her return there simply had to happen sooner or later, memories or not. She had done her best to come to a working arrangement between her guilty conscience and her daily life, a solution which ended up depending more or less upon a burial, or rather a re-burial, of the former so that the later might resurrect with its old vigor. And by all appearances May had succeeded in her rebound; new visitors to the feeders were greeted with her old excitement, and though it was not yet Christmas she had already provided Brad with a list of springtime upgrades and alterations to the environs for him to honey-do once the warmer weather migrated him away from his puzzle table and back to his shovel. But the phrase "by all appearances" was key to fully assessing May's return to her former happy self, for in fact, there still dwelt within her the faulted version of herself she'd met beneath the shade of the Japanese elm, when she had allowed the mosquito to have a taste and thus give her a taste of her own medicine. Discomposing thoughts and images still seeped through her from time to time, like an internal leak badly contained by porous walls. And now those walls, though not quite leaking, were showing signs of fissuring. For when the waxwings finally migrated away later in the winter, the wounded rat still had not; May continued to see the little rat out that window, unendingly spasming in the broken shells, seeing it not only in that place but so many places, anywhere and anytime she allowed her gaze and her thoughts to settle for more than a moment. There it was, still the little bloodied rat, crying and yelping in a voice which only she could hear, a scream arising not only from its pain but as a complaint specifically voiced against Maydelis. Brad, to his credit, was tuned in enough to know that his wife's happyish veneer was covering something darker; there were times while watching television at night when he'd detect an apprehensive disturbance behind her eyes as she glanced nervously at the wall behind the tv as if she heard a sound, at which time he would gently reassure her, "May, there's nothing there. The rats are gone." And they were gone of course- gone from the walls, from the feeders, from the whole property, every one of them- except for the screaming bleeding spasming one, the one who continued to fret and follow her, the one who chased her down and found her out by crawling into her shoes and hiding in her purses and riding atop the fork with every bite of beef. He was still there as the winter's curtain drew to a close, as the springtime awaited its cue just offstage, behind the wings; and there it hesitated before making its entrance, feeling its presence just a bit premature, as if winter still had some final word to speak, some last gesture to make, and until its performance was finished the show could not go on.

It was early in the afternoon on one of those reluctant spring days, a cold wet holdover of stubborn winter in late March, which found Brad unloading his truck in the misty rain and setting out onto the driveway a new adoptee into the Bethke tree family. It was a first for them and for the garden, a topiary tree, a Romano boxwood clipped and trimmed into a curling twisting spiral and standing fully six feet tall. And it was a first in another way as well- unlike every other green thing which had been planted on the premises, the new topiary had been entirely Brad's idea, not May's, and in a most uncharacteristic manner he had announced rather than suggested that the new plant would be installed as a featured addition to the front garden. Thanks to its sculpted uniqueness and its shapely flair for the dramatic, the topiary's new home was to be a place of prominence, the very center of the Bethke garden no less, and the fact that this spot was already occupied by another tree was but a temporary obstacle. Standing center stage at the moment was a seven foot-tall oak leaf holly, a species known and loved for its lustrous and sharply pointed leaves resembling those of the oak and its thickly filled-out and symmetrically-perfect Christmas tree profile. Before ever planting the holly Brad had admired the species from afar, impressed by the richness of its foliage and the uniformity of its shape whenever he'd encountered one. He had never seen an oak leaf holly in fact that had ever disappointed him, and so, when it occurred to him that the middle of the front garden could use a centerpiece, he thought of the oak leaf holly, and brought it home as a small sapling five years ago and eagerly set it in place. For five years it grew, robustly in fact; but as it grew, Brad watched in helpless dismay as the little holly, unlike every other one he'd ever seen, spread itself in a most ungainly manner, with some spots of the tree shooting forth with oversized drooping sprouts while other areas of the plant refused to grow even a little. Patiently/ impatiently he waited and watched, hoping that the holly's misshapened growth pattern was but a period of awkward adolescence and that it would eventually fill out and balance itself into the triangular perfection he'd paid good money for and so had every right to expect. But five years in Brad had accepted the truth: an isosceles-sided Christmas tree the homely holly was not and never would be, and no amount of pruning and reshaping would ever improve its disproportionate appearance. It was an irony not lost on him that the holly was arguably his healthiest tree on the property, and by the glossy-green brilliance of its leaves and the abundance of its new growth each spring the deformed tree seemed to shout out loud just how happy it was to be alive. But one thousand eight-hundred and twenty-five days of looking at the lopsided holly was as many as Brad's eyes could endure. And while he took no pleasure at the prospect of uprooting and destroying a perfectly healthy tree for purely esthetic reasons, Brad reasoned that he labored too hard in his outdoor domain for him to have to put up with things which were not to his liking. It was his yard after all, his more than May's in truth thanks to sweat equity, and he therefore owned the rights over all the plants which by the toil of his hands had been planted there. It was only a tree after all, a faceless tree; it would not complain at his treatment of it, would make no protest or offer any argument that it was feeling healthy and happy and was so looking forward to the years to come. It possessed no eyes which would wince with agony and confusion and fill with water as Brad sawed its trunk away at the roots and it would not cry out in pain. Besides, there would in the end be no loss of a tree, for another tree was taking its place. And what a tree! A lovely topiary, already fully grown, by its very design not meant to grow any more at all, which meant no random whims of Mother Nature that might twist it into something unpleasing to the eye. No, Mother Nature would have no say over the new topiary; Brad was in charge of the topiary, just as he was in charge of everything within the boundaries of his garden, and his snipping and scissoring of the topiary's leaves would keep it just the way he liked it. He'd paid a lot of money for the damn topiary, much more than he paid for the disobedient holly, but he had gladly paid the extra for a tree he could control. It was the certainty of control which he would be planting, and control meant peace of mind. Control was worth paying for.

Heading indoors to change into yard clothes Brad closed the front door behind him, but once in still felt on his face the dampness of cool outdoor air. Heading toward the hallway to check the thermostat he passed by the kitchen, and there he saw Maydelis, standing on her stool at the kitchen window with, to his surprise, the window opened wide and the screen removed, thus the chilly indoor conditions. He blinked with irritation as the first flying ant of the season brushed across his nose.

"May, why are you letting all the bugs in?"

There was no answer; after making two or three steps toward the breezy hole in their defenses he stopped and stared. By her side in her right hand Maydelis held the pellet gun.

"What the hell May?"

Again there was no answer. As the gun was raised it looked grotesquely huge compared to the undersized and delicate hand which wielded it, and as it came up toward the window sill the woman's small arm trembled at the ungainly weight. Brad could only watch, immobilized by surprise and unsure what to do even if he were able to move. Then May's left arm was raised as well, as if preparing to hold onto the sill to steady herself. But instead she turned the barrel of the gun away from the open window and pointed it directly at her raised left arm; and as both hands now shook and shivered, each from very different kinds of overload, May pulled the trigger, shooting herself in the left forearm. She screamed, dropping the gun in the sink as she slipped off the stool, landing in a heap on the kitchen floor with a thin rivulet of red beginning to flow. Brad grabbed a kitchen towel and ran to her, kneeling on the floor beside her and pressing the towel onto the wound.

"May, what the hell? What the hell!?"

She looked up to meet his eyes, and as he peered into hers, Brad's hand could feel the muscles twitching and spasming in her injured arm where he gripped it. Tears welled and ran down her face, but even as they did, Brad thought he could almost see a smile behind them. Yes, Maydelis was smiling. And after lifting his hand away and admiring her wound she finally spoke to him in a voice that was strangely calm and commingled with exhaustion and relief.

"*Now* the rats are gone."

THE HOME BOARD

Greg knew that darts wasn't just a game. Not to him at least. It had started out as just a game of course, fifty long years before, when Santa Claus brought him his first dart board when he was ten years old. It was a real cheapie, the wound-paper dime store variety; after he and his brother nailed it to the wooden post in the basement on Christmas morning they had commenced to pummel the poor thing with the chunky brass-barreled darts so relentlessly that by the end of their Christmas vacation the board had been reduced to little more than pulverized pulp. On his eleventh birthday the dead dart board was replaced by a better, sturdier one, along with sleeker darts of tungsten, and by the time he and his brother were thirteen and twelve respectively they were beating not only all the kids in the neighborhood and the kids at school but also all those kids' dads, and the boys were hungry to find new victims. It was a world of games back then for Greg and his brother, for them and for all the kids they knew, games like ping-pong and bowling and bumper pool as well as the more athletic games which came with balls and bats and baskets. If you asked the kids why they played the games they would say for fun of course, but those same kids would also tell you that the funnest part of any game was winning it. Only the grown-ups would say you should play "for fun" and by that mean that you shouldn't be concerned with winning. Every kid knew that winning *was* the fun; any game that a kid played was all about trying to win it. Greg and his brother played all the games for that same reason, and darts was simply the game that Greg and his brother won the most. Which made darts their most fun game.

Darts was still a game to Greg when he was older, old enough for the bars, which was where he learned the serious darters could be found. At twenty-one Greg thought himself a serious darter too, as did his brother, who was able to join him as Greg's doubles partner in the Monday night bar league the next year when he became old enough for the tavern. Their ambitions expanded beyond the local league in no time; in their early 20's the brothers discovered the tournament circuit, taking them on weekend road trips to such exotic destinations as Fort Wayne and Toledo and Rockford and Cedar Rapids, where they enjoyed a modest but growing level of success (i.e. winning, i.e. fun). They began to make a little noise in the rankings of the American Darts Organization as a doubles team, scoring a handful of Top Four finishes in some smallish Midwest events, and as singles players, both Greg and his brother were establishing themselves as up-and-comers as well, neither brother quite at the level of beating the top-ranked guys but definitely earning those players' respect as young shots not be taken lightly. But in their mid-20's things changed; while his brother's game continued to elevate and he found himself winning events outright and eventually working his way up into the top ten in the ADO, Greg's game flatlined. That certain extra something, that next level of precision and consistency which was needed to get a guy not just into the semifinals but past the semis and into the finals, and then *win* the damn finals, was a level which Greg seemed unable to attain, no matter how he tried to claw his way up to it. Practicing more (and practicing better) didn't seem to help; studying and emulating the styles of the great players only upset his natural rhythm, made him overthink and confuse his arm. Even drinking less at the events did him no good, for without his minimum daily requirement of alcohol he couldn't relax, and drinking more only made him relax too much and get sloppy. And as Greg's status as an also-ran became more firmly established with each new disappointing tournament result, the darters who played the circuit soon began to think of the brothers no longer as Greg and his little brother Ronnie, but as "Big Ron" who happened to have an older brother named Greg. Ronnie's star was ascending and there seemed no ceiling, while Greg had come to the bleak realization that his game was as good as it would ever get and was simply not good enough to win. And without the winning, Greg soon found that the fun of throwing darts was disappearing. With no prospect of winning, the tournaments became dreary and expensive affairs, a down-the-drain waste of entry fees and gas money and hotel bills, one depressing venue after another full of stale smoke and staler juke boxes and piss beer and standing around waiting for the next event with guys whom he felt no simpatico desire to stand around with, entire weekends wasted in a polyester shirt covered with silly patches and nothing on his trophy shelf to show for it. By his late 20's, darts was no longer a game for Greg, because it had become a chore, an obligation; the world of the darter had become odious to him, an endurance test rather than an entertainment or an ambition. And so, at the age of thirty, after languishing long enough as either the greatest of the not very good players or the worst of the very greatest players, take your pick, Greg put his darts away and quit the game he no longer loved. He took up fishing on the weekends instead.

And while his brother Ronnie always said that eventually Greg would "get over himself" and come back to the game he'd once been so invested in, he never did. Greg stayed retired from darts, and felt no pangs of regret. Staying retired from darts was easy for him, because any time he thought of the game- whenever he'd stop into a bar and see a board, or when he'd dig for a t-shirt in his bottom dresser drawer and stumble upon his old dart bag- a sickening wave of anxiety would wash its way across his gut, a wave which carried in its wake all the reminders of wasted weekends and not winning. It was this, the not winning, which the sick feeling in his stomach most reminded him of. And for Greg there was an important distinction to be drawn between *not winning* and *losing*. Losing per se had never been a problem for him, for he'd always been a good loser, a superb loser in fact, a perfect gentleman in defeat who exemplified total sportsmanship while being vanquished and offered sincere congratulatory support afterward to his vanquisher. That was Greg's biggest problem, according to Ronnie that is, that Greg was such a good loser. According to Ronnie, Greg could never be a winner as long as he was so good at losing. It was a difficult point to argue: Ronnie was a bad loser, and Ronnie hardly ever lost. Being such a good loser wasn't something Greg enjoyed of course. Being sportsmanlike and gracious was simply the way he was wired, and to behave in any other way wasn't an option. What was so frustrating for him about not winning- other than the obvious not winning part- was that he knew in his heart of hearts that, if given the chance, he would've shown everyone just what a good and gracious winner he might have been, even more sportsmanlike in victory than he'd ever been in defeat. He would have been a way better winner than "Big Ronnie" at least. *If* Ronnie had ever let him win.

It was just this queasy feeling triggered by reminders of his past darting life which secured Greg's status as a retired darter.

But the truth of the matter was that he'd begun to feel that same sickness in his gut even before he retired, before post-darting encounters with dart boards or dart bags would later trigger it. In his last few events, a sense of dread had gotten mixed in with the beer and bad juke boxes, a hopeless feeling which told him in no uncertain terms that things were not going to go well, even before the weekend's first dart was thrown. And in those events just before his retirement, that feeling proved prophetic. Thanks to that queasy feeling, the dart board began to look smaller and farther away, the darts felt alien in his hand, and his stance at the line incorrectably awkward. In his early days of darts he'd wait eagerly to hear his name called for the next match, but in those last events, to hear over the loudspeaker *On Board 6, Greg Bevington versus Anyone At All It Didn't Matter Who* would cause his belly to churn and send him trudging off like a dead man walking to meet his inevitable Board 6 doom. For Greg, this presumption of failure had become his inescapable reality; as for Ronnie, well, he was kicking ass and taking names on the North American circuit, working his way up to #3 in the ADO rankings in 1988, then #1 in '89, qualifying him for international World Championship match play that year and also in 1990. Greg wasn't jealous of Ronnie, far from it- he knew he'd had all the same opportunities as Ronnie and simply hadn't been able to capitalize when it counted- but it was safe to say that Greg didn't exactly rejoice in Big Ronnie's successes either. For Big Ronnie was a Big Asshole; he'd always been an asshole, even from their boyhood days when they would play chess and Ronnie would laugh in Greg's face at every move Greg made until it flustered him into making some foolish blunder and Ronnie would nail him in a checkmate (at an early age Greg had also retired from chess). It was as if Ronnie had determined early on to not accept his status as younger brother and to usurp the elder position, which his bested older brother meekly accepted without resistance. Greg had always been acutely aware of his demotion and understood full well that he was to follow Ronnie's lead (it was younger Ronnie for example who, when they were teenagers, had entered them both in their first youth dart tournament without Greg even being asked, and then, in that tournament, it was "Little Ronnie" who nailed three straight bullseyes in the finals and carried them to victory). It was no small added benefit therefore, when Greg walked away from the game, that it walked him away for all intents and purposes from his asshole brother as well. For without the common ground of darts, neither brother felt inspired to have anything to do with the other (in Greg's final year of throwing in fact Ronnie would no longer partner with him in doubles, such was Ronnie's opinion of Greg as a dead anchor to his world domination dreams). Ronnie's opinion of Greg as a loser paired with Greg's opinion of Ronnie as an asshole was the perfect recipe for a mutually agreed-upon estrangement, and with his relationship with his brother as good as dissolved, Greg's relationship with his bass boat become virtually exclusive. Life carried on in its daily way, and Greg's dart bag stayed in the t-shirt drawer. Now and then he thought of going online and checking Ronnie Bevington's name in the ADO rankings, but he never followed through with it. Because that thought triggered the queasy feeling too.

And so the years passed, thirty of them in fact. Most of those years he spent as a married man; there were two kids, a son and a daughter, both of whom had grown up happy and healthy and college educated and successfully launched, at which point his wife their mother had launched herself as well, leaving him alone. Despite the divorce, Greg had done very well for himself, including financially- he was an accountant, and in a very typically accountant sort of way had exercised prudence in his investments and frugality in his spending over the years so that by the age of sixty he was able to take early retirement and bass fish as he'd never fished before. In all the ways that lives are usually measured, Greg's was a good one; he'd be the first to tell you that his knees were still sound and his brain was still sharp and that, as far as real problems go, he was happy to report he had none to speak of. Greg's retirement held all the promise of a long and enjoyable one. No queasiness whatsoever loomed on the horizon.

What changes take place in a man when he ages, besides the obvious physical ones? By nature, most of them are gradual, imperceptible in the moment, leaving the man little or no sensation of the changing until one day an easy weight is no longer liftable and the fine print is no longer readable, rather like a man riding a glacier who cannot feel it moving, but then looks up one day and finds he's been carried far down hill. What an unbearable shock it would be, both physically and emotionally, if one day a man were the young version of himself and then, the next morning, he awakened as great-grandfather! No, for all of aging's horrors, it spares us at least by being mercifully motionless in its progression. But not all of aging's aspects are horrific. Aging can actually bring benefits to the man, improvements in fact, even if those improvements are arrived at by the ironic process of deterioration and decay. Consider for example the young man, ambitious by nature, working to get ahead and struggling to succeed in the race of life. To "get somewhere," to win at life if you will, is the young man's goal, or rather, a succession of many goals to be achieved with the hope that, one day, that man will earn a sense of having gained the ultimate goal, to have *won it* (that an ultimate goal does or does not exist is the subject of another discussion). The accomplishment of these milestone goals amount to so many individual wins therefore, and so, in order to keep making forward progress in life, the ambitious young man must keep winning. Since winning is the imperative, for him to then lose, to experience defeat, is acutely felt by the young man, a piercing sting which is only made sharper by the oversupplied irritant of impatience coursing through his veins. But with age comes an adjustment, both for better and for worse; with age, the myth of winning is gradually exposed as the chimera it is, or at the very least the shine of that myth fades to dullness, and so the sting of not winning begins to deaden, even as the man's physical body and life force deaden concurrently. At a certain age the man finally reaches the point where he understands that winning is a young man's game, that to be "over the hill" means his competitive days are over; by no longer competing, winning and losing become faded notions of one's ambitious past. With no more expectations of winning, not winning no longer matters and no longer causes him pain. And so, as a man no longer young, Greg found himself rearranging his furniture and rehanging his pictures one day following the repainting of his downstairs walls; and as he was about to rehang the knick-knack case on a clean and empty wall of the spare back bedroom, it occurred to him that he had always hated those crappy knick-knacks and that the center-spot of that wall was better suited for something other than the case. And when he realized just what it was that would look better on the wall than knick-knacks, it should come as little surprise that, after spending thirty years riding the glacier down, the thought of what should instead hang there did not give him the old nauseous feeling. Within minutes he had carried his old dart board up from the basement and was wiping it down with a dust rag.

When Greg decided that day to restore his old friend and enemy to its rightful spot on the back bedroom wall, his intentions were purely decorative. What mancave is complete without a dart board, he reasoned, especially since his board was set in a lovely 40-inch wooden cabinet? Of course he wouldn't be throwing any darts at it, and that was immaterial; it *looked* damn good there, clearly the certain something which was needed to finish out the look of the room. And after getting the new/old board up and stepping back to admire it, he did not fail to notice that no twist of the stomach tormented him. And why should it? Those miserable tournament weekends wasted in dart dungeons were from some other lifetime, a worn and faded memory. Why should it retain any power these many years later to nauseate him? And besides, hadn't he been pretty damn good at the game, even if he hadn't quite been a winner? The more he looked at his dart board the easier it was on his eyes; and yet, as he stared at it, something about it seemed to be not quite right. But what? Greg double-checked the height of the board, and whether he'd centered it properly on the wall- no, it was all just right. Was the cabinet tilted a little maybe? The bubble of his carpenter's level assured him it wasn't. But still, the look was incomplete in some way... the darts! Well of course! After making a quick trip to his t-shirt drawer, Greg placed one set of three darts in the designated dart holders on the left side of the cabinet, then three other darts in the holders on the right side. He stepped back again and took in the picture- now it was complete. But was it? With all the darts neatly housed in their display holders, the board looked too much like the thing it really was- a non-functional piece of wall decoration. In order for the board to look like an active concern rather than merely ornamental, Greg realized that the six darts shouldn't simply be lined up in a row like tin soldiers, but three of the darts should instead be stuck into the board itself, as if a match had just been finished and the last thrown darts were left where they'd landed. After pulling three of the darts from their holders and then pressing them into random spots on the board (as well as taking up the chalk and scribbling out on the cabinet's scoreboard the fictionalized scoring of a game which never occurred) he once again stepped back to the doorway to check his work. Satisfied finally with the authentic feel of his contrived scenario, Greg resumed his re-assembling of the downstairs' furnishings, but only after first taking the deposed knick-knack case downstairs and exiling it onto the same shelf where the dart cabinet had gathered dust for three decades.

The next morning was a Sunday, the one day of the week when Greg always tried to sleep in until it was light outdoors; and for once his hard-wired habit of being up before the dawn actually relented enough to allow him to do it. What finally woke him, instead of the Carolina wrens which typically served as his choir of alarm clocks, was a steady *thunk thunk thunk*ing sound coming from the general direction of his back yard. As alarm clocks go it was an agreeable one, rhythmic and resonant, and in no hurry to get from one thunk to the next. There was something vaguely familiar about the soft but solid thunking, a sound which seemed to be tied to a sense memory, but what that memory was escaped him in the fuzziness of his nascent consciousness. And then Greg knew exactly what he was hearing: his next door neighbors had a tree stump in their back yard, just across the fence, a big oak tree which had fallen four years ago, and instead of paying to have the stump professionally removed the neighbors had opted instead to take matters into their own hands and chop away at the stump with long-handled axes until there was stump no more. Given the fact that the husband and wife were mere mortals, and underwhelming ones at that, their efforts had produced but little gain; four years of axe-wielding had left the stump no smaller in Greg's eyes than the day they'd first laid into it. But while their efforts at lumberjacking had proven discouraging, these neighbors had refused to get discouraged- about once a week, usually in the morning or early evening when the sun was not so punishing, Greg would hear them thunking away at the unshrinkable stump, for maybe twenty minutes or so at the most, at which point the two would run out of gas and drag their tired axes back up to the house in defeat, only to return a week later and repeat the Sisyphean routine. This then was the thunking which had awakened him. Why his sleepy mind had associated a pleasant sensation to the sound he didn't know, for there was certainly nothing about the stump, the axes or his neighbors which fit any "pleasant" category. Getting up to begin his day, Greg came down the hall, and glanced into the back bedroom at the dart cabinet he'd mounted on the wall the afternoon before. It still looked good there, to be sure, and he was glad he'd gotten over his silly avoidance of the thing and could look at a dart board now without feeling like he'd swallowed a live frog. As he continued to gaze in the direction of the board while deciding between sausage or bacon for breakfast, he heard once again the *thunk thunk thunk* of the neighbors' axes, and in that moment was able to connect the pleasant sense memory associated with the thunking sound to the image now before his eyes. It was the sound of darts, thunking against a dart board, which the neighbors' chopping had resurrected from his recollection; and having made the connection between the sight, the sound and the memory, Greg remained in the doorway and took it all in, his mind launched into a meditation, the chopping sound *thunk thunk thunk*ing through him as a mantra of sorts. With each thunk he pictured a dart striking the board, a single twenty, then a triple twenty, a single nineteen, a double bullseye, one target after another picked off with the unwavering precision of his imagination. And this thunking of the darts was indeed a pleasant sense memory, comforting, soothing even, for the darts he was imagining were not being thrown in the unnerving setting of some desolate tournament venue, where the sound of the dart's thunking is drowned out by the music and the chatter and the clinking of bottles and the nervous thoughts which chirp incessantly in the mind of the nervous competitor. No, this memory was a quiet and private one, preserved from thirty years before, from when he would practice at his home board alone, every day, sometimes for hours, one dart thunking after the other in focused concentration in the relentless pursuit of steel-tip darting perfection. With each thunk of the axe/dart he was drawn deeper into the experience, the feel of the old routine, the rhythm of the throw, the resonance of the strike. But then the thunking stopped- the neighbors' grueling twenty minute workday had come to its end- and with the silence Greg's consciousness returned to the back bedroom and the dart board cabinet where three darts which had not been thrown by him protruded from it, pointing directly at him in an unmistakable invitation/challenge. A moment later, with the darts now pulled from the board and in his hand, he was standing at the throwing line and lining up his stance (*why had you gone ahead and measured out the throwing distance and marked the line* the darts now asked him *if you hadn't planned on throwing us all along!?*); and with his first throw, an attempted triple twenty, the dart wobbled like a one-winged bird and landed four wedges off target into the 14's. But despite the bad miss he felt a warm stirring inside; not the dreaded queasiness mind you, but a good feeling, like a soldier finally making it back home after a long tour of duty. The remaining two darts flew straighter, and the good feeling inside him grew stronger. He retrieved the darts and returned to the throwing line. The sausage would have to wait.

So this was how Greg began throwing darts again. That first Sunday he actually threw more darts than his out-of-condition arm was ready for, and so the alarm clock which woke him up on Monday morning was a sore elbow which stayed sore for three days. But as soon as it felt better he was back at the line, and in very little time the wobble left his arrows and the margins of his misses shrank more and more until, within a few short weeks, Greg nearly felt like a darter again. But the obvious question to ask was, why was he taking up the habit of throwing again at all? For he wanted nothing to do ever again with the tournament scene or the league scene or any competitive scene whatsoever and had not missed it in the least all these years; the imperative of winning and its associated nausea tasted no better in his mouth now than it did back then. No, working up his dart game with the aim of competing was wholly out of the question. Why then was he setting aside a full hour every evening to resume his long-abandoned practice sessions on his home board? It was not in spite of the fact that competition was no longer in the picture that he was throwing, but *because* of it.

For what he was discovering from his renewed relationship with his home board- from throwing darts without the context of an actual game- was, to put it simply, darts for darts' sake. For the old Greg and for every other darter, the idea of practicing without the intention of competing in matches represented an exercise in futility. But the new Greg's second try at darts was showing him a different way to look at things. In the past when he would practice, say on a Wednesday, with a big tournament in Virginia Beach coming up on Friday, the pressure was always on to get his shit together in those two days before the event because his new doubles partner was driving all the way up from Little Rock and he'd be counting on Greg to not suck because that would make the double partner's trip an expensive waste of time and he'd never partner with him again. And if on that Wednesday practice session his game suddenly went south and the darts began to fly badly Greg would panic, and his frantic attempts to fix his throw in time to successfully storm Virginia Beach rather than get washed up on it usually made his errant darts stray even more. But now, without those tightening pressures of performance orientation- without the looming battlefield of a Virginia Beach and a partner with high expectations awaiting him- the new darts-for-darts'-sake Greg's practice session on Wednesday and every other day for that matter was an utterly stress-free experience, no matter how off-course his darts might decide to fly. In fact, the new Greg would often welcome the terrible darts, for they presented to him an aerodynamic puzzle to be solved, a curious wrinkle to be ironed out, one which he could calmly and analytically work on with an unhurried mind until, in due time, the problem in his stroke would be identified and his good dart game would return even better than before thanks to having come through the test. With the dart tournament no longer serving as the reason for practicing, the darts themselves became the reason; from the very beginning, from that first Christmas morning when he nailed the paper dart board to the post in the basement and he'd thrown his first dart, the point of throwing it had been about winning- beating his brother, specifically- and whether he beat him was the measure of the fun. But now the fun was simply in the throwing. Now, for the first time, Greg was discovering the Zen of darts, if you will, an attentiveness to the dart itself and to every aspect involved, physically mentally psychologically and sensorially, in the act of sending that dart and his soul on their airborne journeys. Now he took the time to feel every groove in the barrel's tungsten knurling, exploring the shaft up and down, until thumb, forefinger and middle finger each found their proper places to live where all three could cohabitate in balanced harmony. His stance at the line was not a thing to be arrived at carelessly either; the turn of the front foot, the forward lean, the placement of his center of gravity and angle of the torso all came under scrutiny and were stabilized and tuned within the tolerances of a micrometer. The relaxation of the shoulders, the connecting through-line of eye/dart/target, the elbow pointed like a gun barrel and held steady at the proper unwavering height, the quiet stillness of every body part which was not to move except the hand and forearm, the conscious yet effortless breathing- all of these were accounted for and synthesized into a single purpose; and then the throw itself, not so much a throw as an offering, energy first from the elbow, passing down through the wrist and triggering the soft release of the fingers, those fingers following through the toss with long and forward extension as if attempting to not only reach the board but to pass right through it. Having been liberated from competition, Greg was now able to explore and appreciate the value of each of these instrumental components of his technique, and thus better orchestrate them all together into a single symphony of form. And this new awareness was not just of his stroke, but of himself; beyond the physical action of the throw was the feeling it gave him, a deepening appreciation of himself as a smoothly-operating machine whose function was ever-perfecting, yet with no expectation or requirement to achieve perfection. Had the old Greg not been aware of these mechanics in his first go-round as a darter? Well, yes, of course, he had worked and worked and worked on all these technical aspects of his game back then, and when he was done working he had worked some more. But it was just that: it had been *work*, a pressure-packed discipline of labor, to which he'd submitted himself in order to beat an opponent. Now, the breakdown and tweaking of his technique was a celebration of discovery, unspoiled by any opponent, particularly the ones who had always battled against him in his mind. Practice was now the goal, not the way to a goal. Before, Greg would stand at the line and throw three darts; now, he would stand at the line and throw one dart, three times. And when his throws wandered off-target and feelings of frustration attempted to upset his balance he would now close his eyes and put a finger to his lips as a reminder to quiet himself and breathe the frustrating feelings away. Never before had he felt so much love for the game, now that he so much loved the feel of the game. And over those first few weeks and months of his reacquaintanceship with darts- or rather, his meeting darts for the first time- Greg took notice that his purely pleasurable, stress-free practice sessions were working a very real therapeutic effect on him, and that his meditations upon the *thunk thunk thunk* were leaving him feeling happier and healthier at the end of the practice hour than at the beginning, a phenomena which he couldn't remember ever happening in the anxious bad old days.

And oh yes- there was something else Greg was getting from his practice sessions besides the warm and fuzzy feeling in his soul: his dart game had gotten good. Scary fucking good.

When Greg quit darts the first time it had been partly because his game had hit the wall and he was convinced it could never improve. But now, without him really caring that much if it got any better, it had, dramatically. He remembered painfully well from the past all the winning darts he hadn't been able to throw when it mattered, and now that it didn't matter in the least, here he was throwing them consistently. He found it funny, now that he had such a good game, that hidden away in the inner sanctum of his back bedroom there was no one around to see his transformation but himself. And that suited Greg just fine. Darts was his private pleasure now, all his and not available for anyone else to ruin. Now he completely owned the experience without the depressing trappings of the tournament setting- his music at home was better, his beer at home was better, and his game at home was so much better without the constant scrutiny of others (and without having to hear Ronnie's name announced in the finals instead of his own). His aloneness with his home board proved a better companion than any doubles partner ever was, either of the dart or the marriage variety. And in this aloneness Greg threw his darts, through the autumn, through the winter, happy as a cloistered monk in his back bedroom; but in the spring, when the window which revealed the flowering trees and migrating birds competed with his dart board for his attention, Greg was out on his front porch one April morning with his leaf blower, blowing away the dusting of yellow pollen, when he happened to notice that the floor space of the covered porch and one of its outside walls provided an ideal situation for moving his *thunk thunk thunk* outdoors, a setting which was protected from the breeze and other elements but would afford him the opportunity to both throw his beloved darts and enjoy his equally beloved pastoral distractions without really being distracted by them (what worship service, after all, is not enhanced by the beauty of nature?) In no time he measured out the distances and hung the board, and so it was there on his front porch where he took up his practicing on weather-permitting days. And what a smashing idea it turned out to be! Thanks to the enhancements of the Lady Banks rose and the Jane magnolias, with wrens and hummingbirds swarming above and skinks and chipmunks scurrying about and below, Greg's attainment of darting zen reached unprecedented heights, even as the accuracy of his throwing climbed as well. And there was another added feature which he enjoyed, one which Greg couldn't have guessed he would ever actually have invited upon himself: from his perch out on the porch, he could wave at his neighbors who walked by, neighbors who before he had preferred to hide from, for he took pleasure now at being that somewhat eccentric senior who mounted a dartboard in the great outdoors and threw his darts for all to see. He admitted to himself with some measure of self-embarrassment that he rather liked them to watch (from the detached distance of the sidewalk mind you), that they could see this well-appointed older gentleman who, based on the elegance of his stance and the beauty of his graceful throwing form, was clearly highly skilled at his craft and no doubt a very interesting person overall. But make no mistake- his home board was still his private playground, and no one else was allowed to touch his toys. Still, what harm could it do, he reasoned, to strike a little compromise between his private *thunk thunk thunk* and being noticed just a bit? Because his back bedroom, for all the edifying benefits it had brought him, was a little isolated after all, and now that he was clean and sober from the drug of competition a slight acknowledgement of his fellow man seemed a perfectly safe and non-intoxicating imbibement. All spring and summer then did Greg throw his darts for all the world to see, or at least the world of his cul-de-sac, and into the early fall as the dogwoods lost their leaves and his t-shirt was replaced by a flannel hoodie. But come November the chillier temps brought an icy stiffness to his throwing fingers, and by Thanksgiving, after grudgingly accepting the fact that winter was in for the duration, Greg and his board retreated indoors to await the distant return of the blossoming April dogwoods.

So Greg and his *thunk thunk thunk* moved back to the inner sanctum of his back bedroom, and there he returned to the private throwing routine which had started him so many months earlier on his darts-for-darts'-sake journey. And while it was a return to a familiar home, and by no means an uncomfortable one, it felt different to him now. For he'd been out among the presence of other people, if not actually with them, and so his awareness of being re-immersed in isolation pinched at him acutely, decidedly more than when he'd first moved his game onto the porch to escape it. And a troubling thought accompanied that isolated feeling- while his exclusively locked-in relationship with his home board had done him immeasurable good, he wondered if his internalized practice habits performed in the exact same way every day in the unchanging setting of familiar scenery amounted to an artificial environment in a vacuum, and if so, might his new-found beautiful game be an artificially created one as well? What would happen if he dared throw his darts somewhere else? Was his zen-technique really so unshakably ingrained in his mental and muscle memory, or would a change of surroundings expose his game as nothing but a house of cards? Perhaps he was the new Greg only on his home board and no where else. With a change in location, with different lighting, different music, different flooring under foot, what have you, would all the old bad habits come flooding back in, both the technical and the mental ones? This was not to say that he was backtracking in the least in his resolve to forswear competition; there was no wavering in that regard. It was simply a question of his transformation's authenticity- had he really emerged metamorphosed as a dart butterfly, or had he merely sewn himself and his darts into a back-bedroom cocoon? It was this discomfiting concern, coupled with his cabin-feverish sense of isolation, which moved Greg to consider his options, and in short order he understood that he had but one. There was a dive bar not far from his house where he had downed a bratwurst one lunchtime, and he'd noticed in a darkened side area no fewer than three dartboards (a sight which at the time had predictably triggered the old nausea of course), tucked away almost apologetically from the main area of the establishment. It was as private a public place as he could hope for, and seemed ideal for the experiment which he now felt the need to conduct. If he went to the bar, he would be careful to only go on some unpopular weekday night during off-peak hours, when there would be little chance of curious darters or people in general in attendance. There he could take his game on the road, if only down that road a few short blocks, and see if the signal generated from his back bedroom was strong enough for him to tune in to its *thunk thunk thunk* wavelength. And so it was that on the following Tuesday evening, just as the Christmas lights on the surrounding houses were beginning to twinkle across his neighborhood, that Greg and his dart bag drove down to The Brass Whistle where a clandestine meeting with a foreign board awaited him.

Once inside the establishment he performed a quick scan, and was pleased to see that the environment he'd stepped into was just what he hoped it would be. A glance toward the dart boards revealed no other darters, thank god, and as for the rest of the place, the few early evening stragglers were all sitting at the bar with their backs turned away from the throwing area. After ordering his Guinness he made his way to the boards and checked out the lay of the land. Overall, the conditions were better than he expected, passable for sure- the track lighting was decent enough, the three boards were all fairly new, and the wall to the right was the window onto the street which made the narrow darting nook feel not so claustrophobic. After returning from the bar with his pint, Greg set up shop at the board nearest the window, and with darts in hand, stepped up to the line and stared at the black and red disc on the wall who would be his silent partner for the evening. Well, we'll know soon enough he told himself, as he footed up to the throwing line, whether he really was who his home board said he was or if he was a fraud. Finding his grip on the first dart of the night Greg laughed a little at himself, that the question of legit or fraud should even matter to him. What difference does any of that make if one has adopted a darts-for-darts'-sake philosophy? There is nothing to prove anymore, now that there's no competition; no opponent to prove anything to, and nothing to prove to some doubting doubles partner. Certainly nothing to prove to Ronnie anymore, wherever he might be these days. And so, Greg threw his darts, the first few a little creaky as his elbow loosened up, but soon they were flying smooth and straight, his groove locking in to its familiar rhythm, the machine of his mechanics settling into the cruise-control mode which had become his standard operating procedure these many months. Within ten minutes he was banging his targets at will, picking off doubles, clustering triples, moving over the board with efficiency and precision the same way he did out on his porch or in the back bedroom. He was really doing it, he said to himself, as he sipped his pint with self-satisfaction, just the way he hoped he could do it, in a foreign land away from the safe haven of his home board. No one was observing his mastery on this sleepy Tuesday evening, just as he'd planned and expected they wouldn't, but if they were to turn and watch him, what with him in secure possession of his A-game, he wouldn't mind it in the least; and as he hit first the triple-sixteen, then the triple-fifteen, and then the double bullseye, Greg looked about longingly, thinking it a shame that the barflies on their turned-away stools didn't realize that a virtuoso was performing right behind their backs. By now he'd thrown for nearly an hour and had reached the bottom of his beer; there was no denying that the experiment was a resounding success, and that coming out of his cave had been a capital idea. His dart game had acquitted itself admirably away from his home board, and while he'd experienced no pleasant encounters of the social variety, he had suffered no disagreeable ones either. Sure, there was a pathetic aspect to the whole endeavor, he admitted to himself, coming out to a bar hoping there would be people but also hoping he wouldn't actually have to face them, people he was determined to avoid but then ending up sad about being avoided by them. But he'd always been mixed-minded like that, even in the old days when he needed to pretend he wasn't, when he was an ambitious darter trying to make a name for himself. Fortunately for Greg, Ronnie had never been mixed-minded about anything, so Greg had the benefit of Ronnie to lead him (drag him) into battle; Ronnie always made sure they only went to the busiest dart bars on the busiest nights, entered the biggest tournaments offering the most prize money instead of wasting their time in nowhere spots attended by nobody (had Ronnie seen these three abandoned boards at The Brass Whistle he'd surely have dismissed them as the "bunny boards"). Ah, but it was darts for darts' sake for Greg now, not darts for Ronnie's sake; and as he picked off a single twenty, then another twenty, then a triple twenty, Greg felt with each dart a *thunk* of self-affirmation, each dart a nail in the lid of a problematical box that he was finally sealing for good. He decided that these were a good three darts to end the evening on, so with a final toss-back from his Guinness, Greg walked up to the board to retrieve his flights for the last time of the night.

"Damn. You just hit five twenties!"

It was a female voice which had come from somewhere behind him, over his shoulder. Turning to face it, Greg saw a young woman, mid-twenties probably, pretty enough in a bleached-blonde scruffy and petite sort-of way, wearing a men's flannel shirt unbuttoned over a gray cotton hoodie. "You always hit tons like that?"

He raised an eyebrow in acknowledgement. "So, you know what a ton is."

"Oh yeah." The girl shifted her weight tomboy-style onto her back foot and then counted it out on her ringless fingers. "Five twenties is a hundred which makes a ton, six twenties is ton-twenty, seven twenties ton-forty, and the most you can hit is three triple twenties which is ton-eighty. You hit any ton-eighties tonight?"

"So many ton-eighties."

"Yeah, right!"

Greg walked back to the line and smiled down at the rough-and-tumble little waif. "You're a darter then?"

"Nah." The girl made a quick glance back toward the bar area, then back to Greg. "I just know a lot of darters. So who were you playing against tonight?"

The unintentional poignancy of the girl's innocent question did not escape him. "Well, I wasn't playing *against* anyone. You could say I was playing *for* myself."

"Oh." There was the briefest of pauses as the girl took this in. "Do you always just play for yourself?"

"Oh yes. It's better that way, trust me."

She glanced behind herself once again before continuing. "So you're not on a dart league?"

He pretended to shudder with terror. "Aghgh, leagues! Don't even *mention* leagues!" The girl recoiled just a little, which Greg regretted to have caused. "Sorry, leagues aren't bad. It's just..." She was actually listening, he noticed. " I used to play on a league. I used to... I used to compete. On the tournament circuit. Back in the day."

She tilted her head to the side like a curious parakeet as she processed his answer. "But you don't compete now?"

"No."

"How come?"

It was innocent and simple, the sort of thing a child might blurt out. So he had no problem laughing it off as such. "Well, because I'm an old man now. I had my run."

The girl wrinkled her nose. "You're not *that* old!"

"Well, thanks for that I suppose." It was getting a little awkward; he picked up his dart bag from the table and began loading his arrows.

"And you were pounding those bullseyes too. Not just your twenties."

He looked up from his dart bag. "You were watching me for a while then?"

Now the girl seemed pleasantly flustered. "Well no, not for *a while*, I mean- okay, I watched a little while. I just went to go pee and so I walk by and I see some guy throw a dart and it's a bullseye right away, so I had to stop. And then you hit like three more. Like I said, I know a lot of darters, so..." The girl trailed it off as her hands nervously tousled her already-tousled hair.

"Did you ever go pee?"

Both her hands shot straight up into the air. "Ohmygod, no! I still have to pee!"

"Well go pee!"

"I'm going!" The girl scampered off around the corner, but then scampered straight back. "By the way, I'm CJ."

Greg nodded, even bowing just a little. "Nice to meet you CJ. I'm Greg."

"Okay Greg. You're really good at darts. See you next time!" And CJ was gone again, leaving Greg in her wake where he was moved to make a quick reassessment of his Tuesday night experience at The Brass Whistle: instead of no pleasant encounters of the social variety, there had turned out to be exactly one. And after bagging his last dart and putting on his jacket, he made his way past the bar stools and to the door just as unnoticed as when he had arrived. Well, not completely unnoticed, he reminded himself, as he stopped at the door and glanced back toward the ladies' room before stepping out into the chilly November night air.

It was a slow week which followed Greg's Tuesday night excursion to the dart bar; but then again, most of his weeks at this point in his life were pretty slow affairs, which was how he preferred things after all. What glacier rider who has exhausted all his goals and ambitions wishes the time remaining to pass with haste? But this was one week which he'd have been quite happy to see fly a little more quickly. For his Tuesday night out had been such a successful venture that he had decided even before making it back home that he and his darts would return the Tuesday next; and as such, his practice sessions in the back bedroom on those nights following that Tuesday felt like rehearsals for a return performance. But if he were to say the only reason for a repeat visit was because of how well those darts had flown he'd have been lying to himself. Capping off the evening with his pleasant brush-up with little CJ had proven quite the added attraction; and while he knew he couldn't count on her showing up there again the next Tuesday, her "see you next time" had left him with the hope that such a possibility existed. That she had watched him in action, as it were- and that she noticed his game and appreciated it- pleased him so much that he felt guilty for feeling so pleased. But only a little guilty. What harm was there in it, and why be ashamed of his thoughts and feelings? Darts for darts' sake should be fun after all, fun and nothing else. Whenever during his competitive days had he enjoyed throwing his darts as much as he had that Tuesday night (and whenever had he enjoyed himself so much *after* throwing them, for in the old days, instead of finishing out the evening with chatting up some pretty young thing who complimented his skill, he typically would end his dart night with an ignominious escape from the dart hall with his tail between his legs and a three hour Sunday drive home from Minneapolis spent thinking about what a miserable loser he was)? No, there was nothing wrong with a little Tuesday night rooster-strutting, even if he was an old bird; and if CJ was not to return to The Brass Whistle, well, so be it, for the whole point of the Tuesday night adventure had been about the darts and not the admiring attentions of pretty young women. Still, when the slow-moving Tuesday next had finally arrived, Greg made sure his hair was carefully combed before getting into his car; and despite his resolve to suppress his enthusiasm and behave like the mature gentleman he was, he found himself pulling into his dive bar's parking lot a full hour earlier than he had the week before.

    It was Deja-vu all over again inside the Whistle that second Tuesday night as Greg found the same sparse crowd sitting on the same bar stools as before, and the same unpopulated dart alcove awaiting his follow-up solo engagement. There was no CJ to be seen anywhere, and a pang of disappointment made itself felt; and yet, he also felt a measure of relief at her absence, for now there'd be no danger of his focus being distracted from the mantra of the *thunk thunk thunk,* regardless of how pleasant that distraction might be. With his Guinness tableside, Greg settled into his throwing, and to his delight, the machine of his technique was as well-oiled as ever. Even his bad darts, what few of them there were, were coming from a good place, a place of confidence which told him the that the next dart to follow the bad dart's flight would more than atone for that previous dart's sins. He had just taken out a game of 501 in only eleven darts, no meager accomplishment at any level (Ronnie's best had only been ten after all), and after pulling from the double-sixteen bed the third dart which had closed it out, Greg turned back toward the throwing line to find CJ waiting for him.

"So, you can hit your doubles too. No surprise. It's Greg, right?"

It meant nothing of course, but she remembered his name. "CJ! I didn't see you here tonight."

She held a PBR tall boy, of which half its contents she now poured down her craw. "Well of course you didn't see me. All you see is the dart board. You're focused. Just you and it. You're like- " the remaining beer now rushed after what had gone before- "you're like one of those bullfighter guys, you know, in Spain, those ones..."

"A matador?"

"Matador! Yes!" She bounced up and down on the balls of her feet. "Like how they look so elegant and proper in their matador pose holding out their red flag, that's how you stand holding your dart before you throw. And then they face down the bull all intense and shit, but you're facing down... a bulls *eye*! Oh that's good, right?"

He laughed and laid his darts down on his Guinness table. "Si si CJ, muy bueno. But I don't think I could get even one of my fat old legs into those matador pants."

She wrinkled her nose. "They wouldn't let you into a bar like this wearing 'em anyway." After a quick glance back over her shoulder, CJ made double-sure her PBR was empty, and then, "So you're throwing alone again?"

"Oh yes ma'am." Something approaching a frown shadowed the girl's face. "It's like you say CJ. Just me and my darts. One-to-one focus, right?"

She nodded uncertainly, but then her eyes opened wide. "Oh! Then that means I'm bothering you!" CJ took a quick step or two backwards apologetically. "I'm sorry!"

"No!" Greg waved his hands in protest, laughing aloud. "You're not CJ! It's good to take breaks. You shouldn't always practice in a vacuum. It's not natural."

"You're sure?"

"Positive!"

The young woman relaxed. "Okay. If you say so." In an instant she had plopped herself down on a bar stool near his throwing line. "It's probably rude of me but I like watching you practice. Because you make it look easy, really smooth and nice. Dart throwing actually looks fun when you do it. A lot of other throwers..." At this point CJ picked up one of Greg's darts from the table next to the bar stool and was rolling it absent-mindedly between her fingers. "...sometimes they don't even look like they're having fun. They're, like, all angry at the darts or something. What's the point in that right? That's why I don't throw." The dart was resting in her left hand now, the fingers seeking out comfortable ways to wrap themselves around it.

"So you're a lefty, huh?"

"What?... ohmygod!" CJ suddenly realized what she was holding, and returned the dart quickly but carefully back onto the table. "Sorry, I'm sorry! Did I jinx it?"

He shook his head and picked up his darts. "Are you kidding? The most good luck thing a guy can do is to have a dart wench hold his darts. So, please- "Greg held his darts out to the hesitant girl. "- do me a favor and hold all three. Go on." Warily,

CJ took the darts from Greg's hand, and once again, her left hand took one up in an awkward grip. "So you've never thrown before? Not even a little?"

She shook her head. "Nah. The only time I've been around a dart board has been like in a bar with people all around. It's hard to just get up in front of people and be terrible at something while they're watching you."

"Everybody's terrible at first."

"Oh I'm pretty sure I'd stay terrible."

If the next thing to say hadn't been so painfully obvious he'd have never been so bold to say it. "Well then, what if some fat old matador were to teach you a thing or two about throwing?"

CJ looked up at him wide-eyed, then shook her head vigorously. "What? No! No Greg. Shut up. You're not teaching me. No."

"Why? Because you'd be distracting me?"

"Yes! And because you'd be wasting your time!" She began to dangle and flop her arm about like a rubber hose." Look! Do you see that? That's what you'd be working with!"

He laughed. "I'm pretty sure we can get rid of the flapping thing at least. And as for the distracting me thing- " the childlike way CJ was sitting on the stool and looking up to him with open-eyed attentiveness made him realize the instruction had already begun "- one of the very best ways that a person can get better at something is to teach someone else how to do it. The lesson works both ways. So you'd be doing me a favor."

The slightest wrinkle appeared in her brow. "You really want to do this do you?"

"I really do CJ. Listen, I throw all by myself six nights out of the week, so I can spare the seventh for a rubber-armed girl."

"You throw all by yourself the other six nights too?" The wrinkle in her brow deepened for a moment or two, but then her face brightened. "Okay. You can teach me. But you have to promise me you'll dump me when you've had enough of- " once again CJ flapped her dead rubber arm.

"Fine, fine, I promise. So I assume Tuesday nights are good for you?"

She nodded. "No, yeah, Tuesdays. It has to be Tuesdays."

"Tuesday it is then." Taking a step back he stood at attention, his arms to his sides. "Okay Miss CJ. Are you ready?"

Her eyes blinked with surprise. "Wait, you mean now?"

"Well it's Tuesday isn't it?" At this, Greg took CJ by her elasticated arm and, raising her from her stool, led the hesitant girl to the line. "Okay. Starting at the beginning. This flat thing which your feet are pressing down against, it's called *floor*."

CJ mouthed it back to him carefully, pretending to learn a new language. "Fl-oo-r."

"Very good. And this is the proper way for a darter to stand on it..."

So then began Greg's Tuesday night dart mentorship of his rubber-armed apprentice CJ. Introducing her feet to the floor beneath them was by no means just a joke, for it quite literally reflected his determination to build her game from the ground up. And as he painstakingly worked her through the fundamentals and guided her mechanics with persistence and patience, he came to learn in short order that CJ hadn't overstated her lack of talent. She was, in a word, an oaf, an adorable and delightful oaf to be sure, but as comfortable with three darts in her hand as a walrus in pointe shoes. One entire Tuesday lesson was dedicated to nothing but her stance, or more accurately, her inexplicable inability to maintain one;

another Tuesday amounted to an hour-long wrestling match between Greg and her stumpy fingers as they fought him tooth and nail against being wrapped around the tungsten shafts. But despite all her (their) struggles with the process, each lesson was an enterprise of unmitigated fun for both of them, from the first errant arrow to the last. And this was absolutely by his design; for he had insisted from the start that the sharp objects in their hands were to be wielded strictly for fun, the whole fun and nothing but the fun. Whenever he sensed that CJ was getting frustrated or flustered with her efforts he would perform for her the routine which he'd come to do for himself, would close his eyes and touch his finger to his lips to silence her frustrating thoughts and to bring her back to the fun. There was no argument from CJ that fun was the one and only point; she had no aspirations of becoming competitive at the game (and, thankfully, no delusions of having the remotest *chance* of becoming competitive). And she seemed to have her own troubling issues with the whole idea of competition which she didn't elaborate on, issues springing from her own personal well and not as a result of any anti-competition evangelism from Greg. At all events he found ready-made in CJ an absorbent sponge to soak up his darts-for-darts'-sake approach to the game. But though she was an avid parishioner in the Church of Greg it could not quite be said that CJ was becoming a full-fledged devotee in his religion of the *thunk thunk thunk,* for her staggering lack of darting ability prevented her from reaching such spiritual heights. Still, she was clearly getting the main point, that being the fun, he was sure of that; and rather than simply putting up with Greg's rapturous rants about the Zen philosophy of darts she seemed truly eager to hear them (and if she wasn't then she was a far better actor than a dart thrower).

Occasionally her focus was interrupted by a curious preoccupation of hers which Greg was too polite to ask her about- now and then she would glance back toward the main area of the bar as if waiting or watching for someone, and then immediately return her full attention to the board. But there never was any other someone to be seen, not during the lessons or after them; in fact, it was a mystery to him that at the end of each Tuesday night throw, as he gathered his things and made for the door to leave, there was never any CJ in sight to give a final wave of goodbye to, even though he watched carefully each night to confirm that she hadn't left the establishment before him. But despite her whereabouts being unknown at the end of each Tuesday night he could be sure she'd be there at the next one, eager and oafish with a PBR in one hand and her own darts which Greg had given her in the other, his old backup set which she'd first refused to take but finally relented at his insistence. Nine Tuesday evenings they spent in The Brass Whistle's cozy little dart alcove, or rather, their cozy dart alcove, since no other dart throwers ever once lined up at the two dart boards next to theirs in all those weeks; nine hours of never playing an actual game of Cricket or 501 against each other, the word "against" being banned outright, but instead, nine hours engaged in a different sort of game, the game of fun, which each of them won all the time every time with no keeping score and nary a loser to be found. And while it was only on Tuesdays when Greg would win at the game of fun with his fun-loving dart-throwing friend, it had come to be that he now considered the little dart alcove as his true home board instead of the six-night-a-week board in his dark back bedroom. For nowhere else in his life had his game ever been so on-point. His dart throwing wasn't half bad when he was there either.

At 6:30 on their tenth Tuesday Greg was warming up with his first darts of the evening at their board by the window, awaiting CJ's arrival which was always some minutes after his. He preferred to get to the Whistle before her so that he could get his off-target creaky-elbow tune-up darts out of the way without her seeing them, and on this particular night he was hoping she'd be a little later than usual, for his old man arm was taking its sweet time to warm itself to the task. Of course he was sufficiently self-aware to realize how silly it was, his desire to conceal from young CJ any evidence of his being merely mortal. So what if she saw his crappy warmup throws? Darts for darts' sake had nothing to do with pretending you were someone you weren't. She wasn't hanging out with him on these Tuesday nights because she believed him to be some sort of god. She wasn't there because his darts were always great or that her darts were getting any better, which they weren't. CJ was there- and in this he took a measure of pride, for he knew his mentoring had instilled this in her- because she had discovered the sheer pleasure of the experience, and required no particular skill level or technical achievement to enhance or validate it. Warmed by this thought, Greg threw his next three darts; and as if to underscore what he'd just been thinking, all three darts were sprayed as if thrown by a blind man. Laughing to himself, he walked to the board to retrieve them, and just as he touched the first one, he was surprised to hear just behind him at the next board the familiar *thunk thunk thunk* of three darts landing. He knew exactly who it was, and he smiled, speaking to her without turning to face her.

"I know those darts without even looking. They sound like a drunk girl's darts." He turned around to check out the shrapnel which CJ had sprayed across the neighboring board, but what he saw was nothing less than a perfectly-grouped seven-mark on the 19's: two triple 19's and a single. In amazement Greg looked over to the throwing line, where stood not little CJ but a very tall and very imposing-looking young man sporting a very unapologetic mullet, broad shouldered with both arms fully ink-sleeved and a look of mocking indignation on his goateed face. The loose-fitting shirt he wore was an all-too familiar one to Greg, a polyester relic from his distant past- it was a dart shirt. Complete with dart patches. The tall guy at the line was a goddamn darter.

"So, do they *look* like a drunk girl's darts?" The man stared down at Greg as he made his slow walk to the board where he pulled out all three clustered darts with one big jerk.

Meanwhile, Greg looked up sheepishly at one big jerk. "Sorry man. I thought you were someone else."

The big darter snorted with sarcasm. "Yeah. I know."

Wondering what he might have meant by "I know" but not dwelling on the point, Greg returned to the line, and the two men resumed throwing on their respective boards. Here now was an intruder, an interloper, insinuating himself into Greg's and CJ's private hideaway! How strange it felt, he remarked to himself, to be throwing next to another darter again after all these years, awkward and uncomfortable and yet so very familiar, just like he'd done so many times before. Here was the exact person he had least wanted to encounter, lined up beside him elbow-to-elbow. They continued to throw in silence; and as Greg's bad darts continued to fly badly, a new feeling- to be more accurate, an old feeling, one conjured from the bad old days- began to trouble him, for he was now aware that his neighbor was taking note of the crappy darts Greg was throwing, a realization which only served to make his throwing even worse. That the big darter was unleashing upon his own board a merciless onslaught of accuracy- and that Greg couldn't help but notice the carnage- *and* that the big darter *knew* Greg was noticing it- only added to the older man's discomfiture. A sense of dread and despair he hadn't felt in thirty years now joined forces with the creakiness in his elbow, and the combined effect was one which made him want nothing more than to gather up his darts and run to his truck. For he'd been here many times before, so he knew all too well what this silent standoff between them was leading up to: Mullet Man would soon be challenging him to defend his little alcove and his honor in a match. Of this Greg wanted no part. But before stepping off the panic ledge and fleeing the scene a saving thought reached out and pulled him back to safety- CJ would be here any minute now, and once she was here, the world would be right again. With CJ in the mix, the confrontation would be defused, and the two of them would resume their private party which for nine previous weeks they had enjoyed. To that party the brute invader would not be invited. His incursion could be put off until then.

    The big darter now picked off a double-twenty, a bullseye and then another bullseye, and instead of walking to his board and retrieving them, he stayed at the line and left the darts stuck there like bragging points for all the world to see, like the guy who is the last to jump into the creek with his skinny-dipping friends because he wants them to look back to the bank and see that his is the biggest swinging dick. Just as Greg was about to throw his next set the big dick interrupted him in his motion. "So. Play some 501 maybe?"

    Where the hell are you CJ??? "Nah. Just throwing a little on my own tonight."

Feeling Big Dick's eyes staring down on him, Greg threw his darts- an errant 5, a worse 1, and the third a wire-banging bounce-out which clattered noisily onto the floor.

"Damn. That's a rough-ass three darts." Greg picked up the bounce-out and retrieved his other two disappointments. "A little competition- that's whatchoo need to find your A-game. How 'bout it?"

"Nah." Greg rotated his shoulder with a wince, pretending it was sore, then snuck a quick look back toward the main bar in the same manner his young friend had done so often. "I'm actually meeting up with someone any minute now."

Big Dick finally strode up to his board for his darts. "Oh yeah? Hey, so am I. Until they get here, come on, 501. You, um... you do know how to play 5-oh, right?"

Greg swallowed back his sarcastic response, then shook his head with a meek smile. "Nah, nah. My old ass isn't in the mood to get itself kicked."

"*Your* ass get kicked at 501? By *me*?" His arms were fully outstretched in an incredulous taunt. "How could *I* beat *you* at 5-oh? You're the dart coach, right?"

Greg's throwing hand stopped in mid-air. A fissure now appeared in the lining of his stomach. "No. I'm not a dart coach."

By now Big Dick had breached the invisible border separating their two throwing lanes and was standing defiantly on Greg's lane, hovering somewhat menacingly over his reluctant opponent. "No? That's not what I hear."

"Brian!" It was CJ, finally arrived and clearly flummoxed by the scene she'd stumbled upon. "What are you doing?"

Brian was the picture of innocence. "What? I was just tryin' to play some 501 with your dart coach."

CJ glanced uneasily toward the main bar as per her habit. "Where... why are you out here?"

Brian nonchalantly threw his darts. "The other team read the schedule wrong, went to The Blarney Stone instead. But they're on their way."

Greg was confused, and looked to CJ. "The other team?"

She rolled her eyes with embarrassment. "Yes. Tuesday is league night."

"And league is supposed to play here tonight?"

"Well not- "

"That's right Coach." Brian pulled his darts and then lumbered up to into Greg's personal space. "Atlanta Metro Platinum League plays here on Tuesday nights. But not out here on the bunny boards. In the *real* dart room. Didn't my girlfriend tell you about the real dart room?"

Again Greg looked to CJ, who lowered her eyes guiltily and sighed. "Yes. There's another dart room."

"Go ahead. Show your coach."

Dutifully, CJ led Greg out of the little alcove and walked him across the dimly-lit barroom, all the way to its far wall; upon reaching the end of the dark and grimy paneling she brought him around the corner, and there he beheld a place he would never had known existed had not the girlfriend of some big dick asshole jerk brought him to it: a spacious and in every way inviting game room, dedicated solely to the throwing of serious darts. Eight brand-new Unicorn Eclipse boards, all mounted against octagonal black backings and perfectly lit with angled track lighting, were arrayed against one wall, while well-appointed booths and tables softly illuminated by brass wall sconces lined the wall opposite. Three lumps wearing dart shirts matching Brian's were at the boards with their beers, talking and laughing and tossing their warm-ups. Greg took in the beautiful space with amazement; meanwhile, in a not-so beautiful space in his belly, the steady *thunk thunk thunk*ing on those Unicorn boards was like a leaky faucet which now began to drip out drops of a nearly-forgotten nausea from so many years before. He looked to CJ who shifted nervously from one foot to the other.

"So I was gonna show you this room eventually, when the league- "

"You from the McGiddy's' team we're waitin' for?" It was one the three lumps who had stepped up to address Greg.

"Uh, no, I'm- "

"I was just showing him the room. Let's go." CJ hurriedly turned to leave and gestured for Greg to follow.

"Hey CJ!" She rolled her eyes and turned back; the other two lumps had joined the first and all three were leering at them. "Is this your dart coach we heard about?"

"Yes!" she blurted, then dragged Greg away by the sleeve.

Back in the dark of the main bar, Greg squared up to her face to face. "CJ, explain please what- "

Everything poured out of her in a rush. "So the thing is that Brian has this league every Tuesday night which he says I have to come along and support him since I'm his girlfriend and yet he doesn't like me to watch him when he's throwing because he says I'm bad luck and besides I hate to watch him throw because he's always angry and swearing and who wants to be around that so that first night I was here with him but not *with* him and I wandered out and I saw you not yelling and not swearing and having just a fun quiet time and all by yourself so... yeah. Now you met Brian."

Greg nodded with a smile. *So that was where she disappeared to every Tuesday night.* "Wow. Yeah. Now I met Brian. Nice dart room, I'll say that."

She was just a nudge away from crying. "Are you mad?"

"Mad? At *you*?" She nodded, averting her eyes. "CJ, why would I be mad?"

Now she looked up to him, almost fearfully. "Because some people seem to be mad at me all the time."

He was a little rusty at being a little girl's dad but it came back to him. "Come on CJ. Let's get back. We don't want to make Brian angry. Angri-er." He turned to lead her back to the alcove, but once again she pulled his sleeve, this time to stop him.

"He's not gonna drop it you know."

"What?"

"Playing you. In a match."

"Well, he doesn't get to decide what I'm gonna do. Come on partner."

Back in the little dart alcove, Brian was retrieving the darts of a tight ton-forty he'd just thrown. He was pulling them from Greg's board, which Brian seemed to have claimed as his own. "Nice back there isn't it?"

A sudden thought lifted Greg's eyebrows. "But wait. You say your league has been playing back there all these Tuesday nights? How does that work? Because each week the teams from the different bars rotate their matches around to all those other bars in the league. So you couldn't play every Tuesday night here."

Brian threw three more laser beams, and as he walked to retrieve them, Greg wondered where his own darts which he'd left in his board had gone. "For somebody who doesn't compete against other guys you understand league competition real good. Go get me a beer." Before Greg could ask himself if the big dick had meant for him to bring him a beer CJ scurried off on her errand. Brian went back to throwing. "So yeah, the teams are supposed to rotate to all the bars. But all these other bars in the league have shit throwing setups, bad boards bad lighting and what-not, so it just came down that whoever was scheduled to shoot against The Brass Whistle would always play their matches *at* The Brass Whistle instead of their shitty home bar because the conditions here aren't shitty." He paused, one dart still in hand. "It's funny. Those guys from the other bars, they all kinda think of The Whistle as their home board. These darts ain't bad by the way."

Now Greg looked more closely at Brian's hand. "You're throwing my darts."

Brian weighed the dart in the palm of his hand and made a face. "A little lightweight though."

"Why are you throwing my darts?"

Lumbering his way up to Greg's former board, Brian retrieved the last two of Greg's former darts. "CJ thinks you're some kind of dart god."

"She's a nice kid. She just likes to have fun."

Brian rolled Greg's darts around in his hand. "You like having fun with my girlfriend?"

"Just give me my darts."

Brian held the darts away from him. "501. Best of three."

"I'm not playing you." Greg could feel his face getting warm.

"Why won'tchoo play me Dart God? Whatchoo afraid of?"

"At the moment I'm afraid you're gonna break the flights off my darts, could you just- "

Although he was not reaching for them, Brian held the darts high and away as if Greg was jumping up and down. "If I give 'em back will you play me?

"He doesn't play matches anymore because he throws for the love of throwing now!" CJ was back with her PBR in one hand and Brian's PBR in the other. "Darts for darts' sake. Haven't you heard of zen, Brian?"

"Zen? What, like a fucking Buddhist?" He gulped from his beer in a distinctly non-Buddhist manner. "You're bald like a Buddhist. But shouldn't you be barefoot?"

CJ squared off with him, hands on her hips. "He doesn't compete because competition ruins the experience. Competition kills the beauty of the game. He's beyond competition now."

"*Beyond* competition? Damn, Dart God, what the hell happened to you in the fucking past? You really must've gotcher ass kicked back in the day!"

Greg exhaled slowly to keep calm. "I could hold my own."

"Well yeah, I guess if all you do is play with yourself then you have to hold your own!" Punctuating his remark, Brian grabbed a handful of his junk, then with the same junk-grabbing hand resumed throwing Greg's darts.

"Why does it always have to be about winning all the time?" She spoke straight into Brian's ear as he threw, then stayed in his ear as she walked with him to his board. "Why's it always gotta be about beating some other person? Ugh! It's so tedious!" If felt nice, Greg said himself, to hear her defending him like this, validating him, albeit in vain for her knuckle-dragging boyfriend to ever understand. A little embarrassing, but nice. "Every league night, every match in a tournament, if you don't win, god look out, pissed off and swearing and our whole weekend ruined just because you didn't hit some double-sixteen or something. That's not fun Brian. What Greg does is fun. Fun!"

Brian lined up the next dart to throw, but then lowered his arm and turned to face not CJ but Greg. "Look Dart God. Whatchoo do, out here on the bunny boards, it's fake. Whatchoo do is chicken-shit. There are winners and losers in everything dude. You're way old enough to know that. Winner or loser. You're one or the other. I know which one I am. And we both know which one you are. Here- " Brian reached into his back pocket and came out of it with three darts. "- just to make it fair, you can throw my winner darts, and I'll play you with your loser darts. Maybe some of my winner will rub off on you, who knows?" Greg refused to move, refused even to look at the darts held out to him. "No? Too heavy for you to lift you reckon?"

"Goddammit Brian!" CJ angrily snatched the darts out of her boyfriend's hand. "This, *this* is exactly what I hate about you throwing darts! Why do you always have to be such a, such a- "

"Such a what?" He was daring her to say it, something she had clearly said to him exactly one time before and had learned never to say again.

"Errghghg!" With an irritated whimper CJ thrusted the darts back to him. "You always have to be so mean." She plopped down onto a bar stool in frustration. "Greg isn't mean when he throws. He just throws because he enjoys throwing." She sat up as straight as she could with all the brave defiance she dared show him. "*That*'s why I throw with Greg."

Brian just kept throwing Greg's darts. "That's not whatchoo told me."

"What do you mean?"

Now he stopped, and once again directed his response to Greg. "You told me you threw with him... because you felt sorry for him." He waited a moment to be sure he'd hit his human target, then resumed throwing at the one on the wall.

CJ squirmed and spluttered where she sat. "Wait! No, that's- no, I didn't, I- "

"You just felt sorry for me?"

Brian kept throwing and chuckling to himself as CJ attempted damage control. "No! I mean, no, I- I didn't throw with you *because* I felt sorry for you, it was just- "

Now Brian launched into a cartoonish CJ-imitating voice while making girly fluttering gestures with his hands. "Ohhh Brian, there's this poor old man who comes here to throw, he's all alone, he has nobody to play with, and he's afraid to throw against other *pee*-pul!"

"*I didn't say it like that!*"

From the main bar area, Brian's three lump teammates now came plodding up into the little alcove. "Bri, whatchoo doin' out here on the bunny boards?"

Brian paused from throwing and took a swig from his PBR. "Well, while I was waitin' for the McGiddy's team to show up I thought I might pick up a practice match with an ackshul dart god. You know, learn somethin' from the master. But the dart god don't want to play me."

One of the brontosauri bellied up a little closer and pointed at Brian's hand.

"What are you throwing there B? New darts?"

"Nah nah, check it out- " Brian held the darts out across both palms of his mock-trembling hands as if they were the magic arrows of the Elden Ring. "– these here are *ackshul dart god darts*. Since he didn't want to to throw 'em I was."

"Damn!" One of the other two lumps made big wide eyes and stepped in to join the first. "Can I touch 'em?" The loutish darter ooo'ed and ahh'ed while gently bear-pawing Greg's purloined darts.

The third lump glanced with a smirk toward Greg before chiming in. "So did any of his special dart god shit rub off on you B?"

"Thank fucking god no. Here Dart God." He returned the darts to Greg then took his own darts out of his back pocket. "If I kep' throwin' those, it wouldn't be long 'til I'd only want to play with other guys' girlfriends." As Brian and his teammates yukked it up at Greg's expense, a frustrated CJ stared at him pleadingly, hers eyes trying in vain to explain and apologize.

The lumpiest of the three lumps now insinuated himself between Brian and Greg, addressing the former while turning his back to the latter. "Well since Dart God won't play you, come on, let's do 5-oh dollar-a-game until McGiddy's get here."

"Right. Five-oh. Show me a bullseye."

As Brian and Lump #1 fired up their 501 match on the middle board and Lump #s Two and Three began a match of their own, Greg stood alone at the board by the window and reassessed the situation. Well, so CJ had only felt sorry for him. So much for her then. She was exposed as a fraud, but after all, Greg knew he shouldn't be surprised at learning the true shallowness of her stream. She was staring at him still with her pleading mooncalf eyes, but what more did she need to say, now that his old man blinders were lifted and he saw what should have been so painfully obvious? For CJ it had clearly been nothing more than a ten-week pity party, while for his part, Greg had shared with her his beautiful game and risked sharing as well his deepest feelings for it. What a fool he felt himself now.

At least he'd acquitted himself admirably these ten weeks, at all times the good mentor and perfect gentleman, in that he could take some solace. But now, with his darts returned from the sweaty hand of his tormentor back to his own, there was nothing left to do but to slip past CJ without glancing into her mooncalves and escape the little alcove which had suddenly turned so inhospitable. As he zipped his darts into their bag Greg couldn't help but notice the action taking place on the boards next to his- their match hardly begun, Brian had already demanded of his partner that the stakes be raised to ten bucks a game, and as for the dueling lumps next to Brian, Greg overheard one tell the other that they should also give themselves "a reason for playing" by making their game a money match as well. What stronger kick-in-the-ass message could these guys send to the man who threw darts only for the love of throwing them, Greg thought sardonically, than for them to announce that the only reason for playing was to win money? Having steeled himself for the running of the CJ sad-eye gauntlet he made to leave; but then a thought struck him which held him in place. Yes, it was brutish and typically masculine of these guys, this single-minded blood lust for competition which these cretinous goons were exhibiting. But why should he be so afraid of it? For his own part he'd gotten himself off that drug and was proud of his sobriety- but if it was necessary for him to flee the scene of the drug's very appearance for fear of getting a good whiff of it in his nostrils, was he truly delivered and free of the drug's power over him? If he were really above and beyond the corruptive power of competition, he reasoned, then shouldn't he be strong enough to sip a little of the sauce without fear of getting soused? Now he understood what the final step of his twelve-step program required of him. Instead of shunning these goons, he must show not them but himself that he could stand in their fire and not be ignited by it. In order to win the real game he must lose at the game which was meaningless. He must compete, but without competing.

"Okay Brian. 5-oh. Show me a bull."

On both boards, the play stopped. Brian raised up to his grizzly bear tallest and began sniffing at the air, looking all about the room in every direction except toward Greg. "What? What was that sound? You guys hear that sound?"

"Come on Brian. Let's do this."

CJ was up on her feet. "Greg, what the hell?"

With a snappish look from Brian which hinted at so much violence past, the girl retreated back onto her stool. He then rotated his guns back toward Greg. "Really Dart God? I'm fucking honored. Well okay. I'll show you a bull."

By now the three lumps had backed away from the throwing area like wild west townspeople clearing the street for the high noon showdown. One of the lumps waved at an unseen someone in the main bar, then turned back toward Brian. "Hey B, the McGiddy's team is finally here."

"Tell 'em to wait. Dickheads made us wait after all." Once again Brian sized up the sacrificial lamb which had offered himself up for the devouring. "Need any warmup throws Dart God?"

"No. Don't need any warmup throws" *because unlike you I don't care who wins.*

"Suit yourself." Taking his place at the line, Brian lined up to throw for the cork, and his dart hit the near-center green, a solid single bullseye. With a grin he stepped back from the line and took high-fives from his posse. As Greg stepped up for his try at the bull he took care to avoid eye contact with CJ, but his ears couldn't prevent her words from entering them.

"You don't have to do this Greg."

Something pathetic in the sound of her voice triggered yet another liberating realization: since he no longer needed to avoid competing in a game he wasn't trying to win anymore, why avoid a girl he wasn't trying to win anymore? So he turned calmly to face her. "But you don't know what it is I'm doing." With that, the fat old elegant matador squared off to face the bull, and delivered a toss which missed its mark by more than two inches. He had never been more proud of a shit throw in his life.

Brian shook his head. "Wow Dart God. Helluva miss. Looks like I start this thing off." As Brian lined up to begin the first leg of the match, CJ abruptly leapt up from her stool and made an escape move toward the bar. "Where you going?"

Her feet and mouth skidded to a stop, causing one to trip over the other. "I don't wa- I just- you- you don't like me to watch you throw, right, so I was just-"

"No. I *want* you to fucking watch this. Sit." Like a child put into time-out, CJ trudged back to her stool as Brian lined it up again. His first three darts were shot rapid-fire: triple twenty, single twenty, another trip-twenty. After subtracting his monster ton-forty from 501 and marking his remaining 361 on the scoreboard, Brian repaired to his teammates who commenced to chatter him up.

"That's a big ton, son."

"Way to start him off B."

"Way to finish him off B."

It was Greg's turn now. He had just been splattered in the face by Brian's big ton-forty, yet not a drop of it had touched him. Nothing done to Greg could touch him now, for he was sealed off in his personal space where only the zen of the throw existed, a private experience contained wholly within the practice room of his mind. With the serenity he'd developed over his many months of private throwing Greg stepped to the line to begin his solitary exercise in competitive disengagement in the crowded little alcove occupied by no one but himself. His first three offerings were a twenty, a five and a one for a dismal twenty-six. Happily he collected his darts and stepped back to await his next turn.

"Hey Dart God- you gonna mark your shit score or what?"

"Oh" Greg said with a detached shrug. "Sure. Sorry."

And so proceeded the first leg of 501 on the center board, with Brian hammering away with one high-scoring nail after another and Greg responding with his gracefully delivered but grossly misdirected answers; with each turn at the line, the younger man lopped off ton-sized chunks from his total until after only four rounds he was down to just 24 remaining to win, while after the same number of throws Greg's total had only been lowered to a still-bloated 296. But though Greg's ass was most decidedly getting blistered, that ass was feeling no pain, for its once-sensitive skin was now well protected by a heavy padding of indifference. He watched with dispassionate amusement as the scoring brought him closer and closer to disaster, enjoying the feeling/lack of feeling his nascent disaffection was bringing him. By now the McGiddy's guys had made their way into the cramped little alcove and asked what was going on, the three lumps explaining to them that their league match would need to wait until Brian "schooled some old man that his girlfriend felt sorry for," a remark which didn't hurt Greg's feelings any more than the lopsided score did, since his new-found detachment included (which meant it didn't include) shallow little CJ as well. With each bad dart he threw Greg's spirit felt better and better, and now, as the young man stepped to the line needing only a double-12 to take out his remaining 24, Greg gazed benignly upon his fate with an aloof smile. His death was proceeding promptly and painlessly.

To the surprise of no one and particularly not to himself Brian's first dart split the 12 double ring center-core, giving him the first leg. He and the lumps exchanged fist-bumps all around. When he turned back around he was surprised to find his polite opponent's fist as well, waiting to congratulate him.

"Nice dart Brian."

"Uh, right." Reluctantly the big lummox deigned to allow Greg's fist to touch against his. "I don't miss easy doubles like that one."

Greg's beatific smile exuded inner peace. "Oh I knew you had it. You were on fire the whole leg."

"Yeah. I was. So, second leg, let's go."

Greg nodded. "Second leg. And I'm expecting a ton-eighty out of you!"

"Whatever." Greg continued to smile up at the big block of ice with an inexpressible warmth which did nothing to thaw it. "Okay, loser starts the second leg. You were the loser."

"Right, I'm the loser!" With a lightness in his step, Greg took his place at the line, but then stepped back and once again extended his sportsmanlike fist to his non-opponent. "Shoot well."

"Look old man, I got McGiddy's waitin', can we just get on with your ass whoopin'?"

As Brian's minions and the McGiddy's guys laughed, Greg withdrew his untapped fist and waved it off apologetically.

"Right, right, sorry!" Turning back toward the board, Greg's eye caught a glimpse of CJ on her stool; she was staring straight ahead at nothing and shaking her head, the features of her face pinched tight by what seemed to him a combination of simmering anger and sympathy. Greg wondered- was she upset that the men were laughing at him? Was she upset about Brian's insulting behavior toward him? Was she upset that he was getting waxed so badly in the match? Or was she still just feeling sorry for the pathetic old man? *Well my dear, now it's the pathetic old man feeling sorry for you* Greg said to himself, at seeing her so personally affected while he was feeling nothing whatsoever. Oh he was fully aware of it all of course, the mocking laughter, the rude treatment from the younger man, the thorough darts drubbing he was receiving from same. It simply held no power over him was all. He was free, free from it while immersed in it, unwetted by the piss he was being dunked in, sealed tightly within his deep diving suit of zen impassivity which floated him buoyantly through the troubled sea around him. He had lost the first leg and it didn't matter, he would lose the second leg or maybe he wouldn't *and it did not matter* either way or any way. He would play out the debacle of this final Tuesday and enjoy his beautiful game despite the efforts of these polyester lumps and pitying young women to rob him of that enjoyment, and when his tail thrashing was complete he would sail his tail blissfully back home and resume his *thunk thunk thunk* on his home board as if the match had never happened. For within the insulation of enlightenment it never had.

Greg's first three darts of leg #2 were a dismal continuation of leg #1. "Alright B" Greg said pleasantly as he retrieved his failures and stepped to the side, "let's see that ton-eighty."

Without acknowledging the encouragement from his opponent Brian marched to the line and unloaded his guns: triple twenty, single twenty, trip twenty for yet another ton-forty. High-fives and fist bumps from his posse once again awaited his return.

Greg nodded with admiration as he made his way to the line. "Damn, you nearly did get that ton-eighty! Good darts." Turning to face the board, Greg's glance fell once again upon CJ on her bar stool, and it was obvious to him that her discomfort had by no means eased; in fact, it seemed to him that a new, deeper line of distress was now creasing her brow, one which he perceived was attributable to something more than a mere dart match. And as he heard Brian say under his breath to one of the lumps *why even waste one of my ton-eighties on this bunny?* the cause of her distress dawned on him- in only a matter of minutes, Greg's problematic encounter with boorish Brian would be a thing of the past, never to be revisited, but for young CJ, this evening's unpleasantness merely represented the most recent episode in her general drama of pain, one which would continue for her in perpetual replay for as long as she chose to remain yoked to that drama's author. An involuntary effusion of sympathy now flowed out from him in her direction, one which forgave her in an instant for having let him down in any way, and as if being raised by that sympathy's warmth, CJ lifted her sad face to look upon his. Then, as much for old times sake as for the moment at hand, Greg closed his eyes and put a quieting finger to his lips, and when he opened his eyes she was smiling, actually smiling.

"So you gonna throw or what Dart God?"

CJ averted her eyes guiltily as Greg raised his hand in apology. "Sorry, sorry. Just delaying my death I guess." The point total of his next three darts did not even add up to his opponent's age. "Well, so much for delaying it" Greg laughed, as he and his darts stepped aside for Brian's next turn. "Looks like I'm dead already."

"Oh, you *been* dead" Brian snorted as he toed the throwing line. "I'm fixin' to bury you right now."

Yes Brian. I am a dead thing of the past. You are a dead thing of the past. This is not the present. I am not present. I am not here. You cannot touch me like you used to.

The first of Brian's three darts was poised and aimed to fly, but then the rare experience of a thought showing up in his head made him pause. He lowered his arm and turned toward Greg. "You know, I gotta say Dart God. You're really good at this. Really really good at this."

Greg smiled back at him quizzically, surprised at receiving anything resembling a compliment from such a one. "Well, thanks Brian. Good at what?"

Brian threw three solid single twenties, then turned back to Greg. "At losing. You're really good at losing."

Down in the basement, the string cord below a naked bulb was pulled, lighting up a cheap paper dart board. "I'm good at losing?"

"Yeah. Reeeal good at losing." Brian looked about at everyone in the room for confirmation as he retrieved his arrows. "Ain't he? I mean, he's happy when I throw a ton-forty, happy when he throws a twenty-six, happy to get insulted and laughed at, happy to bend over and take it up the ass. That's being good at losing."

The soft paper of the basement board began unwinding at the edges. Brian kept on his roll and directed it toward CJ. "So is that what'cher dart god taught you? How to be a good loser?

How to suck real bad and be real happy about it?" CJ looked to Greg for some show of encouragement, but his paper board had come completely unraveled and lay in ribbons on the basement floor. Now Brian turned to his three teammates. "Look ya'll, Dart God is right. It's all about bein' a good loser. So let's just call McGiddy's the winner tonight. Don't even play 'em. Show 'em what good losers we are. No wait- McGiddy's, you guys can lose tonight too! Yeah! Nobody wins! That way we can all be good losers!" Having brought the whole room into his big joke, Ronnie finally brought it back home to his older brother. "Hey Dart God. Didja ever think that maybe the reason you *are* a loser is because you're so good at it?"

The string under the light bulb was pulled again. The basement went black.

"Greg?" CJ studied her friend's face for a sign of life. "Are you okay?"

"You still with us Dart God?"

Greg's grimacing mouth never moved when he finally spoke. "My throw."

Brian backed away in mock deference. "Right, right, sorry, your throw."

For a moment, then for another moment, Greg simply stood at the line, not moving. But in fact he was moving, moving in a different way, moving away from something, leaving something behind, leaving himself, going somewhere he'd never gone before. The darts in his hand were something they had never been before, they were weapons now, and he was weaponized. Greg stared down at the dart board, and when the board stared back at him, it could tell by the look in Greg's eye that Greg would no longer be making sweet platonic love to it. The board knew it was about to get raped in the ass. And with his sights trained on the dart board's ass and on assholes past and present, Greg hurled all he had been holding with the graceful finesse of an axe murderer. It was his first ton of the match.

After ripping his darts from the whimpering dart board and marking his score, Greg did not slink off to a neutral corner as was his habit, but stalked straight up toe-to-toe with the taller man and stared up into his Australopithecus face. "Your throw."

Brian nodded, pretending to be impressed. "Damn, an ackshul ton. I guess sometimes even a blind squirrel finds - "

"YOUR THROW!!!"

The smirk evaporated from Brian's face, replaced by something both threatening and threatened. "My throw." After making his way around the Greg obstacle, Brian took aim and threw, the result being a strong score of eighty-five. He rooster-strutted back to his fist-bumping minions. "You're still down over a hun'erd, Dart God." But before Brian's taunt was fully out of his mouth Greg was already firing away, no longer the gentlemanly gamesman but soulless manslayer, not so much throwing his darts as expelling them, ridding himself of them and of everything he'd fooled himself into believing, as if each bad-tempered flick of his hand represented a tossing-off of any traces of darts-for-darts-sake until nothing remained in his arm except the pure anger which moved it and the ugliness which aimed it. His third mean-spirited missile detonated in the heart of the triple-twenty, just as his first two pissed-off darts had before it. Under the mushroom cloud lay the shrapnel of his ton-eighty.

Along the spectator wall Brian's minions stood about nervously, not daring to offer any acknowledgement of Greg's epic toss until and unless their sovereign did, which of course he did not. Instead the younger man strode darkly up to the line and, with three violent ejaculations, punched out a solid one-hundred as a response. The minions were allowed to breathe once more.

"Yeah B good answer B big darts B ."

As Brian slurped up the adoration of his worshippers, Greg took his place once again at the line, and for the first time in the match looked at the chalkboard to check the score. The score had not mattered in the least to him before, but now, with his basement light having gone dark, the stupid score was everything; having lost at the only game which really mattered, all that remained was the score of the meaningless match and the settling of old scores long unsettled. Brian needed one hundred sixteen to win, a big number to be sure, but one which Greg knew the young hotshot was well capable of putting away on his next turn. Greg still had one hundred forty-nine, a giant number, one which Greg was pretty certain he had only taken out in the safe zone of practice but never in actual competition. Had his light not gone out, he would have thought back to the times he'd faced such challenges in the old days, would have remembered how readily he had always resigned himself to the impossibility of taking out a one forty-nine and the certainty of losing and how politely he had always accepted his doom. Had his light not gone out, he'd have remembered how the weight of his generous sportsmanship had always leadened his arm and caused his darts to sag in those critical moments. But that weight was cast off now, thanks to the dousing of the bulb; in this moment the light of his nobler sensibilities had been switched off, replaced by the glare of anger, and so his arm was as light and lithe as a butcher's. Greg's darts flew swiftly through the fresh clear air of rarified hatred. The trip-twenty died without putting up a fight, the trip-nineteen was dispatched as well, and without a pause and certainly without any twinge of nauseous anxiety Greg split the remaining double-sixteen like the legendary apple on William Tell's son's head. The second leg was his.

"Fuck!" A flaming-hot glare from Brian was shot at the hapless lump who had not been able to contain himself, incinerating the lump in a whiff.

"One leg apiece." Greg had retrieved his darts and was back at the line, ready to throw for the bullseye for the right to begin the final leg. "I'll show you a bull." With that, Greg let fly, nailing his dart in the red double bullseye, then spun around to face Brian as if begging him to make some remark. No remark was forthcoming. Instead, Brian wordlessly stepped to the line and tossed his answer, a shot which landed just outside the wire of the single bullseye. He deferred to the older man.

"You start."

Greg waited for something else. "'You start...' Just *you*? That's all?"

"Yeah. That's all. You start."

"You *who*?"

Brian looked about for help that wasn't there, then back to Greg. "You."

"*You*?" You *who*?" Greg cocked his head with feigned bewilderment. "What, I'm not Dart God anymore?"

Brian simmered in his own juices. "Just go."

"No." Greg gestured magnanimously for Brian to step up. "You can go ahead and go first. My treat."

Brian's response was more growl than speech. "I don't need your charity."

"Well you're gonna need somethin'." It felt good, in a Mr. Hyde sort-of way, to flex his smack-talking muscles for the first time ever. Turning toward the board, Greg's glance very briefly met CJ's, and the face that stared back at him was a mix of dismay and horror, as if she were looking not upon the amiable gentleman she'd come to know over ten weeks but some alien replicant which had supplanted him. Ignoring his own dismay and horror at knowing he had indeed become the replicant's host organism, Greg lined up to start the deciding leg, then allowed the replicant to throw the darts which before his light had gone out had been instruments of fun but were now being wielded purely for fratricide. His opening ton-forty was answered by one from Brian, and thus did the final leg proceed, a back-and-forth slugfest more boxing match than darts, with both men exchanging big-point haymakers and neither giving any quarter in the face of his opponent's onslaught. It was, in a word, competition, in all its humorless glory, one man competing against the other in every mirthless and merciless way that the word "against" could be construed. After finishing his fourth round throws Greg was down to needing forty to win, but after Brian's first two darts of his fourth round he was down to just thirty-two, with his third dart in hand for a chance at the double-sixteen which would win the match for him outright. Now there was no hesitation in the younger man to throw that deciding dart, no hitch in his nerves which might delay him nor any wavering in his resolve to give him pause, for understand that Brian was a young man, an ambitious young man, whose hunger for winning propelled him head-first into the fray with no quarter allowed for vacillation. But in that split second before Brian could throw his winning dart Greg was able to launch a missile of negative thoughts, a shit-bomb of mental disruption, designed to intercept that dart mid-flight and by the hindering power of its psychic discouragement deflect the dart away from its double-sixteen target. It is impossible of course for the mind to send out actual shit-bombs loaded with bad thoughts which are really able to blow up someone else's efforts; mental bombs of bad intentions never leave the bomb maker's lab but instead self-detonate in the bomb maker's own face injuring no one but the bomb maker. But it didn't matter that Greg's bad thought shit bomb never made it to Brian's dart, for as it turns out, sometimes shit just happens all by itself. Sometimes guys who never miss simply miss the thing they throw at. Which is just what happened when the ambitious and confident Brian's third dart hit not the needed double but the single sixteen, causing the good-thought encouragement bomb which the minions had simultaneously tried to send their hero's way to blow up in their faces as well.

Now needing only a double-twenty to win the match and three darts in hand to hit it, Greg took his stance at the line and gazed down at the board seven feet-nine and a quarter inches away. The board looked much closer than that now, closer and bigger, thanks to his heightened faculties of perception which the poisonous drug of darkness coursing through his veins was providing him, a drug supplying all the powers and energy one would want from a drug yet oddly none of the pleasures. So big and inviting did the double-twenty wedge look to him that Greg was sure he could just reach out and press his dart into it from where he stood and be done with the whole sordid affair just like that. But in order to defeat assholes past and present he had become the asshole himself, and as such, the asshole within him wouldn't allow him to slaughter his quarry quite so humanely. He sent his first dart flying, and it landed not on the board at all but on the outer cork surrounding it, an intentional miss of the target altogether.

"I didn't need that one."

As Brian silently steamed, unaccustomed with finding himself being cooked in the pot instead of the one doing the cooking, Greg paused before throwing his second dart, still in no hurry to put an end to the younger asshole's simmering. He could feel heat radiating from another direction as well, from where CJ was sitting; by the sidelong glance at her face which he allowed himself to take it seemed that her heat was not the result of a growing fire of anger but rather a warmth which was fading, of something melting away and disappearing. Ignoring her and her face like any good asshole would, Greg refocused upon the dart board, and once again threw a purposefully fucked-up dart, this time missing even the outer cork and sticking into the wall's wood paneling.

Greg shook his head as the dart fell out of the wall and onto the floor. "Damn. Maybe you're right B. Maybe I'm just really good at losing." Holding his third and final dart, Greg rolled it about in his grip while pretending to talk to himself. "Hmm. One dart left." With only the *tercio de muerte* remaining, Greg turned to face the crowd in the grandstands; then, from where he stood in the center of the ring, the matador placed the dart in the palm of his hand and raised it high, a presentation of the *estoque* for all in the arena to look upon. The final moment, the moment of blood, had arrived. No longer was this matador the master of stylismo, the elegant dancer of the *faena*. Now he was reduced to (expanded to) the artless killer, the mechanized agent of doom, and in that role he turned to face the bull that was angered by the sight of its own blood. When he spoke it was the bull and the crowd and himself and the dark of the basement to whom his words were directed.

"*Now* it's time to finish you off."

With that, Greg spun himself to face the board, and without even walking back to the line flung the dart from where he stood with the force of a fastball, ten full feet from the target. Had the double-twenty wedge the benefit of a dying voice it would have screamed with the pain of its impaling. Greg had won the stupid fucking match.

For many long moments no one dared to speak or move. Finally one of the McGiddy's darters (who not so coincidentally stood the farthest from the volcano) broke the silence. "Well come on, we got league to throw. Let's get to the other dart room." With rapid mumbles of agreement the darters nearly trampled one another in their hurry to escape the high tension of the alcove, leaving only CJ still on her stool between the two belligerents. But when Greg returned from pulling his darts from the board the sad-faced girl was up and stood waiting for him at the line. She was holding out the darts he'd given her for him to take back.

"*Now* I feel sorry for you."

"Hey!" Suddenly Brian leapt forward and swatted her outstretched hand. The darts were sent clattering across the floor. "You don't fucking talk to him no more!"

"Don't worry. I'm not."

He was looming over her now, big as a thundercloud. "Get your ass out to the truck!"

Fear and confusion cemented her feet to the floor. "But- but you've still got your league to- "

"Fuck league! *FUCK DARTS!*" His explosion broke the cement to bits and sent CJ running out of the bar. Brian twisted himself back toward Greg and unloaded a spray of spit in his face. "*FUCK DARTS!* Fuck darts and *FUCK YOU MOTHERFUCKER!*" It was only the two of them now in the suddenly smaller alcove, and Greg knew full well what was coming next. He was resigned somehow to the punch in the face which was to come, as if accepting it as an appropriate punctuation to the evening's sentence. But the punch didn't come, at least not to his own face. For as Brian spun away and went stomping out of the bar to follow the pheromone trail of his girlfriend, Greg understood that the punch and probably much worse would be delivered somewhere else soon enough.

It wasn't a long drive home from The Brass Whistle, but it was long enough for Greg's darkness to gradually lift and allow him to process all that had and had not just happened to him. The dark replicant which had taken over his controls had by now relinquished them and departed his body, leaving him with the feeling of being its sole inhabitant once again although in a strangely hollowed-out way. But with that hollowness came a clarity of mind, as when a fever finally breaks and one's thoughts return to their former order. It was in fact no less furious a condition than a fever which had come over him, a rogue wave of delirium washing through his brain and filling every space, and in the course of filling him with its poison had conversely emptied him of his humanity. His brain had rung with the tinnitus of competition, a deafening noise which utterly shut out the sound of his darts for darts' sake *thunk thunk thunk*. More than anything it was disappointment which he was left with on his drive home, disappointment with himself for allowing his emotions to be swept away so easily and utterly. For the final two legs he'd succumbed to the impulse of savagery; during those two legs he had felt no love for his beautiful game whatsoever, no love for anything or anyone. All his calming and center-grounding habits had been put on hold, thanks to the fever- his easy breathing (*had* he even breathed?), his fluid motion, his quiet stance, his long and languid follow-through, his gentle affection for innocent CJ. The zen had left him entirely; no, he had taken the Zen by the scruff of its monkish collar and thrown it the fuck out of the temple. Never in all his years of losing had he felt so defeated as having finally come out the winner on this miserable evening. But even as his drive home was spent lamenting the loss of his darts for darts' sake Zen, the very act of thinking about what he'd lost, of feeling the absence of the pacifying joy he had discovered all those many hours alone on his home board, now triggered within him the realization that there was no reason it could not all be restored. Yes, he had fucked up and fallen off the wagon, but it was simply up to him now to get back on it and fuck up no more. So what if he had allowed the destroyer to pollute his unsullied stream? It would never have happened had Greg not made the foolish mistake of bringing his pure water to mix with his enemy's filthy sewer; but soon, in just minutes, he would be back home, reunited with the pureness of his home board, where the enemy's dirty water could not come flooding in. As long as he stayed away from the Zen destroyers, the thought polluters and the pity partiers, they would stay away from him as well and torment him no more. It would once again be his home board and him, just as it should be. He could almost hear the soothing rhythm of his *thunk thunk thunk* already.

 By the time Greg was turning onto his driveway his mind was in a considerably better place than when he'd left the bar, the drive home providing him the time and space he needed to quite literally leave all the ugliness behind him in the rear view mirror. Unlocking his front door he stepped into his dark house, and quickly disarmed the beeping security system by typing the numeric code onto the keypad by the door. With the rhythmic *beep beep beep* of the system now cut off, the house was silent, and he walked across his unlit living room. But after several steps he stopped and cocked his head, for he was still hearing a rhythmic something despite the alarm's disarmament; and to his horror, the sound he was hearing was one he knew quite well, one he sorely wished he was not hearing, a sound which travelled through his ears and down his gullet and settled in his stomach with the splashing wave of a nausea with which he was also quite familiar. For down the hall, emanating from the unseen dark of the back bedroom, Greg could hear a slow and unmistakable *thunk thunk thunk* upon his home board, like the unending pounding of a gavel on a block, or like an axe which chops and chops against an immemorial stump which can never and will never go away.

TICKET TO HEAVEN

The fishing lures that Lee like most was his crankbaits cause they was the ones that look the mose like fish an anything that was like a fish Lee liked. The crankbaits, they made em outta super-lightweight carve wood an painted with, well he don't know what, like with tiny special brushes or somethin, how anybody could paint all that cool multicolor details an make it look like scales 'n' fins an all the parts of a fish but smooth 'n' curvy, like the lure was some sorta shiny racecar with hooks hangin off it, that was why he like crankbaits. But really all Lee's lures was his favorites cause the best thing about his lures was that he had so many differnt ones, crank baits 'n' spinner baits 'n' plastic worms 'n' beetle spins 'n' Mister Twister soft bodies that was even scented with some fishy chemical juice, an the way he had em arrange in rows side-by-side in his tackle box made it look like he had his own fishing store right there on his bottom bunk bed. Bein able to open it up anytime an look at it all spread out was the bess part of all, cept that ever time he look at his lures it juss made im wish that much more that he was sittin in a big bass boat fishing on Lake Barkley, which was somethin a ten year-old kid in Murray Kentucky whose dad didn't have a boat couldn't make happen on his own. But if Lee couldn't go fishing he could still at lease sit on his bed 'n' look at his lures.

"Liam!" His mom was standin in the doorway of his room, mad as usual. If she called im his real name which she knew he hated then it meant she was mad. "Put that damn tackle box away an get dressed for school, you cain't be late again!"

Lee made sure to close his tackle box slow as he could juss to pisser off. "I won't be late."

"You said that twice this week already an you were late both times. Hurry it up!" His mom was gone again, an he heard her jabberin at his little sister but not in the mad way like she done with him. That's the way it always was for Lee, ever school mornin, him in trouble for this or that 'n' being yelled at by his mom 'n' then when he was at school gettin yelled at by Mizz Reynolds for everything includin breathin the damn air. Showin up late for school shouldn't be a surprise to nobody when bein there juss means gettin yelled at so why be in a hurry? It weren't even a ten minute walk from his house to Froberg Elementary so long as he went a straight line but Lee almose always went crooked, juss because. He had a pretty good idea that today he'd probably go crooked too even though there wasn't nothin between his house an school that was all that interestin to pull im off-track. But goin straight was juss too boring.

When he was dressed 'n' ready to go Lee saw on the kitchen clock he had three minutes leff before he had to leave. So that give im three minutes to try again what he been tryin all week.

"Mom, can we please- "

"Lee don't even ask me about it again!"

This was her new record, cuttin im off at only four words. It juss meaned he had to talk faster so she couldn't butt in. "But the 2023 Music City World Boating 'n' Fishing Expo is gonna be the biggest expo yet with two-hunerd-plus vendors an every kinda boat 'n' three tanks with fish that they let you try to catch an castin lessons 'n' lure demos an the firs 100 kids eleven 'n' under get a free Daiwa rod 'n' reel an maybe get your t-shirt signed by Kevin Van Daam!"

His mom was shakin her head "no" right from when he started 'n' she was still shakin it now. "I swear you don't listen to a thing I say Lee. I done told you over an over why we ain't goin to that expo!" His little sister was sittin on the kitchen counter top while his mom wrestled with gettin her dressed. "One, it's gonna be good weather this weeken so your daddy's gotta work, house painters in January can't pass up good days to make money. An if your daddy can't go then- "

"He can't never go!"

"Work is work Lee!" She was twistin hard at the sleeves of his sister's pullover but wasn't gettin too far with it. "An since your daddy can't go then that's that 'cause I got things I gotta do insteada drive a hundred some-odd miles to Nashville an back in a van thass got shaky ball joints!"

Lee stuck one of his sister's feet inta the leg of her tights to preten like he was bein helpful. "But is only seven dollars to get in an I got the seven dollars."

His mom stopped yankin at the pullover long enough to stare im down. "You don't hear a thing I say I swear. An you know full well the other reason- " His mom went back to pullin the last of his sister's arms through the last of her sleeves, "- you an I an your daddy already had this conversation about your behavior at school an bein' late 'n' how that had to improve if we was to even think about that expo and, well, do I even have to say more on that?"

It was down to two minutes left on the clock. Still plenty a time. "But what if I was to wash Dad's truck or clean up the basement or do the vac'uming next week?"

"Lee we don't need the truck washed or the basement cleaned we need you to do better!" From gettin her legs 'n' arms pulled ever which way his sister was startin to whine almost as much as his mom. "You know we went through this same thing with your brother growin' up an he didn't listen any better'n you 'n' look how he's turned out!"

"If he was here he'd take me to the expo..."

"But he ain't!" His mom stood his sister up on a kitchen chair to give her tights their last pull-up. "An since us tellin' you what you need to do ain't workin' then we're gonna have to try somethin' besides tellin. Instead a juss no expo we might have to say no Playstation on weekends, or maybe take that tackle box of yours 'n' hide it where you cain't stare at it day 'n' night." It weren't the first time Lee's mom had made that threat which was why he knew he better remember to hide his tackle box from her before she could hide it from him. It took im a long time to steal all them lures from Wal-Mart an he wasn't gonna get em stole back by his mom. "Now put a Capri Sun in your back pack 'n' git."

He still had one minute leff but it didn't matter. Another minute wasn't gonna change her mind. Lee shuffled over to the fridge an swang the door open real fast 'n' wide to make all the jars in the fridge door bang aroun, juss so she'd see how mad he was. An when his mom was tyin his sister's shoes an not lookin he grabbed not just a Capri Sun but one of his dad's Yuenglings an put em both in his backpack, then went stompin out the kitchen door slammin it good 'n' loud behine him.

Onced he got around the corner to where he was in fronta the ol abandon gas station Lee dug the can a Yuengling outta the backpack 'n' popped it. He didn't really even like beer, it was bitter an kinda burned his mouth but it was a way for im to get back at his mom but mostly at his dad who was always at work or if not just sittin on his butt watchin TV drinkin Yuenglings. Hidin outta sight behine the gas station Lee took a coupla swigs of the beer but then poured the rest of it onto the concrete. The main thing was the stealin it not the drinkin it, sorta like sayin Okay if you won't take me to the Expo then I'll take your beer. He was back out on the sidewalk again, walkin in the gen'ral direction a school an lookin at people's front yards where he seen the tall green stalks of those yellow flowers which are the firs ones that come up ever spring when it's not even spring yet. Yeah, it was almost kinda warm out, his dad would be paintin a damn house this weeken for sure, an the green stalks comin up an the not-cold air made Lee think how it was even a better mornin for fishing than it was for house paintin. It killed im to hafta be thinkin about fishing when it was only January an there weren't no good fishing you could do til March. That's why they have those fishing expos in winter time, Lee figgered, when ever'body's all stuck at home not able to go fishing but dreamin about it so goin to fishing expos is how they suffer through til Spring. It wasn't fair, that much he knew, to really only want one stupid thing an that be the thing he couldn't have. Then he started thinkin about how it was like that one thing was really three things all stuck together into one, wantin to go to the Expo 'n' wantin to go fishing 'n' wantin a dad who would take im fishing. He had a big brother who would take im to Expos 'n' fishing an even steal a beer for im, yeah, but that wasn't no good since his brother was in jail an accordin to his dad would be there a damn good while. Havin his brother in jail messed things up for Lee in two ways, not juss cause his brother couldn't take im fishing no more but because, ever since he got rested, Lee's mom 'n' dad started gettin all nervous 'n' over protective 'n' stuff with im like they was afraid he'd end up bein a manslaughterer like his brother even though he was only ten. There was times at school when he wanted to be a manslaughterer though, like when kids would call im Lame insteada Liam, god he hated that name Liam, it was cause of some old great uncle over in Irelann name Liam was how he ended up with it. It also sound like some rich kid's name which he definitely wasn't, or like some perfect good-behavin school-on-time little wuss with clean shoes an a fancy haircut. No fancy-haircut Liam kid would know how to hook a live minnow on a #8 hook or steal his dad's beer outta the fridge. But then again from what his dad told im about the Irish maybe a Liam kid might could steal beer after all.

Even though he was draggin his feet to stop from gettin there too soon he could see his stupid school gettin closer, just down the hill a coupla blocks away. He was about to cross Olive Street at the cross walk when a big black pickup drove pass with a mean-face ol man behine the wheel. It was the same black truck an mean-face ol man Lee saw all the time in the neighborhood, an even though he seen im like ever day Lee never knew where the ol man lived but from how the ol man drove it had to be close by cause who could drive that slow an go very far. He look to Lee like he muss eat sharp pieces of glass for breakfass, that was how mean he look, like every mornin he pulled his face off scrunched it up into a ball to wrinkle it up an then smushed it back onto his head all messed up. He never saw the ol man apart from the black truck, an so because the ol man was always in the truck even the truck look mean which Lee knew was stupid but still it did. Drivin that slow all the time made it look to Lee like the ol man was cruisin aroun lookin for children to catch an eat, probly not even cookin em firs, an Lee figgered the mean ol man had a dog at home that was giant 'n' just as mean who chewed on the children's bones when the ol man was through with em. Lee watch as the old man's truck rolled on past im down Olive, where a coupla blocks over his two friends Jake 'n' Rickey live. Jake 'n' Rickey had good normal Kentucky boy names which nobody made fun of an so they didn't have to prove to ever'body all the time that they was normal Kentucky boys. They also had normal Kentucky dads who drank Yuenglings an didn't take Jake 'n' Rickey fishing, same as Lee's dad, so the three of em had to settle with stayin in town to do their fishing by walkin down to shitty little Clarks River which was barely three feet deep an only had bluegills 'n' bullheads not even big as his foot. Well, it was only juss down the block to school now an so Lee thought fuck it might's well go. But when he looked at the winnders of where his classroom was he got a grumpy feelin. So even though Mizz Reynolds would kill'im he knew he wasn't gonna be able to get through a gettin-killed Wednesday until he checked in with what had got him late Monday an Tuesday an which was gonna get him late today too.

It was over on 5th street in the yard of some people he didn't know, just inside a fence that even a short kid like Lee could climb over. They kep it parked at the side a the garage an lucky for him they had took the cover off this week maybe cause they was cleanin it or workin on it. The people's cars was gone which meant they wasn't aroun, so after hoppin the fence an sneakin across the yard Lee jump up onto the wheel well of the trailer and, onced he was on the front deck, slid hisself down into the polstered seat behine the cushiony-grip steerin wheel. As bass boats go it wasn't the latest model but it was still a honey only a few years old, a 19-foot Ranger with a Mercury 250hp motor, not as big a rig as the pro bass fishermen ride but damn close an damn good enough for Lee. Like the other times when he snuck onto the boat he started by lookin at the on-board lectronics, the Lowrance fish finder an the control console 'n' all the light switches, switches he didn't know what they did, then at the front 'n' rear trolling motors an the live well an there was even a bait well to keep your minnows alive, so much cool shit that Lee wonder if he would just faint straight to death if he ever ackshully got to be in this same chair but out on the lake. He put his hand on the throttle an imagine Jake 'n' Rickey sittin in the chairs behine im, maybe with Yuenglings, an after skippin over the lake at 60 mph to get to some quiet back bay of the lake to be standin on the front deck an casting all them lures in his tackle box which he only got to look at in his room thanks a lot dad. His brother'd been savin up for a boat like this but now with him bein a manslaughterer Lee figgered that plan was pretty much not happenin so this was close as he'd ever get. After a few minutes of sittin in the boat pretendin he was Kevin Van Daam Lee finally forced hisself to crawl outta the captain seat jump the fence an get his ass back walkin to school. Yeah he was late as hell now no way round it, Mizz Reynolds'll be callin his mom at lunchtime. An that was when Lee remembered what he forgot to do before he leff the house, which was to hide his tackle box before his mom could steal it. This time she'd take it for sure, he juss knew it, an if he didn't have his tackle box to look at… Lee knew he had to come up with a hellacious excuse for why he was late this time, some lie good enough to rescue his tackle box an not get his ass beat. Or at lease good enough to only get his ass beat.

Mizz Reynolds was juss shuttin the door to the classroom when Lee ran up pretendin to be all flustered 'n' outta breath.

"Don't tell me we're late yet again Leem." *Goddamn her anyway!* How was it that Mizz Reynolds could piss him off so fast in three differnt ways at once? *"Don't* tell me?" I'm NOT tellin you I'm late, I just *am* late! An *"We're"* late? No, *we* ain't late, *I* am! An then *Leem*? Woman, either call me Liam or call me Lee, but Leem is just lazy. Even Lame is better'n Leem. Leem is juss lame. "Do you have an excuse this time?"

Lee did his best fake stammer. "Y-y-yes ma'am I d-d-do."

"Let's hear it."

He only partly knew what he was gonna say since he was juss makin shit up on the spot, an when it come out his mouth he thought that maybe it only made things worse cause when he was done sayin it his butt got took straight down to the princ'pal's office with the door shut an him in a big chair with the resource officer 'n' school couns'llor sittin with em.

The princ'pal Mizz Crandle had a real loud voice you could hear yellin all the way cross the soccer field but when she talk now it was real low an quiet which gave im the all-overs. "So Liam... Mrs. Reynolds tells me you had... an experience this morning. On the way to school?"

"Yes ma'am." Any time he was in trouble Mizz Crandle would sit way back in her chair 'n' stare bullets at im, but this time she was leanin in with kinda-like worried eyes. The resource officer took out a notepad.

"I know it's hard but please tell Officer Paschall and Mr. Ottway what you told Mrs. Reynolds. Can you do that?"

Mr. Ottway the couns'llor nodded with the same creepy eyes as the princ'pal an Resource Officer Paschall had his pen ready to take notes. Lee swallowed a coupla times to make hisself look traum'tized. "W-w-well... I was, you know, on my way to school, an I was like, proud that I got out the house on time, like five minutes early for a change, juss like ya toll me I need to start doin..." He looked aroun to see how it was goin an there was Mizz Crandle smilin at im. So far so good. "... an while I was tryin' to remember in my head the names of all the cont'nents an oceans for the social studies test I was at Olive street and... an this big black truck come along, an then it slowed down, right beside me..."

Officer Paschall look up from his writin. "And who was driving the truck?"

"An ol man. An ol man I seen in the neighborhood before. An when he come up beside me on the street he stop his truck 'n' then he... he l-l-looked at me."

Officer Paschall was scribblin away. Mr. Ottway leaned in. "Liam, would you like a bottle of water maybe?"

"Uh, yeah, tha'd be- " But Ottway was out the door juss like that, then was back with the water fass enough to put out a fire.

"He looked at you. Go on Liam."

"Yeah, well..." Officer Paschall looked up from his pad, waitin. Lee wasn't used to havin all ears listenin to juss him an he kinda liked it. "So I stop from crossin Olive cause the ol man in the truck was blockin my way- oh, an he was real mean-face 'n' scary-wrinkled" Lee added, thinkin that it wouldn't do no harm sprinklin in one or two true things with the lies. "He look juss like Wrinkles the Clown."

Paschall made a face an look to the other grownups. Mr. Ottway was noddin. "Wrinkles the Clown. A real person. He's a wrinkled ol man who dresses like a scary clown and then hires himself out to parents to come to their homes and scare their misbehaving children straight."

"Yessir. That guy. Him drivin' the black truck look like that."

Paschall wrote it down. "Wrinkles the Clown... then what happened?"

Lee took a long drink a the water an notice how comfy his butt felt in the big office chair. Anytime before when he was in the princ'pal's office he was in trouble so he always had to sit on a hard metal fold-out chair, but this'n was cushier than even his grampa's La-z-Boy so he let hisself sink down. Then he remember he was sposed to be traum'tized so he sat back up. "W-w-well, like I said, the Wrinkles the Clown truck was blockin my way an he was juss l-l-lookin at me, lookin me up 'n' down *yeah thass good more shit like that* an smilin, but like a b-b-bad smile... then his winnder come rollin down an he says to me, he says Hey boy, wanna ride to school? An I says no, is juss right down the hill there. An then he says Well I got doughnuts here in my front seat 'n' then he laughed, heh heh heh, you know, like a witch kindof laugh, an I says no thanks. An so I was juss standin there an him sittin in his truck there laughin an whatnot..." Lee could feel hisself runnin outta gas with the story, an Paschall had quit writin an all six eyes was on im. Lee knew he needed to kick his lies up a notch so he did. "An then all a sudden his door come open, an Wrinkles the Clown jumps down outta the truck, an he's standin' there with no pants on an his daggum wiener hangin' there like a little Wrinkles the Clown!" He had got so excited at tellin this lass part that Lee spilt a little of his water from squeezin the bottle so tight but it was prob'ly good it happen cause when he look aroun at the three faces they was all pretty damn startled.

Princ'pal Crandle took a big breath loud enough so you could hear it. "Alright. Then what happened when it jumped out of... when he jumped out of the truck?"

Lee thought he already said enough by that point to save his tackle box but if they was needin' more he'd give em more. "Well, at that point I'm thinkin' he prob'ly don't really have no doughnuts at all so I juss went roun the back of his truck to get on to school so's to be on time. But when I come roun the back here he come roun the front straight at me, Wrinkles the Wiener blockin my way. I got no choice now but to run fast as I can 'n' hearin' im behind me witch-laughin an sayin Come on back, I got doughnuts, look, look at my doughnuts, come look at my doughnuts. An so I was late to school."

There weren't nobody sayin nothin for what seem to Lee a long time. Finally Mizz Crandle shook her head an breathed out another one of her big breaths. "Officer Paschall, you'll file the police report?"

Paschall finished up with his writin. "Yes ma'am." He look down at Lee real serious-faced. "You're a brave young man Liam."

"That's right" Ottway chimed in. "I'll be sure to tell your mom how brave you were."

Lee's face brightened. "You're gonna call my mom?"

"Of course."

"Can you make it soon?"

Ottway looked at Lee with friendly eyes. "Just as soon as we're done here." *Yes! My tackle box is saved!!!*

Mizz Crandle got up 'n' came round her desk then sat right next to im in the metal fold-out chair. Things was switched up now an he liked it, with him sittin comfy an the princ'pal findin out what it felt like in the trouble chair. She was lookin at im with sad funeral eyes like his dog juss got run over. "So Liam. Are you feeling okay? Do you think you can go back to your class?"

It sound to Lee like she was offerin' im the whole day off from school which normally would kick ass but it was sloppy joe day so he figgered he'd stay at least through lunch an maybe save bein traum'tized for the afternoon. "Y-y-yes ma'am, I think I can do it."

Ottway scooted his chair in close which made Lee sink back deeper in his seat. "If you need to talk about this or about anything at all I'll be here for you. We all will."

"So... so I'm not in trouble for bein late?"

Mizz Crandle laughed but in a nice way. "No Liam. You're not in trouble." She lean right into im an talked slow 'n' serious. "You didn't do anything wrong this morning. Do you understand?"

I guess that means she don't smell the beer on my breath. "Yes ma'am."

"Good." Mizz Crandle stood up an so did the other two. "Let's get you back to your class then." Lee dug hisself up outta the swallowin chair an notice for the firs time a jar with hard candies. They was all smilin at im so he thought he'd try. "Is it okay if I get a candy?"

The princ'pal made a face like she was about to cry. "We can do better than that." Goin back to her desk she open her drawer an took out a Snickers bar but not regular it was daggum king-size. "Here you go." Then she kinda winked at im an whispered, "Don't tell the other kids!"

"No ma'am I won't." As Mizz Crandle led him out of her office both Paschall 'n' Ottway patted im on the back which was creepy but better than a ass whoopin. Yeah, Lee figgered he musta come off as pretty traum'tized from the way they treated im, comfy chairs 'n' candy bars an sorry faces the whole time. As he stuff the Snickers into his backpack he thought about how he was gonna wave it right under Jake 'n' Rickey's noses come lunch time. Yep, this was a good day to not go home early.

Once Lee an Mizz Crandle got to his classroom Mizz Reynolds was waitin for him outside the closed classroom door. She was smilin at im. She hadn't smiled at im thataway since the firs day a school, after that day she got to know how much trouble he was an so she stop smilin. "Leem, how are we doing?" *That goddamn Leem and WE again!*

"Fine Mizz Reynolds."

"He's had a rough morning" Mizz Crandle said, her old hand restin on a bony spot of Lee's shoulder. "But he's a trooper." The lass thing Lee wanted to be was a trooper cause the state troopers was the ones who rested his brother out on the front yard. "Okay Liam. I hope the rest of your day goes better than how it started." Then Mizz Crandle whispered but she did it loud like she was too dumb to know Lee could hear her. "I don't know how well he'll be able to concentrate. He's pretty shook up."

When he got into the classroom an into his seat Lee felt Jake's 'n' Rickey's pencils pokin im in each shoulder. "Dude you super late today!" Jake whispered.

"Yeah!" whispered Rickey. "That ass gettin' whooped when you get home for sure!"

"Hey Lame!" It was Keith Pritchett who set across the aisle from Lee. Keith was the first one whoever thoughta callin Lee Lame an he kep on callin im Lame every chance he got. "Where you been Lame? D'joo get locked in the girl's restroom?" Keith threw a Skittles at Lee which was so small not even a hawk could see it but Mizz Reynolds seen it cause teachers see everything.

"Keith Pritchett you head straight for the principal's office."

Keith made a face like he got smacked with a flyswatter. "But it was only a Skittles!"

"Principal. Now!" Keith grumbled his way up an shuffle toward the door. "And if anyone else wants to throw anything at Liam or say anything rude to Liam he or she can just follow Keith to the principal's office as well." The worse part of any day in Mizz Reynolds' classroom was havin to sit cross from Keith Pritchett an so Lee was smilin to hisself big-time. He look back for a quick glance at Jake 'n' Rickey an saw their mouths hangin open. Up in front Mizz Reynolds had picked up a stack a papers an was startin to hand em out to ever'body. "Now this Social Studies test is two parts. The first part is multiple choice questions about continents oceans and seas and the second part is the world map where you need to identify and label the continents oceans and seas." Lee wish now that he'd showed up even later to school cause he hadn't learnt a single one of the cont'nents oceans 'n' seas so he was doomed for an F, maybe he'd lose his tackle box after all. "You'll have thirty minutes to complete it but don't turn it over 'til I say." When Mizz Reynolds got to Lee he reach up to take a test but she shook her head. "Let's hold off on test-taking until you're... not so stressed." As Mizz Reynolds kep movin down the aisle passin out tests Lee look back at Jake 'n' Rickey again an saw their mouths hangin opener than they been before. It was a good thing she thinks he's traum'tized, Lee thought to hisself, cause if she'd a went an made im take that test he'd a been traum'tized for real.

Later on at lunch Jake's 'n' Rickey's mouths was still open as they watch Lee takin his sweet time eatin the king size Snickers bar right in front of em. Jake's open mouth talked first. "Mizz Crandle gave you that Snickers for real?"

"Yep.

"Why?"

"Cause I'm traum'tized."

"Shut up!" Rickey swallered his last bite of sloppy joe an then leaned in closer cross the table. "You gotta tell us the whole story now. You promised." They was both leanin in to hear it, an all Lee wanted to do was to let em in on the joke, to tell Jake 'n' Rickey that he made up a big crazy lie just as an excuse for bein late, but he didn't dare do that cause then they'd tell on im an Lee would lose way more than just his tackle box. Besides, bein child molestered was turnin out to be the best day at school he ever had. An so Lee told em bout Wrinkles the Clown an the wrinkly wiener juss like he told it in the comfy chair, complete with all the stammerin an stutterin. When he was done Jake 'n' Rickey didn't waste no time.

"Bullshit!"

"I call bullshit!"

I know, right? It's a kick-ass lie! But Lee didn't dare say that. "It's true dammitt!"

"Shut up." Jake sat back with his arms crossed. "You was juss sittin in them people's bass boat again this mornin pretendin it was yours is why you was late."

"Nuh-uh!" Lee had showed Jake 'n' Rickey his bass boat one mornin' but they'd been too scared to jump the fence an sit in it. Besides they was name Jake 'n' Rickey so they didn't have nothin' to prove. "I'm prob'ly gonna hafta go to couns'lin."

Rickey was shakin his head. "Ain't fair. Ain't fair you gettin king-size Snickers an not takin tests juss cause of lyin about some ol man wiener."

"An makin up somebody name Wrinkles the Clown."

"Wrinkles the Clown is real!"

"No he ain't!"

"Look it up!"

The resta the afternoon went along pretty much like the mornin, with Mizz Reynolds bein nice to im an givin him special treatment an Keith Pritchett not bein able to bully im even though he was dyin to. Leavin school at 3:00 to walk home Lee was surprise to see his mom sittin out in her van waitin for im. Any time his mom surprise Im like that it meant he was in some big trouble, but not this time, it was cause a Mr. Ottway callin' her about gettin molestered. When he got in the van she had that same funeral face as ever'body in the princ'pal's office, but with her it was like she was about to bust out cryin. On the ride home she made Lee tell the whole story to her, an he juss knew they was gonna get in a wreck cause she look at him the whole time, 'specially when he got to the part about the wrinkly wiener, an onced he got to the house he ran straight to his room an checked- yep, there was the tackle box. Ever'thing was alright his lie had worked. The only bad part was that his mom kep lookin at im with that same bust out cryin face the whole night, but at least at supper she made his favorite thing in the world, sloppy joes, which he didn't tell her he already had cause sloppy joes twice in one day wasn't nothin bad. Sloppy joes twice in one day was what he thought goin to heaven prob'ly was.

On Friday Lee got to school five whole minutes early, not cause he wanted to but his mom drivin him was what done it. She said he weren't walkin to school no more cause it was too dang'rous an so he had to preten she was right. He was thinkin things would be back to normal onced he got to school but no, now it seem like word musta got out about the wrinkly wiener story cause ever'body was kinda lookin' at im an whisperin but not laughin at im, almose like he was a famous person like Kevin Van Daam which was lots better'n hearin "Lame" bein yelled out. He did hafta finally take the social studies test but Mizz

Reynolds give im a whole hour not thirty minutes which didn't make no diff'rence he still didn't know where the Caribean Sea was. Then at lunch the lunch lady had that same creepy funeral face as all the other grownups, an with Jake 'n' Rickey standin there watchin she give Lee not one but two brownies. An on Friday it was more a the same, what with Keith Pritchett sent to the princ'pal again juss for whisperin "Lame" under his breath an double tater tots from the lunch lady an somethin' called a follow up in the comfy chair with Mizz Crandle 'n' Mr. Ottway which got im out of havin to take a math quiz. Yeah bein child molestered was juss about the best thing ever happen to Lee he figgered, even though he Jake an Rickey all three was mad as hell they wasn't goin to the fishing expo that weeken. But Lee wasn't all that mad since his mom already told im he was gettin his secon favorite that night, fried chicken.

When it was still dark out Saturday mornin Lee's mom come into his room shakin' im out like it was a goddamn school day. "Come on Lee , let's get up."

"Wh-why?"

"Well you wanna be one of the first hundred kids in line eleven 'n under for that rod 'n' reel, right?"

Lee rubbed his eyes. Was he still dreamin? "Are you... you mean the fishing expo?"

"Well what else? An I made you waffles to eat in the van."

Now he knew for sure he was dreamin. "An can I have coffee?"

"In one of your dad's travel cups even."

An so it was that Lee found hisself still half asleep ridin in his mom's van with grown-up coffee an a tray of waffles on his lap an headin out for the 2023 Music City World Boating 'n' Fishing Expo in Nashville Tennessee. The whole ride Lee told her bout all the booths 'n' vendors 'n' what-not that was gonna be there, an his mom never complained about him talkin too much or about the van's shaky ball joints even once. As it turn out when the got there the expo itself weren't all that really; they run outta free Daiwa rods 'n' reels at kid number eighty three an he was kid eighty seven, an the famous fisherman they got signin t-shirts wasn't Kevin Van Daam it was juss Ott Defoe. But still Lee was at the expo at lease which Jake 'n' Rickey didn't get to so he could lie to em bout how great it was an they wouldn't know no better, juss like about the ol man an his wiener. An even though he didn't get no Daiwa bein able to go to the expo was still like goin to heaven, even more than sloppy joes twice a day was heaven. Oh an his mom bought im a new Rebel Crawdad crankbait at the expo too.

On Monday mornin Lee was on time again thanks to his mom drivin im, but he didn't mine bein on time now since bein at school was like bein a celeberdy. At lunch (where the lunchlady give im a double dip a corn cause he likes corn) he bragged about the expo to Jake 'n' Rickie an showed em the new Rebel Crawdad lure which he smuggled out of his house in his backpack, an seein that new crankbait got Jake 'n' Rickie real mad, Lee could tell. But then on Tuesday when the mornin nouncements was over an class was started he felt only one pencil pokin him in the shoulder. When he turnt roun he saw Rickey but no Jake. They was all the way done with science an about to start social studies when Mizz Crandle pokes her head into the room an ask Mizz Reynolds to come out to the hall. A coupla minutes later here come Mizz Reynolds back in with a funeral face bein follered by Jake with his hair all messy an lookin like he juss woke up from a nightmare. When he got to his seat he didn't poke Lee with his pencil or nothin, an when

Rickey whisper "Where you been?" Jake didn't answer, juss sat real still in his seat an starin down at his desk.

Keith Pritchett couldn't let it slide so he got a Skittles ready. "Hey Jake, why you so la- "

"To the principal's office Keith Pritchett! *Now!*"

Later on at lunch Lee 'n' Rickey was tryin to choke down the shitty sal'sbury steak while Jake was takin his time eatin a big ass Hershey bar with almonds.

Rickey was pissed off. "No goddamn way Crandle juss give you that Hershey bar! You musta stole it."

Jake lean way back in his chair like he was king a the world an juss kep chewin. "Didn't hafta steal it. I done told ya. They all felt sorry for me."

"Why?"

"Cause I'm traum'tized."

"Shut up!"

An so Rickey made Jake tell em both what the hell happen that made im late for school an got im a Hershey bar. An goddamn but if Jake didn't come up with his own black truck ol man no pants wrinkle wiener doughnut story juss like Lee's! But Jake's ol man story was even better cause in Jake's story the bare-ass ol Wrinkles the Clown man come after im an chased im all the way inta the woods off Pine street to the spot where they foun that little girl who got killt there about a year ago an they never found out whoever done it an Jake was fraid he was gonna get killt there too but by some miracle here he was alive. Lee wanted so bad to juss call bullshit on im same's they had about his story but he couldn't, cause if Lee said Jake's story was bullshit then he'd be sayin his own story was bullshit too an he'd be busted. So instead Lee had to go along with it 'n' say Yeah that ol man's a crazy fucker alright with Rickey juss shakin his head at the both of em. An then sure enough it all startin happenin for Jake just like it had for Lee, with Jake gettin not jus the Hershey bar but special treatment from Mizz Reynolds an special food from the lunch lady, an to top it off that night Lee's supper was back to bein shitty Tuna Helper like before gettin molestered. Now it was Lee's turn to be a Liam nobody again an watch Jake turn into the famous person at school the whole resta the week, an on Saturday when Lee 'n' Rickey went over to Jake's house Jake showed em a bran new Daiwa rod 'n' reel his dad bought im on accounta bein chase by Wrinkles the Clown, but not the cheap $40 rig they was givin away at the expo but a Legalis LT reel on a Fuega Series bass rod. It really made Lee wish he'd a thought a sayin the ol man had chased him to some spot where a girl got killt like Jake done, if he had he might coulda gone not just to the expo but to Opryland too.

So the next week Lee 'n' Rickey was stuck with havin' to watch Jake get treated at school like he was goddamn Kevin Van Daam. Lee notice on his car rides back an forth to school that there was lots of cops now in his neighborhood, drivin aroun real slow an some in unmark cars that didn't fool nobody ever'body knew they was cops. Lee's mom said the cops was out lookin for the ol man was why there was so many an it was somethin Lee hadn't thought of before, that after his story an now Jake's story the cops would be after Wrinkles the Clown to arrest im. He remembered how it was when the cops was all out lookin for his brother for bein a manslaughterer, how he hated them fuckin cops the way they treated im. But Lee had bigger problems than thinkin bout the cops tryin to find some mean face ol man, Lee had to deal with Jake bein a star an hisself bein jus Liam again. Rickey weren't none too happy about it neither, an' after the weeken of the three of em goin down to shitty

Clarks River in the dead of Feb'wary to try 'n' catch shitty bluegills an Lee 'n' Rickey havin to watch Jake cast his beetle spins with that new spensive Daiwa rod 'n' reel, Lee couldn't even say he was surprise when a coupla weeks later it was Rickey who come in late for school with his own ol man Wrinkles the Bare Ass Clown story an bein chase by the wrinkly wiener. Acourse Rickey went bigger still with his lie, sayin that not only did he get chase by the ol man but the ol man caught im an threw im inta his truck an drove im to that killin spot in the Pine Street woods where Rickey was able to kick him right in the doughnuts an escape with his life. An then jus like what happen for Lee 'n' Jake happen for Rickey, he become everb'ody's little pet an' because he got physic'ly accosted was how they put it Rickey got the whole rest a the week off from school. Juss like with Jake's story Lee couldn't call Rickey out for the lie or else get busted hisself. But when Lee 'n' Jake went over to Rickey's house on Saturday to see if he want to go with 'em down to Clark's River an Rickey's mom said Rickey ain't here, his daddy rented a fishin boat an he an Rickey was out crappie fishing on Kentucky Lake which was even better'n Lake Barkley, Lee went away feelin pretty much sick an tired of the whole Wrinkles the Clown thing an was glad he didn't have no friends besides Jake 'n' Rickey, cause that meant there weren't nobody else to keep one-uppin him with bigger 'n' better child molesterin stories.

    The next Monday Lee's mom was drivin him home from school (that day Rickey had showed off the pictures he took of the seventeen fuckin crappie his daddy 'n' him ended up catchin) when down on Spruce Street Lee saw a shitloada blue lights 'n' cop cars at somebody's house. Right next door to that house was where friends of Lee's parents lived so Lee's mom pulled onto their gravel to see what was goin on. The lady friend of his mom was Mizz Lisa an she come out of her house.

"Hey Lisa. What's goin on at your neighbor's?"

Mizz Lisa an Lee's mom walked over to the fence. "Don't know. But that's Mr. Ramsey's house." Lee follered em up to the fence an saw the front door of the house was open, an lots of cops yellin an shit was goin on somewheres inside. An that's when Lee saw the big black truck parked under the house's carport.

Lee's mom leaned over the fence for a better look. "Mr. Ramsey?"

"Yeah." Lee could hear a cop yellin "on your feet!" to somebody in the house. "Nice ol man, lived in that house more'n thirty years. Hope he's okay."

"Does a lot of trouble go on over at that house?"

Mizz Lisa made a face. "Trouble? Never! He's just a quiet old man who lives all alone an walks his little dog aroun the neighborhood wavin hello to everybody." She shook her head kinda sad-like. "His wife died just last year, poor thing."

"Maybe somebody tried to rob him."

"Look, here they come!"

Out the front door now come two a the cops an they was wearin big thick vests like for goin into battle. Then after em come out more cops, couple of em wearing suits, an they was bringin with em the one Mizz Lisa said was Mr. Ramsey, in handcuffs an a cop on each arm. It was the mean face ol man all right, Lee knew that for sure, but as the cops was pullin im out of his house 'n' down his front porch steps Lee didn't see no mean face on the ol man now at all, just a scared face, scared 'n' surprised an cryin out things like "What's all this about?" an "Where's my dog, what about Stanley my dog?"

Mizz Lisa's hands went up to her face the way some grownup women's hands do sometimes. "They're restin im! Whatever for?"

"With three cop cars and six cops, he musta killt somebody."

Mizz Lisa was shakin her head. "But this can't be right. It's juss Mr. Ramsey!"

The cops was off the porch now an on the sidewalk, with Mr. Ramsey lookin loss an afraid. Then up on the porch Lee heard a high pitch "Yip Yip," an there in the open front door was one of them little chiwawa dogs barkin his head off, all mad that they was takin his owner away.

Mr. Ramsey tried to turn back but the cops wouldn't let im. "What about my dog Stanley?"

All the sudden Mizz Lisa went runnin over nex door an went straight up to the cops. "Could I go get Mr. Ramsey's dog to take care of for im?" She turn toward Mr. Ramsey. "Would that be all right?"

It look to Lee like the ol man was about to cry. "Thank you." Mizz Lisa ran up onta his porch an insteada bitin her like chiwawas norm'ly do Stanley juss about jumped up into her arms. Lee knew he was juss imaginin but it look to him like Stanley was about to cry too.

Now it was Lee's mom's hands flyin up to her face. "Ohmygod! Lee didn't you say that man who molested you had a big black truck?"

"Yes ma'am."

She look to the truck an then to Lee then to Mr. Ramsey then back to Lee again. "Lee. Is that him?" But before Lee could decide how to answer Mr. Ramsey tripped or lost his balance someways, fallin straight down on his face onta the sidewalk. The cops musta thought he was resistin arrest or somethin cause one of em got down on the groun an put his knee right into Mr. Ramsey's back an started shoutin at im which made Stanley go to barkin his little ass off again.

But Lee's mom was only lookin at Lee. "Is that him Liam?"

There was only one way to answer unless he wanted to get a fate worser than what Mr. Ramsey was gettin. "Yes ma'am. That's him."

"That sonofabitch!" The cops had pulled Mr. Ramsey up offa the groun an were stuffin im into the back seat of a p'lice car. "I hope they break his damn legs!"

Watchin what was happenin to Mr. Ramsey was startin to bother Lee more an more, an he couldn't help but think Stanley's barkin was meant for Lee just as much as for the cops. "Can we juss go home mom?"

Her pissed off face all the sudden took on a worried mom look. "Oh Liam! Seein that man again must be upsettin you somethin terrible! I am so sorry. Let's go!" An without waitin for Mizz Lisa 'n' Stanley to come back from Mr. Ramsey's Lee was back in his mom's van drivin' off one way just as the cop car carryin Mr. Ramsey was drivin off in the other.

When they got home Lee went to his room an sat on the bed with his tackle box jus the way he always done after school, but even though his fingers was workin a $1/8^{th}$ ounce jighead through a Berkeley Power Grub his brain was workin through somethin else, namely, what he just seen happen with Mr. Ramsey an the p'lice. It was funny to im how differnt a ol man could look sittin behine the steerin wheela their truck than they look when they was layin on their face in their front yard. Well, not funny really, but... Lee remembered how bad he felt that day when the cops had his brother on the groun with a knee in his back, an he felt bad when he seen the cops do Mr. Ramsey the same way. But it was a differnt sorta bad feelin he got when seein it happen to Mr. Ramsey cause when they had his brother on the groun it was cause he really was a manslaughterer at lease. Mr. Ramsey was just a ol man with a little dog. Sittin in his room with his tackle box he was still feelin bad about it, an when his mom tole him to get busy with his homework Lee was glad she done it for the firs time ever because it got his mind off thinkin bout what he was thinkin about. He purdy much didn't think about it no more the rest of the day an night, but then when he come home from school the nex day his mom 'n' dad was both waitin for im at the front door smilin, but kinda scary-like smilin, an when he went to his room an reached under his bed for his tackle box a fuckin clown's arm come out from under the bed an grabbed his hand, an when he screamed 'n' tried to pull away Lee ended up pullin the whole resta the clown out from under the bed an it was Wrinkles the goddamn Clown right there in his room! Lee tried to run away but his mom an dad was blockin the way, an they was laughin at im wild 'n' crazy, an Wrinkles the clown was standin there with the hooks of all Lee's fishin lures stuck all over im, bleedin everywhere, an when Lee look closer Wrinkles the Clown was Mr. Ramsey, an he was screamin at Lee with a Rebel Crawdad hangin off his nose sayin *Whyjoo get me rested Liam? Whyjoo get me rested Liam? Why?* An then Lee woke up feelin all sweaty an out a breath an his mom was there sayin It's all right you juss had a nightmare, go back to sleep. Layin in bed afterwards Lee decided he weren't gonna tell nobody at school that he seen Mr. Ramsey gettin rested even though idd make a good story to tell an a true one for once. If he never mention it maybe he'd be able to forget about it. Maybe then idd all juss go away.

Sittin in Mizz Reynolds class the nex mornin Lee found out right away that it weren't all gonna juss go away. He didn't need to tell nobody bout Mr. Ramsey gettin rested cause Mizz Lisa tole it to Keith Pritchett's mom who then tole Keith who then tole the whole school, an when he done that it set ever'body off the whole resta the day to comin up to him 'n' Jake 'n' Rickey sayin stuff like I betcher glad they got that chile molesterer an I betcher happy he got throwed in jail. Jake 'n' Rickey was sayin Yeah they was happy, that'll teach that crazy chile molesterer a lesson, an even though Lee wasn't feelin none too happy about Mr. Ramsey in jail he had to preten to be happy an so he said he was. By the enda the day nobody was sayin nothin bout it no more an so Lee figgered okay, now it's gonna die down 'n' go away an I can juss go back to bein Lee like before, but when he got home his mom said the p'lice called an that she had to bring im down to the station the nex day to look at pictures an' look at some guys standin in somethin called a lineup which meaned he'd be lookin at Mr. Ramsey right in his face an Lee didn't want no parta that, not cause he was scared since now he knew Mr. Ramsey weren't scary but because goin down to the cop shop meant tellin em Yeah, that's the molesterer that chase me with his wiener an by tellin em that he'd be keepin Mr. Ramsey in jail who knows how long. Cause Lee didn't have no choice now, he'd gone too far with his big lie, if he tole em it wasn't Mr. Ramsey's wiener or anybody else's an admitted to ever'body that he juss made it all up then, goddamn, his punishment be so bad that he'd rather juss have Wrinkles the Clown kill im in the Pine Street woods. Besides if he tole the truth then it would call out Jake 'n' Rickey as liars too an then Lee'd be not only killt 'n' punished but without no more friends. Yeah, Lee knew he done cause this problem an so he juss hadta put up with things like they was an leave Mr. Ramsey in jail for however long they keep chile molesterers in jail. He hoped it wasn't as long as they kep manslaughterers.

When it was morning Lee didn't wanna get outta bed same as ever mornin, an so as usual he juss lay there waitin for his mom to come yell at im to get up an get ready for school. An when he remember that he wasn't goin to school that mornin but instead to the p'lice station he wanted not only to not get up but to hide under the covers. When his mom finally come into his room Lee lay there juss waitin for the hollerin to start.

"Lee?" For some reason his mom wasn't hollerin at all. She was almose whisperin. "You awake?"

"Yes ma'am."

His mom walk up to his bed an sat on it down by his feet. She never done that before cept for the time she come in to tell im his dad run over their dog in the driveway. "You need to get ready for school."

Lee talked from under the sheets. "Ain't we goin to the p'lice station?"

His mom took her time to answer. "Ain't no need to now. The p'lice juss called. That ol man had a heart attack in jail lass night." Lee's head come out from under the covers. "He died Lee."

Now he was sittin straight up. "Mr. Ramsey died? In jail?"

She nodded. "Found im dead in his cell this mornin'. Turns out he had a heart condition. P'lice figgered the stress of gettin rested musta brought the heart attack on." His mom shook her head. "Now I don't wish ill upon anyone, an I specially don't celebrate when someone dies, but that's what comes to a person who does the things that man did." She breathed out one of her "well that's that" breaths an perked up a bit. "Well, at lease now there won't be no more little boys in Murray havin' to deal with what you an your two friends went through." His mom stood up an walk to the door. "But I'm still drivin you to school juss to be safe. Come on, let's you get ready." As he was puttin on his clothes the surprisin news about Mr. Ramsey was bouncin aroun in Lee's head an stirrin his thoughts all aroun. Dead in his jail cell, juss like that. There wasn't nothin to do or say about it really, an it was real quiet between him an his mom in the van on the ride to school. Keith Pritchett wasn't quiet though, he'd heard the news somehow an tole ever'body in Mizz Reynolds class about how they foun "that crazy ol molesterer belly up dead in his bed," an when Lee saw Jake 'n' Rickey they all three didn't say nothin to each other bout it but Lee could see in their faces a queer look that said "I know the truth about things juss like you do" an Lee figgered he prob'ly had that same look on his own face too. For the resta the week his mom 'n' dad didn't say no more about it but they both seem kinda happier now, not like they was happy Mr. Ramsey died but more like cause it was all over 'n' done, no havin to go to p'lice stations an look at lineups an talk to couns'llors an what not. But Lee wasn't no happier. Lee had stuff on his mine that wasn't happy, like thinkin how Mr. Ramsey won't be wavin hi to Mizz Lisa an his neighbors no more, an how Stanley was a poor little orphan dog now. Lee was still feelin no happier that Sunday when he was sittin in church with just his mom since his dad liked church bout as much as Lee did. After the boring songs 'n' the nouncements the preacher started his sermon like always but insteada daydreamin about largemouth bass like he always done in church Lee was hearin the words an listenin to em. On the way home in the van he got all his question askin done cause he knew his dad wouldn't wanna hear no Bible talk in the house.

"So did they really nail that Jesus up on the cross like that?"

His mom look over at im real happy but also like he was a alien. "Liam Lambert that's the firs religion question you ever ask!

"Well did they?"

She settled in like she been waitin a long time for this. "Yes they did. Jesus willingly went along with them crucifyin him an killin him so's he could pay our sinful debt."

Lee made a face. "What exac'ly's a sinful debt?"

"Every bad thing we ever did. People can't go to heaven bein as bad an guilty like we are unless somebody who wasn't bad or guilty of nothin paid for our sins by dyin."

"So the only way you get to go to heaven is if some guy who never done nothin wrong gets killt first?"

"That's right Lee.

"Well that ain't fair!"

"No it ain't son." His mom was noddin her head with her eyes closed even though she was drivin. "It ain't fair that the only person ever who was without sin had to pay the price for all us sinners. But that's how much God loves us, that he would have his only son die for wicked people like me 'n' you."

For God to let his own son get killt to show how much he loved all us was one thing but it didn't soun to Lee like he loved his son too damn much if he went an let it happen. "So even people who tell really big lies get to go to heaven cause of Jesus gettin killt?"

"Yes they do. Liars an robbers an cheaters an all manner of sinners go to heaven thanks to Jesus."

"Even manslaughterers?"

His mom's eyes went closed again. "I pray every night they do Lee. An you should pray for im too."

That night layin in bed Lee wasn't prayin bout nobody cause he didn't know how but he was doin a lot of thinkin which he figgered was pretty close to the same thing. It was mostly all that stuff bout Jesus that was keepin im from fallin to sleep, what with Jesus not doin nothin wrong but gettin killt an all them who did do wrong gettin into heaven because of it. An he knew why it was botherin im. It was because a Mr. Ramsey, dyin in jail like he did, an that ol man doin nothin wrong for such a thing to happen to im. Thanks to Mr. Ramsey Lee didn't get in no trouble for bein late an he got to go to the expo an got a new Rebel Crawdad an sloppy joes twice in one day. It seem to him like Mr. Ramsey's takin the blame an dyin was juss like what Jesus done in order to get people into heaven, cause wasn't goin to the expo an the double sloppy joe day Lee's idea of goin to heaven after all? Layin there in his dark room without no other sounds all Lee could hear was the sound of his brain, an it was tellin im real clear juss how bad a thing it was that he done. An lookin up an seein the bottom of his brother's empty bunk bed gave im an even louder 'n' worser thought- if his big lie is what got Mr. Ramsey into jail an havin a heart attack 'n' dyin then didn't that make him a manslaughterer juss like his brother? His mom said they was worried bout Lee turnin out like his brother, well, it done happen alright. But Lee still got to sleep in his own bed an keep his tackle box an he could go over to Jake's 'n' Rickey's any time he wanted while his brother had to sleep in some metal bed in a jail cell. *And* Mr. Ramsey was dead! It got so loud in his brain that Lee felt like juss leapin outta his bed an runnin into his parents' room an tellin em, It's all a big lie I made up there weren't no Wrinkles the Clown wiener, juss so he could turn off all the loud thoughts an maybe get to sleep. But if he did that then he'd be snitchin on Jake 'n' Rickey. Lee's brother always tole im there weren't nothin worse than snitchin, snitches wear stitches is what he said. An since he was a manslaughterer now juss like his brother Lee reckon he needed to not be a snitch too juss like his brother cause if he snitched then even his brother wouldn't be his friend no more. An so Lee kep layin there in his jail bed juss like his brother was layin in his.

Nobody at school knew Lee was a manslaughterer when he was sittin in Mizz Reynolds room on Monday mornin an he made sure to keep it that way. Meanwhile Jake 'n' Rickey was actin like the happiess kids in the world, still gettin fiss bumps an high fives on accounta the molesterer dyin an goin to hell. All them kids sayin that Mr. Ramsey went to hell made Lee feel even worser than him dyin, an that whole week Lee was feelin so bad about it that his mom 'n' dad notice he wasn't right an so they tried to do little things to make im smile. When his mom made im fried chicken one night an mac 'n' cheese the nex Lee never touch a bite of it, an when they even offer to take im to Applebee's Lee said he didn't wanna go. He knew what they was thinkin, that him bein so traum'tized after gettin molestered was what was makin im sad, an so Lee jus let em think that an said nothin. Then his mom notice he wasn't even lookin at his tackle box no more, to the point that on Thursday she even ask him Hey Lee why don't you show me how you got your tackle box org'nized which she never showed no int'rest in before, an all Lee could do was go outside an hit gravel rocks with his rock hittin stick so she couldn't see he was gonna cry. An on Friday Lee's dad got a call from Rickey's dad sayin he was rentin a fishin boat again on Saturday an would Lee like to come crappie fishin on KenLake with him 'n' Rickey 'n' Jake an get pizza afterwards. When Lee tole his dad he didn't even wanna go fishin on the world's best crappie lake, well, that's when Lee's mom 'n' dad knew shit was real bad for him, an since they believe it was Mr. Ramsey's molesterin which was makin Lee sad it made both his mom an dad say out loud they was glad as hell Mr. Ramsey died in jail an to hell with him. Which only made Lee feel worser.

It was the nex Friday when his mom was drivin Lee home from school that he notice somethin funny goin on with her. As for hisself Lee was still feelin just as bad about manslaughterin Mr. Ramsey as ever, but today there was somethin differnt bout his mom- insteada her worried face an worried sound in her voice that Lee got used to hearin an seein lately she was all happy in a strange way, sayin funny little things that Lee didn't get the meanin of an smilin to herself after sayin it. He didn't know what she was so happy about but as for Lee he weren't in no mood for it.

"Looks like the dogwoods are gettin ready to bloom, aren't they?"

He didn't know what the hell he was s'posed to say after a remark like that so he didn't say nothin.

His mom juss kep smilin. "Yep. Your daddy was tellin me this mornin what it means when the dogwoods commence to bloom."

If she was expectin him to ask her What does it mean when the dogwoods commence to bloom, well, she was gonna hafta wait forever.

"He was sayin that when the dogwoods bloom, that's when the spring crappie run really starts." Now he knew what she was up to. Juss like she tried when she ask im bout his tackle box, she was tryin to talk bout fishing to perk up his mood.

"Yes ma'am" was all he said. Lass week a flat "yes ma'am" like that woulda turned her face all sad an worried, but today it didn't do nothin to keep her from smilin. "He says the largemouth should be spawnin pretty soon too in the shallows." His daddy said all that to his mom bout crappies an largemouth bass? Alright. Now Lee knew for sure what was goin on. Insteada offerin im to go out with Rickey's dad in his rented boat on KenLake it was his own dad who was gonna rent a fishing boat to see if that would draw Lee outta his dark mood. Well unless that boat was big enough to fit them an Mr. Ramsey after raisin im from the damn dead Lee weren't interested.

They was only about a block away from home when his mom started into gigglin. Ackshul gigglin. "It seems a shame to have all them fish wakin up out there in the lake an nobody tryin to throw a, what's it called, throw a crankbait at em, right?" It was gettin embarrassin now, what with his mom even learnin what his lures were called an workin em into conversation. As they turnt the corner before comin up to their house Lee was almos set to tell her to quit tryin, no stupid rented fishing boat on any stupid lake was gonna make him forget about his manslaughterin. An that's when they pull up to the house an he seen the 21-foot Ranger Comanche bass boat on a trailer hooked up to the back of his dad's pickup truck.

His dad was standin on the decka the boat wavin to im with one hand an a Yuengling in the other. "Hey Lee! How you like it?"

Somehow Lee's numb fingers foun a way to get his car door open. "What- whose boat's this?"

"Well it's ours. *Yours!* Or it's the bank's I s'pose until I finish makin the payments. Wanna come aboard?" Lee's legs was too rubbery to work right so his dad had to help pull im up. "Go on an sit behine the captain's wheel. *Your* captain's wheel."

Lee slid down onto the bucket seat an put his hands on the steerin wheel, then look aroun. This here boat was ever bit as fancy an nice as the boat he snuck up onto those other times, maybe even nicer. That boat didn't have nothin that this boat didn't have. That boat was even two feet shorter'n this boat. Than *his* boat.

"Hey Shirley! What's this here?"

His mom walked up closer. "What's what?"

His dad pointed at Lee. "Whatever's on Lee's face. What is that thing?"

She preten like she was shocked. "Well I do believe it's a smile!" It was true. Lee could feel his face smilin. He hisself couldn't believe it neither.

"So it's really ours? For real?"

His dad sat in the seat nex to Captain Lee's. "For real." Leanin back in the seat he closed his eyes for just a secon, then look down an talked into his Yuengling. "I know I been workin too damn much, not bein aroun to take you places 'n' do stuff withya. I don' know, maybe that's why you an your brother…" Now he look back up to Lee, an his eyes was jus a little shiny wet. "I ain't been aroun much for you while you been goin through all this ugly business lately. I guess when your brother was aroun I kinda left it to him to do my dad job for me. But he ain't here now, an so…" He shook hisself out of it real quick like, then laughed . "Well if I'm workin all that goddamn much I guess it means I can buy my boy a bass boat, right? Right!" He slap Lee on the knee an laughed again. "Damn that smile looks good on you son!" Lee's mom was up at the side of the boat now, an he notice she an his dad was holdin hands which was somethin they never done. "Baby I'm gonna hafta paint every house in Murray if we're gonna make these boat payments. Every house in Calloway County!" He took a long slurp of the Yuengling an then smiled at Lee. "But it's worth it. Even if I gotta pay for it the resta my life."

That whole Friday night turned out to be one big ol party for Lee an his family. To celebrate the new boat they all went to Applebee's an Lee ate so much mac 'n' cheese he thought he was gonna splode. Then at home his mom made popcorn an they all watch *Top Gun Maverick* with his dad gettin drunk in a goofy happy kinda way insteada the angry throwin shit aroun way he got drunk mose Friday nights. When it was late ever'body finally went off to bed, an when he knew his mom 'n' dad 'n' sister was sleep Lee got up an tiptoed his way through the house so as not to wake em, then snuck out the front door into the dark nighttime. The boat was parked at the side a the house, an when he hop up onto the trailer an then onto the deck a the boat Lee slid down behind the wheel an looked aroun at all the trollin motors an live wells an electronics an cool gadgets, jus takin it all in an makin sure to not miss a thing. That afternoon when he firs come home an there the boat was Lee didn't really see it all that clear cause he was like in a trance, it surprise an amaze im so much that all he could think at the time was that he musta died an gone to heaven, way more than sloppy joes 'n' fishing expos was heaven. Yeah, his mom 'n' dad really got im good he reckon, goin so far as to sit his butt in a kick-ass bass boat juss to trick him outta bein sad. They done dump so much heaven on im all at once it made im drunk on heaven right there on the spot, an he stayed drunk on heaven all the way through Applebee's an *Top Gun Maverick*. But he was sober now, juss like how his dad is a happy drunk for now but in the mornin he's gonna wake up an be his sober not so happy self. Cause even a kid like Lee know that you might get away with tellin a lie an manslaughterin a nice ol man without nobody knowin about it, but you yourself know about it, an no Applebee's or bass boat can ever make you forget. An juss because some nice ol man's dyin makes a way for you to get into heaven it don't make it right for you to stay there. That was why he come out in the middle of the night 'n' sit in the boat an soak it all in an make sure to never forget no part of it, because it would be the lass time for the rest of his life that he would ever sit in this here boat, period. It was his lass look at heaven before stayin away from it forever after. He didn't want no part of any heaven thatchoo only get to go to if some person better'n you has to die firs. It wasn't right that bein a manslaughterer gets you into heaven. Bein a manslaughterer got his brother sent to jail not heaven an Lee wasn't no better than his brother. So to hell with heaven, to hell with the boat. Lee's dad said he was gonna hafta pay for it for the resta his life. Well Lee reckon he'd be payin for it the resta his life too.

THE BIG DAY

As the town which people from bigger towns would call small waited for the sun to rise in what for that town was the east to mark the beginning of its big day- and, at the same time, as some other town half a world ahead (or behind) waited for that same sun to sink into what for them was the west and put an end to its big day (unless of course those people slept during sunlight hours and awakened at night, which meant their big day was just beginning, if you are one of those people who believe that day begins when one awakens and ends when one sleeps that is)- the approaching dawn/someone else's departing sunset carried in its breeze an air of buzzing expectancy, which was scientifically impossible. An all-enveloping sense of awareness and appreciation of the weight of the incomplete sentence which it was and would be. The individual blades of grass in the town square had all been shaved down to a uniform height, despite their hopes and dreams of one day growing up to their full potentials; the square's sidewalks had been swept and the park benches scraped clean of all the chewing gum and human butts which had been stuck to them, leaving no incriminating evidence of the acts which had been committed there the day before. And somewhere out there (wherever "there" was) a black limousine sped along on an otherwise empty highway, getting closer and closer to something just as rapidly as it was getting farther and farther away from something else, its engine purring in silent efficiency and moving toward its target which was locked in its sights and lay some indeterminate number of miles ahead. Or behind.

Over at the Carlson's, Jimmy Carlson was proud of the springy bush of pubic hair which had sprouted in the bathroom mirror.

"Lookin' good Jimmy."

"Thanks Mirror."

"The big day today?"

"You bet it is!" After carefully sliding one of his many secrets back into its holster, Jimmy came out to the kitchen, where his mom was lining up on the counter top all the boxes of cereal to choose from. "Do we have Crunchberries?"

Mom winced a little from the pain she never felt down there. "Well, yes, but your little brother ate all the crunchberries out of it so now it's only Cap'n Crunch."

"Okay, so then we have Cap'n Crunch."

"Well, no. Because the box says Crunchberries."

"Crap." Jimmy could hear things being moved around out in the garage, probably not by burglars but maybe. "Is Dad getting everything ready?"

Mom was pouring Jimmy a bowl of Rice Krispies. "Oh you know he is. He started last night. This is his big day."

Jimmy sat down at the counter with the Krispies who had no idea what was about to happen to them. "Isn't today everybody's big day?"

"Well sure. But it's his big day in the way that it is for him. Today is your big day in the way it is for you, my big day the way it is for me, and on and on and on."

"And on and on and on?"

"And on and on and on." Jimmy poured the milk on the Krispies, who at that moment realized their fate and began screaming in terror with snaps crackles and pops. "I wonder how today will be my big day."

"I'll bet it'll have something to do with Toni Jansen!" Dad had just come in from the garage and was carrying two folded-up lawn chairs.

Jimmy rolled his eyes. "Dad!" Jimmy was in love with Toni Jansen. But Toni Jansen didn't even know that Jimmy was alive.

"Well, am I wrong?" Dad set the lawn chairs down on the kitchen floor, which caused the lawn chairs to open up and become lawn chairs.

Mom backed away in disgust. "Ugh! Lloyd, get those things out of my kitchen!"

Dad laughed. "Don't worry, I cleaned 'em up first. Gonna load 'em into the car for the big day."

Jimmy swallowed a mouthful of dead Krispies before speaking. "Why don't you like those lawn chairs in here Mom?"

"Because they're lawn chairs Jimmy. *Lawn* chairs." Mom made a face as she glared at the alien objects. "I mean, just look at them. Don't they look wrong indoors? *Look* at them."

Jimmy looked at them. His mom was right but he didn't know why. "Mom, can I take one of the kitchen chairs out onto the lawn?"

"Of course not! Why would you want to do that?"

"To see what it would look like."

Jimmy's dad looked at the kitchen chairs, then back at the kitchen Jimmy. "But that's dumb Jim! You already know what it would look like. You can see what it looks like right now!"

"Can I?"

"Eat your Rice Krispies."

Suddenly Mom's eyes darted all about the room. "Lloyd! Where's Stevie?"

Dad folded up the lawn chairs which made them chairs no

longer but they still were but they weren't. "Ha! Little guy's already out in the car buckled into his car seat."

"Already in his car seat! Whyever for?"

Dad tucked the remains of the lawn chairs under his arm. "That's how excited he is about the big day. He can't wait to get it started."

"Why is he's so excited about the big day?"

"Because I told him to be."

Mom finished up with the dishes while Jimmy put all the cereal boxes back up in the cupboard where they could mourn the loss of their Krispies colleagues in privacy. Jimmy was still sporting the boner he got when his dad had gone and mentioned Toni Jansen, so Jimmy was hoping his mom could help him take care of it the way she always did. "Mom, tell me the story of Rice Krispies."

"Again?"

Jimmy and his boner nodded their heads.

"Well alright." Mom and Jimmy sat in the kitchen chairs which might never ever get the chance to become lawn chairs. "It all begins with the rice Jimmy. And rice is just a seed. But after it's harvested and dried the rice is really dense and solid and tough to get into. And so they needed to figure out a way to change the rice into something better. Here's what they did. First they took the rice to a mill where they removed the bran and the germ (the bran and germ is the healthy part but it really gets in the way). Then they cook down what's left with malt flavoring and sugar to make a rice and sugar paste. When this paste is ready they then form it into little kernel-shaped lumps which aren't rice kernels anymore but just shaped to look like the very same rice which they started out as. Then they toast those sugar-paste pretend-rice kernel-lumps which makes them expand and fill up with air and it gives them their thin outer shells that snap crackle and pop in the milk so that anybody can eat it even if they don't have teeth. Rice Krispies are bigger and puffier and noisier and emptier than real rice which is why we love them! And that's how rice the humble seed grows up to become Rice the noble Krispie. Is your boner gone now?"

"No it's even bigger. Thanks Mom!"

"Hey you two!" Dad was standing out on the driveway because that's where the car was. "Time for the big day! Let's go!" With a flurry of water bottles and key jangles and pocket stuffing and dog collaring and Stevie tickling and gun loading and jacket grabbing and door locking they were all finally ready to set out on their big day; and as Dad seized control of the car and offered it no choice but to back down the driveway, each member of the Carlson family was blissfully unaware of the possibility that at the end of their big day their home might not be there when they returned to it. Which, if it wasn't, they wouldn't.

Toni Jansen was standing in the middle of her bedroom, crying her eyes out.

Her mom poked her head in. "Toni, why are you crying?"

"Because I'm in love!"

The rest of Mom's body followed her head into the room. "Just in general, or with a specific person?"

"With Jimmy Carlson!" Toni plopped down onto her bed and laid herself out for embalming. "But he doesn't even know I'm alive!"

Out on the distant highway, the black limousine continued on its course, its destination looming ahead. Or behind. Mom sat in the lawn chair next to her daughter's corpse. "But you're on the debate team with him aren't you?"

Toni sniffed. "Yes."

"Well, then, he knows you're alive."

Toni's face brightened. "Hey. You're right!" She was sitting up now and drying her eyes.

Mom's wrinkled brow wrinkled even more. "But that's only 'if.'"

"'If' what?"

"*If*, when you're on the debate team... you're alive." Mom stared deeply into her daughter's red eyes. "Are you?"

Toni's lip began to quiver. "No!" She jumped up from the bed and ran out of her room, weeping once again. "Daaaaaaaaaad!"

"Whush wong wisch er?" It was Toni's twin brother Tony, who was brushing his teeth.

Mom sighed. "Oh, she's in love. Which means she's miserable. And on the big day, too!"

"Nah wi shat Szimmy Garlson ishee?"

"Yes, with Jimmy Carlson."

Tony sprayed Aquafresh halfway across the room. "Buh heesh nah daytabuhl! Heesh on duh duhbay team!"

"Well I won't argue that point with you." Outside the house, the surrounding world of humanity had recklessly plunged itself into an irreversible spiral of self-immolation, its inexorable march toward annihilation and the inglorious ending of the Anthropocene by this time an unavoidable certainty. But Mom had bigger problems. "Tony, don't talk with your mouth full of toothpaste, go rinse out. Then come back so we can talk." While Tony went to the bathroom to spit out the remaining Aquafresh, Toni was running from room to room, crying and wailing and looking for her dad who was the identical twin of Tony's dad. Tony and his now-empty mouth came back to Toni's room and sat on the park bench across from his mom. "Now Tony. You're going to be a senior next year so we need to talk about college."

"Ahm nah gowee tah cawage."

Mom sat upright. "Not going? But why not?"

Tony sat up straighter still. "Ahm jone-ing dah Ahmee."

"What???" Mom stood and began pacing back and forth across Toni's yard. "The Army? Have you talked to your father about this?"

Tony shrugged. "Yeth. Buh yuhno Dahd. Iz lahk ah talk tah im buh ee dozuhn unnustamee."

Mom stopped pacing and regarded her son. "Tony, where were you when you talked to your father?"

Tony thought. "We wuh in thuh caw. Ahways in thuh caw."

"So you talk to your dad when he's driving and you're sitting next to him?"

"Uh huh. So wuh?"

"Tony." Mom shook her head sadly, then took aim at the young soldier. "That means whenever you've talked to your father you were talking into his right ear. That's Toni's ear."

"Toni's ear?"

"Toni's ear. Your ear is his left ear. *That's* the Tony ear."

Tony's eyes filled with an emotion that short-story writers might describe as despair. "Buh- buh tha meenth- "

"That means Tony that your dad hasn't heard a thing you've said for seventeen years because you've been speaking into the wrong ear. And since you've been talking into the Toni ear all this time- " Mom took Tony's hand with every intention of returning it, "- your dad now thinks you're Toni."

"Whaaah???" Now it was Tony who jumped on his feet and began pacing about. "Buh den... den oo duth he thing Toni ith?"

Mom's voice was soft and horrible. "He thinks Toni is Toni too. He thinks you're *both* Toni. Because you both talk into his Toni ear." Tony stood in the middle of the room, blinking back tears. "Can you imagine how badly you've confused him?"

"Buh... buh wuh do ah do nah?"

Mom folded her hands across her lap. "All you can do from this day on is to try your hardest to be the best daughter and sister you can be." Mom stood and gave exactly one-half of her children a hug. "Now go fix your mascara, it's all streaked from crying. And brush your teeth. It's the big day after all!"

Walking back out to the kitchen, Larry the beagle yelped when his head was stepped on by Mom who was also walking back out to the kitchen. The birth Toni was sitting on a stool at the breakfast island, looking at her phone while finishing her Rice Krispies and grinning broadly. "Well Toni, you sure look happier."

"I am happier!" Toni held up her phone. "Text from Jimmy. He says he has a big surprise for me for the big day today."

"I see!" Mom dropped anchor at the island next to her daughter and ignored Larry's cries for help. "Did Jimmy tell you what the surprise was?"

A gear slipped in Toni's brain. "Well it... it wouldn't be a surprise anymore if he told me. Would it?"

"Sure it would be silly! If it turns out to be something completely different than what he told you, or if it turned out to be nothing at all, that would *really* be a surprise, right?"

Larry was lying in a puddle of his own urine, shuddering and gasping. "But Mom, why would Jimmy tell me what it was only for it to be something different?"

"Toni, people say they have something for you and it turns out to be something different all the time."

The girl wrapped her hands around her head in anguish. "But hold on. Hold on! None of this matters anyway! Because he *didn't* tell me what the surprise was."

"Great!" Lawrence departed from this world leaving it no better and no worse for having taken many shits upon it. "So that means it *will* be a surprise for you after all."

Mom stood to leave, but Toni grabbed her arm. "But wait! No! No it won't. Because now you got me thinking that the surprise might be the thing Jimmy didn't say or it might be some other thing *or* it might be nothing at all, and so now I'm thinking it could be *any* of those which means I'm expecting any and everything so it really won't be a surprise now no matter what it turns out to be. That's what you've got me thinking now. Thanks."

Mom paused, and then made sure she was speaking into Toni's Mom ear. "That's why you should never think Toni. Because if you don't think then you'll always be surprised by what you get."

The artist formerly known as Tony joined them in the kitchen. "Ohgay Mom. Ahm weddy foh dah bih day." He was wearing a very empty-looking backpack.

"You're wearing a very empty-looking backpack."

Non-Tony smiled despite his crushing sadness. "Weh it won be emppy fah wong." He looked to his sister who was once again staring at her phone. "Ahwent you gonna ass me whu ahm puh-ing innih?"

"Toni, don't provoke your sister, she's in love. I'll ask instead. What are you puh-ing innih?"

"Iss uh seeket." The once and future Toni groaned and rolled her eyes. "Iss foh duh bih day." He leaned in toward his sister and whispered. "So don tehwel ay-one wuh mah seeket iss."

Toni 1.0 pushed her face up to his which for them as identical twins was redundant. "*How the hell can I tell anyone your secret if I don't know what it is?*"

"Now Toni, what did I tell you about provoking your sister? Please go check on your dad."

"Ah don knee to. Hiss aweddy behiynna wheew innis cawsea, stapped in."

"In his car seat?" Mom looked out the kitchen window where, out on the driveway, she saw Dad strapped in on the driver's seat of the car, staring straight ahead with his hands on the wheel as if already driving. "Why is he strapped in already?"

"Thass how essiyaad he ithabow the bih day."

Mom shrugged. "Well alrighty then. Let's go!" Mom grabbed her very full-looking purse, but then stopped at the kitchen door and turned back. "Oh, and Toni- you did check Dad's straps didn't you?"

Toni rolled his eyes in the way his sister Toni did which shouldn't come as much of a surprise. "Yeth Mom. Don wuhwee, he won geh ow of zem ziss time."

"Then off we go. You too Toni."

"Whatever." Toni reluctantly pocketed her phone, and then looked up with a start. "Wait a minute! Why have you been calling *him* Toni?"

"Resolved: that the United States Federal Government should reverse the earth's revolution on its axis and spin the planet in the opposite direction which would turn back time and thereby forestall the demise of the human race." This was the

National Speech and Debate topic for the current academic year, and for Mr. Benham, the debate coach at the high school, it was his job to prepare his young team to be able to argue both sides of the question effectively and by doing so win speaker points and plastic trophies and forget about their acne for a few hours. Whether it helped them forget about their acne Mr. Benham didn't know; debating never made Mr. Benham forget his own acne back when he was in high school, and now, some 12,045 earth revolutions later, here he was, thinking about acne once again. For at this implausible point of his midlife Mr. Benham's acne had returned, just as bright and bubbly as it had been when he was 5840 earth revolutions old, a speckly mountain range of red bumps staring back at him now in his bathroom mirror and sharing the spotlight with the other miraculous new changes to his body which the mirror was also reflecting. Acne again, at his age? And on the big day, too!

Sitting down at the kitchen table with his bowl of hard granola (because of his extensive dental work he had always avoided crunchy cereals and instead went with Rice Krispies, but now that so many new strong teeth had recently sprouted up in his mouth in place of the repaired ones he found he could once again eat anything), Mr. Benham thought about the thing which he knew was not at all the thing he should be thinking about. What he should be thinking about of course was this year's debate topic; it was his job to think about it after all, the one and only topic which his debate team would focus on the entire debate season. Each year the topics were chosen because of their universally-recognized importance, because they were issues that mattered and deserved to be at the forefront of any thinking person's thoughts. But no matter what the topic was from one year to the next, no matter how compelling the issue it represented, Mr. Benham could never bring himself to think about the debate topic except when forced to, when the pimply faces of the debate team depending on his guidance met for practice. Mr. Benham didn't feel guilty in the least about not thinking about the topics because he knew that nobody else thought about them either. "That Congress should do this" or "That the government should do that-" what person, what normal everyday person sitting at his job or staring into his bathroom mirror or riding in his big black limousine speeding down a lonely highway toward an unknown destination thought about those big important debate topic questions? Congress and the rest of the government didn't even think about them, even though they made speeches about them and did interviews about them and voted about them and wrote books about them. The people in the government were thinking about the exact same thing that Mr. Benham and everybody else was thinking about. They thought about That Thing which everyone knows everyone else is thinking about and so doesn't even need to be mentioned because it's too obvious. As he crunched on the granola Mr. Benham thought about this truth; and as he thought, he realized that all the thinking he was doing about what people think about had caused him to forget what it was that he'd been thinking about. It was yet another reason why one shouldn't think.

 When the earth and the sun had each moved to their respective points in the Milky Way galaxy to permit the sun's beams to shine directly into Mr. Benham's eyes the startling brightness reminded him what had been thinking about: the big day. Well of course that's what had been on his mind. He'd been looking forward to it for the longest time now, just as everyone in the town had been looking forward to it and thinking about it since, well, since as long as he or anyone else could remember. You never had to ask, if you saw someone staring out their window or into their coffee cup or through the windshield when they were stopped at a red light, what was on their mind; the big day was what was on everyone's mind, all the time, the unspoken subtext which captioned everything that was said, the ever-present invisible ink indelibly written between every line. Christmas was inconsequential compared to the big day. Birthdays and graduation days and marriage days and holidays were nothing days by comparison, merely incremental milestones to be passed along the road whose ultimate destination was the big day. There were some who grew so impatient with waiting for the big day to arrive that they chose to end their lives out of despair, opting to settle for death as their big day and by so doing miss out on the real big day's payoff altogether. The day of one's dying was by no means the big day; death was simply the last day, the day when sunrises and sunsets and earth revolutions and big debate topics and bigger limousines on distant highways all disappear into a hell of emptiness where nothing fills the void. But Mr. Benham was not ready in the least for any hell of empty nothingness. Because Mr. Benham had acne again. And new teeth.

After placing his granola bowl in the sink Mr. Benham went through his checklist of preparations for the big day before grabbing his keys and heading out the door; and in an instant was chuckling to himself upon realizing he had no such checklist, unlike the one which everyone else in town was certainly going over at this very moment. The truth of the matter was that Mr. Benham had no need to bring anything along for the big day, unless bringing along or leaving behind one's own mind was an option. For it was all right there in his head, everything he would need for the big day; it was his debating skills, so long wasted on teaching the dead-eyed young but now sharpened anew and ready to be weaponized by himself for himself and his own selfish ends. It was to be the first time in his life that debating would not be a vain and pointless exercise. And what a pointless exercise debate was indeed! All that working on arguments and researching evidence and building cases and rehearsing rebuttals just for one school's flock of adolescent nerds to flap and squawk against another school's nerds and at the end of all that *sturm und drang* over some important issue which really needed to be seriously dealt with by someone who wasn't a squawking high school nerd the debate tournament would come to an end and then everyone would just go back to thinking about what people always think about with nothing whatsoever being done to bring action to that all-important resolution which everyone had just been debating. For twenty-five earth years Mr. Benham had been an enabler of this sort of absurdity, but today, on the big day, the absurdity would come to an end. Today his talents would not be wasted in vain. The wielding of his debating skills would have nothing at all to do with any stupid National Debate and Speech topic- today his skills would be applied exclusively to That Thing Which Everyone Always Thinks About. Besides, he had long ago wearied of this year's National Debate and Speech topic, just as he always wearied with every debate topic every year. The nature of his boredom with the debate topic this year was considerably different however, for it had nothing to do with a disinterest in the topic per se but with the charade of it having to be debated at all. For unlike past years, this year's resolution was one which he knew full well had already been settled and resolved. "*That the government should reverse the spinning of the earth and* reverse time?" What a laugh! It had become quite obvious to Mr. Benham- obvious to anyone who, like him, was not in denial of the truth- that the direction of the spinning of the earth had already been reversed and time was now in a full and hasty retreat. What other explanation could there possibly be for the fresh eruption of acne on his long-dormant face, the new teeth which had popped into his mouth, the buoyant bounce in his no-longer achy knees and the springy bush of thick pubic hair which had replaced the wispy gray beard straggling below his wispy gray penis (which had itself snapped back to attention, toned and taut and curved in steely readiness like an unsheathed scimitar)? No, time had been reversed, the signs of it were unmistakable; and it was still reversing, revisiting itself and dialing back the hours (even now he found himself tightening his belt another notch as he felt the ripples returning to his resurrected six-pack), yet somehow time was also still moving forward, closer and closer to the big day. And now that the big day was finally almost here Mr. Benham was ready to seize it by the short hairs. He had no intention of missing this window of opportunity. Not again. He'd missed it on the first go-round way back when but he wouldn't miss it this time. Back then he saw his acne as a hideous and shameful scourge; now he saw it as so much uncontainable buildup of life force and youthful vitality that the very pores of his face were bulging with it. No, this time things would be different. This time Mr. Benham had a plan. He had researched and compiled his evidence. He had built his case and his arguments. He'd rehearsed his cross-exams and rebuttals. He had sheathed his sleek new scimitar. With keys in hand and his past awaiting him, Mr. Benham stopped before getting into his car to check his drivers license to see if he was still old enough to drive. He was not. But it wouldn't stop him from getting behind the wheel. It was the big day after all. And Toni Jansen was nearly within reach.

"Jimmy, go help your father bring the lawn chairs from the car."

Jimmy's mom was casting hundreds of unsuspecting insects into total darkness by spreading a big blanket across the grass of the town square. Jimmy's little brother Stevie was eating some of those insects. Dutifully, Jimmy walked back to the car, knowing that his dad not only didn't need help carrying the lawn chairs but would refuse any help with the lawn chairs because his dad was the god of the lawn chairs and he was very monotheistic. When Jimmy got to the car his dad was waiting for him.

"Jim." Dad stared down at Jimmy with his sternest god face. "When I took the lawn chairs out of the trunk I noticed there was something else back there, hidden under a tarp. Care to tell me what it is?"

"It's a- "

"I know what it is!" The lawn chairs were leaning against the bumper of the car, folded up and small, just as Jimmy wished he could be at the moment. "Now I don't know what tomfoolery you're up to Jim but what's under that tarp is gonna stay under the tarp. It is *not* coming out. Is that clear?"

"Yes sir." In his peripheral vision Jimmy could see that the Jansens had arrived. There was Toni Jansen, climbing out the car along with her new sister.

"Now get on back to your mother. We've got the big day ahead of us." As Dad carried the lawn chairs to the Carlson's blanket, Jimmy watched as the Toni of his boners followed the rest of her family onto the square where they opened lawn chairs just like the ones his dad had brought and sat in them the same way that his family sat in them. Jimmy gazed upon the half-recumbent form of his paragon, then glanced back at his badly-kept secret which slept beneath the dark green tarp in the trunk of the Carlsons' car. Oh, it was coming out alright. There was nothing his dad could do to stop him. And when he whipped it out he would make sure Toni Jansen took a good long look at it.

The prettiest of the Jansen girls watched Jimmy Carlson as he joined his family on their blanket. "Wook, deh iss yo bohfrehn, Jimmah Cawson. Whuddah douchebah." Pretending to ignore her twin, Toni kept her eyes on her phone while staring longingly at Jimmy with her mind. *Would this be the day he finally speaks to me?* It was ridiculous of her, Toni knew full well, to be so desperate for Jimmy, or for any boy for that matter. Besides, he'd sent her the text after all about bringing her a surprise, but texting wasn't the same as talking- sending words without also sending your eyes and your face isn't talking so much as it is hiding. And of course Jimmy's face and eyes did speak to her, every day at debate practice, when she would argue the affirmative and he would argue the negative. But that was just debate, not real speaking; debate was just talking at someone and being talked at. Toni would get so lost in his dreamy eyes while he cited the experts who opposed the reversal of the earth's rotation that she was always grateful for her prepared notecards and evidence which told her what to say, for without that she'd just stammer and stutter and stare stupidly at his kissable mouth. That was the thing which Toni liked about debate, the way it equipped a person so that you could be able to talk even if you had nothing to say. Maybe that was the reason Jimmy could only speak to her with typing fingers instead of face and eyes, because he had the same problem of not having anything to say. Or maybe because his fingers had more to say than his mouth. Or maybe- a little shudder of dread washed over Toni as she considered the possibility- maybe he really *did believe* that the earth should just go on spinning the same way that it always had. If so the big day was doomed.

"Toni!" Mom was snapping her fingers an inch away from Toni's face. "Did you hear anything I said?"

"You mean ever?"

Mom crossed her arms in exasperation. "I *said*- isn't that your debate friend Jimmy Carlson over there with his family? You should go say hello."

"Ughghg, we've been over this Mom!" Hazarding a glance toward the Carlsons, Toni saw Jimmy standing ten feet away from his lawn chair and staring at it. "I'm not gonna go over and embarrass myself with somebody who doesn't even know I exist."

Mom put on her sunglasses which allowed even less light to enter her mind. "Well that's no kind attitude. What's the point of the big day if you don't take some chances?"

Suddenly Toni looked about and realized that except for the ten billion other people also in the world they were all alone. "Wait. Where'd my brother go?"

Mom nodded her head slowly. "Exactly Toni. Where *did* your brother go?"

Back in the parking lot, ToniBoy was sitting in the front seat of their car, checking the straps which kept his father securely in place behind the wheel. It was important for Toni to check the straps on a regular basis, considering the many times his father had tried to escape in the past. "Theh. Thuh staps ahnt too tot ah dey Dah?"

Dad looked all about as if he was hearing voices, which clearly he wasn't. "What?"

"Nevah mine." The two strangers stared straight ahead as the surrounding silence splattered against the windshield. Toni had learned long ago that there was no point in saying anything else to his dad but that part of her learning was disabled, so they kept speaking to him. "Todaytha bih day Dah."

Dad continued to stare straight ahead, his hands at ten and two.

"Mom seth ah should go tah cowage, nah duh Ahmy. Whudduh you thing Dah?"

At this, Dad's head began to turn, very slowly, until the front part of that head was facing the face part of Toni's head. The dim light of Dad's eyes was barely visible behind the fog. "Packers 27, Bears 14." Having expressed his deepest feelings, Dad rotated his central processing unit back to the forward position and returned his attention to his non-driving. From his lonely perch on the passenger seat, Toni thought about his dad and how it felt to not have one.

"So Dahd..." Out on the open highway the black limousine was still speeding along, its engine purring and its destination not in doubt. "... if ah undo yo stapps ah you gohnna wun away?"

Dad understood nothing which Toni had said but knew exactly what to answer. "Yes."

Toni unstrapped his dad from the car seat. "Theh. Wun away."

Dad jumped out of the car and ran away.

Sitting behind the wheel with her hand at nine and his hand at three, Toni gazed out through the windshield upon the unseen landscape of roads which awaited them. Those roads all belonged to him now; from this moment on the man in the driver's seat would know exactly who he was and would understand him perfectly. From now on it would be his car to drive, his destination to choose, his army to join and his orders to obey. On the seat beside him he saw his empty backpack, from which he removed Larry's dead and broken body (had Larry been alive the backpack would not have been empty but full of course). Toni had brought along the remains of Larry with the intention of placing them in the earth; not as a burial but as a planting, knowing that the big day was the best day of all for germinating new life, be it his own or a dead dog's. Out on the square he could see the big day unfolding like so many blankets across an endless sea of smothered insects, and on one of those blankets, he saw those members of his family who had not yet run away, and he stared at them with impunity, knowing that it was impossible for them to see him in the least. And across the square he saw the big round world, beckoning for him to drive his brand new car off the edge of the too-flat earth and dive headlights-first into the big day.

Across that same square, Jimmy Carlson squeezed the car key which he'd pickpocketed from his dad's insensate pants and popped open the trunk of the car. Pulling back the tarp, he was thrilled and surprised to see that the kitchen chair he'd snuck out of his house was still in the trunk and had not made its escape; surprised that the kitchen chair which looked so very out-of-place anywhere but in the kitchen (and therefore felt the kind of self-conscious panic we all feel when we find ourselves dropped into strange and alien places) had not succumbed to the impulse to just run back home. But it was just for this out-of-place strangeness that Jimmy had brought the chair; looking at it now against the incongruous background of the car trunk, he found the simple chair interesting, almost captivating and unique in its incorrectness. In its usual place in his mother's kitchen the chair had existed as an invisible thing, an anonymous and harmonious ingredient of the everyday background, so perfectly appropriate in its functionality that any distinction it may have possessed as a stand-alone object had been blended away by the dullness of familiarity. Jimmy was this same kind of kitchen chair, or at least had felt so all semester on the debate team, so ordinary and bland and blended into the background that of course Toni Jansen barely knew he was alive. Oh sure, they talked now and then and even texted, but it was stuck in sameness, just like his mother's kitchen, safe and predictable and never a chair out of place. But Jimmy longed to knock those chairs about a bit; his springy bush of pubic hair had whispered to him that he was more than just another kitchen chair, and Toni would finally know it if only she could see him somewhere besides the kitchen. And so he had brought the kitchen chair out-of-doors for the big day, that he might place it on the grass of the town square and sit his springy bushy ass upon it, bethroning himself in the chair so absurdly situated, but an absurdity which would clearly define him at last, framed by glorious weirdness, so that Toni might finally see him as the stand-alone object he truly was. And his Toni would have no choice then but to climb up onto the chair and sit behind him in the saddle, and they would ride off on their kitchen chair into the sunset of the big day and ride that way forever.

This then was the developing scene spreading itself across the town square on the morning of that big day, an absurd young lover in love with a young lover of absurdity, an intrepid first-time driver and a trunk which held kidnapped furniture, with the ghost of a departed dog and a departed ghost of a dad and the three-fourths remaining parents hovering above while the insects whose blanketed lives would in the final analysis amount to no less value than the lives of those who trampled over them cowering below. Somewhere out on the highway the black limousine continued to speed along, drawing nearer and nearer to its inevitable somewhere, even as the optical illusion of a rising sun climbed higher and higher toward a goal no less certain than the limousine's. And now there rolled up onto the scene one last car, parking next to the square, and from the car emerged the final player of the *dramatis personae*- Mr. Benham, or rather, the one who had come to be known as Mr. Benham in the graying sunset of his middle age. But the world was spinning backwards now, and so the reversal of time had rendered Mr. Benham a thing of the future. For he was Chad now, Chad the Younger, slayer of opportunity and conquistador extraordinaire, resplendent in his acne and skilled in the art of debate. He had come to the square on the big day that he might shed his tattered Benham and, cloaked in his new Chad, seize by the power of his words and the unassailability of his arguments that which had eluded him all his Benham lifetime: the girl, the young and nubile girl, a girl who was older than him now thanks to the reversal but still young of course. And despite his youth he would win the young older girl; despite his inexperience he would persuade the older young girl that he was worthy of her love, and she would submit not only to his youthful desires but to the new direction of the spinning earth (hadn't she argued the affirmative case all semester after all?), and so reverse *her* rotation as well, forsaking the orbit which could never take her to Benham but a new orbit that could take her ever Chad-ward. Toward the prosecution of this mission then did Chad come galloping onto the square astride his resurrected morning; and as if it were aware of its role in the setting of the scene, the sun now took the stage at the centermost spot of the sky, for it was high noon, that classic moment of showdown in every gunslinging western film, when the forces of good and evil and love and hate face off for the ultimate confrontation which marks the climax of the events and produces outcomes that are irreversible, unlike the capricious spinnings of the changeable world. Yes, it was high noon at the town square on the big day. And every hand was pressed against a trigger.

\`\`

The thin wisp of clouds which drifted in over the ridge of boreal spruce was barely visible against the faintly glowing backdrop of winter sky, an illumination so dim and unspecific that to refer to it as "light" required a stretch of the imagination. To accept that the source of this feeble light was the sun required imagination as well, considering that in this frozen wilderness one hundred and fifty miles north of the arctic circle the sun would not be seen again for many weeks to come. Daryl watched the clouds as they crept in from the northwest, and while they appeared innocent enough as thinly-strewn nothings, he knew that not far behind them the bigger clouds were following, bringing the big weather, an impending knife-slash of snow and wind which was business as usual along these foothills of Alaska's Brooks Range. Trudging over the snow while pulling behind him his toboggan loaded with marten traps, Daryl checked down in his mind all the various jobs in and around the cabin which he had set out to finish before the blizzard hit, and realized happily that he'd successfully dealt with them all. It had been a good day, a productive day; or, if you prefer, it had been a productive night, since day and night did not exist in a world where the winter sun neither fell nor rose. He had tacked up the metal sheeting along the base of his cabin's outer walls to keep the gnawing porcupines out, as well as nailing down the last of the insulation strips onto the cabin floor to keep the precious heat in; he'd found the cause of the draught seeping in through his window and puttied over the whistling crack which had appeared there; he had struggled for an hour with his sputtering generator which he feared was ready to fail altogether, only to find that after simply cleaning the air filter the generator was once again running good as new. Now, with getting his marten trapline baited and set before the onset of the heavy weather being his only pre-blizzard duty remaining, Daryl allowed himself the luxury of taking in some feeling of self-satisfaction, but only a small serving of it. For while all indications were that he was staying one move ahead in the survival chess game between himself and the Alaskan winter, Daryl knew that his opponent's resourcefulness at finding ways to kill him were limitless, and to prematurely celebrate a victory not yet won was the sort of overconfident foolishness which played right into the White Queen's checkmate gambit.

Having arrived at the brushy knoll which he'd chosen as the location for his first marten trap, Daryl set his .270 bolt-action Winchester down on the opposite end of the toboggan and opened the box which held the trap baits, which consisted mostly of deer fat and pieces of leg bone. Scanning his eyes up and down the long unbroken stretch of dense willow thicket to check for any inquisitive predators who might be taking an interest in his work or in the plumpness of his leg, Daryl also took note of the snow cover, which he found to be ideal- not so soft as to make his tobogganing difficult, but soft enough to clearly show any and all animal tracks. Sure enough, there were marten tracks aplenty, all along the willows just where he hoped they would be. Encouraged by this promising sign, he set out his first baited gripper trap on the trunk of a fallen balsam, then took up his Winchester and resumed his toboggan pull toward the next trap site a hundred yards down. The willows held a lot of small game, but they were a problem as well; Daryl's favorite high spot for scouting caribou was on the other side of the willows, but their denseness prevented passage through them, which meant a two-mile detour all the way around the willows to make it to his scouting spot. That would be his first job after the storm, he now decided, to chainsaw a path through the hundred yards-thick willows to make a shortcut from his cabin to the high ground, a path that would shorten the route down to a mere quarter-mile and save him valuable time and energy. As he came up on his second trap site, a branchy pile of fall-down timber, he laughed to himself at how presumptuous he was being to assume that, before the storm even hit, he would be the one who would decide what his first job would be after it. Daryl knew full well that the White Queen would dictate what Job One would be after her storm, just as she dictated all his behavior and every decision he made. He thought back to his previous life in Ohio, before moving to Alaska five years ago, and how alarming and precarious it would have felt to that old Daryl to be living every day, every hour of every day, at the disposal of a capricious and unpredictable natural world, an existence focused on the emergency of the moment and the necessities of the here-and-now. He had wondered at the beginning of his adventure in the Arctic how he would adjust to that sort of life, afraid that perhaps he'd be escaping the bondage and daily grind of the corporate world only to be enslaved by a new taskmaster more demanding still, and that the freedom he was seeking by fleeing the world of encroaching humanity would feel like no freedom at all. But Daryl had found his freedom after all, not in spite of the demands of his new master but because of them- to have all thoughts and concerns other than those which were directly tied to staying alive stripped away, to live a life so focused on basic survival that one was freed of all non-essential mental and emotional distractions, was liberating to him. Although his life in Ohio was physically easier than in the Arctic, it was far more anxiety-ridden and stressful, since so much of his activity in that world felt meaningless and intangible, disconnected from one's physical existence. There was nothing intangible above the Arctic Circle; everything which was done in the Arctic had meaning and mattered in a practical, tangible way. Each problem to be solved was a three-dimensional one, not an abstraction, and every solution arose from the rationality of his mind and the dexterity of his hands. What a curious thing it was, Daryl thought to himself, as he wedged the second trap into a well-placed nook amongst the tangled timber and set off with his toboggan toward the next spot down the willow line, that in Ohio, where his day-to-day survival was a foregone conclusion and never threatened, he had so little appreciation for, even awareness of, surviving; and how by contrast in this beautiful but deadly world which poised in waiting like a marten trap for him to make just one mistake so it could snap his fragile existence away, he understood that fragility, accepted and embraced the terms of engagement, and as a result took no moment of his survival for granted. He appreciated the sturdy toboggan loaded with high-quality traps which he pulled with one hand, just as he appreciated the classic American firearm he held with the other; he appreciated the crunch of the snow beneath his feet and the not yet stormy skies above his head. He would appreciate the wind at his back on the walk home to the cabin (provided a wolverine didn't chew off his foot enroute) and would appreciate the hot cup of gloriously terrible coffee which the hotplate powered by the newly-restored generator would heat for him. And he would appreciate more than anything that it would all be on his terms. With the White Queen's permission of course.

As he positioned the third trap just below the covered bait which he had first nailed onto the leaning spruce tree, Daryl noticed that the clouds which only an hour earlier had appeared as little more than feathers had swollen somewhat, by no means threatening yet but clearly foreshadowing the threat to come. The timing of his trap setting was perfect, Daryl thought to himself; he'd finish them all up and be back in the protection of his cabin just before the first flakes would fall. Or rather, he'd be safely back in the cabin provided nothing deterred him along the way. For even now, as he studied the many marten tracks which led in and out of the willow thicket, a different sort of track, broader in width and longer in its stride, came to his attention as well: wolf tracks, not yet filled with drifted snow which indicated that they were freshly created, and clearly put down by more than just one animal. It was common for martens to follow the wolves, trailing them in hopes of scoring sloppy seconds from the bigger animals' kills; and while Daryl was glad to see that these tracks were a full mile away from his cabin, the sight of pack activity so near where he happened to be standing at the moment made him grip his Remington with renewed vigilance. That so very few wolf attacks on humans had been recorded in North America was of little comfort to him, for his experience with the gray wolf had taught him to be wary. More than once had he observed a wolf slithering toward him on his belly, a move reserved solely for the stalking of prey, and the fact that the wolves grew bolder and ventured nearer and nearer to his cabin during the hungriest times of the year caused him no small amount of unease as well. The fact that he loved the wolf dearly was purely sentimental and beside the point; Daryl understood that in a starving wolf's eyes he was 200 pounds of delicious carcass, and he and his .270 would do whatever they had to do for him to remain a living carcass. No, sentimental feelings had no place north of the Arctic Circle. Sentimental feelings cause a man to vacillate in times of action, to doubt and hesitate when decisions had to made. Reflection and deep thoughts and writing poetry were all well and good, but only after the firewood was chopped and the rifle was cleaned. Dreaming was fine as well, but only when you were asleep. The White Queen ate daydreamers for lunch.

Within an hour Daryl had put out the last of his marten traps, and pulling what was now a considerably lighter toboggan he began the two and a half-mile trek back to the cabin. The busy marten activity which all the tracks indicated was an encouraging thing; the cash he'd earn from the pelts would go a long way toward paying for supplies later in the season. But even this undertaking as simple as putting out marten traps had nearly resulted in disaster; at the site of his last trap, Daryl had caught a bootlace on a tree trunk and, being tripped up, twisted his ankle, a rookie blunder which, had he not fallen into the soft snow to his left but off the steep ledge to his right, could have meant a broken ankle instead of the mild sprain he felt now as he walked. A broken ankle, an injury which would've stranded him more than two miles from home utterly alone, with a Siberian northwester packing 40+ mph winds and wind chills of nearly 100F below zero due to arrive in a couple of hours- this then was the reality of his relationship with the White Queen, the tightwire-thin margin of error which she required him to walk if he was to continue his tenancy within her domain. But he hadn't fallen off the ledge and he had not frozen to death; he'd stood back up and brushed himself off, completely alive, and now he was pulling a light toboggan without even a limp, with the northwest wind at his back and a warm cabin waiting. When he got to the cabin he would work on the smokehouse he'd recently begun building, work until the weather told him it was time to stop working that is. Then he would go inside, and when his stomach told him he was hungry he would eat. When his eyelids told him he was sleepy he would sleep. And when his bladder told him he had to pee he would get up again. Life in a world which had no day nor night was a continuum, an unbroken event of taking what your environment gives you and responding to it in its timeframe, not your own. How quaint and uselessly sentimental to Daryl now were notions such as "the dark of night" or "the dawn of a new day," how obsolete were such reference points as tomorrow or the day after tomorrow or two weeks from now. What was once "tomorrow" was now "when I'm next awake." Even the word "yesterday" had disappeared from his vocabulary; in his old life, yesterday more often than not represented a reminder of regrets, of opportunities missed and mistakes he'd made. The imminent approach of a killer blizzard afforded the cabin dweller no time to dwell upon regrets, unless of course one had failed to repair the cabin's roof. But the dangers were so real above that Arctic Circle that such lack of preparation was simply out of the question, beyond imagination. And despite his most meticulous preparations there were always surprising calamities popping up in his path. Nothing had ever been truly surprising in his life back in Ohio; how desperate was his need in those days to find entertainment and amusement to break the unsurprising monotony of sunup-to-sundown. Not only was life in the Arctic surprising, but the surprises here were life-affecting, even life-threatening. The idea of seeking entertainment was ludicrous to Daryl now, just as was the idea of looking forward to some big defining event someday in the future. The present was engaging enough all by itself. Of course he did still look forward to things, like the first bearberries of the season and the return of the nesting ptarmigans, but even these "events" were surprises in that one never knew just when or where such firsts of the season would appear. No, what Daryl no longer looked forward to was some mythical future day when he would finally feel that he'd arrived, when he would believe his journey toward self-actualization had been completed. The steady constancy of the winter solstice and its sunless unchangeability had exposed the myth of "arriving" for the lie it was; there was no such thing as arriving, only continuing, moving and working in the world of Now instead of waiting and watching the sky for the dawn of Then. This walk through the snow, these thickening clouds above him, this long willow thicket to his right and the ridge of spruce behind it, this was the truth, the truth of here and now in the Church of the Here and Now, the destination and the journey and the risk and the reward all rolled into one painfully pleasurable experience. And when he saw his sturdy little cabin just up ahead and felt the nearing blizzard's intensifying northwest wind pushing him toward it, Daryl once again allowed himself to enjoy just a small serving of self-satisfaction in light of the success of his undertakings- the traps were all set, the cabin was readied for the weather, and the wolves had been kind enough to not invite themselves along on his walk home. And when he reached the inviting front door Daryl went to lift the latch, but then he paused for just a moment, slowly moving his hand away from the latch and wrapping a finger around the trigger of his Remington. For in the snow in front of the door and in the snow all about the cabin and in the snow which surrounded all sides of him Daryl saw wolf tracks, nothing but wolf tracks, deep and crisp and as new as they could be. The self-satisfaction he had swallowed began to burn a small hole in his stomach. For the White Queen had been setting out traps as well.

\`\`\`

As the noonday sun stared down upon the building drama developing in the terrestrial scene below it, Jimmy Carlson quietly closed the trunk of the family car and, hunkering down behind it and peering across the square to make sure the coast was clear, removed the tarp from the kitchen chair which now lay shivering on the ground next to him. Confirming that his dad was nowhere to be seen, he rose to his feet, and with one hand tucking the chair under his arm and the other hand covering the chair's protesting mouth, Jimmy bravely lowered his head and stormed the blanket-strewn beach where he hoped his stolen cargo would soon be planted. Toni Jansen, the pearl of great price who provided the reason for all his efforts, sat forlornly on her family's blanket, staring at her silent phone and sadly wondering where on earth Jimmy could be and why he had so cruelly forsaken her. Her sister Toni, having so recently established herself behind the steering wheel as the new man of the house, wrapped his fingers around the ignition key and debated amongst his many selves which direction the key should be turned, even as Larry's chrysalis lay in perpetual waiting on the seat beside him, buckled in for safety. Somewhere beyond the square, the former father of the redundant Toni's ran and ran some more, tearing up the road like a speeding limousine and leaving behind him abandoned mothers and baby brothers while thinking of nothing else but of getting as far away as possible before the fuse of the big day was lit and the whole shittery of cars and chairs and picnic blankets and silent phones exploded. But fleeing dad was far too late; the fuse was already lit and burning. And as the northwesterly winds of the impending storm fanned its bellows breath over the fizzing flame, a lone figure of once-and-future provenance stood at the top of the square like a statue of pock-marked chivalry, the wind blowing the tilted windmills of his arms into a frantic spinning which announced his arrival with a flourish and spelled out the meaning of his intentions in a swirling utterance of semaphore.

That so very few wolf attacks on humans had been recorded in the town square was of little comfort to Chad as he studied the tracks in the snow between the blankets which surrounded his cabin. There was but one thing to do of course- get inside, where the safety of her inner danger would protect him from ravenous teeth and where the freezing winds and blinding snow of the big day could not reach him. But when he reached for Toni's latch he was dismayed to find that, try as he may, he could not lift it; she was stuck, unresponsive to his hand, and instantly Chad understood the problem. He'd been so proud of himself for remembering to do everything else in preparation for the big blizzard, the porcupine-proofing and the floor-insulating and the generator-fixing and the new tooth-growing, but one last job- unsticking the latch- had slipped his mind, and now, with wolf tracks blanketing the grass all around him and the blizzard of the big day just about to hit, Chad was excluded from safety and exposed to the elements. Popping the latch and getting in had only gotten more and more difficult for him over the years, had been difficult for him from the very beginning in fact, and as he tried the stubborn latch once again but to no avail he could feel the sun no longer directly above him but moving away, scampering off toward the west, as if trying to get as far away as possible from the brewing disaster which was beginning to look both inevitable and inescapable. He tried the latch again, but there was nothing doing; no matter which way he turned the key his former father's car just would not start. Toni sat immobilized behind the disabled steering wheel, frustrated with his inability to unleash the hundreds of horses which slept under the hood, a herd of fuel-injected stallions waiting only for an igniting kiss to awaken them and carry their new master to places he'd never even dared to dream of seeing. Why had he never learned to drive before now? Why hadn't his father taught him? And why was it he should even *have* to be taught? Aren't there some things which should just come naturally, Chad wondered to himself, which one should be able to do without having to be shown how? It all seemed too easy and obvious: when a door latch is touched, it should yield to him, simple as that. And yet, here he was, stranded behind a steering wheel with the body of a dead dog who had selfishly died before imparting to Toni the mystery of his instinctual abilities which he shared with all canines: the ability to get what a dog needs without first having to watch a tutorial. The snow was falling in earnest now, not falling so much as spraying horizontally as if blasted from a cannon, covering the windshields of the cars parked around the square and burying inch by inch Toni's uncovered legs where she sat on the family blanket along with her freeze-dried mother. But Toni cared nothing about the onslaught of the blizzard or the curious phenomenon of an east-retreating sun; Toni's only thought was of Jimmy, wondering why he had so cruelly lied to her in his earlier text about bringing a big day surprise for her. Chad was wondering this as well, for despite the dozens of tracks which quite strangely were not filling in despite the driving snow, no wolf had yet to show itself or make its presence known. But now, even as he turned the stubborn key one more time and pumped the pedal of a girl who simply would not start, a shape emerged from the willows and slowly approached the cabin, low to the ground and slithering on its belly in a move reserved solely for the stalking of prey, its teeth bared and its kitchen chair dragged along behind it through the snow by a trailing paw. And while the horses beneath Toni's hood fled in terror from the approaching predator, Chad could do nothing but stand his ground, his hand still resting on the unfriendly latch, watching in paralyzed dread as Jimmy Carlson crept in across the square, his every muscle loaded for action and all his senses focused exclusively upon the exposed underbelly of the big day.

    Up on the high ridge, the martens and the caribou took their seats in the grandstands, eager to watch a show which for once might have a happy ending. Chad steeled himself for his fate, understanding that the course of true love never did run smooth and that getting eaten alive in the pursuit of a devouring passion was a perfectly reasonable outcome. Larry was ready for the worst as well, but unlike Chad, the worst had nothing to do with getting eaten, for if Larry was eaten he'd at least then serve as nutrient for some other continuing lifeform and thus not feel his existence had been meaningless. No, the worst for Larry was knowing what dead meat he really was, for instead of being planted in the earth as was his wish he found himself strapped into a lifeless car whose horses had fled and whose driver's pronouns were hopelessly stuck in neutral. And now from the grandstands a cheer rose up from the martens and the caribou, for from the tangled arms of the willows and from under the bellies of the sleeping parked cars there now appeared other wolves, emboldened by the Alpha Jimmy who had slithered out from under the brushy cover of pubic bushes and had dared to be seen, who had dared to bring the chair and would dare to be seen sitting in it. Larry's glassy eye also saw the wolves, and his decomposing spirit was instantly encouraged- perhaps the wolves would pick up the scent of his rotten situation and he'd be eaten after all. And then an even more exciting thought struck Larry: it was true that the humans had systematically bred the wild wolf completely out of him, leaving him as domesticated and docile as a middle-aged high school debate coach, but perhaps if Chad could be eaten by the wolves his essence might be passed down through their offspring, and he'd be resurrected as the true wolf he had started out as so many generations before and longed to be again. Through the windshield, Toni also saw the wolves, but their sister Toni did not see them, for she could not tear her eyes away from her silent phone and so had not yet noticed her slithering young Jimmy snaking his way in her direction across the snow of drifting blankets. As for Jimmy's dad, he could see nothing but the steady advance of a non-conforming kitchen chair which was creeping dangerously nearer and nearer to his utterly defenseless lawn chairs, and as he lined up the kitchen chair in the crosshairs of his Remington .270 he resolved that if necessary he would stop it in its tracks with a single shot of pictorial realism, son or no son. Which was when the thing which changed everything else that was happening happened.

Up to this point the sun had managed to remain pretty much in the shadows, avoiding detection; and as the big day drew nearer and nearer with each tug at the latch and each crank of the key, the sun had moved further and further away from it all, distancing itself as much as it could from what it viewed as the tawdriness of petty planetary affairs. It had therefore gone unnoticed that the sun's celestial disassociation with the proceedings had brought the solar system's one-and-only star to a point in the sky which from one of the earth's twenty-four time zone's point of view was commonly referred to as sunset. It would by rights be a premature sunset, thanks to the sun's decision to slip away from the party early, before the wine glasses were thrown against the wall and the police were called. And as the sun stood at the door and prepared to leave the party in the manner that it always did, ie, without acknowledgement, with none of the guests paying heed to his comings and goings with even so much as a "good night," the sun looked down upon it all and reflected with sadness on what had become for him a rather sorry state of affairs. In recent eons the sun had begun to dwell upon the fact that it was dying; and while it was true that it still had a few good years remaining, seven or eight billion to be precise, it was approaching middle age, and as such had begun to feel a sense of its own mortality, and with that a deep sadness for how little it had accomplished in that time. *What have I done so far*, the sun lamented to itself, *other than serve as the light bulb for one insignificant little planet, and that planet a particularly ingrateful and self-destructive one at that!* So although the big ball of hot gas still had plenty of gas left to give, the sun believed itself to be passing its gas for naught, and that the selfish and short-sighted earthlings (so short-sighted that if they dared take even one precious moment out of their day to so much as *look up* at the sun it blinded the poor babies) had come to take the sun's unwavering reliability completely for granted. Out of the excruciating boredom of its routine and the thanklessness it received in the performance of it therefore the sun had decided that the time had come for it to show its ass, so to speak, by delivering a little wake-up call to the wretched men of earth and remind them that it was his cosmos they were sailing in, not theirs. And the way that the aging sun had decided to show its ass was to surreptitiously reverse the direction of its path across the universe, which would then result in the earth's rotation being necessarily reversed as well. The sun had timed this reversal to occur during the World Cup finals, when the earth's human animals would be far too enrapt and self-absorbed by the little white ball to notice any change in the big yellow one; having thusly fucked shit up, the sun stood back to enjoy what was sure to be the cataclysmic fallout of his fuckery. But in those days which immediately followed the rotation reversal the sun observed with bewilderment and horror that the big celestial Fuck You he'd contrived for the human race had created no impact upon it whatsoever- the heads of the humans which before the change had been shoved far up into their own asses had not come out of those asses after the change to see what had happened but had remained shoved-up as ever, the only difference being that those heads-in-asses now faced in the opposite direction. There were those very few observant exceptions of course who'd noticed the reversal of the earth's rotation, but rather than be frightened and troubled by the change as the sun had hoped and expected, those aware humans actually saw nothing alarming about it but rather welcomed the rollback of time, thrilled with the prospect of growing younger and exploiting the phenomenon as their chance to grow new teeth and rejuvenated penises and to relive their misspent youths, concerned only with getting a second try at adolescence, too foolish to understand that human adolescence lived once was having lived it one time too many. So here then was the sun, a forsaken flame, starved for attention despite the showing of its ass, standing once again at the door of the party and poised to leave it in the same sulky way that it always did every night by simply slinking off over the horizon and casting the humans into darkness, thereby cutting short their self-centered daytime activities and forcing them to remain in that darkness for hours on end, then showing up again at an ungodly hour of the morning and with its rude light forcing them out of their comfortable beds and impelling them toward the grind of their daily toil. It was a petulant little habit of the sun's, this ill-tempered shuffling out the door and snapping off the lights as it left, and the sun knew it; a petty gesture which amounted to little more than pouting. But this was all the sun had at its disposal in the way of expressing its frustrations, and now it was about to express those frustrations in like manner once again. Today of course was a little different; today the sun would give the humans just a little extra donkey punch by cutting off the lights a few hours earlier than scheduled, right at the moment when they all felt so sure that their big day was about to arrive to the party, only for it to be turned away from the door at the last minute. For this was the curious way that the humans were programmed, a contradictory configuration of cross-wiring, in which their lives were lived utterly oblivious of the sun above them yet thoroughly conditioned and controlled by its every movement. Knowing the crushing effect which his early exit would have upon the big day activity down on the square was of little solace to the sun, even though he knew full well that when it happened it would be the thing which changed everything else that was about to happen. What did it matter to him, the sun pondered ruefully, that by turning off the light the alpha boy would not sit in his chair, that the key would not start the car, that the newly-pimpled scarlet pimpernel would once again not get the girl, that teenage love would not connect and that a dead little dog would not rise in resurrection? But although his early departure from the inconsiderate humans provided the sun with but an unsatisfying shot of watered-down self-amusement, the sun proceeded with tossing the shot back; and as a single tear of hydrogen trickled down his orange face, the lonely star departed, taking with it the time of day and the speed of life and imbuing the players in the matinee melodrama of the square with the universally-felt sensation that the stage lights had been dimmed to black and the curtain had been closed. And so it was over, just like that, over before it had really begun. Yet there was no sadness among the people as they folded their melted blankets and drove home in their cars that pseudo-summer evening; it had been quite a day all-in-all, even if it had not been the big day, for no one could deny they had given it their very bestest effort. They had only run out of time was all, and really, what was new about that? There would be more time some other next time for the big day, for there had always been more time for the next time and the sun still had seven billion years of time to give them. And as they sped on down the road toward the homes which they had no reason to believe did not exist, their cars flattening and splattering into roadkill the martens and caribou which had no place to hide, the townspeople felt a great sense of relief, to be honest, at how the day had ended, the same sort of relief they always secretly felt every day which always turned out to not be the big day- for despite how big they knew the big day would be they were just a little afraid that they might not know the big day when it happened. If it had not happened already. And so once again they had escaped the crushing disappointment of the big day. There was no escape for Daryl, however, for he was in the timeless land where no appearing and disappearing sun existed which might put an end to the proceedings and thereby rescue him from life, which in his case of course was death. And as he felt his body being torn apart by the wolves which so very rarely ever ate a man, he was not surprised in the least, for he knew full well that he lived in the land of surprises, and so, surprises like these were to be expected. As his flesh and blood and muscles and tendons were removed by the mauling teeth, Daryl permitted himself to enjoy just a small serving of self-satisfaction despite his considerable pain, for it was a life-affirming pain, a confirmation that his existence had served a useful purpose in that he was being transubstantiated into food for ongoing, future life, and so he did not feel that his efforts to survive to this point had been in vain. But for all those bloodless souls who were driving home from the sun-abandoned square there would be no surprise for them, just as there never was; and it would serve as no surprise when, the next morning, the sun would rise as it always did and their belief in the big day would be reignited by the sun's life-perpetuating rays. The people loved the sun after all, even if the sun was always proving how much it hated the people by burning and sometimes blinding them. It would be their new morning once again under their beloved hateful sun, even as it was someone else's sunset.

Tomorrow would finally be the big day, they just knew it. And as those people crawled into their comfortable beds and underneath their snowy blankets and dreamt of their big day just up ahead and days of misspent sunburnt youth so far behind, an escaped herd of frightened horses and an escaping father too frightened to ride them galloped headlong across an open land in pursuit of a speeding car which they would never ever catch, a black limousine which neither rose nor set but sailed straight ahead in a seamless continuum along an unending tangling stretch of arctic willows.

Printed in the USA
CPSIA information can be obtained
at www.ICGtesting.com
LVHW041100260823
756385LV00036B/535